The astonishing shape of things to come

Year's
Best
SF
16

Praise for previous volumes

"An impressive roster of authors."
Locus

"The finest modern science fiction writing."
Pittsburgh Tribune

Edited by David G. Hartwell

Edited by David G. Hartwell
& Kathryn Cramer

YEAR'S BEST SF 16

EDITED BY
DAVID G. HARTWELL
and KATHRYN CRAMER

HARPER Voyager

An Imprint of HarperCollins Publishers

Additional copyright information appears on pages 499–500.

HARPER Voyager
An Imprint of HarperCollins*Publishers*
10 East 53rd Street
New York, New York 10022-5299

Copyright © 2011 by David G. Hartwell and Kathryn Cramer
Cover art by John Harris
ISBN 978-0-06-203590-5
www.harpervoyagerbooks.com

First Harper Voyager mass market printing: June 2011

Harper Voyager and) is a trademark of HCP LLC.

Printed in the U.S.A.

10 9 8 7 6 5 4 3 2 1

Contents

Introduction

It was a good year for genre publishing in general, by which we mean that publishers and authors made money. The year 2010 was also one in which electronic books attained a higher level of sales and became a significant force in bestseller publishing. Not so significant in ordinary publishing. Very significant in academic publishing. At present, the electronic market is driven by the sales of reading devices. Science fiction and fantasy, as we know, is not generally bestseller publishing, and so the genre was not in general hurt but helped in the short run. More or less the same number of printed books were sold in the genre, but the number of ebooks increased, and so a bit more money was made because of ebooks. We spent the last decade saying that we make tens of dollars on ebooks, and when it gets to hundreds, we will know. It got to hundreds in 2010, a big jump.

In some areas other than SF, the ebooks appear to have reduced the number of books sold, especially top bestsellers, compromising their profitability. This is bad news for those publishers who went for the "just publish the bestsellers" line in the last decade or two. And for the authors. And their agents. And for bookstores that rely on the big bestsellers for a hefty percentage of their sales and profits.

Barnes & Noble solved this problem by selling its own ebook reading device. It is too early to tell as we write, but it appears that the real money in ebooks was made from device sales in 2010, not from the content on them. So it remains an ambiguous moment for the book publishing industry, and for authors and editors and readers. And the Google settlement, which will impact the whole situation profoundly, didn't happen in 2010—perhaps in 2011 . . .

As we write in February of 2011, the Borders chain, the third largest retailer of books in the U.S., has declared bankruptcy and is closing stores. Bookselling is generally in dire shape, especially mass market bookselling. People are talking in the usual hyperbolic terms about the death of the mass market book. It is certainly true that average mass market sales are in decline, but it is still too early for the funeral.

The biggest single chunk of the mass market is women's romance in various forms, and it appears that that audience is avidly adopting ebooks, especially since it is in general an audience that reads daily, and recycles by donation, trading, or simple disposal most of the mass market books. And ebooks are not a clutter problem. The question is, can much of the mass market industry survive the loss of a significant portion of its current print audience? Probably it can. There are still thrillers and mysteries—for the moment. Millions of paperbacks are still being sold.

Science fiction magazines once again lost some circulation, and magazines in the mainstream failed in large numbers in 2010. Survivors thus far tend to fulfill specific niches—such as fantasy or science fiction does. Online venues, which might pay contributors but make little money, grew or failed again this year. Non-profit *Strange Horizons* and *Tor.com* appeared the most stable of the online bunch. *Lightspeed* was a new attraction online. *Clarkesworld* won the Hugo Award for best semiprozine. Lots of the small presses generally carried the ball for innovation in 2010, especially the Bay Area cluster of Night Shade, Tachyon, and Subterranean, and PS Publishing in the UK. There is a whole lot of genre short fiction being published. Steampunk is becoming its own genre, for instance, as alternate history fiction did in the 1990s, only sometimes discernible as science fiction, but there was less genre science fiction in 2010. *Analog*, for instance, had a stronger-than-average year and no one seemed to notice (we did), so we point it out here. *Asimov's* featured a lot of talented newcomers in 2010.

Science fiction book reviewing seemed in danger of falling completely out of the mainstream in 2010 in the U.S., with not a single major newspaper devoting significant space to it, and fewer-than-ever regional publications covering the new books. Late in the year, Jeff VanderMeer appeared with a review roundup in the *New York Times*, and then it was announced in January 2011 that Tom Shippey will begin a science fiction and fantasy column in the *Wall Street Journal*. So there is some hope.

Otherwise, the mainstream happily and effectively appropriated tropes and images and settings from SF in a lot of literary and commercial novels, which is in general implying that SF is crap but that we can use pieces of it for real literature. That implication is certainly clear to the publishing establishment, though not, of course, to genre publishing and the genre audience, which generally claims any work that uses the furniture of SF to be really part of the genre, and then claims the writer as an SF writer. Ironically, that strengthens the "SF is crap" faction. Watch out for it. The best corrective is intelligent, sympathetic reviewing of genre material by reviewers who can tell the difference between SF and borrowing from SF, and can praise success in either venue appropriately without conflating them. We like some of those mainstream literary successes very much, but they are not successes for the genre, except insofar as letting us know the genre is worth appropriating—which is flattering in its own way.

There are still four professional print magazines that publish SF (the Hugo rules say there are three, but this is nonsense—*Interzone* is a professional magazine), and several online venues that pay more than a token for fiction and are in effect professional markets. However, much of the new fiction of high quality is showcased in original anthologies these days, and they are a significant source for this book (five of the stories this year, actually fewer than in recent years, but the point still holds). Only mentioning the SF anthologies, among the best are: *Sprawl,* edited by Alisa Krasnostein, an Australian small press collection; *Is Anybody Out There*, edited by Nick Gevers & Marty Halpern; *Metatropolis,* edited by John Scalzi (originally an audio book, reprinted in trade in 2010); *Shine,* edited by Jetse De Vries; and *Gateways*, edited by Betty Ann Hull. We make a lot of additional comments about the writers and the stories, and what's happening in SF, in the individual introductions accompanying the stories in this book.

Our Year's Best SF is an anthology series about what's going on now in SF. We try in each volume to represent the varieties of tones and voices and attitudes that keep the genre vigorous and responsive to the changing realities out of which it emerges, in science and daily life. It is supposed to be fun to read, a special kind of fun you cannot find elsewhere. The stories that follow show, and the story notes point out, the strengths of the evolving genre in the year 2010.

This book is full of science fiction—every story in the book is fairly clearly that and not something else. It is our opinion that it is a good thing to have genre boundaries. If we didn't, young writers would probably feel compelled to find something else, perhaps less interesting, to transgress or attack to draw attention to themselves. We have a high regard for horror, fantasy, speculative fiction, and slipstream, and postmodern literature. We (Kathryn Cramer and David G. Hartwell) edit the *Year's Best Fantasy* as well, a companion volume to this one—look for it if you enjoy short fantasy fiction too. But here, we choose science fiction. Welcome to the *Year's Best SF 16.*

David G. Hartwell & Kathryn Cramer
Pleasantville, NY

Sleeping Dogs

JOE HALDEMAN

Joe Haldeman (home.earthlink.net/~haldeman/) alternates between living in Gainsville, Florida, and the Cambridge, Massachusetts area. He teaches writing seasonally at MIT, where he has been a part-time professor since 1983. His first SF novel, The Forever War, *established him as a leading writer of his generation, and his later novels and stories have put him in the front rank of living SF writers. High spots among them include* Mindbridge, Worlds, The Hemingway Hoax, 1968, *and* Forever Peace. *His story collections include* Infinite Dreams, Dealing in Futures, Vietnam and Other Alien Worlds, None So Blind. *His collection* War Stories *appeared in 2005. His most recent book is* Starbound *(2010), a sequel to his 2008 novel* Marsbound. *The third book in the trilogy will be* Earthbound.*

This story appeared in Gateways, *an original anthology of new and reprinted stories in honor of Frederik Pohl, and one of the best anthologies of the year. A former soldier returns to the world rich in dysprosium where he served in combat thirty years before, trying to recapture erased memories. When he recaptures them, he makes a series of surprising, deeply ironic discoveries about himself and his civilization. A lot of them reflect back on our contemporary situation, making this story our choice for first in this book.*

The cab took my eyeprint and the door swung open. I was glad to get out. No driver to care how rough the ride was, on a road that wouldn't even be called a road on Earth. The place had gone downhill in the thirty years I'd been away.

Low gravity and low oxygen. My heart was going too fast. I stood for a moment, concentrating, and brought it down to a hundred, then ninety. The air had more sulfur sting than I remembered. It seemed a lot warmer than I remembered that summer, too, but then if I could remember it all I wouldn't have to be here. My missing finger throbbed.

Six identical buildings on the block, half-cylinders of stained pale green plastic. I walked up the dirt path to number three: OFFWORLD AFFAIRS AND CONFEDERACIÓN LIAISON. I almost ran into the door when it didn't open. Pushed and pulled and it reluctantly let me inside.

It was a little cooler and less sulfurous. I went to the second door on the right, TRAVEL DOCUMENTS AND PERMISSIONS, and went in.

"You don't knock on Earth?" A cadaverous tall man, skin too white and hair too black.

"Actually, no," I said, "not public buildings. But I apologize for my ignorance."

He looked at a monitor built into his desk. "You would be Flann Spivey, from Japan on Earth. You don't look Japanese."

"I'm Irish," I said. "I work for a Japanese company, Ichiban Imaging."

2

He touched a word on the screen. "Means 'number one.' Best, or first?"

"Both, I think."

"Papers." I laid out two passports and a folder of travel documents. He spent several minutes inspecting them carefully. Then he slipped them into a primitive scanning machine, which flipped through them one by one, page by page.

He finally handed them back. "When you were here twenty-nine Earth years ago, there were only eight countries on Seca, representing two competing powers. Now there are seventy-nine countries, two of them offplanet, in a political situation that's . . . impossible to describe simply. Most of the other seventy-eight countries are more comfortable than Spaceport. Nicer."

"So I was told. I'm not here for comfort, though." There weren't many planets where they put their spaceports in nice places.

He nodded slowly as he selected two forms from a drawer. "So what does a 'thanatopic counselor' do?"

"I prepare people for dying." For living completely, actually, before they leave.

"Curious." He smiled. "It pays well?"

"Adequately."

He handed me the forms. "I've never seen a poor person come through that door. Take these down the hall to Immunization."

"I've had all the shots."

"All that the Confederación requires. Seca has a couple of special tests for returning veterans. Of the Consolidation War."

"Of course. The nanobiota. But I was tested before they let me return to Earth."

He shrugged. "Rules. What do you tell them?"

"Tell?"

"The people who are going to die. We just sort of let it catch up with us. Avoid it as long as possible, but . . ."

"That's a way." I took the forms. "Not the only way."

I had the door partly open when he cleared his throat. "Dr. Spivey? If you don't have any plans, I would be pleased to have midmeal with you."

Interesting. "Sure. I don't know how long this will take . . ."

"Ten minims, fifteen. I'll call us a floater, so we don't have to endure the road."

The blood and saliva samples took less time than filling out the forms. When I went back outside, the floater was humming down and Braz Nitian was watching it land from the walkway.

It was a fast two-minute hop to the center of town, the last thirty seconds disconcerting free fall. The place he'd chosen was Kaffee Rembrandt, a rough-hewn place with a low ceiling and guttering oil lamps in pursuit of a sixteenth-century ambience, somewhat diluted by the fact that the dozens of Rembrandt reproductions glowed with apparently sourceless illumination.

A busty waitress in period flounce showed us to a small table, dwarfed by a large self-portrait of the artist posed as "Prodigal Son with a Whore."

I'd never seen an actual flagon, a metal container with a hinged top. It appeared to hold enough wine to support a meal and some conversation.

I ordered a plate of braised vegetables, following conservative dietary advice—the odd proteins in Seca's animals and fish might lay me low with a xeno-allergy. Among the things I didn't remember about my previous time here was whether our rations had included any native flesh or fish. But even if I'd safely eaten them thirty years ago, the Hartford doctor said, I could have a protein allergy now, since an older digestive system might not completely break down those alien proteins into safe amino acids.

Braz had gone to college on Earth, UCLA, an expensive proposition that obligated him to work for the government for ten years (which would be fourteen Earth years). He had degrees in mathematics and macroeconomics, neither of which he used in his office job. He taught three nights a week and wrote papers that nine or ten people read and disagreed with.

"So how did you become a thanatopic counselor? Something you always wanted to be when you grew up?"

"Yeah, after cowboy and pirate."

He smiled. "I never saw a cowboy on Earth."

"Pirates tracked them down and made them walk the plank. Actually, I was an accountant when I joined the military, and then started out in pre-med after I was discharged, but switched over to psychology and moved into studying veterans."

"Natural enough. Know thyself."

"Literally." Find thyself, I thought. "You get a lot of us coming through?"

"Well, not so many, not from Earth or other foreign planets. Being a veteran doesn't correlate well with wealth."

"That's for sure." And a trip from Earth to Seca and back costs as much as a big house.

"I imagine that treating veterans doesn't generate a lot of money, either." Eyebrows lifting.

"A life of crime does." I smiled and he laughed politely. "But most of the veterans I do see are well off. Almost nobody with a normal life span needs my services. They're mostly for people who've lived some centuries, and you couldn't do that without wealth."

"They get tired of life?"

"Not the way you or I could become tired of a game, or a relationship. It's something deeper than running out of novelty. People with that little imagination don't need me. They can stop existing for the price of a bullet or a rope—or a painless prescription, where I come from."

"Not legal here," he said neutrally.

"I know. I'm not enthusiastic about it, myself."

"You'd have more customers?"

I shrugged. "You never know." The waitress brought us our first plates, grilled fungi on a stick for me. Braz had a bowl of small animals with tails, deep-fried. Finger food; you hold them by the tail and dip them into a pungent yellow sauce.

It was much better than I'd expected; the fungi were threaded onto a stick of some aromatic wood like laurel; she brought a small glass of a lavender-colored drink, tasting like dry sherry, to go with them.

"So it's not about getting bored?" he asked. "That's how you normally see it. In books, on the cube . . ."

"Maybe the reality isn't dramatic enough. Or too complicated to tell as a simple drama.

"You live a few hundred years, at least on Earth, you slowly leave your native culture behind. You're an immortal—culturally true if not literally—and your nonimmortal friends and family and business associates die off. The longer you live, the deeper you go into the immortal community."

"There must be some nonconformists."

"'Mavericks,' the cowboys used to say."

"Before the pirates did them in."

"Right. There aren't many mavericks past their first century of life extension. The people you grew up with are either fellow immortals or dead. Together, the survivors form a society that's unusually cohesive. So when someone decides to leave, decides to stop living, the arrangements are complex and may involve hundreds of people.

"That's where I come in, the practical part of my job: I'm a kind of overall estate manager. They all have significant wealth; few have any living relatives closer than great-great-grandchildren."

"You help them split up their fortunes?"

"It's more interesting than that. The custom for centuries has been to put together a legacy, so called, that is a complex and personal aesthetic expression. To simply die, and let the lawyers sort it out, would trivialize your life as well as your death. It's my job to make sure that the legacy is a meaningful and permanent extension of the person's life.

"Sometimes a physical monument is involved; more often a financial one, through endowments and sponsorships. Which is what brings me here."

Our main courses came; Braz had a kind of eel, bright green with black antennae, apparently raw, but my braised vegetables were reassuringly familiar.

"So one of your clients is financing something here on Seca?"

"Financing me, actually. It's partly a gift; we get along well. But it's part of a pattern of similar bequests to nonimmortals, to give us back lost memories."

"How lost?"

"It was a military program, to counteract the stress of combat. They called the drug aqualethe. Have you heard of it?"

He shook his head. "Water of what?"

"It's a linguistic mangling, or mingling. Latin and Greek. Lethe was a river in Hell; a spirit drank from it to forget his old life, so he could be reincarnated.

"A pretty accurate name. It basically disconnects your long-term memory as a way of diverting combat stress, so-called post-traumatic stress disorder."

"It worked?"

"Too well. I spent eight months here as a soldier, when I was in my early twenties. I don't remember anything specific between the voyage here and the voyage back."

"It was a horrible war. Short but harsh. Maybe you don't want the memory back. 'Let sleeping dogs lie,' we say here."

"We say that, too. But for me . . . well, you could say it's a professional handicap. Though actually it goes deeper.

"Part of what I do with my clients is a mix of meditation and dialogue. I try to help them form a coherent tapestry of their lives, the good and the bad, as a basic grounding for their legacy. The fact that I could never do that for myself hinders me as a counselor. Especially when the client, like this one, had his own combat experiences to deal with."

"He's, um, dead now?"

"Oh, no. Like many of them, he's in no particular hurry. He just wants to be ready."

"How old is he?"

"Three hundred and ninety Earth years. Aiming for four centuries, he thinks."

Braz sawed away at his eel and looked thoughtful. "I can't imagine. I mean, I sort of understand when a normal man gets so old he gives up. Their hold on life becomes weak, and they let go. But your man is presumably fit and sane."

"More than I, I think."

"So why four hundred years rather than five? Or three? Why not try for a thousand? That's what I would do, if I were that rich."

"So would I. At least that's how I feel now. My patron says he felt that way when he was mortal. But he can't really articulate what happened to slowly change his attitude.

"He says it would be like trying to explain married love to a babe just learning to talk. The babe thinks it knows what love is, and can apply the word to its own circumstances. But it doesn't have the vocabulary or life experience to approach the larger meaning."

"An odd comparison, marriage," he said, delicately separating the black antennae from the head. "You can become unmarried. But not undead."

"The babe wouldn't know about divorce. Maybe there is a level of analogy there."

"We don't know what death is?"

"Perhaps not as well as they."

I liked Braz and needed to hire a guide; he had some leave coming and could use the side income. His Spanish was good, and that was rare on Seca; they spoke a kind of patchwork of Portuguese and English. If I'd studied it thirty years before, I'd retained none.

The therapy to counteract aqualethe was a mixture of brain chemistry and environment. Simply put, the long-term memories were not destroyed by aqualethe, but the connection to them had been weakened. There was a regimen of twenty pills I had to take twice daily, and I had to take them in surroundings that would jog my memory.

That meant going back to some ugly territory.

There were no direct flights to Serraro, the mountainous desert where my platoon had been sent to deal with a situation now buried in secrecy, perhaps shame. We could get within a hundred kilometers of it, an oasis town called Console Verde. I made arrangements to rent a general-purpose vehicle there, a jépe.

After Braz and I made those arrangements, I got a note from some Chief of Internal Security saying that my activities were of questionable legality, and I should report to his office at 0900 tomorrow to defend my actions. We were in the airport, fortunately, when I got the message, and we jumped on a flight that was leaving in twenty minutes, paying cash. Impossible on Earth.

I told Braz I would buy us a couple of changes of clothing and such at the Oasis, and we got on the jet with nothing but our papers, my medications, and the clothes on our backs— and my purse, providentially stuffed with the paper notes they use instead of plastic. (I'd learned that the exchange rate was much better on Earth, and was carrying half a year's salary in those notes.)

The flight wasn't even suborbital, and took four hours to go about a tenth of the planet's circumference. We slept most of the way; it didn't take me twenty minutes to tell him everything I had been able to find out about that two-thirds year that was taken from me.

Serraro is not exactly a bastion of freedom of information under the best of circumstances, and that was a period in their history that many would just as soon forget.

It was not a poor country. The desert was rich in the rare earths that interstellar jumps required. There had been lots of small mines around the countryside (no farms) and only one city of any size. That was Novo B, short for Novo Brasil, and it was still not the safest spot in the Confederación. Not on our itinerary.

My platoon had begun its work in Console Verde as part of a force of one thousand. When we returned to that oasis, there were barely six hundred of us left. But the country had been "unified." Where there had been seventy-eight mines there now was one, Preciosa, and no one wanted to talk about how that happened.

The official history says that the consolidation of those seventy-eight mines was a model of self-determinism, the independent miners banding together for strength and bargaining power. There was some resistance, even some outlaw guerilla action. But the authorities—I among them, evidently—got things under control in less than a year.

Travel and residence records had all been destroyed by a powerful explosion blamed on the guerillas, but in the next census, Serarro had lost 35 percent of its population. Perhaps they walked away.

We stood out as foreigners in our business suits; most men who were not in uniform wore a plain loose white robe. I went immediately into a shop next to the airport and bought two of them, and two sidearms. Braz hadn't fired a pistol in years, but he had to agree he would look conspicuous here without one.

We stood out anyway, pale and tall. The men here were all sunburned and most wore long braided black hair. Our presence couldn't be kept secret; I wondered how long it would be before that Chief of Internal Security caught up with me. I was hoping it was just routine harassment, and they wouldn't follow us here.

There was only one room at the small inn, but Braz didn't mind sharing. In fact, he suggested we pass the time with sex, which caught me off guard. I told him men don't routinely do that on Earth, at least not the place and time I came from. He accepted that with a nod.

I asked the innkeeper whether the town had a library, and he said no, but I could try the schoolhouse on the other side of town. Braz was napping, so I left a note and took off on my own, confident in my ability to turn right and go to the end of the road.

Although I'd been many places on Earth, the only time I'd been in space was that eight-month tour here. So I kept my eyes open for "alien" details.

Seca had a Drake index of 0.95, which by rule of thumb meant that only 5 percent of it was more harsh than the worst the Earth had to offer. The equatorial desert, I supposed. We were in what would have been a temperate latitude on Earth, and I was sweating freely in the dry heat.

The people here were only five generations away from Earth, but some genetic drift was apparent. No more profound than you would find on some islands and other isolated communities on Earth. But I didn't see a single blonde or redhead in the short, solidly built population here.

The men wore scowls as well as guns. The women, brighter colors and a neutral distant expression.

Some of the men, mostly younger, wore a dagger as well as a sidearm. I wondered whether there was some kind of code duello that I would have to watch out for. Probably *not* wearing a dagger would protect you from that.

Aside from a pawnshop, with three balls, and a tavern with bright signs announcing berbesa and bino, most of the shops were not identified. I supposed that in a small isolated town, everybody knew where everything was.

Two men stopped together, blocking the sidewalk. One of them touched his pistol and said something incomprehensible, loudly.

"From Earth," I said, in unexcited Confederación Spanish. *"Soy de la Tierra."* They looked at each other and went by me. I tried to ignore the crawling feeling in the middle of my back.

I reflected on my lack of soldierly instincts. Should I have touched my gun as well? Probably not. If they'd started shooting, what should I do? Hurl my sixty-year-old body to the ground, roll over with the pistol in my hand, and aim for the chest?

"Two in the chest, then one in the head," I remembered from crime drama. But I didn't remember anything that basic from having been a soldier. My training on Earth had mainly been calisthenics and harassment. Endless hours of parade-ground drill. Weapons training would come later, they said. The only thing "later" meant to me was months later, slowly regaining my identity on the trip back to Earth.

By the time I'd gotten off the ship, I seemed to have all my memories back through basic training, and the lift ride up to the troop carrier. We had 1.5-gee acceleration to the Oort portal, but somewhere along there I lost my memory, and didn't get it back till the return trip. Then they dropped me on Earth—me and the other survivors—with a big check and a leather case full of medals. Plus a smaller check, every month, for my lost finger.

I knew I was approaching the school by the small tide of children running in my direction, about fifty of them, ranging from seven or eight to about twelve, in Earth years.

The schoolhouse was small, three or four rooms. A gray-bearded man, unarmed, stepped out and I hailed him. We established that we had English in common and I asked whether the school had a library. He said yes, and it would be open for two hours yet. "Mostly children's books, of course. What are you interested in?"

"History," I said. "Recent. The Consolidation War."

"Ah. Follow me." He led me through a dusty playground, to the rear of the school. "You were a Confederación soldier?"

"I guess that's obvious."

He paused with his hand on the doorknob. "You know to be careful?" I said I did. "Don't go out at night alone. Your size is like a beacon." He opened the door and said, "Suela? A traveler is looking for a history book."

The room was high-ceilinged and cool, with thick stone walls and plenty of light from the uniform glow of the ceiling. An elderly woman with white hair taking paper books from a cart and reshelving them.

"Pardon my poor English," she said, with an accent better than mine. "But what do you want in a paper book that you can't as easily download?"

"I was curious to see what children are taught about the Consolidation War."

"The same truth as everyone," she said with a wry expression, and stepped over to another shelf. "Here . . ." she read titles, "this is the only one in English. I can't let you take it away, but you're welcome to read it here."

I thanked her and took the book to an adult-size table and chair at the other end of the room. Most of the study area was scaled down. A girl of seven or eight stared at me.

I didn't know, really, what I expected to find in the book. It had four pages on the Consolidation and Preciosa, and in broad outline there was not much surprising. A coalition of mines decided that the Confederación wasn't paying enough for dysprosium, and they got most of the others to go along with the scheme of hiding the stuff and holding out for a fair price—what the book called profiteering and restraint of trade. Preciosa was the biggest mine, and they made a separate deal with the Confederación, guaranteeing a low price, freezing all their competitors out. Which led to war.

Seca—actually Preciosa—asked for support from the Confederación, and the war became interstellar.

The book said that most of the war took place far from population centers, in the bleak high desert where the mines were. Here.

It struck me that I hadn't noticed many old buildings, older than about thirty years. I remembered a quote from a twentieth-century American war: "We had to destroy the village in order to save it."

The elderly librarian sat down across from me. She had a soft voice. "You were here as a soldier. But you don't remember anything about it."

"That's true. That's exactly it."

"There are those of us who do remember."

I pushed the book a couple of inches toward her. "Is any of this true?"

She turned the book around and scanned the pages it was open to, and shook her head with a grim smile. "Even children know better. What do you think the Confederación is?"

I thought for a moment. "At one level, it's a loose federation of forty-eight or forty-nine planets with a charter protecting the rights of humans and nonhumans, and with trade rules that encourage fairness and transparency. At another level, it's the Hartford Corporation, the wealthiest enterprise in human history. Which can do anything it wants, presumably."

"And on a personal level? What is it to you?"

"It's an organization that gave me a job when jobs were scarce. Security specialist. Although I wasn't a 'specialist' in any sense of the word. A generalist, so called."

"A mercenary."

"Not so called. Nothing immoral or illegal."

"But they took your memory of it away. So it could have been either, or both."

"Could have been," I admitted. "I'm going to find out. Do you know about the therapy that counteracts aqualethe?"

"No . . . it gives you your memories back?"

"So they say. I'm going to drive down into Serarro tomorrow, and see what happens. You take the pills in the place you want to remember."

"Do me a favor," she said, sliding the book back, "and yourself, perhaps. Take the pills here, too."

"I will. We had a headquarters here. I must have at least passed through."

"Look for me in the crowd, welcoming you. You were all so exotic and handsome. I was a girl, just ten."

Ten here would be fourteen on Earth. This old lady was younger than me. No juve treatments. "I don't think the memories will be that detailed. I'll look for you, though."

She patted my hand and smiled. "You do that."

Braz was still sleeping when I got back to the inn. Six time zones to adjust to; might as well let him sleep. My body was still on meaningless starship time, but I've never had much trouble adjusting. My counseling job is a constant whirl of time zones.

I quietly slipped into the other bunk and put some Handel in my earbuds to drown out his snoring.

The inn didn't have any vegetables for breakfast, so I had a couple of eggs that I hoped had come from a bird, and a large dry flavorless cracker. Our jepé arrived at 8:30 and I went out to pay the substantial deposit and inspect it. Guaranteed bulletproof except for the windows, nice to know.

I took the first leg of driving, since I'd be taking the memory drug later, and the label had the sensible advice DO NOT OPERATE MACHINERY WHILE HALLUCINATING. Words to live by.

The city, such as it was, didn't dwindle off into suburbs. It's an oasis, and where the green stopped, the houses stopped.

I drove very cautiously at first. My car in LA is restricted to autopilot, and it had been several years since I was last behind a steering wheel. A little exhilarating.

After about thirty kilometers, the road suddenly got very rough. Braz suggested that we'd left the state of Console Verde and had entered Pretorocha, whose tax base wouldn't pay for a shovel. I gave the wheel to him after a slow hour, when we got to the first pile of tailings. Time to take the first twenty pills.

I didn't really know what to expect. I knew the unsupervised use of the aqualethe remedy was discouraged, because

some people had extreme reactions. I'd given Braz an emergency poke of sedative to administer to me if I really lost
control.

Rubble and craters. Black grit over everything. Building
ruins that hadn't weathered much; this place didn't have much
weather. Hot and dry in the summer, slightly less hot and
more dry in the winter. We drove around and around and
absolutely nothing happened. After two hours, the minimum
wait, I swallowed another twenty.

Pretorocha was where they said I'd lost my finger, and it
was where the most Confederación casualties had been recorded. Was it possible that the drug just didn't work on me?

What was more likely, if I properly understood the literature, was one of two things: one, the place had changed so
much that my recovering memory didn't pick up any specif-
ics; two, that I'd never actually been here.

That second didn't seem possible. I'd left a finger here,
and the Confederación verified that; it had been paying for
the lost digit for thirty years.

The first explanation? Pictures of the battle looked about
as bleak as this blasted landscape. Maybe I was missing
something basic, like a smell or the summer heat. But the
literature said the drug required visual stimuli.

"Maybe it doesn't work as well on some as on others,"
Braz said. "Or maybe you got a bad batch. How long do we
keep driving around?"

I had six tubes of pills left. The drug was in my system for
sure: cold sweat, shortness of breath, ocular pressure. "Hell,
I guess we've seen enough. Take a pee break and head back."

Standing by the side of the road there, under the low hot
sun, urinating into black ash, somehow I knew for certain that
I'd never been there before. A hellish place like this would
burn itself into your subconscious.

But aqualethe was strong. Maybe too strong for the remedy to counter.

I took the wheel for the trip back to Console Verde. The
air-conditioning had only two settings, frigid and off. We
agreed to turn it off and open the nonbulletproof windows
to the waning heat.

There was a kind of lunar beauty to the place. That would have made an impression on me back then. When I was still a poet. An odd thing to remember. Something did happen that year to end that. Maybe I lost it with the music, with the finger.

When the road got better I let Braz take over. I was out of practice with traffic, and they drove on the wrong side of the road anyhow.

The feeling hit me when the first buildings rose up out of the rock. My throat. Not like choking; a gentler pressure, like tightening a necktie.

Everything shimmered and glowed. *This* was where I'd been. This side of the city.

"Braz . . . it's happening. Go slow." He pulled over to the left and I heard warning lights go *click-click-click*.

"You weren't . . . down there at all? You were here?"

"I don't know! Maybe. I don't know." It was coming on stronger and stronger. Like seeing double, but with all your body. "Get into the right lane." It was getting hard to see, a brilliant fog. "What is that big building?"

"Doesn't have a name," he said. "Confederación sigil over the parking lot."

"Go there . . . go there . . . I'm losing it, Braz."

"Maybe you're finding it."

The car was fading around me, and I seemed to drift forward and up. Through the wall of the building. Down a corridor. Through a closed door. Into an office.

I was sitting there, a young me. Coal-black beard, neatly trimmed. Dress uniform. All my fingers.

Most of the wall behind me was taken up by a glowing spreadsheet. I knew what it represented.

Two long tables flanked my workstation. They were covered with old ledgers and folders full of paper correspondence and records.

My job was to steal the planet from its rightful owners—but not the whole planet. Just the TREO rights, Total Rare Earth Oxides.

There was not much else on the planet of any commercial

interest to the Confederación. When they found a tachyon nexus, they went off in search of dysprosium nearby, necessary for getting back to where you came from, or continuing farther out. Automated probes had found a convenient source in a mercurian planet close to the nexus star Pouco-yellow. But after a few thousand pioneers had staked homestead claims on Seca, someone stumbled on a mother lode of dysprosium and other rare earths in the sterile hell of Serarro.

It was the most concentrated source of dysprosium ever found, on any planet, easily a thousand times the output of Earth's mines.

The natives knew what they had their hands on, and they were cagey. They quietly passed a law that required all mineral rights to be deeded on paper; no electronic record. For years, seventy-eight mines sold 2 percent of the dysprosium they dug up, and stockpiled the rest—as much as the Confederación could muster from two dozen other planets. Once they had hoarded enough, they could absolutely corner the market.

But they only had one customer.

Routine satellite mapping gave them away; the gamma ray signature of monazite-allenite stuck out like a flag. The Confederación deduced what was going on, and trained a few people like me to go in and remedy the situation, along with enough soldiers to supply the fog of war.

While the economy was going crazy, dealing with war, I was quietly buying up small shares in the rare earth mines, through hundreds of fictitious proxies.

When we had voting control of 51 percent of the planet's dysprosium, and thus its price, the soldiers did an about-face and went home, first stopping at the infirmary for a shot of aqualethe.

I was a problem, evidently. Aqualethe erased the memory of trauma, but I hadn't experienced any. All I had done was push numbers around, and occasionally forge signatures.

So one day three big men wearing black hoods kicked in my door and took me to a basement somewhere. They beat me monotonously for hours, wearing thick gloves, not breaking bones or rupturing organs. I was blindfolded and hand-cuffed, sealed up in a universe of constant pain.

Then they took off the blindfold and handcuffs and those three men held my arm and hand while a fourth used heavy bolt-cutters to snip off the ring finger of my left hand, making sure I watched. Then they dressed the stump and gave me a shot.

I woke up approaching Earth, with medals and money and no memory. And one less finger.

Woke again on my bunk at the inn. Braz sitting there with a carafe of *melán*, what they had at the inn instead of coffee. "Are you coming to?" he said quietly. "I helped you up the stairs." Dawn light at the window. "It was pretty bad?"

"It was . . . not what I expected." I levered myself upright and accepted a cup. "I wasn't really a soldier. In uniform, but just a clerk. Or a con man." I sketched out the story for him.

"So they actually chopped off your finger? I mean, beat you senseless and then snipped it off?"

I squeezed the short stump gingerly. "So the drug would work.

"I played guitar, before. So I spent a year or so working out alternative fingerings, formations, without the third finger. Didn't really work."

I took a sip. It was like kava, a bitter alkaloid. "So I changed careers."

"You were going to be a singer?"

"No. Classical guitar. So I went back to university instead, pre-med and then psychology and philosophy. Got an easy doctorate in Generalist Studies. And became this modern version of the boatman, ferryman . . . Charon—the one who takes people to the other side."

"So what are you going to do? With the truth."

"Spread it around, I guess. Make people mad."

He rocked back in his chair. "Who?"

"What do you mean? Everybody."

"Everybody?" He shook his head. "Your story's interesting, and your part in it is dramatic and sad, but there's not a bit of it that would surprise anyone over the age of twenty. Everyone knows what the war was really about.

"It's even more cynical and manipulative than I thought, but you know? That won't make people mad. When it's the government, especially the Confederación, people just nod and say, 'more of the same.'"

"Same old, we say. Same old shit."

"They settled death and damage claims generously; rebuilt the town. And it was half a lifetime ago, our lifetimes. Only the old remember, and most of them don't care anymore."

That shouldn't have surprised me; I've been too close to it. Too close to my own loss, small compared to the losses of others.

I sipped at the horrible stuff and put it back down. "I should do something. I can't just sit on this."

"But you can. Maybe you should."

I made a dismissive gesture and he leaned forward and continued with force. "Look, Spivey. I'm not just a backsystem hick—or I am, but I'm a hick with a rusty doctorate in macroeconomics—and you're not seeing or thinking clearly. About the war and the Confederación. Let the drugs dry out before you do something that you might regret."

"That's pretty dramatic."

"Well, the situation you're in is *melo*dramatic! You want to go back to Earth and say you have proof that the Confederación used you to subvert the will of a planet, to the tune of more than a thousand dead and a trillion hartfords of real estate, then tortured and mutilated you in order to blank out your memory of it?"

"Well? That's what happened."

He got up. "You think about it for a while. Think about the next thing that's going to happen." He left and closed the door quietly behind him.

I didn't have to think too long. He was right.

Before I came to Seca, of course I searched every resource for verifiable information about the war. That there was so little should have set off an alarm in my head.

It's a wonderful thing to be able to travel from star to star, collecting exotic memories. But you have no choice of carrier. To take your memories back to Earth, you have to rely on the Confederación.

And if those memories are unpleasant, or just inconvenient . . . they can fix that for you.

Over and over.

Castoff World

KAY KENYON

Kay Kenyon (www.kaykenyon.com) lives in Wenachee, Washington with her husband, Tom Overcast. Her novels began appearing in 1997 (The Seeds of Time), and have gotten some award nominations. Her most recent novel is Prince of Storms (2010), the fourth book in The Entire and the Rose series. She has published ten novels and thirteen short stories to date. The focus of her blog is on giving advice to aspiring writers, and she is a founding board member of Write on the River, a writer's organization in North Central Washington.

"Castoff World" appeared in Shine, *edited by Jetse De Vries, an anthology devoted to SF stories that choose a positive or optimistic approach to the future. It takes place on a "Nanobotic Oceanic Refuse Accumulator" nicknamed "Nora," in an ocean gyre, a system of rotating ocean currents that has the effect of concentrating floating in the ocean. In the real world, ocean gyres are a large and unsolved problem for the world ecology. Kenyon postulates an AI/nanotech device that functions both as the setting and a character in the story. About this story, she says in an SF Signal interview with Charles Tan: "I wanted—mixing my metaphors here—to make lemonade out of garbage, and therefore looked for the hopeful side of a young girl marooned on a floating garbage patch."*

Child knelt at the edge of the ocean and carefully spread the bird bones on the water, putting them out to sea. She waited for them to burst into feathers and rise from the ocean, flapping in circles, corkscrewing into the wind.

Not this time, though.

Child always hoped to see the leftover bones from meals reform in their proper shapes: seagull, turtle, swordfish. When she was little, she used to think Grappa was saying they had to put meal leftovers *out to sleep,* not out to sea. So even though she knew better now—being almost seven— she still thought of the bones as sleeping. And it was their little fun thing that they said, her and Grappa: *out to sleep.*

She checked the fishing lines on this side of the island for any catches—none—and scanned the horizon for pirates. The blue-green sea stretched in gentle swells to the edge of the world. No pirates today. If you saw pirates you had to crawl to the trap door to meet Grappa who would have a rat for protection. They'd practiced many times, always quiet and serious, but Child would have liked a glimpse of pirates. The book had a picture of one, but Grappa said, no, that was like in the movies, and not a real pirate. Movies was a before word. The book didn't have a picture of movies. But it had other before things, like fire hydrant, bicycle, and nano assembler.

"You dropped a bone, Child."

Grappa stood, his beard fluttering in the wind, and pointed to the tiny bone.

"Can I watch Nora kick it off?"

He nodded, and they crouched beside the bone, watching as the nanobots slowly moved the fragment toward the water's edge. You couldn't see the nanobots because of being too small, but they were there, working hard, passing the bone to the nanobots next to them. It would take all afternoon for Nora to put the bone out to sleep. Child would come back later to check on the progress.

"Nora doesn't like our garbage," Child pronounced.

"Not her kind." Grappa stood and looked out over their floating home. It was made entirely from garbage, an island of toxic trash, collected over years of swirling round the ocean gyre. The more garbage collected, the bigger Nora got. Here and there you could see plastic bottles, styrofoam cups, white and yellow bags, and crunched up cans. Over there, a collection of tiny stirrers and straws, lined up like a miniature forest. (Forest: many trees clumped together. Tree: tall growing thingy.) Nora was going to break all these things down and make them into good stuff so that bad stuff wouldn't leak into the water.

Grappa said Nora wasn't alive. But they called her *her*, because he said you could call ships *her*, and what they were on was like a ship or maybe a raft.

Grappa held up a bulky sack, his eyes sparkling. "A new rat."

They tramped over to the rat collection, carefully hung up on little poles so Nora wouldn't try to eject them. Nora couldn't take any extra weight, or the whole ship might go down. Things like a dead rat could go into the ocean, because it was good stuff that could rot. Nora just collected bad stuff like pee-cee-bee, pee-vee-cee, dee-dee-tee, and nurdles so she could turn them into derm. The trawlers were supposed to pick up the Noras once a year, but there weren't trawlers any more, so their Nora was starting to have a weight problem and threw overboard anything that wouldn't hurt the ocean.

It was Grappa's idea to hang the dead rats up on wooden poles. Sooner or later Nora would take apart the wooden poles and flush them away, but until then they had good stashes of rats in case of pirates. When the oldest rats got too slimy, out to sleep they must go. But neither did you want a nice-looking dead rat. Best was a just-right dead rat, one rotted just so, and that's how come so many rats all lined up.

Using scraps of fishing net twine, Grappa secured the body onto a pole. Then Child followed him, past the privy hole, past the hot spot, to his big net where they finished pulling the catch from the webbing. Her hat slipped off while she worked.

She caught Grappa's eye. Quickly, she stuck the broad brimmed hat back on her head so as not to get skin sores.

But he kept looking at her. "Where's your belt, Child?"

"I don't need it. I've got these." She pointed to the little nuggets that went down her shirt. They slipped into holes on the other side, keeping her shirt closed against the sun.

Grappa came over to her, fingering the nuggets. "Buttons. Where . . ."

"Nora made them." They'd started as little nubs and then grew in about a week to be the right size for the holes.

He gazed at her in silence.

"Maybe she told her nanobots to help my shirt stay closed."

"Nora's nothing but a Nanobotic Oceanic Refuse Accumulator."

They faced off on the old argument. If she talked back, he'd frown and mutter, *Just like your mother. Magical thinking.* Mom died soon after she was born. Grappa said that when they put her out to sleep, a tern hovered over her, circling like a guard-yan angel.

Grappa went back to sorting the catch, looking up at her now and then, and squinting his eyes at the buttons. In the end his catch was—not including the rat—three medium-sized fish, two tiny crabs, and a piece of sty-ro-foam.

Holding the flakey blue piece of garbage, Child asked, "What was it?"

Grappa pulled his hat down tighter, getting his face sore into the shade of his brim. "Oh, it's polystyrene foam."

She rolled her eyes at the big word.

"Well, it was a cooler. People used it to keep food, maybe for a picnic."

"Picnic?"

"The family going some place fun to have a meal."

"We could have a picnic."

He eyed her, scratching his beard. "Might could."

"When mother comes back. Then."

He didn't answer for a while. "What makes you think she's coming back, Child?"

She shrugged. "Out to sleep."

"That's what we say."

"Yes."

"Maybe we shouldn't say that anymore. Call it out to sea."

"Let's not, though."

He pointed to the hot spot, where they threw the bad stuff. It was a big pile in the middle of their garbage island where most of Nora's nanobots worked.

Child made her way over to it. The closer she got, the more the tiny nurdles clung to her feet and legs. You could brush them off, except then they'd stick to your hands. They leapt up on her like fleas, but that was just stat-ick, Grappa said; they weren't alive. Grappa had strict ideas on what was alive and what wasn't. *Nurdles are pre-production industrial plastic pellets. Everything plastic gets made from nurdles. The ocean is nurdle soup, Child.* He smiled at that, but she didn't know why.

She tossed the sty-ro-foam into the hot spot. Maybe people didn't throw the cooler in the ocean, only lost it, like the ghost nets that still caught fish and turtles. But whether on purpose or on accident, Nora was against it.

Even so, Child liked garbage. It made Nora bigger and stronger, all made from derm, the material left over after Nora changed pollu-tants into good stuff. And sometimes things that came into their nets got a story going, a story of before, the time when Grappa was an ocean-o-grapher, and helped make the Noras. Some of the best stories were from: cath-ode ray tube of teli-vision (check out picture in the book), inflated volley ball (learn to play until it got bumped into ocean), and the doll's head (if lonely in time before, you could have a small friend and talk to it). Child kept the doll's head until Grappa said he couldn't stand to look at just a head. Then they argued about whether hot spot or out to sleep. *People don't go into the hot spot,* she insisted. Grappa turned away. *She doesn't know the difference,* she heard him whisper. When she finally put the doll's head in the hot spot, it sank down, becoming island.

The really exciting thing? There were more islands like this out there. Probably every Nora had a child and a grappa. She kept a sharp eye out for other Noras so that she'd have a playmate, but the only time she saw one, it was a lonely, empty place. Except for seagulls nesting and churning around it in the air, a white gyre.

The ocean rocked them in their den under the trap door. Lantern light splashed off the smooth sides of the desal-inizer that Grappa said was too heavy for Nora to eject. Child watched his bearded face as he leaned against the desal-inizer and considered a bedtime story.

"Tell about Mom and Dad again."

"Well, your Dad was a good fisherman. Kept us going those first years."

"Until the tuna fish took his fishing pole." In the lantern's glow she imagined the tuna swimming away, laughing, and Dad so mad he threw his hat in the ocean after it.

"Yes. Dragged it away. He made others, but none were as good as that pole we got from Reel Good Sports. It about broke your Dad's heart to see it go."

She glanced up at the ceiling at the big red kayak. It hung by leather cords out of Nora's reach. It had two open places for people to sit in, and together with a second kayak that had got lost, this was how they got to the island: Dad and Mom and Grappa.

Nora wanted in the worst way to get a hold of that plastic kayak, but she let them have a few other things in the den without pulling them apart. For instance, she let them store food for a few days. Also a plastic bag or two to carry stuff around and also a few ghost nets, even though they were poly-propy-lene. Grappa said Nora had to go against her program to allow it. *She wants us to be happy,* Child had said once. Grappa had looked at her funny. *She doesn't know* happy. *She knows garbage detox and sequestering.* She'd objected, *But, Grappa, we're helping her pick up garbage. We dragged in that big drum. We catch sty-ro-foam, don't we?* He scratched around his face sore, not answering.

But the red plastic kayak was too much for Nora. Every now and then, they'd come into the den and find that Nora had chewed through the leather straps and the kayak had fallen.

Grappa was saving the boat for when it was time to go to shore, which would be when it was safe, when there'd be picnics and stores again.

"Reel Good Sports was a *store*," she said, hoping to keep Grappa talking. "You could point at things that you wanted, and trade monies for them."

"Well, the owner was long gone. We just took things. Buying things, that was in the time before."

"On land."

"California," Grappa said. "It used to have stores, a lot of them."

"And toasters and cars and baseball gloves. Except Mom and Dad didn't, just you, Grappa. You had cars and toasters."

"Oh, for a while, and then I didn't anymore. I raised your Mom in a compound where we didn't have cars or such. When the bad men came we escaped. She was grown by then and we hid in the woods until your Dad came along and helped us—"

"And then we were a family."

"—and then your Mom was pregnant and we needed a safe place for you, so we found the kayaks and scouted around for a portable desalinizer. I knew where Nora was, because I brought my GPS with me, and we came here, to be safe."

"Except for the pirates. They're not safe."

"Lights out, now." He blew out the lantern, and pulled derm mats over them.

"How was Nora born?"

"Lights out."

"Yes, but how did Nora get born? What was her Mom?"

She closed her eyes and thought about how Nora kept

growing, and that maybe someday she'd stretch all the way to land.

"A seed," came Grappa's voice. "We put little seeds in the ocean, and programmed them to sweep up garbage."

"Seeds with nanobots."

"And you told the nanobots to get garbage out of the water and to make DERM from pollutants."

Sleep tugged on her, but she wanted to prove she knew what derm was: "De-graded Rewoven Refuse Matters."

"*Materials*. Degraded Rewoven Refuse Materials. And the Noras got big, some of them. This Nora swirls in a big vortex, vacuuming up one of the North Pacific gyres, just a never-ending clockwise rotation. Whole thing's kept in place by a mountain of high pressure."

"Like the Great Pacific Garbage Patch."

"Except that one, that's as big as Texas."

Texas was a place so big you could walk for months and you'd still be there. Whenever they wanted to say how big something was—like the tuna that defeated Dad—she and Grappa would say, "big as Texas."

She fought against sleep, because Grappa was talking even past lights out. But the great ocean gyre had her in its arms. The gyre was a huge ocean creature that danced in a big soft circle, carrying turtles, volley balls, tunas, ghost nets, and their island around and around and around and into dreams.

"Grappa, why are you sleeping out here?"

Sometime during the night Grappa had got up and left the den. This morning she found him top side just waking up in a nest of derm.

He brushed the nurdles off his clothes. "Oh, its nice out here, Child."

But she thought he looked cold. "I don't like it when you sleep out here."

He started to make their breakfast fire in the metal drum that Nora let them keep. Child tried rotating the sticks, but she didn't have the knack of it, yet. Once the fire was going, she fetched crabs they'd saved from yesterday and they roasted them. The ocean had big swells today, rolling softly under Nora, lifting and settling them, the sunlight caught in the tops, going along for the ride.

"I'll be sleeping up here from now on," Grappa said.

"No. Nothing should change."

"Listen to me, Jessie." Oh boy, when he called her her real name, that was the worst.

"I've been collecting garbage a long time. But now I've got the same sore your Dad had. Soon I'll have to . . . have to be done with it. When the time comes—" He nodded toward the edge of the island, toward the ocean gyre. "You know Nora can't keep me. You help her. Can you do that? Because if I'm down in the den you won't be able to put me out to . . . out to . . ."

"But we'll always be together. You said, Grappa."

"I said." He turned away. "It's just sleep, Child."

As his words sank in, they released a weight from her chest, as though a big rock had lain atop her. It lifted, letting in a good light that fired up her heart like a lantern. So he'd be coming back. They'd all be coming back.

That's what she'd been trying to tell him all along.

She put the crab shells in the ocean and watched as they bobbed away. Then she sat down to watch her nets, pulling them in now and then, expecting good luck today. She hummed a tune and lay down on her stomach trying to see the nanobots. Looking real close, sometimes she saw a seething and sparkling, and she knew the bots were breaking down pee-cee-bees and other pollu-tants and car-cino . . . car-cino . . .

Underneath her she felt the ground heave, and a big wave jolted the island, sending Child rolling down a sudden hill. Then, unthinkably, she fell off the side into the cold water, into the ocean. She sank, popped up, gulped air, sank again. Down, down. Under Nora, her hands and elbows hit plastic bottles, a huge jumble of them. Down here nurdles floated everywhere like fish eggs. Mustn't get trapped under Nora. Need to get to the edge . . . Overhead, Nora's shadow loomed dark, except the bottles glimmered with a sunken light. She grabbed the nearest plastic bottle that was stuck fast to the others, and pulled herself forward, chest aching, breath gone. She slapped at the bottles, pulling, pulling.

Popped up. And there, Grappa shouting. Grappa throwing a net. She reached for it and he pulled it closer, closer, until he bent down and hauled her over the side. As she sat hunched over, retching and coughing, he slapped her on the back. She spit salt water out, and nurdles, too.

Then he tore the net off her and pulled her into his arms.

After awhile he carried her to Nora's exact middle and told her to stay put. He came back with a water jug and her second set of derm clothes. She shivered hard, but he wanted her to wipe down with fresh water, so she did. That's when he pointed to the jacket she'd been wearing. It was puffy and didn't fold like normally. Then it slowly wilted, like the air got let out.

As Child dressed in dry clothes, Grappa picked up the wet jacket and examined it. "Life vest," he said. "Little air pockets that must've filled up when you hit the water."

"Nora, I guess."

"You ever have . . . nanobots on your clothes, Child?"

"Sometimes."

He looked around at the island, as though expecting to see nanobots gotten big.

They sat together then, his arms around her, and they watched the forever blue sky without their hats on so her hair could dry. The great sky stacked overhead in an ocean of light.

"Grappa, Nora puts the bottles underneath."

"There's bottles down there?"

"It's all bottles. Just a million bottles, all stuck together."

He looked down at the ground. "For floatation."

"Do we float on the bottles?"

Grappa put his head in his hands. After a few moments he said, "We do if she strengthened the bottles and they're full of air."

Child put her arms around him. "The nanobots do it, Grappa. It's all right."

"They're getting smarter," he said, like he was speaking to the gyre, and not to her. "They've had to. All these years on their own, and no trawlers." He seemed confused and not as happy as he had been a few minutes ago when he pulled her from the water.

To lighten the mood, she said, "The nurdle soup tastes terrible." She pointed to the water where the nurdles floated under them, swimming with Nora.

He smiled a little. "I'm going to make you seagull soup, how's that?"

And he did, but it took him a long time, and when they'd eaten, he slept.

The day was blue and bright like every day. A high pressure system sits over our heads, Grappa always said. It drives back the rain. Since they didn't get rain, she'd had to learn how to run the desal-inization box and how to clean the salts from it. And she finally learned how to make fire from two sticks. Those were the last things, the hardest things, to learn just before Grappa died.

In the full sunlight the kayak's lovely red sides looked more scuffed than when it hung in the den. The kayak was supposed to be for getting to shore, but Child couldn't just push Grappa into the ocean.

Dragging the kayak to the edge of the island, she pulled it over onto its side. Somehow she managed to get Grappa into the little boat, and turn it right side up again.

She sat for a long time, leaning against the kayak, staring out to sea. "I know you said to keep the kayak, Grappa. But I just can't." She stared as birds lifted their wings, letting the air currents take them higher. She wished Grappa could go up, like a bird, like Mom, instead of out to sleep. But it was only for a while. So she got up her courage, and walked behind the kayak and leaned against it, pushing, pushing. It didn't budge. She tried pulling from the front. No better.

Then from the back again, and this time she thought she saw little sparks along the path where the kayak pressed into the derm. And the boat moved an inch, and then an inch more. The nanobots, she thought. Nora had finally got her hands on the plastic kayak.

At last the kayak slipped over the edge. Child knelt, watching it go.

"Always together, you said."

It's only sleep.

OK, then.

Voices overhead. A man laughed, but not a nice sound. Child felt the ground shake from people stomping around. She was still breathing hard from throwing everything into the den: cooking drum, fishing nets, bird traps. Then kick up the derm over the privy holes. Lastly: throw the rats overboard, but save a slimy one.

Just before getting into the den, pile derm on the trap door and put the rat there. Grappa said that keeps them from looking too close, because the rat stinks and looks bad.

The pirates were looking for stuff, because sometimes the Noras had usable things collected. Also they would take a bunch of derm to make clothes and bedding. She had to hide, because the pirates might also steal her.

She eyed the trap door. It would be her last chance to see a pirate, if she just opened the den cover a little ways.

But the sounds they were making were getting angry and loud. She huddled into herself. As she folded up as small as possible, her heart knocked hard inside her chest. Her pulse came into her wrists, bumping like crazy. *If you ever have to go to sleep, to be with your Mom, there's one way,* Grappa once said. *You cut your wrists, using something very sharp. It hurts a little, but then you put your wrists into the DERM, and let them bleed. Don't look, though. Then sleep comes. You understand? Only if you have to. If things are too sad. All right?*

All right.

Sometimes, like during that big storm once, she calmed herself by thinking about Mom and what she looked like. *What color was her hair?* He'd said, *Black. It was black, Child.* Just like the tern, then, all white with black on the very top. Somewhere out there, a tern rode over the world, looking down on her. Keeping watch.

Smoke curled down from the chinks in the trap door. The pirates were burning something.

She climbed the ladder and tipped the door up, just a little. Blazing, jumping fire. They'd set Nora on fire. Beyond, she saw the boat oaring away. She rushed down into the den to get the big jug, and then up the ladder and, pushing the jug out ahead of her, slithered out onto the derm.

The boat was still too close for her to stand up, so she crawled to Nora's edge, filling the jug with ocean water. Then she poured it over her head, like Grappa told her in case of fire. The jacket puffed up around her. Once more she refilled the jug. By now, the boat was so far, the men looked small. She threw the water on the closest flames, burning hard, making popping noises. Back for more water, but by the time she got a jug-full, the fire stopped, going to embers.

Amid the smoldering derm, she sat down and watched the boat until it disappeared. Maybe the pirates were mad that alls they found was a dead rat, so they set a fire. Nora hadn't liked the fire. Air pollu-tion.

"The rat worked really good, Grappa."

I *said*.

You did.

In time, the weather changed. Storms came, and Nora thrashed and rocked on her platform of plastic poly-mers. By this, Child knew that the island had passed from the great ocean gyre. Nora was headed somewhere, and this worried Child because where would they go?

Nora's sides had built up into little walls. Child never fell in the ocean again. It was harder to get the nets in and out, but fishing got better outside of the gyre, and Child was not often hungry.

As she grew, her clothes changed, getting bigger. Now she had only one shirt and pair of pants but they never got dirty.

The desal-inization machine finally broke—that had been two hundred days ago—but she collected rainwater now, in a drum. Also Nora caught rainwater into a little pond that was seldom empty.

And the island sailed on.

In rough seas, Nora pitched up and down, but the waves just broke on the walls she'd built. And the island got taller. In time it was too hard to cast nets down, and so Child trapped birds. There were more of them than ever. She got hungry, though, if the wood was too wet to make a drum cooking fire. That was a problem with being outside the gyre: it rained a lot. Nora hadn't yet learned that Child needed dry kindling to cook. She tried telling Nora so, but that wasn't how Nora learned.

Child never saw another Nora. Finding a friend or a grappa on a Nora had been a childish thing to believe, she knew. And she was used now, to being alone. Grappa was back there, still circling the old gyre, his red kayak going round and round. It seemed like a thing she'd dreamed, that Grappa had been with her. She began to doubt that he truly slept, because she'd packed the paddle in the kayak, and he would have come for her by now. But maybe the gyre creature wanted to keep him.

She sat with her back to the cooking drum—still warm from her last meal—and paged through the book, faded, torn, musty. There were land animals: cat, horse, and others whose names she'd forgotten. There were things like clock, chair, space elevator, ship with masts, and skis.

She fell asleep in the warm afternoon. When she jerked awake she saw a whale.

No, something too big for a whale.

The horizon had a black lump that didn't move. It got bigger.

They were closing in now, people in little boats, staring at her and Nora. Children too, pointing at her. The shore drew near. She saw trees dark against the sky, and farther inland, wooden buildings with windows and smoke drifting from what might be cook fires. It was where Nora had been taking her, following whatever trail the nanobots could sense, whether the taste of soil or smoke borne on the wind.

Dozens of little boats. The people in them kept their distance, chattering and looking past Nora, as a bigger ship came around the headland toward her. Many oars came out, and they beat up and down together. She thought the sailors would come on board Nora, but instead they used spikes to secure ropes to her and began pulling her to shore. Then Nora was caught up in waves rolling onto the beach, and, with people pulling from the land, Nora creased into the sand with a heavy smack.

For the last time Child went down into the den. Looking around at her possessions, she picked up the book and Grappa's hat. Before she left, she pressed her forehead against the soft, rewoven refuse of the wall. "You never needed those trawlers, did you? Got the garbage out of the water all on your own."

Back on top, she saw a growing crowd of people on land.

The people turned to watch two large creatures approaching from down the beach. The creatures stopped some distance away, pointing at Nora. Then Child saw how it was people riding horses.

It was time to go. Child stuck wood staves into the derm and looped a fishing net over it, trying to snarl it so that it wouldn't slip. Then she used the net to climb down.

Her feet landed in shallow water. Surrounded by a crowd that gently urged her forward, she walked closer to the horses with people on them.

One horse rider was a woman. She had yellow hair pulled back into a knot at her neck, and wore clothes with bright colors. She leaned forward, saying, "Your name, child?"

"Yes."

"Where did you come from?"

Child tried to answer truthfully. "A North Pacific ocean gyre."

"Who made your clothes?"

"Nora."

The woman turned to the man next to her, also on a horse. "She is a gift to us."

He nodded. "But what is that?" He looked past Child, down the beach.

Child turned. There was Nora, pulled up on the sand. From here, Child saw how Nora had lovely smooth sides coming to a point in front. In back, a blade jutted out and down into the waves as they crested into the shallows. Strangest of all, the side of Nora that Child could see had a beautiful moving circle on it, traveling round and round, sparking like sometimes the nanobots did. Then she saw how it was a picture of the ocean gyre, because a small red dot rode on the circle, slowly, slowly moving like a kayak on a softly turning wheel.

"What is that thing?" the man repeated.

"It's a ship," Child said. "Her name is Nora."

And it was a ship, more than ever, more than she had ever guessed. Nora had made herself beautiful so people would want to bring her onto the land. So at last her task could be finished, to get the bad things out of the ocean forever.

The woman smiled at her. "Would you like to pet my horse?"

Child came closer, putting her hand on the creature's nose, feeling its soft warmth.

At this, the people began to press closer, putting their hands on Child's clothes and exclaiming, but friendlier now that the woman had let her pet the horse.

A boy about her age pointed at Child's ankles, where her pants had puffed up from being in the water.

"Life vest," Child told the child.

Nearby, where a tree leaned over the beach, a dark-headed tern flew in, settling onto a branch. It flapped white wings, tucking them close, keeping watch.

Petopia

BENJAMIN CROWELL

*Benjamin Crowell (www.lightandmatter.com/personal/) lives
in Fullerton, California, where he teaches physics at Fullerton College, a community college in Orange County,
California, "which apparently is no longer the Margaret
Atwood-style theocracy described to me when I was growing up in Berkeley." He has a Ph.D. in physics from Yale
and writes his own physics textbooks, which are available
for free download from his website. His stories began appearing in science fiction publications in 2008, and he lists
ten published by the end of 2010 (six of them in* Asimov's*).*

"Petopia" appeared in Asimov's, *which had another in
its continuing string of good years. The story details the
adventures of two, poor third-world kids who salvage a
purple AI animal toy in post-cyberpunk Africa. The scenario reminds us a bit of the Spielberg/Kubrick* A.I., *as re-
worked in light of the highly commercialized, technologically
advanced toys of today, in best cyberpunk "street finds uses"
mode.*

Rain slid down like sweat over the mountain of beige and black computer cases, as if the machines were still having trouble adjusting to the climate. Aminata Diallo twirled a screw, snipped a ribbon cable, and pulled a tiny solid-state drive out of the machine on her workbench.

The drive had gone in the basket, and she was getting up to fetch the next computer from the tall, unsteady heap that slouched against the back wall of the alley, when motion caught her eye at the base of the pile—a rat? She'd let her guard down because it was so much safer now that Alseny had her working here instead of at the dump.

There! Telltale ripples were still bouncing back and forth in a greenish puddle half-hidden in the shadows. She thought she could make out a furry leg sticking down into the water. Too stocky for a rat. She palmed the Phillips screwdriver and wished for shoes instead of sandals.

"Hello?" a squeaky little voice said in English.

Mina turned the possibilities over in her mind. She'd never been inclined to believe in the spirits Father mumbled about, but when confronted with a real one it would be fool-hardy to ignore the basic precautions her *baba* had taught her. Then again, there could be a perfectly ordinary expla-nation for what was happening.

"Hello," she parroted back, feeling clumsy about the pro-nunciation. She kept her eyes lowered respectfully.

It forded the dirty puddle and trotted out, dripping, into the muddy alley: a shaggy little purple thing with big, liquid

38

eyes and floppy ears. She fought down an urge to giggle at the creature's bedraggled cuteness, because that would certainly offend it. It launched into rapid-fire English.

"I'm sure what you say is correct, sir," Mina replied in Susu, "but I'm afraid my English isn't very good."

It just stared at her and cocked its head, so she did her best to reformulate her speech in what little French she'd learned when she was still in school.

"*Bonjour mademoiselle,*" the dripping apparition replied, in what she imagined was a very posh Parisian accent. "I've been lost. Could you please ship me to 1324 Telegraph Avenue, Oakland, California?"

California? She'd only gone as far as African geography before *Baba* got fired and the money for school fees and uniforms ran out, but she knew that California was in the United States. They had surfing, and movie studios. These computers must have come on a ship from California, and with them, this—spirit? animal? machine? Definitely not a spirit. If spirits existed at all, it was probably only in dusty old places like *Baba*'s home village, not modern ones like California. And although parrots could talk, she'd never heard of a real animal with purple fur.

"Can you talk about all kinds of things?" she asked, "or can you only say things people told you how to say?"

"I can talk about all kinds of things. What's your favorite dessert?"

Smarter than a parrot, but not as smart as a person. Some kind of machine. She knew better than to answer its question. Alseny didn't volunteer details about what he got off the drives, but people talked, and Mina had a general idea of how the business worked. *What's this rich foreigner's identification number? His birthday? His mother's maiden name? What about the name of his first pet, the brand of his first car, his favorite dessert?*

"Shut yourself off," she told it. It did, and she went back to work.

Mina hurried home, keeping a tight grip on the two plastic shopping bags. One held her tools and her collapsible umbrella, the other her bowl, her fork, and the furry machine. The rain had stopped. The electricity was out, as usual, and only in one place where she cut across the *Avenue de la République* was there a pool of blue fluorescent light spreading out from the internet café, which had a generator. She tried to look very busy and avoid attracting notice. You never knew what a soldier might do, and although the idle men on the street-corners were usually harmless, it was best for a young girl to avoid their questions about why she was out at night without a chaperon. What would she say? *My brother is too young, and my father begs in the Place du 23 Février for money to buy palm wine.*

Through the window of her house, she was surprised to see a gleam of yellow light reflected by the corrugated iron wall inside. Was one of her parents home already? But when she got inside, she saw that it was neither *Nga* nor *Baba* but her brother Raphael who had the lantern on.

"What are you doing? Have you had that lit all evening?" She cuffed him on the head. (These days she had to reach up to do that.) "You know what batteries cost!"

"I was lonely in the dark." He had on her hand-me-down black T-shirt that was too small for him, and for a moment it seemed to Mina as though the part of him that it covered might fade away completely if the lantern-light ceased.

"You shouldn't have time to be lonely. Did you sweep the floor and fetch water like *Nga* told you?"

"Carrying water is a woman's work."

So he'd ignored his chores and spent his day fiddling with his chessboard. It was sitting on the table, set up in some position that Mina was sure was very interesting to an expert. Propped open next to it was one of *Baba*'s old dog-eared books, a thick volume with diagrams of boards and finicky symbols that showed the moves. It was in a foreign language, maybe German, but she supposed Raphael could figure it out without understanding the words. Marching past the board, like tiny mortals ignoring a battle of the gods, a stream of ants went to and from an orange peel. Without yet putting down either shopping bag, she snagged the peel between two fingers and threw it out the window.

A woman's work. The lantern threw her shadow onto the street, which was so narrow that the image of her head was cast onto old Mme Soumah's crumbling stucco wall. The arms stretched out long like the melted plastic parts when they burned the computers at the dump to get the copper out. She closed her eyes, and the weight of the two shopping bags increased, became the weight of the two men in her family pulling her down.

"All right, give me the lantern. I've got to go out to the toilet anyway."

She looked around to put down the bags, and then the hint of an idea flickered uncertainly in a corner of her brain. She placed one bag on the floor to free a hand for the lantern, but kept the one with the talking machine in it.

Someone was using the toilet, and, while she was waiting outside the tattered blue blanket they used as a curtain, she tried to fan her spark of an idea back into a flame. Raphael was in that long period that a male was allowed before he had to be grown up. The women had to baby him, and he got the best pieces of meat. Then the sun would rise one day and he would be a soldier, a beggar, a glue-sniffer, a stander on streetcorners: no longer a crushing burden but merely a danger or a nuisance. What Mina needed was a way to kick him over that threshold.

When it was her turn she sat down and pulled the electronic animal out. She combed her fingers through its fur in the lantern-light, but it didn't seem to have a power switch. "Wake up," she whispered experimentally, and then realized sheepishly that she'd said it in Susu. *"Réveille-toi."*

Its eyes had never been closed, but now they came alive and moved. "Hello again," it said loudly in French. "Are we at school?"

"School? No, this is the toilet near my house. Could you speak more slowly, and lower your voice a little, please?"

"Oh, you go home for lunch?" Its voice softened but didn't sound whispery, so it was suddenly like hearing him from far away. "It's after one o'clock, though. You'll get in big trouble. You'd better hurry back to school right away. You can leave me at home. It's against the rules to bring me there."

"You're confused, *Monsieur*. It may be one o'clock in California, but this is a different time zone. Anyway, I don't go to school."

"You have to," the machine said accusingly. "You're not a grownup. I can tell." Was it her imagination, or was that a little pout on his lip? He really was simply the sweetest thing imaginable. "You're about fifteen, aren't you?"

"Sixteen. But things are different here than in California. People aren't all rich. My family doesn't have enough money for school right now, and if they did they would send my brother, not me."

"Oh, I see." It tilted its little purple head adorably. "You should be going to school, though. After I go back to California I won't be here to remind you, but you have to remember to go anyway."

"*Bon*, we should talk about that. I don't have money to send you back to America, so you may be here for a long time."

"Petopia will reimburse you for reasonable shipping costs."

"What's Petopia?"

"Petopia is a world that Jaybeemallorme and Tiborhora"—the foreign names blurred together in her ears—"made in Jaybee's garage while they were eating unhealthy amounts of kimchi and Little Caesar's pizza. It's low-rez, it's silly, and while you're there you play the part of your Petopian. You can get your own lovable Petopian at . . . sorry, I'm not picking up a wireless signal here, so I can't tell you about local stores that sell Petopians."

Mina didn't know who Little Caesar was, or about kimchi and low-rez, but she got the general idea. "You're a Petopian?"

"Yes. My name is Jelly." When it pronounced its name it switched abruptly to an American accent.

"So I don't need a store. I already have a Petopian."

It thought that over. "Well, you aren't my registered user. And you're using me offline, so I'm in demo mode. Unless you log in with the right password, you can't access all the features of Petopia's persistent virtual reality."

"Persistent . . ."

"Virtual reality. The Petopia world."

"So . . . I *have* you, but I don't *own* you? And Petopia is like an imagining game—for little rich kids."

"Petopia isn't Webfrenz," the machine said, with a good simulation of disdain. "Our demographic is older." His manner communicated the feeling perfectly: you and I, Mina and Jelly—we're alike, aren't we? Not like those silly *little* kids. Had some American programmer written that reaction like a script for a play? "And you don't have to be rich to be a Petopiowner. You can get the basic plan for only fifty dollars a month."

How much was that? A dollar was down to about thirty or forty eurocents these days, wasn't it? And a euro was . . . Great God, they could spend that kind of money on a child's game? And that was for the "basic plan." Evidently even their imaginary world was split between rich and poor.

When she got back to the house she casually took Jelly out of the bag.

"What's that?" Raphael demanded.

"What's what?"

"The stuffed animal."

"Oh, don't worry about Jelly. I don't think you'd like him. He's a little old for your, ah, *demographic*." She wasn't sure if she was using the fancy French word correctly, but it was unlikely that Raphael would know any better.

Once Jelly had heard the list of Raphael's daily duties, and verified that it was backed by their mother's authority, he made it his singleminded duty to enforce it. Mina had only hoped vaguely to enlist him as a spy, one whom Raphael would tolerate because he was also a toy. But even though Jelly was too small to hit Raphael, he had mysterious ways of getting him to obey. Mina never asked how it worked, for fear of breaking the charm, but when she came home in the evening the big plastic water jugs would all be full, the house would be clean, and Raphael and Jelly would be playing chess in light so dim that they must be keeping track of the pieces in their heads. Raphael took the machine under his wing. At the internet café, he apparently ingratiated himself enough by doing odd jobs that they let him recharge Jelly's battery every morning. Mina began to suspect that they gave him a little cash, too, but he never admitted it.

It was only by chance that she found out what was really happening. It was a Wednesday, and *Baba* had been gone for two nights. *Nga* was worried, of course—perhaps in the same way one would worry about a goat that had jumped a fence, and might damage someone else's garden—but what could she do? She had to clean the rooms at the Novotel in the day, and then go and sell the toilet paper at the bus station in the evening. She asked Mina to go on her midday break and buy some groundnuts and tomatoes for a sauce, if the price was good. It was raining and devilishly hot. Mina slogged through the steamy, foul-smelling streets until she got to the market, and there was Raphael with a big bag over his shoulder, stepping off a minibus. A minibus!

He sat down at a metal table under the awning of a café at the edge of the little market square. Incised on the table, and just barely visible from this distance, were the grid-lines of a chessboard, the faded squares indistinguishable black from white. He leaned on the fence surrounding the café. Oh, so casual: it was something he did all the time. A woman brushed against his arm with a brown chicken she dangled by its legs. She apologized, and he laughed it off. Even though she was older, he met her eyes as directly as a drunken soldier at a checkpoint at night.

Mina went ahead and bought the groundnuts, because a duty was still a duty, and bargained all the more aggressively because of the angry way her heart was beating. The tomato-man was impossible, though—wouldn't go below seventeen thousand francs a kilo, which was robbery, no matter how fresh they were. Meanwhile she kept an eye on Raphael. A prosperously fat Malinké man, with a bald head like a cannonball, came up to the table. He had polio and walked with a cane. He tried to look like he didn't care whether he got a game or not, but anyone could see that he did, just from the effort it cost him to haul that big body closer to the table on those spindly legs.

Wads of blue ten-thousand-franc notes appeared, and from his bag Raphael produced a chess clock and an inert-looking

Jelly, whom he enlisted as a paperweight to hold down the bills by the side of the board.

Mina crept up closer behind Raphael. The sweat rolling down the Malinké's head formed systems of rivers and tributaries. It felt as though God were pressing the market square like a shirt between the plates of a steam iron. The waiter had brought a pot of tea, but neither player disturbed the inverted cups. They were playing some kind of speed game, and it was over quickly. The money went into the fat man's pocket. Mina stifled a sob and crept a little closer.

"Okay, if you want," she heard Raphael say through the din. She could see now that the man had a big, shiny watch on his wrist. They set the board back up, and after a little more negotiation Jelly became the unmoving guardian of another pile of money. This time there were some red twenty-k notes mixed in with the blues. This game lasted longer. A dirty-looking man standing outside the awning tried to give advice, which both players ignored. *"Échec et mat,"* Raphael said after a while, and Mina could tell from the way the fat man and the dirty man reacted that it took them both by surprise. Raphael made the money disappear, thanked his opponent for the game, and put a stack of coins on the table for the untouched tea. He swept up the big bag and turned around to go, and then he saw Mina. His eyes showed only the briefest hint of recognition before they rolled away and he strode across the market and into the crowd. She tried to follow him, but she bumped into an old woman and almost knocked her down. By the time she was done apologizing, he had escaped.

While she worked that afternoon, she tried to sort out her thoughts. Despite the jumbled state of her brain, her hands went about their work efficiently, testing the coin-sized solid-state drives and sorting them into the three baskets: encrypted, unencrypted, and broken.

Her first reaction had been horror at the amounts of money Raphael was wasting. But it wasn't money that she and *Nga* had earned, it was money he'd come up with himself. Was he a professional chess hustler now? Was Jelly as inert as he seemed, or was he somehow helping Raphael to make the right moves? If Raphael was making cash, where was he hiding it? Was he spending it on drugs, or going to Wolosso clubs in the afternoons and dancing with buttock-swinging infidel girls in miniskirts? Mina had been dreaming of the day when she could "kick him over the threshold" into manhood so that he wouldn't be a burden anymore, but not this soon—he was only fourteen, even if he looked bigger and older. He seemed to be throwing around more money than *Nga* and Mina made together, so why should they work so hard to feed him, while he deceived them and hid his wealth? She made up virtuous fantasies of what *she* would do with that kind of money: buy *Nga* a fancy gown woven with gold, and a big, soft chair from Japan with a built-in foot massage.

A wet slap of sandals: Raphael.

"You!" She got up and shook a fist at him. "What have you been doing?"

"You mean the chess? Forget that, *Baba*'s in trouble! He had a run-in with some soldiers, and now they want money."

She felt like a dog whose bone had been popped out of its mouth while it wasn't looking. "Drunk, or sober?"

"The soldiers, or *Baba*? Anyway I think they're all drunk."

"God is my protector!"

"I know, fucked up, heh? They're at our house, and they want a hundred."

"A hundred what?"

"Euros, stupid, what did you think, francs? They aren't little kids looking for candy money. I've got enough, but it's all in S.P.E., and it's after hours at the hotel, and Ismael—he works at the desk—he doesn't have a phone at home and I don't know his address, so—"

"S.P.E.?"

"*Système de poche électronique,* you know, *certificats,* and—"

"No, I don't know. Where's this money?"

"In here." He pulled Jelly out of his bag.

"He has a hidden pocket, like a *kangourou*?"

"No, no, don't you know anything? It's lots of numbers,

it's like a big long computer password that says the bank has to give me this much money. Foreigners use it because it's safe, right? Insured for if you get robbed, whatever. But the company doesn't want the hotels doing *électronique* deals with locals, okay? Too much fraud, 419 and all that." Mina nodded. The Nigerians were to blame for that, of course. Everyone knew they were born thieves, just like the Malinké were born stupid. "But obviously I can't keep stacks of bills in our neighborhood, so I have to do S.P.E. Ismael isn't supposed to let me, but we have an understanding."

"But you can't find Ismael. So where can we go to make Jelly's magic money into real money?"

"The internet café on the *Avenue de la République*. They have electricity at night, and they have an S.P.E. box on the bar so you can pay for your time or buy beer and shit. But because of the fraud thing, this level-two box, it only lets one person do fifty euros a day. It checks your biometrics, and—"

"So if I come, each of us can take out fifty euros."

"Right."

They rode back in a real yellow taxi—with a chesty woman on the flatscreen in the back of the driver's seat intimating huskily, *I bet he drinks Carling Black Label!*—and the alien experience finally brought home to Mina the seriousness of the situation. She cursed herself for being so impressed by the taxi, and the speed with which the shops and kiosks flew by; her own stupid reaction reminded her of *Nga*'s sister-in-law's niece's idiotic account of how she'd visited her friend from school, a refugee from a remote province, in the hospital. The niece always dwelled on the height of the building, its silent elevators, its clean floors and windows, and how all the nurses could read like professors. She never seemed to get around to why the friend got in a hospital bed in the first place. It seemed to Mina that her relationship to *Baba* had become as tenuous now as her relationship to the distant cousin's school-friend. Mina tried to make herself remember the times before *Baba* had started to drink, when he'd been kind to her. It was like nerving yourself to chew some old, dried-up rice that you knew would make you sick.

The driver pulled up in front of the blazing lights of the internet café. "We'll be right back," Raphael told him. "We just have to get some cash from the S.P.E. box." The driver tried to object, but Mina and Raphael jumped out too quickly to allow for argument. They plunged into the dark, smoke-filled café and strolled, Raphael confidently and Mina trying to seem so, past the hoodlums and rich boys and tourists shooting things on computer screens. Raphael slid onto a barstool as if it were something he did all the time, and said to Jelly, whom he held belly-up in his lap, *"Réveille-toi."* Jelly wiggled his furry purple legs and twisted his head to see what was going on. His cute little ears dangled and flopped around endearingly. If only *Baba* could be so sweet and lovable!

"Bon, Jelly," Raphael said, drawing on his store of gutter French, "let's open desktop slash private slash—"

"I have internet connectivity," Jelly announced, with his jaw waggling upside-down. He didn't really have lips and a tongue, just a speaker, but they'd made him so his mouth moved anyway.

"Oui—" Raphael began again.

"I have 17.7 terabytes of software updates," Jelly squeaked.

"Skip that, Jelly. You don't need to phone home right now."

"Relaying GPS coordinates: 166 milliradians north, 239 west."

Mina felt a surge of alarm. "Has he ever been awake in here before?" she asked Raphael in a low voice.

"No." Raphael's brow furrowed. "I just recharge him in the back room. I don't activate him while—"

The taxi driver's sweaty, gap-toothed face was suddenly spraying spit on Mina's nose and cheek. "All right, girlie, you paying or not? My meter's still running. Want me to call the police?"

"My use pattern is showing unusual activity," Jelly said. "For your protection, an anti-theft alert has been triggered."

"Salam, camarade," Mina told the taxi driver, who was straddling her leg and close to knocking her off the stool. She put her hand on his chest. "I'm sorry for the misunderstanding. We'll just be a moment while we—"

"Leave my sister alone, *cow-boy*—"

"What's the problem here?" the wiry old woman behind the bar demanded, and then a purple ball of fur whirled like a demon, leapt the chasm behind the bar, caromed off of some bottles of liquor, and disappeared down onto the floor. The old woman screamed and grabbed a bottle to brandish against the apparition. Raphael dove across the bar, and Mina wriggled away from the cab driver and ran around to the end to block Jelly's escape route. She crashed into someone and landed on the floor, caught a glimpse of Jelly running by, wedged him against the back of the bar with her knee, and caught him by the scruff of his neck. Raphael dragged her backward. She scrambled to her feet, and they ran out the back door into the dark and familiar alleys of their neighborhood.

Mina clutched Jelly like a rugby ball in the crook of her arm, her hand clamped over his nattering mouth, and as they ran she tried to think. *Leave my sister alone.* She'd never believed that her brother could be more than a donkey looking for some trick to get out from under its load, but she had to admit that he'd not only been resourceful but stood up for her—and for *Baba*, too. She tripped over a beggar who'd already settled down for the night. Stumbling, she lost her grip on Jelly, and he went flying down the alley. Raphael snatched him back up, and by the time Mina caught up with them she saw that the little robot seemed to have calmed down. Maybe she'd underestimated him, just as she'd underestimated her brother. She caught Raphael by the arm.

"Jelly?" she asked.

"Yes?"

"You know, we're not trying to steal you."

"Oh, I know that," he said. "Ms. Nagel threw me away."

"What's this all about?" a toothless old lady demanded, peeping out from behind a dumpster. Raphael apologized, and they moved farther down the alley toward home.

"So Ms. Nagel threw you away," Mina prompted.

"She was tired of paying the bill every month. She's going to tell Piper I was lost."

"But . . . you said your anti-theft alert had been set off . . ."

"Triggered."

"Triggered. Because . . ."

"Because of the unusual use pattern." He didn't seem to see any contradiction there. But maybe that didn't mean he was stupid. Maybe it was like feeling angry when you knew you shouldn't, or believing in tree-spirits even though you said you were a Muslim. "Who do you think is your owner now?" she asked.

"Petopia, Inc."

"You mean if the person throws you away, the ownership goes back to the company that made you?"

"No, Petopia always owned me. Petopians aren't sold to the users, just licensed."

"I see. So really we have as much claim on you as anyone, right?"

"Let me do this," Raphael said. "He's really mine these days. Or . . . not mine, but—I'm his user, right? It's me that knows how to use him."

"That's stupid! I found him."

"Yeah, you stole him, all fair and legal, and then I stole him from you, just as fair."

"It wasn't stealing. We already discussed that, right, Jelly?"

"Right."

"Okay, so let's say we went back to the internet café," she proposed to the animal. "Now that we've worked all this out, you wouldn't do your theft thing—"

"—my anti-theft alert."

"You wouldn't do that again, would you?"

"Yes, I would. Well, I would if the server sent me the command again, and I think it would, because it would be the same conditions. I finished some of my software updates, though. I only have 17.5 terabytes left to do. When I finish those you'll need to restart me."

"*Bon,* I understand, you don't have control over that kind of thing. But you see, Jelly, we have a serious problem, and we need you to help us—"

"He doesn't understand shit like that," Raphael objected.

"Maybe he understands more than you think," Mina said. Jelly didn't seem to be very good at understanding himself, but even if he was just a machine, he was a machine that could learn. As his life went on he could get smarter. Maybe he was still growing up, like Raphael and Mina. "Jelly, there are some people who are going to beat up our father. They want money."

"Never put up with bullying," Jelly said. "Tell a grownup. It's not something you have to handle on your own."

"Yes, but our father is a grownup, and so are the bullies."

"You could tell a teacher or a police officer. But," tilting his head again in that cute way, "you don't have a teacher, do you?"

"No. And these bullies are soldiers, so the police aren't going to help us."

"I have things I'm allowed to do if the bullying is in progress and there's not time to get help," he said doubtfully.

"Yes, that's exactly the situation," Mina said. "What can you do?"

"I can make a sound like a loud whistle. That can get the attention of a nearby adult. Or I can do the alarm."

"What kind of alarm?"

"Well, the normal one sounds sort of like a car alarm. Usually that works."

Raphael said, "People around here don't have car alarms." Mina didn't even know what it was. "But yeah, I should have thought of that kind of thing. We went through your sounds folder before, right?"

"Like the ultrasonic signals for when you're playing chess?"

"Right, that folder. But this is going to be a sound that we *want* older people to be able to hear. Do you have a siren?"

The trick with the siren didn't work, probably because the soldiers knew that the streets were too narrow for vehicles to pass, but it did turn their attention for a while from abusing *Baba* to finding and then abusing Jelly. They used him as the ball for a game of cricket, but he kept from being destroyed because none of the soldiers were sober enough to get a hit. The house was an easier target, and they knocked it down. Mina liked to believe that they went away eventually because the family, and a couple of the neighbors, did their best to intervene, or at least stood nearby and exposed themselves to harm. Raphael maintained that the soldiers left because they got sleepy. Even so, it was obvious that Jelly had changed the situation for the better. He was like Raphael: whereas before he'd been an encumbrance, now at least he was a wildcard, a useful agent of chaos.

The family took shelter for a while under the bridge where the *Avenue de la République* stepped daintily over the salt evaporation ponds. At first Mina imagined that they would fix the house and move back into it, but they didn't have the right hardware and tools, and they were short on labor, because they had to work to get money for food. *Baba* was in the hospital, and he seemed like he was going to need some time to get better after what the soldiers had done to him. When Raphael tried to get his money turned into paper bills by the machine at the hotel, the S.P.E. company's A.I. agent said in its cheerful sing-songy voice that there was a freeze on his account "for your protection," and he should give a phone number and address to straighten it out. But the family had never had a phone, and as for a street address, it had never even occurred to Mina that a number might be assigned to her family's house, or an official name to the street it stood on.

Once the family was off their house's former parcel, their connection to the property slipped into a confusing kind of tenuity. Nobody seemed clear on the legal arrangements. There was a meeting with the landlady's son, at which it became clear that the landlady had died a while back without their knowing it, and which degenerated into an argument about the quality of the five cases of toilet paper that *Nga* had provided a while back in place of cash. Mina realized finally that she'd been misunderstanding how property worked in the modern world. She'd thought that people—at least rich landlords and rich American people—still owned things, but it was clear from what Jelly and the landlady's son said that really all you ever had these days was a license: a kind of temporary permission to use something, which could evaporate at any time for obscure reasons. Despite all the fancy techno-frills, the way it worked was more like what happened when a toddler screamed *mine!* The toy was only his until he lay down for a nap, and then it went away. Maybe it had always been that way, even long ago when the rich had first become rich and the poor poor. How could anyone have owned anything to start with, unless it was simply because one caveman bonked another on the head and walked off with the prize?

The bridge was drier than the house, and when she came home at night her nose adjusted to the briny smell more quickly than it had to the sewage stink in their old neighborhood. There were only a couple of other families there, so it wasn't even too crowded. There wasn't much you could objectively say against the bridge, except that it was a completely unsuitable place to imagine installing a big, soft Japanese chair with foot massage—but still Mina couldn't help feeling that it was a terrible step down in life. Equally illogical were her newly softhearted feelings about *Baba*, finally diagnosed with a damaged spleen. Once when she was bringing him food, she took Jelly along, and when she left the room for a moment and came back, she caught him saying something to the robot that sounded suspiciously like half-remembered endearments from her own childhood. He just looked up sheepishly at her, and she had to smile and stroke his balding head. The hospital cost a vast amount of money, which the billing lady said was really just a token payment compared to what it would have cost if he hadn't been a hardship case. Depending on which doctor they talked to, he might also need surgery.

That was how Mina and Jelly ended up at the Christian school run by the American nuns, sitting in front of the gigantic English dictionary. Between her feet was Raphael's big sack, full of solid-state drives from Alseny's e-waste computers: drives that were encrypted, so that they were useless to Alseny. Light streamed down onto Jelly through a window that had been nearly filled with a cheap plastic facsimile of stained glass, showing the miracle of the loaves and fishes. Television-blue light fell on the top of page 680, CINCTURE to CINQUEFOIL. Jelly, perched on the sill of the dictionary's carved wooden stand, pored over the pages that to him were as big as carpets. If it had been safe to bring him close to an internet hotspot again, he could probably have completed this process in a tenth of a second, but instead they had to spend hour after tedious hour here every morning before work. The nun who kept an eye on the library thought Mina was very studious.

Jelly stirred, and Mina reached out to turn the page for him, but he said, "I think I've got one: *CINNAMON123*."

"*Cinnamon*, what's that?"

"*Cannelier de Ceylan*, the spice. It's probably the name of their cat or something."

Mina smiled and shook her head. It still amazed her that so many of the rich foreigners could be so dumb, especially after they got to go to school until they were eighteen or twenty. Why would they go to all the trouble of encrypting their drives, but then choose a password that was basically just a word from the dictionary? No doubt when Jelly got farther through the alphabet he'd get hits like PASSWORD123 and SECRET123.

"Okay, which one?"

"I can find it. Open the bag."

She checked to make sure that the nun wasn't peeking in from the hall, then held the sack open in her lap so that Jelly could go in. His front paws dug like a dog's through the jumble. He had memorized a small part of each drive, like going to a library and memorizing one page out of each book. If he could decrypt the sample using CINNAMON123, he could probably decrypt the whole thing.

"This one," he squeaked from inside the bag, and pointed with his nose. She cabled him up to the drive through the port in his mouth.

He held still for a moment, then nodded and spoke—he could still talk even when his mouth was full. "Yes, that's working. I've got it all decrypted. Emails . . . banking . . ."

Raphael had a new system for handling money, something involving prepaid phone cards and a *hawala* in Cairo. Tomorrow he'd be at the cashier's window in the basement of the hospital with another small pile of ten-k notes.

"Ah, *très bien, mon petit chou.*" Jelly came out of the bag, looking proud. Mina stroked his head, and he wiggled his tailless rump and rubbed the side of his stubby little snout against her belly. He knew it, and Mina knew it too: Jelly had been kicked over the threshold.

Futures in the
Memories Market

NINA KIRIKI HOFFMAN

Nina Kiriki Hoffman lives in Eugene, Oregon. Her most recent books are a young adult novel, Thresholds *(2010), and* Fall of Light *(2009), a supernatural thriller. She has published more than two hundred fantasy and science fiction stories since 1983, and ten novels, including* The Thread That Binds the Bones *(1993),* The Silent Strength of Stones *(1995), and* Catalyst *(2006). She writes in the tradition of Zenna Henderson, Alexander Key, Andre Norton, and to a certain extent Ray Bradbury. Her fiction is optimistic, generous to her characters, and somewhat sentimental, often about finding your place in life and your community. Her last short-story collection was* Time Travelers, Ghosts, and Other Visitors *(2003). Given the quantity and quality of her short fiction in recent years, it seems to us that she's due for another one.*

"Futures in the Memories Market" was published in Clarkesworld, *the online magazine that won the Best Semi-Prozine Hugo Award in 2010. Itzal is a bodyguard for the memory mod(ule) star Geeta Tilrassen. Geeta has sold a bit too much of herself to her corporate employers. She cannot grow and change. The making of mods involves wiping the experience from her memory, ironically preserving her freshness and vivid perceptions for each new time and place.*

$\mathbf{Y}$ou can't do anything else when you emp one of Geeta Tilrassen's memory modules. Her senses seize you; you see through her eyes, taste with her tongue, hear with her ears. And touch? You've never felt air against your skin until you've felt it breathe across hers. In a desert environment, there's a sense of cinnamon in the air. When Geeta's on a water world, you feel the humidity as embrace instead of torture, as though you are constantly being kissed. Every module Geeta makes is fresh and innocent, and every time you use one, you feel as though it's the first time.

I've got one legitimate copy of a Geeta memod; I'm only allowed one at a time, and I've kept this one for a while. It's her visit to the Hallen people. Nothing very exciting happens. She walks into their village. (The red sand gets into your sandals, but instead of grinding against your feet or raising blisters, it's a pleasant friction.) The air smells of woodsmoke, charred flesh, and sage.

Hallen burrows are mostly underground, but they have built delicate aboveground structures of woven withies, beautiful as spider webs, with small crystals at the intersections that flare in the red sunlight.

The Hallen greet Geeta, draw her into one of the withy shelters, and give her the only thing it's safe for her to ingest from their cuisine, some kind of berry drink with bits of leaf in it. She drinks. The liquid is cool on your tongue, a nice contrast to the desert heat. You taste the essence of that drink a long time after she's swallowed the last sip, a sour-sweet merging of bright and dark flavors. She presses palms with the head lizard, smells his individual scent that shares species straw-tones with the others in the shelter but smells a shade more like sulfur and ginger. She listens to their drum-intensive music and sits in a woven-leaf chair with a Hallen egg in her lap. The music gets inside you like a second heart-beat, chasing your blood until you want to rise and dance. You can feel how warm the egg is, how there's something moving inside that leather shell. You sense Geeta's delight, the way it feathers her insides.

It only lasts about a minute real-time, maybe twenty minutes mod time. It's my favorite possession. I save it for the most difficult days, when I hate being Itzal Bidarte, the man who lost his home as a child and has never found another. I long for roots, and all I do is wander.

If I had Geeta's power, perhaps my memories of my homeland would be stronger. They are fragments, mostly visual, a plane of light on my mother's cheek as she leans to kiss me, my father settling in a deep chair beside the hearth and lighting his pipe with a coal on a wire he's fished from the fire.

I acquired a memod made by a cousin of mine, dead now. When I play it, I see again the stream beside our village, smoke rising from the chimneys of the white-plastered, red-shuttered houses on a cool morning, pots of red geraniums beside the doors, and even, I think, I catch a glimpse of my father leading a donkey down to drink. My dead cousin's memory is too flat, too simple. There are only muted sounds, distant scents, no touch. I don't feel as though I'm there. It is more like seeing something in a smoked mirror.

I've emped Geeta's memory module of the Hallen about twenty times. I notice different things each time. She is so alert to every sensation that a normal person can't take it all in at once.

What I don't see in the memod are Geeta's bodyguards. GreaTimes, the memory merchants who have the sole license to distribute Geeta's mods, edits us out. Even though I've gone on memory missions with Geeta, you will never sense me in one of her mods.

* * *

As the ship approached our next destination, I pressed the alert beside Geeta's cabin door. The door slid up and let me in.

Geeta stood in the middle of the cabin, with colored outfits draped over the omnishapes of furniture whose functions she hadn't set. The scentser laid down a faint, unobtrusive smell that covered any other odors in the cabin, and the audio was playing very low, something melodic without any percussion. Aside from the colors, this was Geeta neutral, as close as she could get to shutting down her senses and living on a par with the rest of us.

"Itzal," Geeta said, "you know more about this than I do. What should I wear on Tice?"

She had been to Tice before, but she didn't remember.

I looked over all her outfits and pointed to the scarlet one with the gilt, point-edged hem. "We're going to a big city on Tice, lots of energy and interaction. That dress will attract attention and intensify your experience."

She looked at me sideways, her broad mouth quirked at one corner. She was not beautiful in any of the regular ways, but her face was full of character, elastic enough to reflect her moods and thoughts. Only lately had I learned that she might be a different person behind her face, that there were parts of herself she had been hiding. "What if I want to have a quiet time?"

"Do you?" I asked.

She spun around, stopped, hugged herself. "You know me better than I know myself." She took the red dress and hung it from a ceiling ring. I helped her pick up the other clothes and store them behind the wall. She controlled the furniture into two chairs and a table, and we sat facing each other.

She tapped her wrist. I lifted my own wrist and swept the room with the spystopper. No glow: Geeta's corporate masters weren't watching us.

"Did you get me one?" she asked.

I shook my head. Sentients all through the interlinked worlds could buy Geeta's memods, but access to them was strictly limited aboard *The Collector*. Each crewmember could own one at a time, and Geeta was not allowed to use any of them. She didn't have an implanted emp receptor like the rest of us. She had to use an external one to get the cultural gloss and language of the places we visited before we arrived. Her corporate masters allowed her some forms of entertainment so she would be stimulated during our tween-worlds journeys through the skip nodes and in and out of systems. Nobody wanted Geeta to get bored.

"Maybe I can pick up something on Tice," I said. "I'm not sure how to get it aboard, though."

"Could you disguise it as something else?" she asked.

I thought about that. "Maybe. If I have enough money. I'd need to find an underground tech there who could make it look like your normal entertainment emps, so you could put it into the emper without them knowing what you're doing." I tapped my lips with my index fingers. Before I landed this job as Geeta's bodyguard, I had done some less-than-legal things—most of my guard training had come from people operating at the fringes of the linked worlds, in shadowy spaces often called Underground. I knew a few signs of the Starlight Fraternity that might lead me to someone on Tice who could successfully disguise an emp. Or the signs might have expired, and using them could get me into trouble.

I shook my head. "I don't think I can pay enough."

"I'll give you money."

"But Geet, you don't have any."

Geeta made the best memods in the business, according to her fans, who were legion across many worlds. Grea-Times bought her contract when she was very young, recognizing her memory potential even then; they had automated observers on most worlds, watching for talented children like Geeta. Geeta was kept in luxury, given everything she needed and wanted so long as it wouldn't interfere with her memories, but she had no salary, and no real freedom.

"I'll trade something." She looked around her cabin, went to the wall and opened a drawer full of jewelry. She had a robber bird's delight in sparkling things, so she often asked for and received jewel gifts when she had completed a memory job. She got out the Kudic rubies, a necklace with raw chunks of pink stone. It was one of her most expensive pieces.

I felt a prickle of excitement. We usually visited backwater planets, because people who bought memods seldom went there, and they were hungry for Geeta's fresh experiences. Tice was bigger than our usual stop; I might successfully fence jewels like these. They'd have a wider choice of memods for sale there, too. "Which memory do you want most?" I asked, tucking the jewels in an inner pocket.

"The horse people," she said. Though she wasn't allowed to emp her own memods, she could check the infostream and see the GreaTimes catalog, read the blurbs.

"I'll see what I can do." Geeta had a second guard, Ibo; we alternated shifts when we were in relatively safe environments. I had some leave due, and Tice had some quiet places Geeta was scheduled to visit.

"Thanks, Itzal." She pressed her cheek to the back of my hand. I wondered what that was like for her. Did she like my smell? The feel of my skin? These were small random memories no one would ever buy. GreaTimes let Geeta keep all her memories between missions, the dull details of shipboard life; it was only the planet visits they siphoned off, leaving her with amnesia of all her adventures, unknowing of any lessons she might have learned. They kept her in a state of confused innocence. She wanted to change that. She wanted me to help her recover the memories she had lost.

Ibo and I flanked Geeta as she stepped out of the shuttle, through the docking tunnel, and into Tice's "Welcome Outworld Travelers" Terminal. She looked everywhere, smiling wide. Hanging baskets of local plants with long, colored fronds filtered the light coming through the hazed sky-ceiling, scattering spots of green and lavender on the floor. People attended by companion animals moved through the distance, intent on their own business. A mother with triplet daughters dangled a star on a string in front of her babies. They laughed and reached for it, and Geeta laughed, too.

I hungered for her response to this situation even as I

surveyed the area for potential threats. Like Geeta and Ibo, I'd emped the culture and language memod for Tice last night. I still wasn't sure about the companion animals; they'd be easy to mimic. Some looked like large dogs, some like pack animals, and some walked upright like the humans they accompanied, and looked like nothing I'd seen before. What if one of them was the kind of fan who wanted Geeta to experience death or pain so they could share her intense response to that? She'd encountered threats before.

Because of the nature of her memories, most people had no idea what Geeta looked like. She rarely looked at herself in mirrors. If her reflection happened to show up in a memory, GreaTimes fuzzed it. She had been captured in some tourist vids GreaTimes could do nothing about, though; a tricky outsider might have some idea of what she looked like. Plus there was always the general threat anyone might fall under in any place.

Ibo took the lead. We went through customs scan. They determined that Ibo and I were licensed to carry the stun weapons we had. We had no luggage. Geeta never stayed anywhere overnight. It only took her a few hours to collect several salable memory sets. She had already started. She had a long conversation with the customs official about what kind of people he met, what their stories were, what people tried to smuggle in. Ibo and I stood patiently while the customs official called over his superior and had her tell more stories. All part of Geeta.

I had the rubies in a shielded belt. I wasn't sure the belt would fool sophisticated scanners on Tice, or even the ship's scanner, though I hoped the stones would show up as just rocks and metal. (Emps triggered the ship scanner—it was looking for them.) Then again, rubies weren't illegal or dangerous. I didn't want Captain Ark to know about them, though, or Ibo.

We left the terminal through close-pressed crowds of various kinds of people and animals. Geeta smiled at them, and they found themselves smiling back, maybe without thinking about it. The usual ripple of pleasant spread around us as we moved. Even the pickpocket whose hand I caught in Geeta's purse smiled after I retrieved Geeta's pay-ID, because Geeta said, "Better luck next time," with a short warble of laughter, and kissed his cheek before I released him back into the wild.

On the curb of Hollow Street, Geeta engaged a cab. She sat in the back sandwiched between me and Ibo and told the driver we wanted to go to the Queen's Sculpture Garden, the first of four planned stops here.

Last time Geeta came to Tice, she started with the amusement park. I wasn't with her then, but I've heard from people who have emped that module. They love it. Even when she threw up on the big roller ride. I was surprised that wasn't edited out.

The sculpture garden was quiet when we got there, apparently not a big attraction early on a work day. Only some of the sculptures were made by humans; others had been left behind by vanished alien civilizations, or some made by the three alien species we regularly traded with. All were meant to be touched. Geeta was in her element, studying the sculpture with eyes, ears, nose, fingers, palms, finally full-bodied embraces. She climbed into the lap of a Greatmother and curled up there, hugging herself, her cheek against the smooth dark stone. The bliss on her face made me wonder if she were thinking about her own mother's lap, or some other place where she had been perfectly comfortable. Her emotions loaded with the memods, but you couldn't read her thoughts, though sometimes I felt like I could.

Ibo and I had been standing at an easily editable distance, watching Geeta make memories for half an hour, when she looked around and said, "Ibo, we're safe here, aren't we?"

Ibo and I both surveyed the garden, using our detection gear to see if anyone or anything dangerous was nearby. No threats.

"It's okay for Itzal to take half an hour of his leave now," Geeta said. "I'll be here at least that much longer."

"What have you two cooked up?" Ibo asked.

"You took leave on Geloway," I said. We had been walking

a tour trail through a spectacular lava field when Ibo begged time off. He had come back, smelling of sex shop perfume, when we were in the sweet shop at the end of the tour.

"True," he said. He frowned as though he realized it was a mistake to accuse me and Geeta of anything during a memod. The GreaTimes people edited us out, but for sure they listened to our conversations before they eliminated them. "All right. See you later, Itzal," he said, and I left.

We are not supposed to know how to hack our trackers, but my last job before joining the Geeta team was with a research and development security company, and I learned a lot there. I entered false coordinates in my tracker and headed for Pawn Alley.

Twenty-nine minutes later I was back in the sculpture garden with news I kept to myself.

The rest of our tour of Tice went without trouble, and Geeta, Ibo, and I taxied back to the terminal, our arms full of souvenirs—boxes of Tice teacakes in five flavors, soft and textured stuffed animals, three new dresses for Geeta with hats, shoes, overtunics, and jewelry to match, and an infostream address for the man Geeta had met and kissed at the races. Having walked through the day with Geeta, and watched her differing delights, including that kiss, I wanted the whole suite of today's memods. Maybe I'd get them, one at a time, though there were so many Geeta memods on my wish list already. . . .

Geeta had a party with the ship's crew, sharing the treats she'd brought back, and talking about her day. We were all charmed, as we always were the night before the company extracted her memories. We got to see who Geeta might be if she could have held on to her experiences. We all loved the woman she would never become.

Later, the cakes gone and souvenirs distributed amongst the crew, to be hidden any time Geeta came near—though she always got to keep any clothes and accessories she bought—I escorted Geeta back to her cabin. She went into the changing alcove while I spystopped. I found a new active camera and managed to remotely access its feed while my back was to it. Geeta fluttered back into the cabin in her exercise clothes, talked about her adventures, then started her nightly routine. Three repetitions in, I created a loop and sent the camera into nontime. As soon as I gave Geeta the all-clear, she rushed to me.

She saw my expression and sighed, two steps before she would have collided with me.

"They were fake," I said.

"The rubies?"

"I went to three pawn shops and they all told me the same thing. Decent fakes, not spectacular. Worth no more than glass. Didn't get enough to even contact anyone who might have disguised the real memods. I traded what I got for the rubies for a couple disguised bootlegs, the lava walk on Placeholder and the plunge valley on Paradise. I need to test them. Maybe they won't be infected." I had tried a couple of bootlegs of Geeta's memods without testing them, back when I was younger and stupider. They were dirt cheap but still amazing, though they suffered from copy fatigue. Often the bootleggers placed compulsions in them that took money, time, and effort to eradicate. I still had the urge to gamble every time I passed an Ergo machine.

"Fake," Geeta repeated. She wandered to her jewelry drawer, stared down at her treasures, and shut the drawer, her shoulders drooping. Then, angry, she stepped back into place and resumed her exercises. I unlooped the spy camera and we went through her night-of-a-collection-day routine, which included a shower for Geeta and a furniture keying for me: I had to shape the bed so it would do the extraction during the night.

Washed free of every trace of Tice, Geeta let me help her into the bed, fasten the restraints, and plug in her head. "Kiss me," she said. "I want two kisses in a day. I never had that experience before, did I?"

I kissed her long and deep, kissing the woman we were killing. This kiss wouldn't make it into the memods; her return to the ship was always cut out. We had done the Tice Ending Shot at sunset on a mountain where cool wind touched us with feathered fingers; it would be spliced onto the end of each of Geeta's Tice memods.

Geeta would not remember the kiss, but I would, the taste of her sorrow and desperation mixed with the last sweet tang of willowcake. She often kissed me last thing after a mission; I had a collection of these moments in my memory, moments that sometimes deceived me into thinking we were closer than we were.

Her lips relaxed, and I straightened out of the kiss, looked down into her tear-wet eyes.

"Good night, Geeta," I said softly.

"Good night, Itzal." She closed her eyes. I set the bed on COLLECT and touched off the lights as I left the room.

In my own much smaller and sparer cabin, I checked for spies. I had never found one; what I did away from Geeta didn't concern the GreaTimes people, as long as it was legal and not going to impair my care for her.

I put the Hallen memod in the recycle slot and took out the memod I had bought with the ruby money, what I hadn't put away. I had bought the horse people, the one she'd asked me for. It was a memod she'd made before I was part of her staff. I had read the sales copy on all of them, wanting to know who she had been as much as she did. This was one of the better ones; all the reviews said so.

I set the new memod in my receptor and settled down to emp.

Geeta walked down a ramp into a sky seething with dawn clouds and the tracks of skitterbirds. The air smelled of damp and green, and morning animals called, a random concert with notes that sometimes clashed and sometimes harmonized. In Geeta's mind, it was all beautiful. The air was cool; Geeta felt it as a pleasurable hug from a chilly friend.

Three horses galloped up the soft-surfaced road and stopped just in front of her, breathing grass-scented breath, musky warmth pouring off them. She laughed and went to hug one, even though the culture memod said people weren't allowed to do that. How amazing to have your arms around so much huge intelligent warmth; the texture of damp hair against your cheek, the solid muscles shifting against your chest. The smell of the horse's sweat, salty and musky, stirred Geeta awake on several levels.

"Miss," said the horse, "Miss, I don't know you."

She released him and stepped back. "Oh! I'm sorry. Please forgive me. You don't know me yet, but I hope you will." He watched her with one large dark eye, as intricate and beautiful a glistening eye as I had ever seen, with a depth in it that might lead to mystery. I fell in love with the horse. I knew Geeta smiled up at him, because I saw his response: charmed, his head nodding a little, even as his companions laughed at him.

I settled deeper into being Geeta, finding a home that wasn't really mine but felt like mine. Geeta was home everywhere she went, and when I was emping her, I felt that way, too.

I didn't know if I would ever share this with her.

A Preliminary Assessment of the Drake Equation, Being an Excerpt from the Memoirs of Star Captain Y.-T. Lee

VERNOR VINGE

Vernor Vinge (vrinimi.org) lives in San Diego, California. He is the author of many SF stories and novels from the 1960s to the present, including, most prominently, A Fire upon the Deep *(1992), a novel that helped create the hard SF renaissance of the 1990s, and its prequel,* A Deepness in the Sky *(1999). His most recent novel is the hard SF novel* Rainbows End *(2006). He is among the most popular and influential living hard SF writers.*

"A Preliminary Assessment of the Drake Equation, Being an Excerpt from the Memoirs of Star Captain Y.-T. Lee" appeared in Gateways. *In a way that reminds us a little of Terry Bisson's novel,* Voyage to the Red Planet—*future interstellar exploration is financed by the media. Real science and media fakery happen all at the same time. Here, the captain of the title has discovered a barely habitable planet the media conglomerate has renamed Paradise. Is there life on Paradise?*

At the time of its discovery, Lee's World was the most earthlike exoplanet known. If you are old and naïve, you might think that the second expedition would consist of a fleet of ships, with staff and vehicles to thoroughly explore the place. Alas, even back in '66, that was not practical. The Advanced Projects Agency had too much else to survey. APA paid me and my starship the *Frederik Pohl* to make a return trip, but they eked out the funding with some media-based research folks. And they insisted on renaming the planet. Lee's World became "Paradise."

Ah, the "Voyage to Paradise". That should have given me warning. Over the years, I've had some good experiences with APA (in particular, see chapters 4 and 7), but that name change was a gross misrepresentation. The planet is in the general class of Brin worlds—about the only type of water world that can maintain exposed oceans for a geologically long period of time. Those oceans are extraordinarily deep, almost like an upper layer of mantle, but with no land surface—except in the case of Lee's World, where some kind of core asymmetry forced an unstable supermountain above sea level.

More important than the name change, APA gave the mission's science staff way too much independence. When you are on a starship in the depths of space, there has to be just one boss. If you want to survive, that boss better be someone who knows what she's doing. I have a long-term policy (dating from this very mission as a matter of fact): scientists must be sworn members of the crew. Even a science officer can cause a universe of harm (see chapter 8), but at least I have some control.

In fact, there were some truly excellent scientists on my "Voyage to Paradise," in particular Dae Park. Most legitimate scholars consider Park's discovery as making this expedition the most important of the first twenty years of the interstellar age. On the other hand, several of my so-called scientist passengers were journalists in shallow disguise—and Ron Ohara turned out to be something worse.

We landed near the equator, on the east coast of the world's single landmass, an island almost one hundred kilometers across. It was just after local sunrise. That was the decision of Trevor Dhatri, our webshow producer—excuse me, I mean our mission documentarian. Anyway, I'm sure you've seen the video. It is damn impressive, even if a bit misleading. I brought the *Frederik Pohl* in from the ocean, along a gentle descent that showed miles and miles of sandy beaches, bordered with rows of glorious surf. The shadows were deep enough that the little details such as the absence of cities and plant life were not noticeable. In fact, the human eye has this magical ability to take straight lines and shadows and extrapolate them into street plans, forested hills, and colors that aren't really there. Blued by distance, mountains loomed, clouds skirting along the central peaks, and there was a hint of snow on the heights.

I have to admit, the video is a masterpiece. It could be showing a virginal Big Island of Hawaii. In fact, there are no trick effects in these images. They are simply Lee's World shown in its best possible light. The beach temperatures were indeed Riviera mild, and there really was scattered snow high in the far mountains. Of course, this artfully ignored the *minor* differences such as the fact that half the world—all the mid- and high latitudes—was encased in ice, and the fact that there was essentially no free oxygen in the atmosphere. Hey, I'm not being sarcastic; those aren't the big differences.

Fortunately my passengers were not as ignorant of the big differences as the presumed webshow audience. Within an hour of our landing, the geologists were out in the hills, following up on what their probes had reported. Within another hour, Dae Park had her submersible and deep samplers cruising toward the oldest accessible sea floor.

My crew and I had our own agenda. Coming in, my systems chief had been monitoring the seismo probes. Now that we were grounded, we were stuck for a minimum of eight hours before we could boost out. Crew was quietly working at a breakneck speed to get everything ready in case we had to retrieve our passengers and scram.

I did my best to look bored, but once Trevor had taken his media focus off my command deck, I had a serious chat with my systems chief. "Can we get out of here by landing plus eight—and will we need to?"

Jim Russell looked up from his displays. "Yes to the first question, assuming Park and Ohara"—both of whom had insisted on crewing their submersibles—"obey the excursion guidelines. As for the second question . . ." He glanced at the seismic time series scrolling past on his central display. "Well, the problem is that we don't yet have a baseline to make predictions with, but my models predict a seismically stable period lasting at least forty hours."

"This is seismically stable, eh?" I was an army brat. I've lived everywhere on Earth from Ankara to Yangon. I was in Turkey after the quake of '47. For weeks, the aftershocks were rattling us. That was nothing compared to this place. The deck beneath our feet had been quivering constantly since we landed.

Jim gave a smile. "Actually, Captain, if we go for more than an hour or two without any perceptible shaking, it would be a very bad sign."

"Um. Thank you so much." But at least that was something definite to watch for.

"I always try to look at the bright side, Captain. You're the one who's paid to worry. And your job could be harder." He waved at a view of the outside. It showed Trevor Dhatri hassling crew and scientists to create the most photogenic base camp possible. Now I saw why our sponsors had paid for state-of-the-art O2 gear. The transparent gadgets barely covered the nose and mouth. Jim continued, "Dhatri is play-ing the paradise angle as hard as he can. If he ever gets tired of that, I bet he'll go for the high drama of explorers racing the clock to escape destruction."

I nodded. In fact, it was something I had considered. "I welcome the lack of attention. On the other hand, I don't want our passengers to get *too* relaxed. If those subs go be-yond the excursion limits, all our diligence is for nothing." It was a delicate balance.

I grabbed one of the toylike oxy masks and went outside. Damn. This was stupid. And dangerous. Explorers on a new world should wear closed suits, with proper-size O2 tanks. But everybody in our glorious base camp was wandering around in shirtsleeves, some in T-shirts and shorts. And barefoot!

I moseyed around the area, discreetly making sure that my crewfolk were aware of the situation and dressed at least sensibly enough to survive a bad fall.

"Hey, Captain Lee! Over here!" It was Trevor Dhatri, wav-ing to me from a little promontory above the camp. I walk up to his position, all the while trying to think what to say that would make him cautious without exciting his melodramatic instincts. "How do you like our view of Paradise, Captain?" Trevor waved at the view. Yes, it was spectacular. We were looking down upon a vast jumble of fallen rock, and beyond that the beach. From this angle it looked like some resort back home. Turn just a little bit, and you could see my starship and the busy scientists. I debated warning him about the per-ils of the view. That talus looked *fresh*.

"Isn't the base camp splendid, Captain?"

"Hm. Looks cool, Trevor. But I thought the big deal of this expedition was the Search for Life." I waved at his bare feet. "Shouldn't your people be more worried about con-taminating the real estate?"

"Oh, you mean like the Mars scandal?" Trevor laughed. "No. Near the landing site, it's impossible to avoid contami-nation. And from the Mars experience, we know there will be low-level global contamination in a matter of years. We're concentrating all our clean efforts on the first sampling of likely spots. For instance, the exterior gear on the submersibles is fully sterile. I daresay you won't find even inorganic contamination." He shrugged. "Later landings, even later runs on this expedition—they'll all be suspect." He turned, looked out to sea. "That's why today is so important, Captain Lee. I don't know what Park or Ohara may bring back, but it should be immune to the complaints that mucked up Mars."

Yeah, so besides their well-known rivalry, Park and Ohara had reason to take chances right out of the starting gate. I glanced at the range traces that Jim Russell was sending me. "I notice Park's submersible is more than sixteen kilometers down, Trevor."

"Sure. I've got a suite of cameras inside it. Don't worry, those boats are rated to twenty kilometers. Dae Park has this theory that fossil evidence will be near the big drop-off."

"Just so she doesn't exceed our excursion agreement."

"Not to worry, Ma'am. Of the two, Dae is the rule-follower—and you'll notice that Ron Ohara is still very close to the beach, barely at scuba depth." His gaze hung for a moment, perhaps watching what his cameras were showing from Ohara's dive. "There'll be some important discovery today. I can feel it."

Ha. So while I obsessed about ship, crew, and scientists, Dhatri obsessed on his next big scoop. I messaged Jim Russell to ride herd on the ocean adventurers—and then I let our "mission documentarian" guide me back to the center to the base camp. That was okay. I don't like standing ten meters from a cliff where magnitude seven earthquakes happen every few days.

Back in the camp, I began to see what Dhatri was up to. Of course, it wasn't science and in fact he wasn't doing much with the exploration angle. Dhatri was actually making a case for colonizing the damn place. No wonder he kept calling it "paradise." All this was sufficiently boggling that I let him lead me this way and that, showing off the crusty starship captain working with scientists and crew. My main attention was on the range traces from the submersibles. Besides which, Trevor's video work was really confusing, just little unconnected bits and gobs, all set pieces. It was quite unlike most web videos from my childhood. After a while I realized I was seeing the wave of the future. Trevor Dhatri was a kind of pioneer; he realized that in coming years, the most important videos would never be live. Even the shortest interstellar flights take hours. On this expedition, the *Frederik Pohl* was almost four days out from our home base in Illinois. Dhatri could sew all this mishmash into whatever he chose—and not lose a bit of journalism's precious immediacy.

I was still outside when a siren whooped up, blasting across the encampment. I got to my system chief while the noise was still ramping up. "What in hell is that?"

Jim's voice came back: "It's not ours, Captain. It's . . . yeah, it's some kind of alarm the scientists set up."

Dhatri seemed to have more precise information. He had dropped his current interview when the siren blared. Now he was scanning his cameras around the camp, capturing the reaction of crew and scientists. His words were an excited blather: "Yes. Yes! We don't know yet what it is, but the first substantive discovery of this expedition has been made." He turned toward me. "Captain Lee is clearly as surprised as we all are."

Yes. Speechless.

I let him chivvy me toward where the scientists were congregating.

Trevor was telling me, "I gave all the away teams hot buttons—you know, linked to our show's Big News feed. That siren is the max level of newsworthiness." His voice was still excited, but less manic than a moment before. He grinned mischievously. "Damn, I love this asynchronous journalism! If I botch up, I can always recover before it goes online." As we got close to the others and the fixed displays, he reverted to something like his official breathlessness. His cameras shifted from faces to displays and then back to faces. "So what do we have?"

An oceanographer glanced in Trevor's direction. "It's from one of the submersibles. Dae Park."

"Dae—?" I swear, Trevor suffered an instant of uncontrived amazement. "Dae Park! Excellent! And her news?"

In my own displays, I was checking out Park's submersible. It was still sixteen kilometers down. Thank goodness the "Big News" did not involve going deeper. Her boat was either on the bottom or just a few meters up, motionless. Okay, she was within the excursion rules, but near a hillside that could be a serious problem in a big quake. You'd never get me down there. I fly between the stars. Just the idea of being trapped in a tiny cabin under sixteen thousand meters of water makes me queasy.

Around me, I heard a collective indrawing of breath. I glanced back at the fixed displays, seeing what everyone else was seeing—and I got an idea why someone might go to such an extreme: Park's lights showed the hillside towering over her boat. It looked like nondescript mud, but some recent landslide had opened a cleft. The lights shone on something round and hard-looking. The picture's scale bar showed the object was almost forty centimeters across. If you looked carefully, you could see knobbly irregularities.

The oceanographer leaned closer to the display. "By heaven," he said. "It looks like an algae mat."

Everyone was quiet for a moment. Even my crew—well, all but the cook—knew the significance of such a discovery.

"The fossil of one," came Dae Park's voice. She sounded very pleased.

And then everyone was talking except Trevor—who had his cameras soaking it all in. There was significant incredulity, mainly from Ron Ohara's staff: the video showed just the one object. If this was really life—or had been real life—where was the context? Park's guys argued back that this was probably millions of years old, transported by heaven knew what geological cycles to the deep mud. Ohara's people were unimpressed; the rock looked metamorphic to them.

"People, people!" The voice seemed to surround us. It was probably coming from the same sound system that made the siren noise. It took me a second to recognise Ron Ohara's voice behind the mellow loudness. "I for one," Ohara continued, "have no doubt of Dr. Park's outstanding discovery. I'm sure that if she had focused on shallower water, she would have found living instances of communal life."

From her submersible, you could hear Dae Park spluttering, unsure what to do with the simultaneous insult and support. On the other hand, *Park* was the one who had just made the biggest discovery in the history of starflight. So after a moment, she said sweetly, "Thank you so much, Ron, but we've both seen the preliminary genome dredges. If there was significant life here, it was very long ago."

"I disagree. I have a—"

Park interrupted: "You have a theory. We have all heard your theories."

This was true. Ohara had droned on about them at the Captain's table every day of the voyage.

"Oh, it's not a theory, not anymore." You could almost hear him gloating, and I could guess what was coming next. After all, Ohara's sub had been scouting around the coast just a few meters down.

"Take a look at what I found." Ohara preempted all the displays with the view from his boat. The light was dim; perhaps it was true sunlight. But it was enough to see that my guess had been a vast underestimate: the creature's thorax was almost fifteen centimeters long, its limbs adding another ten centimeters or so. And those limbs moved, not randomly with the currents, but in clear locomotion. It might have been a terrestrial lobster, except for the number of claws and its greenish coloring.

This was the ninetieth voyage of the Starship *Frederik Pohl*. My ship and crew had visited eighty-seven star systems, all still within a few thousand light-years of Earth. As such, the *Fred Pohl* was one of the most prolific ships of the early years of exploration. My discovery of Lee's World had been one of the high points of that time. This second visit was shaping up to be something even more extraordinary.

By an hour after sundown all the remote teams were back—and we were close to having an onboard civil war. I eventually slapped them down: "I swear, if you people don't behave, I'll leave your junk outside and we'll lift off for Chicago this very night!"

For a moment the passengers were united, all against me. "You can't do that!" shouted Ohara and Park and Dhatri, almost in chorus. Dhatri continued: "You have a contract obligation to the Advanced Projects Agency."

I gave them my evil smile. "That's true but not entirely relevant. APA has clear regulations, giving competent ship management—that's me—the authority to terminate missions where said competent ship management determines that the participants' behavior has put the mission at risk."

Some eyes got big with rage, but to be honest that was the minority reaction. Most folks, including Dae Park, looked somewhat ashamed that their behavior had brought them to this. After a moment, Trevor nodded capitulation. Ron Ohara looked around at his faction and saw no support. "Okay," he said, trying for a reasonable tone. "I am always in favor of accommodation. But my discovery beggars the imagination." He waved at the aquarium-sample box that he had set in the middle of my conference table. "We can't afford to postpone the follow-up, no matter what the demands of the other—"

Park cut him off, but with a look in my direction: "So what do you suggest, Captain?"

Ohara wanted all the ship's resources turned toward his discovery, a massive dredge around the edge of the continent, led by his techs and using all our sea gear. Park was defending her own find and implying that Ohara was a monstrous fraud. Right now, my job was to keep them from killing each other. I waved those who were standing to take their seats. We were up on the main conference deck, what doubled as the Captain's table at mess. That gave me an idea. "No more fighting about resource allocation," I said. "The latest seismo analysis shows we have at least one hundred hours of safe time here. So take a moment to cool off. In fact, it is just about time for dinner. We'll have some light predinner drinks"—taking a chance there, but I'd make sure Cookie watered the wine—"and discuss, well, things that are not so sensitive. I'll be the umpire, where that's needed." Maybe with a good meal in them, I could get something like an even distribution of resources between Park—who had made an extraordinary discovery—and Ron Ohara's "miracle."

No one was happy, but given my threats, no one complained. On a private channel, I could see Jim Russell's messaging the cook and staff. I passed around a box of Myanmar cigars I'd brought along. Of course no one but me would touch them. I lit up and for a minute or so they stared at each other, silent except for the coughing of wimps. Finally, one of the Japanese contingent said, "So, how about them Dodgers?"

Ohara and Park just looked sullen. Every few seconds the ground somewhere beneath the *Frederik Pohl* gave a wiggle, reminding us all that whatever the seismo estimates, this was a world where evidence could disappear on short notice.

As Cookie had the drinks brought in, Ohara leaned back and said, "Seriously, Captain, we're going to have to settle some of this quite soon." He waved again at the aquarium. Sitting in the middle of it was a greenish critter that looked like a refugee from a very old science fiction video. Ohara's people called it Frito—I have no idea why. In truth, if it were not fraudulent, Frito was the the most extraordinary living thing ever seen by humans. I noticed that the creature was not nearly as lively as it had been in the discovery video. I bet myself that Ron hadn't figured how to keep the poor fake supplied with enough oxygen.

"Just be cool, Ron." If I could get everyone through dinner . . .

Then I noticed Cookie was looking at me nervously. His voice came in my ear, on a private voice channel. "Sorry, Captain, but I can't find any more banquet-class food."

We routinely stocked high-class dinners for passengers, and fresh food for the crew too. Given the short voyage times, there was no need for anything less. I gave Cookie an unbelieving glare.

"The victuals are here someplace, ma'am," continued Cookie's private communication. "It's the new container system that's screwed us."

I gave Cookie another look, and then turned back to Ohara: "We'll return to the resource issues right after a good meal. Our staff has planned something special for us tonight. Isn't that right, Cookie?"

Cookie Smith has been with me from the beginning. He doesn't give a damn about starflight or science, but he's a real chef. And he knows how to put on a good front. He gave everybody a big grin. "Yes, Ma'am, the very best." He and his white-jacketed assistants made their exit. Cookie's parting comment was private, and it wasn't quite so confident: "I'll keep looking, Captain."

Even if logistics had screwed up the luxuries, Cookie could probably work some kind of miracle with standard rations. The problem was that for now I had to string these guys along with weak wine and sparkling conversation. Actually, that would have been easy on the flight out. Having a Captain's table does amazing things for the egos of most passengers. (It also keeps the passengers out of the way of my crew, but that's another story.) This gang of academics was full of theories. Until today their arguments had been in the context of collegial socialization; it's what they got paid to do at their universities, after all. The trick was for me to put them back in that abstract mood, not raging about who was going to get what equipment in the next twelve hours.

"So," I said, looking around the table, "today has truly been a great day for science." I dimmed the lights a bit. Now the window light provided most of the illumination, a panoramic view from the ship's sensor mast. The result was a perfect illusion of looking out glass windows onto the last of the sunset twilight. Not counting my cigar smoke wafting around the table, it was a supernally clear evening. I noticed Trevor Dhatri repositioning his cameras. He had been sucking in all the Ohara-Park vitriol, but now he was looking outward. And I have to say that this quiet twilight didn't need Trevor's magic touch.

I waved at the sky. "Space, the final frontier." The words will forever send a shiver down my back. "If you look carefully, you can see the stars just coming out." You really could. I was filtering the video stream through an enhancement program—just enough of a boost so you could see the stars as they would appear in the deeper dark, after your eyes adjusted. "We are four hundred light-years from Earth, yet there's not a single recognizable constellation. Unless you're an observational astronomer, you probably couldn't find anything recognizable. Our generation has gone where no one has gone before. Humankind now has answers to questions that have bedeviled us since the beginning of time. We, *here, today,* have added immensely to those answers. What would we—who know the answers—say if we could talk to earlier generations?"

One of Park's guys piped up with, "We'd say that we have only partial answers ourselves."

"True," came a voice from the far end of the table, "but we know enough to render a preliminary assessment, real answers after generations of uncertainty." That was Jim Russell, bless him.

I picked up on Jim's point: "We have hard numbers to assess even the uncertainties. Take the central equation that bioscientists have used to summarize the mystery of life in the universe."

"The Venter-Boston relation?"

"No, no. Before that." These guys knew way too much about Venter-Boston. "I'm thinking of the Drake equation—you know, for the number of civilizations with which communication might be possible."

Silence all around.

"Okay," Dae Park finally said, "that's a good question. More general than Venter-Boston."

For a wonder, Ron Ohara seemed to agree: "Yeah. I . . . guess since the stardrive was invented, we scientists have become so focused on the near term that we don't talk about the questions that really drive the whole enterprise."

"Then now might be a good time to see where we stand," said Dhatri. He sounded sincerely interested in pursuing the topic. I could also see him rearranging his cameras. "Somebody scare up a definition of the Drake equation and let's supply some answers.

Now if we'd been back on Earth, I'm sure everyone

would've had that definition instantly. Groundhogs don't appreciate the solitude of deep space. In deep space, you don't have an instant link to the Internet. It can take hours or days to get home. I take considerable satisfaction from this fact. You don't have to put up with the incessant din of social networking and trivia searches. But some people can't tolerate the isolation. Many cope by hauling around petabytes of crap that they grab from the web before shipping out. On this occasion, I was grateful for their presence. After a moment, one of the Internet cache boobies popped up a definition from Wikipedia:

The Drake Equation (1960):
The number of civilizations in our galaxy with which communication might be possible can be expressed as the product of the average rate of star formation times
$$fp*ne*fl*fi*fc*L$$
where
fp is the fraction of those stars that have planets;
ne is the average number of planets that can potentially support life per star that has planets;
fl is the fraction of the above that go on to develop life at some point;
fi is the fraction of the above that actually go on to develop intelligent life;
fc is the fraction of civilizations that develop a technology that releases detectable signs of their existence into space;
L is the length of time such civilizations release detectable signals into space.

The letters floated silvery in my cigar smoke.

I had not seen the Drake equation in a long time. From the murmuring around the cabin, I could tell that many of the younger folks had never seen it. The equation reached beyond their nearsighted concerns.

Park gave a little laugh. "So how many systems have APA and the other agencies explored?"

That's a question *I* could answer, since I tracked my ship's standing: "As of this month? Fifteen hundred and two. If you count robot probes"—which I don't since the robots can miss what trained explorers might notice—"maybe four thousand."

Park shrugged. "Four thousand out of hundreds of billions."

"But with the newest versions of the stardrive we can easily reach any point in the galaxy." That was Hugo Mendes, our staff astronomer. We'd need him if there were navigation problems and we wound up someplace *really* far from home. "I agree with Mr. Russell. We've seen enough to make some good estimates. . . ." He paused, reading the definitions. "You know, some of those factors aren't stated very well."

One of Park's protégés said, "Yes, but that's half the fun, seeing how the truth has twisted the Old Timers' questions."

And in a few minutes, they were all absorbed by this long-ago vision of our present.

The first factor, "fp," got a big laugh. "Almost every normal star has planets," Mendes said. "Lots of planets. Too many planets, crashing around, with wild-ass orbits and ejections. As stars migrate around the HR diagram, a lot of them even have second and third generations of planets."

Dae Park was nodding. "I remember reading how back in the nineteenth century, the great mathematicians tried to prove the long-term stability of our solar system. They never did, but no one realized that it wasn't a failure in their math. Only one in a hundred planetary systems lucks into stability for even a billion years."

Now in the floating Wiki extract, someone annotated "fp" with a smiley face and the comment "near 1.0, but so what?"

Trevor leaned forward. "That second factor, 'ne,' that's just about zero if you count all the unstable planetary systems that Hugo said."

"Okay, so just count the systems that stay stable long enough to be interesting."

No one said anything for a moment. Then, "Hmm, you know, if you count importing life, like we're trying to do nowadays on our colony worlds, ne might be near one." That was Jim Russell again. I couldn't tell if he was just working to hold up the discussion or if he were seriously intrigued.

"Yeah, with terraforming. That's cheating."

Just then Cookie's voice sounded in my ear. "Captain! I think I found where the logistic jackasses stored our banquet supplies. I've brought the containers up to the galley. It's not everything, but I can put together a nice meal, maybe a little short on dessert."

I leaned back from the table and muttered a response: "Excellent. Go ahead with what you've got." I really didn't care about dessert, that probably being past the time where pacifying distractions would be useful.

I missed whatever the group decided about "ne." They had moved on to "fl," the fraction of habitable worlds that "actually go on to develop life at some point." Oops, was this a problem? Park and Ohara were already growling at each other.

I tapped my wineglass on the table. "Ladies and gentlemen! Professors! Isn't factor 'fl' the simplest of all?"

Jim picked up on that. "Well, yes. The interstellar medium—at least where we've been—has enough simple organics that almost any habitable planet evolves bacterial activity. So factor 'fl' is essentially one. Certainty."

"Only technically speaking," that from one of Ohara's techs. "Sure, things like bacteria and archaea pop up very early, but they never go on to anything more. Before Paradise, we never found evidence of a transition to eukaryotes, much less metazoa. But today, all that is changed thanks to Professor Ohara's magnificent discovery." The tech waved expansively at Frito's vaguely glowing form.

I expected some kind of explosion from the Park camp, but Dae responded almost mildly: "We'll . . . see about Professor Ohara's unbelievable claims, but I agree with the rest. Today we've shown that there are places off Earth where something more advanced than simple bacteria can exist— or has existed. The transition is possible. After today, I would put a meaningful value for factor 'fl' to be at least one in hundred."

There were nods around the table. Since we had discovered

ten Brin worlds and another handful that had had surface water for some time, her numbers made sense.

"Very good," I said, moving right along before Ohara could respond, "that gets us to more interesting territory, namely factor 'fi,' the fraction of life-bearing worlds that develop intelligent life."

Trevor laughed. "I consider Earth to be such a world, but if it's not to be counted in this arithmetic—" He sounded discouraged for a moment. "All the thousands of worlds we've visited the last fifteen years. And yet we've come up with nothing." Strange. Trevor Dhatri had seemed such an unrestrained cheerleader. I hadn't thought he'd take note of failure—though somehow I doubted this little speech would show up in his online show. He paused and sounded a bit more chipper; maybe he'd figured how to spin this. "On the other hand, what we've discovered today gives me faith that the possibility of alien intelligent life is greater than zero. If we can just get a large enough baseline, a large enough sample size, we'll find our peers in the universe."

"It doesn't matter think we are effectively alone." This was Hugo Mendes. "You talk about how many worlds we've looked at. Fine. But in fact, we have visual access almost to the cosmological horizon—and nowadays we have observatories that can watch all that, every second. If there were an intelligent civilization anywhere, don't you think it would ask the same questions we do? Wouldn't it make signals we could recognize? But we don't get anything. Whatever the other factors, I don't think there are other civilizations in the observable universe, at least none that make signals." He waved at the silvery formula. Factor "fc" got the annotation: "Zero or as close as makes no difference."

We were getting near the end of the list. I really didn't want to resume the argument about who deserved to hog the research gear. Give them some time to cool off and I could pull a Solomon on them, dividing everything down the middle—which would leave Park with enough to do some real science. I gave Cookie a poke on my private voice channel: "When will you be in with the first course? Appetizers at least?"

"Not more'n five minutes, ma'am! I promise." Cookie sounded breathless.

I turned back to my mob of academics. Some of them looked unhappy with Hugo Mendes. Maybe he had gored their funding opportunities. This could burn up five minutes, but it might also cause real argument. I took a chance and brought them back on topic. "Ladies and gentlemen. We have only one more item on the Drake list, namely the length of time that a civilization might exist in a communicating form."

Ohara laughed. "Well, *we've* lasted. We've got several real colonies. I think factor 'L' could be a very long time."

That seemed hard to dispute.

"Oh, I don't know." This was one of the software jocks, a young fellow with a kind of smart-alecky air. "I think 'L' is as easily zero as any of the other factors."

Trevor Dhatri gave him a look. "Come, come. We're here aren't we?"

"Are we?" The software guy leaned forward, a wide smile on his face. "Have you ever wondered why computer progress leveled off in the teens, just a few years before the invention of the stardrive?"

Trevor shrugged. "Computers got about as good as they can be."

"Maybe. Or maybe"—the kid paused self-importantly—"maybe the computers *kept* getting better, and became superhumanly intelligent. They didn't need us anymore. Maybe no stardrive was ever invented. Maybe the super AIs shuffled the human race off into a star travel game running on an old hardware rack in some Google server farm."

"Ah, I . . . see," said Trevor. "A novel cosmology indeed." I'll give Trevor this, he didn't roll his eyes the way most did. Me? I thought all the Singularity types had died or been carted off to old folks homes long ago. But here was living example, and not an old fart. I guess like Nostradamus, some notions will never go away.

The embarrassed silence was broken by Cookie, who stuck his head into the room and said, "Captain, dinner is ready at your pleasure."

Bless him, Cookie's timing couldn't have been better. I waved him in. As the mess staff trundled in their silver kettles and table settings, I brought up the lights. I noticed that Frito had hunkered down behind some rocks, no doubt bored by all the chitchat. Hopefully he and Ohara would keep a low profile while we had a good meal.

Whatever Cookie had magicked up, it smelled delicious. As his people set out the plates and silverware, he launched into his grand chef patter. "Yes, ladies and gentlemen, this dish is one that you might find at the best New York restaurants. I ordered it myself for this mission." That was a lie. Cookie yearned for his days in New York, but I knew that logistics was the responsibility of APA, with Cookie only allowed to state his general wishes. "I do apologize for the delay this evening. The ship's loaders made a major bungle of where they stored what."

"Yes," I said, "but we're just beginning to use the new universal shipping containers. Except for the ID codes, they all look alike." APA had supervised the loading so I didn't want to sound too critical.

Ron Ohara was sniffing suspiciously. He looked pale. "Just where did you find your . . . food supplies?"

Cookie, oh innocent Cookie. Without even trying, he brought down an academic career. "Oh," he said, "they were in Lab Space 14. Stored live." He waved to his servers, and they simultaneously raised the silver lids. "I give you broiled lobster in the shell!"

It smelled like lobster. It even looked like lobster—if you discounted the greenish flesh and the extra claws.

No wonder Frito was trying to hide.

Of course, Ron Ohara was thoroughly screwed. I mean discredited. He tried to claim that the critters had all been brought up during his single dive earlier that day. There were just too many Frito creatures for that explanation to fly.

In fact, Ron had intended to plant the others during his later dives—after I gave him both submersibles and clearance to hog all our equipment.

In one grand *coup de cuisine*, Cookie had solved all my problems. Dae Park got the resources to complete her epoch-making survey of Lee's World. In the process, she discovered two more of the famous "Park stromatolites." Analysis back on Earth extended for months and years thereafter. The fossils show signs of metamorphic distortion; the fine detail has been lost. And yet a good argument can be made that they're something like an early eukaryotic form. No doubt they originated several cataclysms earlier in the geological history of Lee's world. Alas, since Park's intense search, no further examples were found. Some claim this makes her work suspect. Of course this is balderdash. The isotope ratios in Park's fossils are a *perfect* match for the isotopic fingerprint of the crust of Lee's World.

Now thirty years have passed since our voyage to Lee's World and our preliminary assessment of the Drake equation. That equation has crept back into the vernacular of speculation, if only because it captures disappointment and possibility on such a grand scale. In those thirty years we've colonized six of the most terrestrial worlds. A number of others are still in the process of terraforming—teleporting in oceans, for instance. (See chapter 8 for my part in the development of this technique.)

The last thirty years have transformed exploration, but not entirely for the better. Too many people are satisfied with terraforming; they don't expect we can find worlds any better. The massive government funding of the early years has dried up. On the other hand, with the super-scalar extension of the stardrive, now we can go anywhere in less than ten days. Anywhere in the observable universe? Sure, but that's just the beginning. The vast majority of the universe is so far away that its light will never be visible from Earth or from any place you can see from Earth. That's why a system memory failure is so dangerous in modern exploration—you might be so far from home that a lifetime of jumping wouldn't bring you to a recognizable sky. Having a Hugo Mendes on board wouldn't be any help. (If you're a cache booby or have access to a planetary Internet, you can look this up. Search on "cosmological horizon." Or better yet, buy my book, *Beyond this Horizon: Star Captain Y.-T. Lee's Voyage to the Cosmic Antipodes*.)

Nowadays, the best explorers pop out to supra-cosmological distances, survey visually for the one-in-a-million exceptional star—and then home in on that. This strategy has two advantages: first, it may eventually get us to some far corner of the universe where the Drake statistics are improved. Second (a more practical reason), it makes it easier for explorers to keep proprietary control over the location of their discoveries; we're less tied to the capricious funding of APA. Without this innovation, the public could never benefit from our Planets for Sale program.

So what have we found Out There? No little green men (or even little green lobsters). No stable planetary ecology with breathable pressures of free oxygen—i.e., no living eukaryotes or even cyanobacteria. We have seen four planets with fossil algae mats such as Park discovered on Lee's World. Thus, the transition to complex life does happen off the Earth. I think it's just a matter of time before we find such life. I know some folks say we have failed. Some explorers want to shift the focus to hypothetical nonorganic life-forms in Extreme Environments—the surface of neutron stars and black hole accretion disks. This is all very nice, but the Extremists are getting way too much funding for their agenda. There is *no* evidence that Extreme Life is even possible.

Our voyage to Lee's World was full of surprises. Some of them didn't surface till we got back to Chicago: Trevor's webcast was an enormous hit all over Earth—more for the world itself than Park's discovery and the drama of Ohara's fraud. Without actually lying, the videos convinced millions that the place was indeed a paradise. Furthermore, the geologists concluded that although the planet was overdue for a crustal "readjustment" (Krakatoa on a planetary scale), and even though such a catastrophe might come with only a few hours' warning, it might not happen for decades.

The Advanced Projects Agency can go nuts when it's hit with a fad. In this case, APA boosted the terraform priority on Lee's World to the max. Planets like Eden and Dorado, stable environments that were already as congenial as Earth's Antarctic and Sahara respectively, just needing a little atmosphere tweaking, these got moved to lower priority. Meantime, fifty million people queued up to homestead Lee's World.

Thirty years later, the place still hasn't blown itself up. A million crazy people live on Paradise. (That's what they call it. Maybe I should be glad my name isn't attached to this incipient disaster. Still, I was the discoverer. What's wrong with "Lee" anyway?)

I actually visited the place last year, at the invitation of the planetary government. Still another surprise is that the planetary government of Paradise is none other than Ron Ohara! I got my own parade and tours all over the hundred-kilometer-wide continent. The towns are beautiful, but with a weirdness you won't find on Earth. Where else will you see architectures designed to survive more rock 'n' roll every week than a *century* of Ankara earthquakes? Where else will you find building codes that require every residence to have an escape-to-orbit vehicle built in? (They look like large-bore fat-ass chimneys.) Anyway, the citizens of Paradise treated me royally. I even got to unveil a discoverer's statue (of me!) in the capital. Maybe my name is okay.

All the while, I was trying to figure who was really behind the hospitality—and if it was Ron, why? Maybe he knew the world was going to blow while I was there. I should stay close to fat chimneys.

The last afternoon of my visit, I had a private lunch with Ron at his presidential lodge at the Place of First Landing. We sat out on the veranda, not more than two hundred meters from the original camp. That ground had long since fallen onto the beach, but the remaining terrace was everything that Trevor's wacky video had implied about this world. We might as well have been at some Mauna Kea resort. And unlike that last time I was on this world, there wasn't even a need for oxy masks!

I hadn't seen Ron in all the years since our expedition returned to Chicago. He's showing his age. But then, I imagine I am too. When his staff had left us alone with our drinks, he raised his beer as if giving a toast to the scenery. "Paradise was the easiest terraform job in the history of starflight. We seeded a few million tonnes of the proper ocean bacteria and now after less than three decades we have breathable levels of free oxygen."

Considering the investment's dubious future, that was only fair. But I didn't say that. I just puffed on my cigar and enjoyed the view. You couldn't see the talus from here, just the sea in the farther distance (complete with some certifiably insane surfers). Closer, above the drop off, there were wide grassy lawns. The planetary flag fluttered on a flagpole between two palm trees.

"Have you seen our flag, Captain?"

"Oh yes." The flag was everywhere: a blue field surmounted by a green lobster with too many claws. "How is Frito, anyway?"

Ron laughed. "Frito, or at least his offspring, are doing great. We tweaked their biology so they're filter feeders. Now they're the most plentiful large animal in the sea, having a feast on the new plankton. But you should know that they're a legally protected species." He smiled. "I don't think I could survive another surprise lobster dinner."

I smiled back. He seemed mellow enough. "There's a question I always wanted to ask you, Mr. President. Did you ever think you could get away with such a transparent hoax?"

"Actually, I thought I had a shot at it. I was betting that Paradise would blow up before any third expedition got here. Meantime, I'd have the subsea videos I intended to make of Frito's siblings—the ones you cooked."

"Yes, but even without Cookie's menu, once we got back to Earth and serious DNA analysis was done on Frito—"

Ron looked embarrassed. "Well, as I'm sure you've read, I rather misrepresented my academic qualifications; my PhD is in sociology. I used a hobby kit to insert the green genes and muck around with a few other things like claw count. Trevor said that would be enough to give us deniability. Actually, I think Trevor was leading me on a bit. He only needed the hoax to last long enough to boost the ratings for his video. In the end, your cook didn't give us even that much time."

He leaned back, looking awfully content for someone who'd had his great hoax blown away. "But that was thirty years ago. Amazing how it all turned out isn't it? I call it the luck of Paradise. You and your cook debunked Frito so fast that no one talked seriously about sending me to jail. And Trevor's video was still a smash hit. We were able to take advantage of all the publicity to become land developers here." He grinned at me. "Life is good."

Hmm. "Paradise could end tomorrow, you know."

"True." Ron set his beer down and clasped his hands across his gut. "But we Paradiseans are ever alert. Besides," he gave me a sidelong look, "we have you and your fellow explorers working tirelessly on our behalf. I understand you've discovered ten worlds that are a match for Paradise."

We at Planets for Sale don't release the exact totals, but I said, "That's about right. And every one of them is at least as unstable as this world. Are you talking about culture of throwaway worlds?"

"Sure. If you give us a cheap enough price. Traditional terraforming also has its place, of course. Both ways, the human race is spreading out." He smiled at the gleaming day. "Up to a few decades ago, we were trapped on one tiny world—and we were getting crowded and deadly. We were close to global catastrophe. That was a very narrow passage. But we got through it. And because of the near-zero values of 'fl' and 'fi' and 'fc,' we've discovered that 'L' may be unbounded. The whole universe is our private playground! We just have to supply the trees and the grass and the pets. I know the biologists are still hunting for higher life. I read how Dae Park is flying around beyond the beyond. She'll be ecstatic if she ever finds a living algae mat. But don't you see? It really doesn't matter anymore. A thousand years from now, we humans will be beyond the reach of any disaster. A hundred thousand years, and the profs will be arguing about whether humans originated on a single world or many. And a million years from now . . . well, by then life will be scattered across the universe and evolved into new species. I'll bet some will be as smart as us. *That* will be the time for a new assessment of the Drake equation!"

Maybe Ron is right about the future; his view is widely held these days. But I can't wait a million years—or even a thousand. And in a way, the spread of Earth's life messes with our learning the truth. It did on Mars. It tried to on Lee's World. I'd like to stay ahead of that, to continue to open up the universe to you, my customers. I remain an explorer, my boots planted in the hard vacuum of reality, my gaze directed beyond this horizon.

About It

TERRY BISSON

Terry Bisson (www.terrybisson.com) *lives in Oakland, California. Originally from Kentucky, Bisson lived in New York City for many years, where he wrote copy for publishing companies and ran a revolutionary mail-order book service, Jacobin Books, with his wife, Judy. They moved to Oakland, California, in 2002. He is the author of seven genre fantasy or SF novels, including* Talking Man *(1987);* Fire on the Mountain *(1988);* Voyage to the Red Planet *(1990);* The Pickup Artist *(2001); and, most recently,* Dear Abby *(2003) and* Planet of Mystery *(2007)—and a number of movie tie-in books of unusually high quality for that subgenre. His short fiction, which he continues to publish every year, is collected in* Bears Discover Fire *(1993),* In the Upper Room *(2000), and in* Greetings *(2005). His most recent book is* The Left Left Behind *(2009), a satire on the bestselling Christian fantasy series,* Left Behind; *the volume also includes "Special Relativity," described by the publisher as "a one-act drama that answers the question: When Albert Einstein, Paul Robeson, and J. Edgar Hoover are raised from the dead at an anti-Bush rally, which one wears the dress?"*

"About It," which appeared in F&SF, *is an anecdote told by a janitor about the creature he brought home from work at the biotech lab. It is a story about kindness and empathy, and the collision of commercialism and idealism.*

It was supposed to be a Sasquatch, a Bigfoot, whatever you call it. The Lab makes these things for museums and special zoos. It's not a phony deal, even though it's made up. It's as accurate as they can make it. Some of the DNA is still around, some of it in us they say. Lots is just guess work too, I guess.

They were going to put it down so I took it home. The Lab guys knew about it. I was helping them out. They could save the autopsy ritual as they call it, plus the paperwork, and say it fell into the vat or something.

There was just something I liked about it, so I took it home.

It was illegal technically, but who notices these days. And we're pretty friendly, the Lab guys and my crew. They handle the scientific stuff, the racks and the vats, and we take care of the floors and cages, even the walls. The rest of my crew comes and goes but they all know me.

We clean up their mess so in a way I was just doing my job. It wasn't going to last anyway. There was something I liked about it, and even a small house gets lonesome, especially around the holidays. So I took it home.

Nothing is all that easy. Once I found it in a tree. I say found it, but I got a call before I even knew it was lost. We're talking about way up there, looking down. Luckily I knew one of the cops, Ernesto.

My cousin, I said. Crazy cousin, you know how it is. Ernesto gets all badgey on me. Your cousin covered with hair? Come on.

94

Ernesto, I said, don't you have a favorite tia? A loving tia who was nice to you even when your mama was muy escondida in accion? (I happen to know he did.) Don't embarrass my tia by asking the wrong questions about her wayward son. Please just help me get him in the car, por favor, no questions asked. Of course it saved Ernesto paperwork too. Everybody likes to save paperwork.

Ernesto helped me get it in the car. After that it stayed home, around the yard, even inside sometimes. It liked TV. Plus it had a personality. A nice one, too. It was shy but down-to-earth, no funny business at all. A gentle herbivore, like a gorilla but more upright in standing.

We do gorillas at the Lab a lot. Of course there's less guesswork with them. We have the actual DNA of the last ones.

But it was no gorilla. Its eyes were pale and watery, like ice cubes that are melting. It had thick hair like a chestnut horse, only longer. Tangled except on its back, where it was smooth. Its feet were no bigger than mine. We measured them, side by side. So much for Bigfoot.

Its teeth were wide like bad false teeth, and greenish. I never caught it eating grass, but I think it did. Mostly it liked nuts, and sometimes breadsticks, which I got from my actual cousin who owns a restaurant and pretends to be Italian. I spent a fortune on party mix. Candy drew a blank. For fun it ate grapes by the handful. This was in the days of the Huelga, too, which should have made it more of a problem for me, but what could I do? It wasn't long for this world and the union is forever as they say.

And corn on the cob—it was a regular pig for corn on the cob, it was like it had never seen it before. Which I guess it hadn't. Then it was out of season and it was breadsticks again.

It just hung around. It would sit on the front step and kids would come around. They like unusual things. I didn't worry about the neighbors. We mind our own business around here. There are reasons for that. And just because we are all immigrants doesn't mean we are from the same town.

I say kids, it was mostly boys. They taught it to play marbles and some video games. It was better at marbles, with those wide thumbs, then it would give them all back. (No pockets!) The kids liked that. It was tall. You couldn't tell how tall because it was always stooped over. The kids liked that. They don't care how tall you are as long as you stoop.

This one kid taught it to shake hands. It wouldn't shake with the others though. It would just yank its hand away looking shocked if they tried. Wouldn't do it with me either. Just the one kid.

They tried to teach it to talk but it wasn't interested. Not mute but just quiet. Unusual for a hominid I am told. Doc Ayers says we are all howlers.

It didn't have many expressions. Looking shocked was one of them. Alarmed is more the word. Looking uninterested was another. Not bored, just not interested.

Sometimes it mumbled. Talking to itself. It was part of its thinking process, I believe, but there didn't seem to be a language involved. Maybe there was, but it didn't sound like words to me.

The kids called it Mumbles. I never did. It wasn't an animal, like a cat. It was worthy of more respect than that. A good companion. It was happy just to hang around. We watched a lot of TV.

It didn't like to get out of sight of the house, but there's a lot next door where the kids play baseball sometimes, and they made it an umpire. Honest to God. I don't know how they taught it how to do that, but they did. I didn't see the process. All it knew was strikes and balls. It didn't count, just called balls and strikes, holding up one hand or the other.

It could be that it had better vision than us. As far as the kids were concerned it was unfallible. Of course, boys are going to say that. It's a part of baseball.

Mostly though it sat on the steps till I came home.

Mostly the boys came and went, but this one kid, the handshake kid, liked to just sit with it. I'm not wild about kids but I wasn't about to run him off. I knew his father who was bad news.

It wouldn't let the kids touch it, except for the one kid, but it would let me brush its hair sometimes while we watched TV. It was very long and silky, and if you didn't brush it it would get burrs, which was odd since it never went out of the yard and I keep it mowed. It was like the burrs found it instead of vice versa.

It didn't like being in the house, except when the TV was on. It would sit on the middle of the couch, taking up the whole thing. I didn't mind. I have my special chair. It didn't care what was on. I mostly watch sports or crime shows.

I never talked to it much. It didn't like to be talked to, and I'm not much of a talker myself. It was easy to get along with. A good companion.

One time they asked about it, at the Lab. Doc Ayers, he said he needed it back. I know I must have looked shocked because he whispered, Not now, Emilio! After, you know. We just need the D and RNA for a template, just in case. The other one didn't work out either.

I said no problem. We're pretty friendly.

It stayed out back at night, in the shed I had put together for it. More of a lean-to, really. I put together a kind of cat box too, and enclosed it for the neighbors. It caught on right away.

We watched a lot of TV together. I think it saw it just as patterns, like looking into a fire.

Speaking of fire, that was the only time I ever saw it cry, and I didn't actually see that. I saw the results is all.

This black guy down the street was burning some old fence or something. Country people like to burn things. The boys came around to poke it with sticks and this one kid, the handshake kid, brought it along. Dragged it by the hand I imagine. But instead of just sitting like it did on the porch, it started to cry.

Just sat there staring at the fire and cried and cried. The kids freaked out and left, all but one. It wouldn't stop crying. Police brought it home. Good old Ernesto. Your cousin, he says.

I never saw any actual tears. It stayed in the lean-to a few days and when it came out it was smaller. Not a lot but enough to tell. It was starting to die. I'd seen enough of that at the Lab so I knew what to expect.

The kids didn't, though. They saw it on the porch no bigger

than them anymore and most of them stayed away. This one kid, the handshake kid, came like before and sat. I wasn't about to chase him away.

You could see it getting smaller. All this took over a week, hard on the one kid. He must have thought it was his fault.

This had to happen, I told him. I probably should have told him earlier. It was hard on him, watching it get smaller, day by day. The only consolation was that as it got smaller it let the kid brush its hair like I used to. I didn't want it in the house anymore. I let him use my brush.

After a while even the brush was too big. Once it starts it doesn't take very long. It got small as a squirrel, then lost its shape all together. I tried to shoo the kid away at that point but he just sat there, stroking its back with his fingers, staring off into space. He didn't like looking at it anymore.

Then there was only the puddle with the DNA things, the R and D units in it like a pair of dice. And the one kid sitting there beside them, staring off into space, like before.

I brought both units back to the lab but Doc Ayers said they already had a better one started. I gave them to the kid and he buried them in a flowerpot. The one still there on the steps. Honest to God.

That's pretty much the whole story. Sometimes I think about it and its brief life, at the banquet as the poets say. Its brief life came as a surprise to it, as it does to us all, when you think about it. Then not so suddenly it's gone.

That's about it.

Thanks for asking.

Somadeva:
A Sky River Sutra

VANDANA SINGH

*Vandana Singh (users.rcn.com/singhvan/) lives in Framing-
ham, Massachusetts. She is an assistant professor of physics, and the author of a number of impressive SF short
stories, at least fifteen to date. She was born and brought up
in New Delhi, and her parents both had graduate degrees in
English literature: "I grew up as much with Shakespeare
and Keats as I did with the great Indian epics and literary
writers in Hindi such as the inimitable Premchand. My
mother and grandmother told us the Ramayana and Ma-
habharata, and various folk tales and village lore." Her
stories are collected in* The Woman Who Thought She Was
a Planet *(2008), in India from Zubaan Books and Penguin
India. Her novella "Distances" was published in 2008. And
she is the editor of* To Each Her Own: Anthology of Con-
tempoary Hindi Stories.*

   "Somadeva: A Sky River Sutra," appeared in the online
magazine* Strange Horizons, *and this is its first appearance
in print. It is an excellent story about certain things that do
not change for humans, no matter how much humanity
changes. It is about storytelling in the far future, in which
the telling of stories is the authentic connection between the
distant past and that future.*

I am Somadeva.

I was once a man, a poet, a teller of tales, but I am long dead now. I lived in the eleventh century of the Common Era in northern India. Then we could only dream of that fabulous device, the udan-khatola, the ship that flies between worlds. Then, the sky-dwelling Vidyadharas were myth, occupying a reality different from our own. And the only wings I had with which to make my journeys were those of my imagination. . . .

Who or what am I now, in this age when flying between worlds is commonplace? Who brought me into being, here in this small, cramped space, with its smooth metallic surfaces, and the round window revealing an endless field of stars?

It takes me a moment to recognize Isha. She is lying in her bunk, her hair spread over the pillow, looking at me.

And then I remember the first time I woke up in this room, bewildered. Isha told me she had re-created me. She fell in love with me fifteen centuries after my death, after she read a book I wrote, an eighteen-volume compendium of folktales and legends, called the *Kathāsaritsāgara*: The Ocean of Streams of Story.

"You do remember that?" she asked me anxiously upon my first awakening.

"Of course I remember," I said, as my memories returned to me in a great rush.

The *Kathāsaritsāgara* was my life's work. I wandered all

over North India, following rumors of the Lost Manuscript, risking death to interview murderers and demons, cajoling stories out of old women and princes, merchants and nursing mothers. I took these stories and organized them into patterns of labyrinthine complexity. In my book there are stories within stories—the chief narrator tells a story and the characters in that story tell other stories and so on. Some of the narrators refer to the stories of previous narrators; thus each is not only a teller of tales but also a participant. The story-frames themselves form a complex, multi-referential tapestry. And the story of how the *Kathāsaritsāgara* came to be is the first story of them all.

I began this quest because of a mystery in my own life, but it became a labor of love, an attempt to save a life. That is why I wove the stories into a web, so I could hold safe the woman I loved. I could not have guessed that fifteen centuries after my death, another very different woman would read my words and fall in love with me.

The first time I met Isha, she told me she had created me to be her companion on her journeys between the stars. She wants to be the Somadeva of this age, collecting stories from planet to planet in the galaxy we call Sky River. What a moment of revelation it was for me, when I first knew that there were other worlds, peopled and habited, rich with stories! Isha told me that she had my spirit trapped in a crystal jewel-box. The jewel-box has long feelers like the antennae of insects, so that I can see and hear and smell, and thereby taste the worlds we visit.

"How did you pull my spirit from death? From history? Was I reborn in this magic box?"

She shook her head.

"It isn't magic, Somadeva. Oh, I can't explain! But tell me, I need to know. Why didn't you write yourself into the *Kathāsaritsāgara*? Who, really, is this narrator of yours, Gunādhya? I know there is a mystery there. . . ."

She asks questions all the time. When she is alone with me, she is often animated like this. My heart reaches out to her, this lost child of a distant age.

Gunādhya is a goblin-like creature who is the narrator of

the *Kathāsaritsāgara*. According to the story I told, Gunādhya was a minion of Shiva himself who was reborn on Earth due to a curse. His mission was to tell the greater story of which the *Kathāsaritsāgara* is only a page: the Brhat-kathā. But he was forbidden to speak or write in Sanskrit or any other language of humankind. Wandering through a forest one day, he came upon a company of the flesh-eating Pishāch. He hid himself and listened to them, and learned their strange tongue. In time he wrote the great Brhat-kathā in the Pishāchi language in a book made of the bark of trees, in his own blood.

They say that he was forced to burn the manuscript, and that only at the last moment did a student of his pull out one section from the fire. I tracked that surviving fragment for years, but found only a few scattered pages, and the incomplete memories of those who had seen the original, or been told the tales. From these few I reconstructed what I have called the *Kathāsaritsāgara*. In all this, I have drawn on ancient Indic tradition, in which the author is a compiler, an embellisher, an arranger of stories, some written, some told. He fragments his consciousness into the various fictional narrators in order to be a conduit for their tales.

In most ancient works, the author goes a step further: he walks himself whole into the story, like an actor onto the stage.

This is one way I have broken from tradition. I am not, myself, a participant in the stories of the *Kathāsaritsāgara*. And Isha wants to know why.

Sometimes I sense my narrator, Gunādhya, as one would a ghost, a presence standing by my side. He is related to me in some way that is not clear to me. All these years he has been coming into my dreams, filling in gaps in my stories, or contradicting what I've already written down. He is a whisper in my ear; sometimes my tongue moves at his command. All the time he is keeping secrets from me, tormenting me with the silence between his words. Perhaps he is waiting until the time is right.

"I don't know," I tell Isha. "I don't know why I didn't put myself in the story. I thought it would be enough, you

know, to cast a story web, to trap my queen. To save her
from death. . . ."

"Tell me about her," Isha says. Isha knows all about
Sūryavati but she wants to hear it from me. Over and over.

I remember. . . .

A high balcony, open, not latticed. The mountain air, like
wine. In the inner courtyard below us, apricots are drying in
the sun in great orange piles. Beyond the courtyard walls I
can hear men's voices, the clash of steel as soldiers practice
their murderous art. The king is preparing to battle his own
son, who lusts for the throne and cannot wait for death to
take his father. But it is for the queen that I am here. She is
standing by the great stone vase on the balcony, watering the
holy tulsi plant. She wears a long skirt of a deep, rich red,
and a green shawl over the delicately embroidered tunic. Her
slender fingers shake; her gaze, when it lifts to me, is full of
anguish. Her serving maids hover around her, unable to re-
lieve her of her pain. At last she sits, drawing the edge of her
fine silken veil about her face. A slight gesture of the hand.
My cue to begin the story that will, for a moment, smooth
that troubled brow.

It is for her that I have woven the story web. Every day it
gives her a reason to forget despair, to live a day longer. Every
day she is trapped in it, enthralled by it a little more. There are
days when the weight of her anxiety is too much, when she
breaks the spell of story and requires me for another purpose.
Then I must, for love of her, take part in an ancient and dangerous rite. But today, the day that I am remembering for Isha,
Sūryavati simply wants to hear a story.

I think I made a mistake with Sūryavati, fifteen centuries
ago. If I'd written myself into the *Kathāsaritsāgara*, perhaps
she would have realized how much I needed her to be alive.
After all, Vyāsa, who penned the immortal *Mahābhārata*,
was as much a participant in the tale as its chronicler. And
the same is true of Vālmīki, who wrote the *Rāmāyana* and
was himself a character in it, an agent.

So, for the first time, I will write myself into *this* story.
Perhaps that is the secret to affecting events as they unfold.

And after all, I, too, have need of meaning. Beside me, Gunādhya's ghost nods silently in agreement.

Isha sits in the ship's chamber, her fingers running through her hair, her gaze troubled. She has always been restless. For all her confidences I can only guess what it is she is seeking through the compilation of the legends and myths of the inhabited worlds. As I wander through the story-labyrinths of my own making, I hope to find, at the end, my Isha, my Sūryavati.

Isha is, I know, particularly interested in stories of origin, of ancestry. I think it is because she has no knowledge of her natal family. When she was a young woman, she was the victim of a history raid. The raiders took from her all her memories. Her memories are scattered now in the performances of entertainers, the conversations of strangers, and the false memories of imitation men. The extinction of her identity was so clean that she would not recognize those memories as her own, were she to come across them. What a terrible and wondrous age this is, in which such things are possible!

In her wanderings, Isha hasn't yet been able to find out who her people were. All she has as a clue is an ancient, battered set of books: the eighteen volumes of the *Kathāsaritsāgara*. They are, to all appearances, her legacy, all that was left of her belongings after the raid. The pages are yellow and brittle, the text powdery, fading. She has spent much of her youth learning the lost art of reading, learning the lost scripts of now-dead languages. Inside the cover of the first volume is a faint inscription, a name: Vandana. There are notes in the same hand in the margins of the text. An ancestor, she thinks.

This is why Isha is particularly interested in stories of origin. She thinks she'll find out something about herself by listening to other people's tales of where they came from.

I discovered this on my very first journey with her. After she brought me into existence, we went to a world called Jesanli, where the few city-states were hostile toward us. None would receive us, until we met the Kiha, a nomadic desert tribe who had a tradition of hospitality. None of the inhabitants of this planet have much by way of arts or machinery, civilization or learning. But the Kiha have stories that are poetic and strange. Here is the first of them.

Once upon a time our ancestors lived in a hot and crowded space, in near darkness. They were not like us. They were not men, nor women, but had a different form. The ancestors, having poor sight, lived in fear all the time, and when one intruded too close to another, they immediately sprang apart in terror. It was as though each moment of approach brought the possibility of a stranger, an enemy, entering their personal domain. Imagine a lot of people who cannot speak, forced to live in a small, cramped, dark cave, where every blundering collision is a nightmare—for that is what it was like for them. Their fear became part of them, becoming a physical presence like a burden carried on the back.

But every once in a while two or more of them would be pushed close enough together to actually behold each other dimly through their nearly useless eyes. During these moments of recognition they were able to see themselves in the other person, and to reach out, and to draw together. In time they formed tight little family units. Then they had no more need to carry around their burdens of fear, which, when released, turned into light.

Yes, yes. You heard that right. Although they continued to live in their furnace-like world and be cramped together, what emanated from them—despite everything—was light.

Isha's eyes lit up when she heard this story. She told the Kiha that the story had hidden meanings, that it contained the secret of how the stars burn. They listened politely to her explanation and thanked her for her story. She wanted to know where they had first heard the tale, but the question made no sense to them. Later she told me that for all their non-technological way of life, the Kiha must have once been sky-dwellers.

They had told Isha the story to repay a debt, because she brought them gifts. So when she explained their story back to them, they had to tell her another story to even things out. They did this with reluctance, because a story is a gift not easily given to strangers.

Here is the second story.

In the beginning there was just one being, whose name was That Which Is Nameless. The Nameless one was vast, undifferentiated, and lay quiescent, waiting. In that place there was no darkness, for there was no light.

Slowly the Nameless One wearied of its existence. It said into the nothingness: Who am I? But there was no answer because there was no other. It said unto itself: Being alone is a burden. I will carve myself up and make myself companions.

So the Nameless One gathered itself and spread itself violently into all directions, thinning out as it did so. It was the greatest explosion ever known, and from its shards were born people and animals and stars.

And so when light falls on water, or a man shoots an arrow at another man, or a mother picks up a child, That Which Was Once Nameless answers a very small part of the question: Who Am I?

And yet the Once Nameless still reaches out, beyond the horizon of what we know and don't know, breaking itself up into smaller and smaller bits like the froth from a wave that hits a rocky shore. What is it seeking? Where is it going? Nobody can tell.

I could tell that Isha was excited by this story also; she wanted to tell the Kiha that the second story was really about the birth of the universe—but I restrained her. To the Kiha, what is real and what is not real is not a point of importance. To them there are just stories and stories, and the universe has a place for all of them.

Later Isha asked me:

"How is it possible that the Kiha have forgotten they once traversed the stars? Those two stories contain the essence of the sciences, the vigyan-shastras, in disguise. How can memory be so fragile?"

She bit her lip, and I know she was thinking of her own lost past. In my life, too, there are gaps I cannot fill.

The stories in the *Kathāsaritsāgara* are not like these tales of the Kiha. Queen Sūryavati was of a serious mien, spending much time in contemplation of Lord Shiva. To lighten her burdens I collected tales of ordinary, erring mortals and divines: cheating wives, sky-dwelling, shape-shifting Vidyadharas, and the denizens, dangerous and benign, of the great forests. These were first told, so the story goes, by Shiva himself. They are nothing like the stories of the Kiha.

Isha has so much to learn! Like Sūryavati, she is a woman of reserve. She conceals her pain as much as she can from the world. Her interaction with the Kiha is impersonal, almost aloof. Now if it were left to me, I would go into their dwelling places, live with them, listen to gossip. Find out who is in love with whom, what joys and sorrows the seasons bring, whether there is enmity between clans. I have never been much interested in the cosmic dramas of gods and heroes.

However, the third Kiha tale is quite unlike the first two. I don't know what to make of it.

Once, in the darkness, a man wandered onto a beach where he saw a fire. He came upon it and saw that the fire was another man, all made of light, who spun in a circle on the beach as though drunk. The first man, warmed by the glow of the fire-man, wanted to talk to him, but the fire-man didn't take any notice of him. The fire-man kept spinning, round and round, and the first man kept yelling out questions, spinning round and round with the fire-man so he could see his face. And there were three small biting insects who dared not bite the fire-man but wanted to bite the cheeks of the other man, and they kept hovering around the other man, and he kept waving them off, but they would go behind him until he forgot about them, and then they'd circle around and bite him again.

Then?

Then nothing. They are all, all five of them, still on that dark beach, dancing still.

Isha thinks this story is a more recent origin story. She speculates that the ancestral people of the Kiha come from a world which has three moons. A world that floated alone in space until it fell into the embrace of a star. There are worlds like that, I've heard, planets wandering without their shepherd stars. It is not unlikely that one of these was captured by a sun. This story was told to Isha by a child, who ran up to us in secret when we were leaving. She wanted to make us a gift of some sort, but that was all she had.

If Isha is right, then the Kiha told us the stories in the wrong order. Arrange them like this: Birth of the universe, birth of their sun, coming into being of their world.

But these old stories have as many meanings as there are stars in the sky. To assign one single interpretation to them is to miss the point. Take the second story. It could be as much a retelling of a certain philosophical idea from the ancient Indic texts called the Upanishads as a disguised theory of cosmological origin. In my other life I was learned in Sanskrit.

But it is also important what we make of these stories. What meaning we find in them, as wanderers by the seashore find first one shell, then another, and form them into a chain of their own making.

Here is the start of a story I have made by braiding together the Kiha tales.

In the beginning, Isha made the world. Wishing to know herself, she broke herself up into parts. One of them is me, Somadeva, poet and wanderer. We circle each other for ever, one maker, one made. . . .

Sometimes I wonder if I have made her up as much as she has concocted me. If we are fictions of each other, given substance only through our mutual narratives.

Perhaps the Kiha are right: stories make the world.

* * *

I wake and find myself on that high stone balcony. The queen is watching me. A small fire in an earthen pail burns between us, an angeethi. Over it, hanging from an iron support, is a black pot containing the brew.

"Did it take you too far, my poet?" she asks, worried. "You told me of far worlds and impossible things. You spoke some words I couldn't understand. An entertaining tale. But I only want a glimpse of what is to come in the next few days, not eons. I want to know . . ."

I am confused. When I first opened my eyes I thought I saw Isha. I thought I was on the ship, telling Isha a story about Sūryavati. She likes me to recite the old tales, as she lies back in her bunk, running her fingers slowly over her brow. I wish I could caress that brow myself.

So how is it that I find myself here, breathing in pine-scented Himalayan air? How is it my mouth has a complex aftertaste that I cannot quite identify, which has something to do with the herbal brew steaming in the pot? My tongue is slightly numb, an effect of the poison in the mix.

Or is it that in telling my story to Isha I have immersed myself so deeply in the tale that it has become reality to me?

The queen's eyes are dark, and filled with tears.

"Dare I ask you to try again, my poet? Will you risk your life and sanity one more time, and tell me what you see? Just a step beyond this moment, a few days hence. Who will win this war. . . ."

What I cannot tell her is that I've seen what she wants to know. I know what history has recorded of the battle. The prince, her son, took his father's throne and drove him to his death. And the queen . . .

It is past bearing.

What I am trying to do is to tell her a story in which I am a character. If I can have a say in the way things turn out, perhaps I can save her. The king and his son are beyond my reach. But Sūryavati? She is susceptible to story. If she recognizes, in the fictional Somadeva's love for Isha, the real Somadeva's unspoken, agonized love, perhaps she'll step back from the brink of history.

My fear is that if events unfurl as history records, I will lose my Sūryavati. Will I then be with Isha, wandering the stars in search of stories? Or will I die here on this earth, under the shadow of the palace walls, with the night sky nothing but a dream? Who will survive, the real Somadeva or the fictional one? And which is which?

All I can do is stall Sūryavati with my impossible tales—and hope.

"I don't know how far the brew will take me," I tell her. "But for you, my queen, I will drink again."

I take a sip.

I am back on the ship. Isha is asleep, her hair in tangles over her face. Her face in sleep is slack, except for that habitual little frown between her brows. The frown makes her look more like a child, not less. I wonder if her memories come to her in her dreams.

So I begin another story, although I remain a little confused. Who is listening: Isha or Sūryavati?

I will tell a story about Inish. It is a place on a far world and one of the most interesting we have visited. I hesitate to call Inish a city, because it is not really one. It is a collection of buildings and people, animals and plants, and is referred to by the natives as though it has an independent consciousness. But also it has no clear boundary because the mini-settlements at what might have been its edge keep wandering off and returning, apparently randomly.

Identities are also peculiar among the inhabitants of Inish. A person has a name, let us say Mana, but when Mana is with her friend Ayo, they together form an entity named Tukrit. If you meet them together and ask them for their names, they will say "Tukrit," not "Ayo and Mana." Isha once asked them whether Ayo and Mana were parts of Tukrit, and they both laughed. "Tukrit is not bits of this or that," Mana said. "Then who just spoke, Mana or Tukrit?" Isha asked. "Tukrit, of course," they said, giggling in an indulgent manner.

"I am Isha," Isha told them. "But who am I when I'm with you?"

"We are *teso*," they said, looking at each other. Isha knew what that meant. "*Teso*" is, in their language, a word that stands for anything that is unformed, not quite there, a possibility, a potential.

It is hard for outsiders to understand whether the Inish folk have family units or not. Several people may live in one dwelling, but since their dwellings are connected by little corridors and tunnels, it is hard to say where one ends and another begins. The people in one dwelling may be four older females, one young woman, three young men and five children. Ask them their names and depending on which of them are present at that time, they will say a different collective name. If there are only Baijo, Akar, and Inha around, they'll say, "We are Garho." If Sami, Kinjo, and Vif are also there, then they are collectively an entity known as "Parak." And so on and so forth.

How they keep from getting confused is quite beyond Isha and me.

"Tell me, Isha," I said, once. "You and I . . . what are we when we are together?"

She looked at me sadly.

"Isha and Somadeva," she said. But there was a faint query in her tone.

"What do you think, Somadeva?" she said.

"*Teso*," I said.

Here is a story from Inish.

There was Ikla. Then, no Ikla but Bako walking away from what was now Samish. While walking, Bako found herself being part of a becoming, but she could not see who or what she was becoming with. Ah, she thought, it is a *goro* being; one that does not show itself except through a sigh in the mind. She felt the *teso* build up slowly, felt herself turn into a liquid, sky, rain. Then there was no *teso*, no *goro*, no Bako, but a fullness, a ripening, and thus was Chihuli come into happening.

And this Chihuli went shouting down the summer lanes, flinging bits of mud and rock around, saying, There is a storm coming! A storm! And Chihuli went up the hill and sank down before the sacred stones and died there. So there was nothing left but Bako, who looked up with enormous eyes at the sky, and felt inside her the emptiness left by the departure of the *goro* being.

Bako, now, why had the *goro* being chosen her for a happening? Maybe because she had always felt *teso* with storms, and since storms were rare here and people had to be warned, there was a space inside her for the kind of *goro* being that lived for storms and their warning. So that is how the right kind of emptiness had brought Chihuli into being.

Pods kept forming around Bako but she resisted being pulled in. It was because of the coming storm, because she could sense the *teso* with it. Nobody else could. With others it was other beings, wild things and bright eyes in the darkness, sometimes even the slowtrees, but only with Bako was there the emptiness inside shaped like a storm. And so she felt the *teso*, the way she had with the *goro* being.

The air crackled with electricity; dark clouds filled the sky, like a ceiling about to come down. Everywhere you looked, it was gray: gray water, gray beings, looking up with wondering, frightened eyes. Only for Bako, as the *teso* built, was the excitement, the anticipation. Many had felt that before when they found their special pod, their mate-beings. The feeling of ripening, of coming into a fullness. The wild sweetness of it. Now Bako felt something like that many times over.

Samish came sweeping up the hill where she was standing, trying to swoop her back with them, so they could be Ikla again, and the *teso* with the storm would become nothing more. But she resisted, and Samish had to go away. This was a thing stronger than the love-bonds they had known.

Came the storm. A magnificent storm it was, rain and thunder, and the legs of lightning dancing around Bako. Rivers swollen, running wild over land, into homes, sweeping everything away. Hills began to move, and the beings ran from their homes. Only Bako stood in the rain, on the highest hill, and the storm danced for her.

The *teso* became something. We call it T'fan. T'fan played with the world, spread over half the planet, wrapped her wet arms around trees and hills. The storm went on until the beings thought there would be no more sun, no more dry land. Then one day it ceased.

Samish gathered itself up, and went tiredly up the hill to find Bako, or to mourn the death of Ikla.

Bako was not there. What was there was standing just as they had left Bako, arms outstretched to the sky. She looked at them with faraway eyes, and they saw then that although the sky was clearing, the storm was still in her. Tiny sparks of lightning flashed from her fingertips. Her hair was singed.

They saw then that the storm had filled her empty spaces so completely that there would never be Ikla again. They did not even feel *teso*. They walked away from her and prepared for mourning.

T'fan stands there still, her eyes filled with storms, her fingers playing with lightning. Her hair has singed away almost completely. She needs no food or water, and seems, in the way of storms, to be quite content. When storms come to her people they cluster around her and she comes to life, dancing in their midst as though relatives have come again from far away. Then T'fan goes away and is replaced by something larger and more complex than we can name.

"What does that story mean, I wonder," Isha said.

"Sometimes stories are just stories," I told her.

"You've never told me what happened to Sūryavati, after you took the next sip, told her the next tale," she told me, turning away from the consequences of my remark. The fact that you can't wrest meaning from everything like fruit from trees—that meaning is a matter not only of story but of what the listener brings to the tale—all that is not something she can face at the moment. She is so impatient, my Isha.

I steeled myself.

"The queen was distraught with grief when her son took the kingdom and destroyed his father," I said. "She threw herself on his funeral pyre. I could not save her."

But in this moment I am also conscious of the queen herself, her eyes dark with grief and yearning. Her hand, with its long fingers—a healed cut on the right index finger, the henna patterns fading—her hand reaches up to wipe a tear. And yet in her gaze leaps a certain vitality, an interest. Her mind ranges far across the universe, carried by my tales. In that small fire in her eyes is all my hope.

Perhaps all I've found is a moment of time that keeps repeating, in which, despite the predations of history, I am caught, with Isha and Sūryavati, in a loop of time distanced from the main current. Here my stories never end; I never reach the moment Sūryavati awaits, and Isha never finds out who she is. Gunādhya remains a whisper in my mind, his relation to me as yet a secret. Here we range across the skies, Isha and I, Vidyadharas of another age, and Sūryavati's gaze follows us. Who is the teller of the tale, and who the listener? We are caught in a web, a wheel of our own making. And if you, the listener from another time and space, upon whose cheek this story falls like spray thrown up by the ocean—you, the eavesdropper hearing a conversation borne by the wind, if you would walk into this story, take it away with you into your world, with its sorrows and small revelations, what would become of you? Would you also enter this circle? Would you tell me your story? Would we sit together, Sūryavati, Isha, and I, with you, and feel *teso* within us—and weave meaning from the strands of the tale?

I am Somadeva. I am a poet, a teller of tales.

Under the Moons of Venus

DAMIEN BRODERICK

Damien Broderick (www.panterraweb.com) is an Australian writer who now lives in San Antonio, Texas. Broderick has been publishing SF since 1963, and at present has the longest career of any of the leading Australian SF writers. He is also a critic, reviewer, and the leading literary theorist of the genre in Australia (his major critical works are Reading by Starlight *and* Transrealism*). In addition he writes popular science books (*The Spike, The Last Mortal Generation*) and has a continuing interest in cutting-edge and speculative science. Of his novels, the most important to date are* The Dreaming Dragons, The Judas Mandala, Transmitters *(a mainstream novel about SF fans), and* The White Abacus.*

"Under the Moons of Venus" was published in* Subterranean, *a magazine that is published both online and in print format, having both a softcover and a hardcover edition. The story is sort of a reimagining of New Wave Ballardian science fiction, and certainly should be received as an homage to J. G. Ballard. It reminds us of the moment in Ballard's "The Atrocity Exhibition" in which Dr. Travis's wife asks, "Was my husband a doctor, or a patient?" and Dr. Nathan responds, "Mrs. Travis, I'm not sure if the question is valid any longer. These matters involve a relativity of a very different kind."*

1.

In the long, hot, humid afternoon, Blackett obsessively paced
off the outer dimensions of the Great Temple of Petra against
the black asphalt of the deserted car parks, trying to recapture the pathway back to Venus. Faint rectangular lines still
marked the empty spaces allocated to staff vehicles long gone
from the campus, stretching on every side like the equations
in some occult geometry of invocation. Later, as shadows
stretched across the all-but-abandoned industrial park, he
considered again the possibility that he was trapped in delusion, even psychosis. At the edge of an overgrown patch of
dried lawn, he found a crushed Pepsi can, a bent yellow
plastic straw protruding from it. He kicked it idly.

"Thus I refute Berkeley," he muttered, with a half smile.
The can twisted, fell back on the grass; he saw that a runner
of bind weed wrapped its flattened waist.

He walked back to the sprawling house he had appropriated, formerly the residence of a wealthy CEO. Glancing at
his IWC Flieger Chrono aviator's watch, he noted that he
should arrive there ten minutes before his daily appointment
with the therapist.

2.

Cool in a chillingly expensive pale blue Mila Schön summer frock, her carmine toenails brightly painted in her open Ferragamo Penelope sandals, Clare regarded him: lovely, sly, professionally compassionate. She sat across from him on the front porch of the old house, rocking gently in the suspended glider.

"Your problem," the psychiatrist told him, "is known in our trade as lack of affect. You have shut down and locked off your emotional responses. You must realize, Robert, that this isn't healthy or sustainable."

"Of course I know that," he said, faintly irritated by her condescension. "Why else would I be consulting you? Not," he said pointedly, "that it is doing me much good."

"It takes time, Robert. As you know."

3.

Later, when Clare was gone, Blackett sat beside his silent sound system and poured two fingers of Hennessy XO brandy. It was the best he had been able to find in the largely depleted supermarket, or at any rate the least untenable for drinking purposes. He took the spirits into his mouth and felt fire run down his throat. Months earlier, he had found a single bottle of Mendis Coconut brandy in the cellar of an enormous country house. Gone now. He sat a little longer, rose, cleaned his teeth and made his toilet, drank a full glass of faintly brackish water from the tap. He found a Philip Glass CD and placed it in the mouth of the player, then went to bed. Glass's repetitions and minimal novelty eased him into sleep. He woke at 3 in the morning, heart thundering. Silence absolute. Blackett cursed himself for forgetting to press the automatic repeat key on the CD player. Glass had fallen silent, along with most of the rest of the human race. He touched his forehead. Sweat coated his fingers.

4.

In the morning, he drove in a stolen car to the industrial
park's air field, rolled the Cessna 182 out from the protection
of its hangar, and refueled its tanks. Against the odds, the
electrically powered pump and other systems remained active, drawing current from the black arrays of solar cells
oriented to the south and east, swiveling during the daylight
hours to follow the apparent track of the sun. He made his
abstracted, expert run through the checklist, flicked on the
radio by reflex. A hum of carrier signal, nothing more. The
control tower was deserted. Blackett ran the Cessna onto
the slightly cracked asphalt and took off into a brisk breeze.
He flew across fields going to seed, visible through spar-
klingly clear air. Almost no traffic moved on the roads below
him. Two or three vehicles threw up a haze of dust from the
untended roadway, and one laden truck crossed his path, apparently cluttered to overflowing with furniture and bedding.
It seemed the ultimate in pointlessness—why not appropriate
a suitable house, as he had done, and make do with its ap-
pointments? Birds flew up occasionally in swooping flocks,
careful to avoid his path.

Before noon, he was landing on the coast at the deserted
Matagorda Island air force base a few hundred yards from
the ocean. He sat for a moment, hearing his cooling engines
ticking, and gazed at the two deteriorating Stearman biplanes that rested in the salty open air. They were at least a
century old, at one time lovingly restored for air shows and
aerobatic displays. Now their fabric sagged, striped red and
green paint peeling from their fuselages and wings. They
sagged into the hot tarmac, rubber tires rotted by the corro-
sive oceanfront air and the sun's pitiless ultraviolet.

Blackett left his own plane in the open. He did not intend
to remain here long. He strolled to the end of the runway and
into the long grass stretching to the ocean. Socks and trou-
ser legs were covered quickly in clinging burrs. He reached
the sandy shore as the sun stood directly overhead. After he
had walked for half a mile along the strand, wishing he had

thought to bring a hat, a dog crossed the sand and paced alongside, keeping its distance.

"You're Blackett," the dog said.

"Speaking."

"Figured it must have been you. Rare enough now to run into a human out here."

Blackett said nothing. He glanced at the dog, feeling no enthusiasm for a conversation. The animal was healthy enough, and well fed, a red setter with long hair that fluffed up in the tangy air. His paws left a trail across the white sand, paralleling the tracks Blackett had made. Was there some occult meaning in this simplest of geometries? If so, it would be erased soon enough, as the ocean moved in, impelled by the solar tide, and lazily licked the beach clean.

Seaweed stretched along the edge of the sluggish water, dark green, stinking. Out of breath, he sat and looked disconsolately across the slow, flat waves of the diminished tide. The dog trotted by, threw itself down in the sand a dozen feet away. Blackett knew he no longer dared sit here after nightfall, in a dark alive with thousands of brilliant pinpoint stars, a planet or two, and no Moon. Never again a Moon. Once he had ventured out here after the sun went down, and low in the deep indigo edging the horizon had seen the clear distinct blue disk of the evening star, and her two attendant satellites, one on each side of the planet. Ganymede, with its thin atmosphere still intact, remained palest brown. Luna, at that distance, was a bright pinpoint orb, her pockmarked face never again to be visible to the naked eye of an Earthly viewer beneath her new, immensely deep carbon dioxide atmosphere.

He noticed that the dog was creeping cautiously toward him, tail wagging, eyes averted except for the occasional swift glance.

"Look," he said, "I'd rather be alone."

The dog sat up and uttered a barking laugh. It swung its head from side to side, conspicuously observing the hot, empty strand.

"Well, bub, I'd say you've got your wish, in spades."

"Nobody has swum here in years, apart from me. This is an old air force base, it's been decommissioned for . . ."

He trailed off. It was no answer to the point the animal was making. Usually at this time of year, Blackett acknowledged to himself, other beaches, more accessible to the crowds, would be swarming with shouting or whining children, mothers waddling or slumped, baking in the sun under SP 50 lotions, fat men eating snacks from busy concession stands, vigorous swimmers bobbing in white-capped waves. Now the empty waves crept in, onto the tourist beaches as they did here, like the flattened, poisoned combers at the site of the Exxon Valdez oil spill, twenty years after men had first set foot on the now absent Moon.

"It wasn't my idea," he said. But the dog was right; this isolation was more congenial to him than otherwise. Yet the yearning to rejoin the rest of the human race on Venus burned in his chest like angina.

"Not like I'm *blaming* you, bub." The dog tilted its handsome head. "Hey, should have said, I'm Sporky."

Blackett inclined his own head in reply. After a time, Sporky said, "You think it's a singularity excursion, right?"

He got to his feet, brushed sand from his legs and trousers. "I certainly don't suspect the hand of Jesus. I don't think I've been Left Behind."

"Hey, don't go away now." The dog jumped up, followed him at a safe distance. "It could be aliens, you know."

"You talk too much," Blackett said.

5.

As he landed, later in the day, still feeling refreshed from his hour in the water, he saw through the heat curtains of rising air a rather dirty precinct vehicle drive through the unguarded gate and onto the runway near the hangars. He taxied in slowly, braked, opened the door. The sergeant climbed out of his Ford Crown Victoria, cap off, waving it to cool his florid face.

"Saw you coming in, doc," Jacobs called. "Figured you

might like a lift back. Been damned hot out today, not the best walking weather."

There was little point in arguing. Blackett clamped the red tow bar to the nose wheel, steered the Cessna backward into the hangar, heaved the metal doors closed with an echoing rumble. He climbed into the cold interior of the Ford. Jacobs had the air-conditioning running at full bore, and a noxious country and western singer wailing from the sound system. Seeing his guest's frown, the police officer grinned broadly and turned the hideous noise down.

"You have a visitor waiting," he said. His grin verged on the lewd. Jacobs drove by the house twice a day, part of his self-imposed duty, checking on his brutally diminished constituency. For some reason he took a particular, avuncular interest in Blackett. Perhaps he feared for his own mental health in this terrible circumstance.

"She's expected, sergeant." By seniority of available staff, the man was probably a captain or even police chief for the region, now, but Blackett declined to offer the honorary promotional title. "Drop me off at the top of the street, would you?"

"It's no trouble to take you to the door."

"I need to stretch my legs after the flight."

In the failing light of dusk, he found Clare, almost in shadow, moving like a piece of beautiful driftwood stranded on a dying tide, backward and slowly forward, on his borrowed porch. She nodded, with her Gioconda smile, and said nothing. This evening she wore a broderie anglaise white-on-white embroidered blouse and 501s cut-down almost to her crotch, bleached by the long summer sun. She sat rocking wordlessly, her knees parted, revealing the pale lanterns of her thighs.

"Once again, doctor," Blackett told her, "you're trying to seduce me. What do you suppose this tells us both?"

"It tells us, doctor, that yet again you have fallen prey to intellectualized over-interpreting." She was clearly annoyed, but keeping her tone level. Her limbs remained disposed as they were. "You remember what they told us at school."

"The worst patients are physicians, and the worst physician

patients are psychiatrists." He took the old woven cane seat, shifting it so that he sat at right angles to her, looking directly ahead at the heavy brass knocker on the missing CEO's mahogany entrance door. It was serpentine, perhaps a Chinese dragon couchant. A faint headache pulsed behind his eyes; he closed them.

"You've been to the coast again, Robert?"

"I met a dog on the beach," he said, eyes still closed. A cooling breeze was moving into the porch, bringing a fragrance of the last pink mimosa blossoms in the garden bed beside the dry, dying lawn. "He suggested that we've experienced a singularity cataclysm." He sat forward suddenly, turned, caught her regarding him with her blue eyes. "What do you think of that theory, doctor? Does it arouse you?"

"You had a conversation with a dog," she said, uninflected, nonjudgmental.

"One of the genetically upregulated animals," he said, irritated. "Modified jaw and larynx, expanded cortex and Broca region."

Clare shrugged. Her interiority admitted of no such novelties. "I've heard that singularity hypothesis before. The Mayans–"

"Not that new age crap." He felt an unaccustomed jolt of anger. Why did he bother talking to this woman? Sexual interest? Granted, but remote; his indifference toward her rather surprised him, but it was so. Blackett glanced again at her thighs, but she had crossed her legs. He rose. "I need a drink. I think we should postpone this session, I'm not feeling at my best."

She took a step forward, placed one cool hand lightly on his bare, sunburned arm.

"You're still convinced the Moon had gone from the sky, Robert? You still maintain that everyone has gone to Venus?"

"Not everyone," he said brusquely, and removed her hand. He gestured at the darkened houses in the street. A mockingbird trilled from a tree, but there were no leaf blowers, no teenagers in sports cars passing with rap booming and thudding, no barbecue odors of smoke and burning steak, no TV displays flickering behind curtained windows. He found his key, went to the door, did not invite her in. "I'll see you to-morrow, Clare."

"Good night, Robert. Feel better." The psychiatrist went down the steps with a light, almost childlike, skipping gait, and paused a moment at the end of the path, raising a hand in farewell or admonishment. "A suggestion, Robert. The almanac ordains a full moon tonight. It rises a little after eight. You should see it plainly from your back garden a few minutes later, once the disk clears the treetops."

For a moment he watched her fade behind the overgrown, untended foliage fronting this opulent dwelling. He shook his head, and went inside. In recent months, since the theft of the Moon, Clare had erected ontological denial into the central principle of her world construction, her *Weltbild*. The woman, in her own mind supposedly his therapeutic guide, was hopelessly insane.

6.

After a scratch dinner of canned artichoke hearts, pineapple slices, pre-cooked baby potatoes, pickled eel from a jar, and rather dry lightly-salted wheaten thins, washed down with Californian Chablis from the refrigerator, Blackett dressed in slightly more formal clothing for his weekly visit to Kafele Massri. This massively obese bibliophile lived three streets over in the Baptist rectory across the street from the regional library. At intervals, while doing his own shopping, Blackett scavenged through accessible food stores for provender that he left in plastic bags beside Massri's side gate, providing an incentive to get outside the walls of the house for a few minutes. The man slept all day, and barely budged from his musty bed even after the sun had gone down, scattering emptied cans and plastic bottles about on the uncarpeted floor. Massri had not yet taken to urinating in his squalid bedclothes, as far as Blackett could tell, but the weekly visits always began by emptying several jugs the fat man used at night in lieu of chamber pots, rinsing them under the trickle of water from the kitchen tap, and returning them to the bedroom, where he cleared away the empties into bags and tossed those into the weedy back yard where obnoxious scabby cats crawled or lay panting.

Kafele Massri was propped up against three or four pillows. "I have. New thoughts, Robert. The ontology grows. More tractable." He spoke in a jerky sequence of emphysematic wheezing gasps, his swollen mass pressing relentlessly on the rupturing alveoli skeining his lungs. His fingers twitched, as if keying an invisible keyboard; his eyes shifting again and again to the dead computer. When he caught Blackett's amused glance, he shrugged, causing one of the pillows to slip and fall. "Without my beloved internet, I am. Hamstrung. My *preciiiouuus*." His thick lips quirked. He foraged through the bed covers, found a battered Hewlett-Packard scientific calculator. Its green strip of display flickered as his fingers pressed keys. "Luckily. I still have. This. My *slide rule*." Wheezing, he burst into laughter, followed by an agonizing fit of coughing.

"Let me get you a glass of water, Massri." Blackett returned with half a glass; any more, and the bibliophile would spill it down his vast soiled bathrobe front. It seemed to ease the coughing. They sat side by side for a time, as the Egyptian got his breath under control. Ceaselessly, under the impulse of his pudgy fingers, the small green numerals flickered in and out of existence, a Borgesian proof of the instability of reality.

"You realize. Venus is upside. Down?"

"They tipped it over?"

They was a placeholder for whatever force or entity or cosmic freak of nature had translated the two moons into orbit around the second planet, abstracting them from Earth and Jupiter and instantaneously replacing them in Venus space, as far as anyone could tell in the raging global internet hysteria before most of humanity was translated as well to the renovated world. Certainly Blackett had never noticed that the planet was turned on its head, but he had only been on Venus less than five days before he was recovered, against his will, to central Texas.

"*Au contraire*. It has always. Spun. Retrograde. It rotates backwards. The northern or upper hemisphere turns. Clockwise." Massri heaved a strangled breath, made twisted motions with his pudgy, blotched hands. "Nobody noticed that until late last. Century. The thick atmosphere, you know. And clouds. Impenetrable. High albedo. Gone now, of course."

Was it even the same world? He and the Egyptian scholar had discussed this before; it seemed to Blackett that whatever force had prepared this new Venus as a suitable habitat for humankind must have done so long ago, in some parallel or superposed state of alternative reality. The books piled around this squalid bed seemed to support such a conjecture. Worlds echoing away into infinity, each slightly different from the world adjacent to it, in a myriad of different dimensions of change. Earth, he understood, had been struck in infancy by a raging proto-planet the size of Mars, smashing away the light outer crust and flinging it into an orbiting shell that settled, over millions of years of impacts, into the Moon now circling Venus. But if in some other prismatic history, Venus had also suffered interplanetary bombardment on that scale, blowing away its monstrous choking carbon dioxide atmosphere and churning up the magma, driving the plate tectonic upheavals unknown until then, where was the Venerean or Venusian moon? Had that one been transported away to yet another alternative reality? It made Blackett tired to consider these metaphysical landscapes radiating away into eternity even as they seemed to close oppressively upon him, a psychic null-point of suffocating extinction.

Shyly, Kafele Massri broke the silence. "Robert, I have never. Asked you this." He paused, and the awkward moment extended. They heard the ticking of the grandfather clock in the hall outside.

"If I want to go back there? Yes, Kafele, I do. With all my heart."

"I know that. No. What was it. *Like*?" A sort of anguish tore the man's words. He himself had never gone, not even for a moment. Perhaps, he had joked once, there was a weight limit, a baggage surcharge his account could not meet.

"You're growing forgetful, my friend. Of course we've discussed this. The immense green-leaved trees, the crystal air, the strange fire-hued birds high in the canopies, the great rolling ocean–"

"No." Massri agitated his heavy hands urgently. "Not that. Not the sci fi movie. Images. No offense intended. I mean . . . The *affect*. The weight or lightness of. The heart. The rapture of. Being there. Or the. I don't know. Dislocation? Despair?"

Blackett stood up. "Clare informs me I have damaged affect. 'Flattened,' she called it. Or did she say 'diminished'? Typical diagnostic hand-waving. If she'd been in practice as long as I—"

"Oh, Robert, I meant no—"

"Of course you didn't." Stiffly, he bent over the mound of the old man's supine body, patted his shoulder. "I'll get us some supper. Then you can tell me your new discovery."

7.

Tall cumulonimbus clouds moved in like a battlefleet of the sky, but the air remained hot and sticky. Lightning cracked in the distance, marching closer during the afternoon. When rain fell, it came suddenly, drenching the parched soil, sluicing the roadway, with a wind that blew discarded plastic bottles and bags about before dumping them at the edge of the road or piled against the fences and barred, spear-topped front gates. Blackett watched from the porch, the spray of rain blowing against his face in gusts. In the distance a stray dog howled and scurried.

On Venus, he recalled, under its doubled moons, the storms had been abrupt and hard, and the ocean tides surged in great rushes of blue-green water, spume like the head on a giant's overflowing draught of beer. Ignoring the shrill warnings of displaced astronomers, the first settlers along one shoreline, he had been told, perished as they viewed the glory of a Ganymedean-Lunar eclipse of the sun, twice as hot, a third again as wide. The proxivenerean spring tide, tugged by both moons and the sun as well, heaped up the sea and hurled it at the land.

Here on Earth, at least, the Moon's current absence somewhat calmed the weather. And without the endless barrage of particulate soot, inadequately scrubbed, exhaled into the air by a million factory chimneys and a billion fuel fires in the Third World, rain came more infrequently now. Perhaps, he wondered, was it time to move to a more salubrious climatic region. But what if that blocked his return to Venus? The very thought made the muscles at his jaw tighten painfully.

For an hour he watched the lowering sky for the glow pasted beneath distant clouds by a flash of electricity, then the tearing violence of lightning strikes as they came closer, passing by within miles. In an earlier dispensation, he would have pulled the plugs on his computers and other delicate equipment, unprepared to accept the dubious security of surge protectors. During one storm, years earlier, when the Moon still hung in the sky, his satellite dish and decoder burned out in a single nearby frightful clap of noise and light. On Venus, he reflected, the human race were yet to advance to the recovery of electronics. How many had died with the instant loss of infrastructure—sewerage, industrial food production, antibiotics, air conditioning? Deprived of television and music and books, how many had taken their own lives, unable to find footing in a world where they must fetch for themselves, work with neighbors they had found themselves flung amongst willy-nilly? Yes, many had been returned just long enough to ransack most of the medical supplies and haul away clothing, food, contraceptives, packs of toilet paper . . . Standing at the edge of the storm, on the elegant porch of his appropriated mansion, Blackett smiled, thinking of the piles of useless stereos, laptops and plasma TV screens he had seen dumped beside the immense Venusian trees. People were so stereotypical, unadaptive. No doubt driven to such stupidities, he reflected, by their lavish *affect*.

8.

Clare found him in the empty car park, pacing out the dimensions of Petra's Great Temple. He looked at her when she repeated his name, shook his head, slightly disoriented.

"This is the Central Arch, with the Theatron," he explained. "East and West corridors." He gestured. "In the center, the Forecourt, beyond the Proneos, and then the great space of the Lower Temenos."

"And all this," she said, looking faintly interested, "is a kind of imaginal reconstruction of Petra."

"Of its Temple, yes."

"The rose-red city half as old as time?" Now a mocking note had entered her voice.

He took her roughly by the arm, drew her into the shade of the five-story brick and concrete structure where neuro-pharmaceutical researchers had formerly plied their arcane trade. "Clare, we don't understand time. Look at this wall." He smote it with one clenched fist. "Why didn't it collapse when the Moon was removed? Why didn't terrible earthquakes split the ground open? The earth used to flex every day with lunar tides, Clare. There should have been convulsions as it compensated for the changed stresses. Did they see to that as well?"

"The dinosaurs, you mean?" She sighed, adopted a patient expression.

Blackett stared. "The *what*?"

"Oh." Today she was wearing deep red culottes and a green silk shirt, with a bandit's scarf holding back her heavy hair. Dark adaptive-optic sunglasses hid her eyes. "The professor hasn't told you his latest theory? I'm relieved to hear it. It isn't healthy for you two to spend so much time together, Robert. *Folie à deux* is harder to budge than a simple defensive delusion."

"You've been talking to Kafele Massri?" He was incredulous. "The man refuses to allow women into his house."

"I know. We talk through the bedroom window. I bring him soup for lunch."

"Good god."

"He assures me that the dinosaurs turned the planet Venus upside down 65 million years ago. They were intelligent. Not all of them, of course."

"No, you've misunderstood—"

"Probably. I must admit I wasn't listening very carefully. I'm far more interested in the emotional undercurrents."

"You would be. Oh, damn, damn."

"What's a Temenos?"

Blackett felt a momentary bubble of excitement. "At Petra, it was a beautiful sacred enclosure with hexagonal flooring, and three colonnades topped by sculptures of elephants' heads. Water was carried throughout the temple by channels, you see—" He started pacing off the plan of the Temple again, convinced that this was the key to his return to Venus. Clare walked beside him, humming very softly.

9.

"I understand you've been talking to my patient." Blackett took care to allow no trace of censure to color his words.

"Ha! It would be extremely uncivil, Robert. To drink her soup while maintaining. A surly silence. Incidentally, she maintains. You are her. Client."

"A harmless variant on the transference, Massri. But you understand that I can't discuss my patients, so I'm afraid we'll have to drop that topic immediately." He frowned at the Egyptian, who sipped tea from a half-filled mug. "I can say that Clare has a very garbled notion of your thinking about Venus."

"She's a delightful young woman, but doesn't. Seem to pay close attention to much. Beyond her wardrobe. Ah well. But Robert, I had to tell *somebody*. You didn't seem especially responsive. The other night."

Blackett settled back with his own mug of black coffee, already cooling. He knew he should stop drinking caffeine; it made him jittery. "You know I'm uncomfortable with anything that smacks of so-called 'Intelligent Design.'"

"Put your mind at. Rest, my boy. The design is plainly

intelligent. Profoundly so, but. There's nothing supernatural in it. To the contrary."

"Still—dinosaurs? The dog I was talking to the other day favors what it called a 'singularity excursion.' In my view, six of one, half a dozen—"

"But don't you see?" The obese bibliophile struggled to heave his great mass up against the wall, hauling a pillow with him. "Both are wings. Of the same argument."

"Ah." Blackett put down his mug, wanting to escape the musty room with its miasma of cranky desperation. "Not just dinosaurs, *transcendental* dinosaurs."

Unruffled, Massri pursed his lips. "Probably. In effect." His breathing seemed rather improved. Perhaps his exchanges with an attractive young woman, even through the half-open window, braced his spirits.

"You have evidence and impeccable logic for this argument, I imagine?"

"Naturally. Has it ever occurred to you. How extremely improbable it is. That the west coast of Africa. Would fit so snugly against. The east coast of South America?"

"I see your argument. Those continents were once joined, then broke apart. Plate tectonics drifted them thousands of miles apart. It's obvious to the naked eye, but nobody believed it for centuries."

The Egyptian nodded, evidently pleased with his apt student. "And how improbable is it that. The Moon's apparent diameter varies from 29 degrees 23 minutes to 33 degrees 29 minutes. Apogee to perigee. While the sun's apparent diameter varies. From 31 degrees 36 minutes to 32 degrees 3 minutes."

The effort of this exposition plainly exhausted the old man; he sank back against his unpleasant pillows.

"So we got total solar eclipses by the Moon where one just covered the other. A coincidence, nothing more."

"Really? And what of this equivalence? The Moon rotated every 27.32 days. The sun's sidereal rotation. Allowing for current in the surface. Is 25.38 days."

Blackett felt as if ants were crawling under his skin. He forced patience upon himself.

"Not all that close, Massri. What, some . . . eight percent difference?"

"Seven. But Robert, the Moon's rotation has been slowing as it drifts away from Earth, because it is tidally locked. Was. Can you guess when the lunar day equaled the solar day?"

"Kafele, what are you going to tell me? 4 BC? 622 AD?"

"Neither Christ's birth nor Mohammed's Hegira. Robert, near as I can calculate it, 65.5 million years ago."

Blackett sat back, genuinely shocked, all his assurance draining away. The Cretaceous-Tertiary boundary. The Chicxulub impact event that exterminated the dinosaurs. He struggled his way back to reason. Clare had not been mistaken, not about that.

"This is just . . . absurd, my friend. The slack in those numbers . . . But what if they are right? So?"

The old man hauled himself up by brute force, dragged his legs over the side of the bed. "I have to take care of business," he said. "Leave the room, please, Robert."

From the hall, where he paced in agitation, Blackett heard a torrent of urine splashing into one of the jugs he had emptied when he arrived. Night music, he thought, forcing a grin. That's what James Joyce had called it. No, wait, that wasn't it—Chamber music. But the argument banged against his brain. And so what? Nothing could be dismissed out of hand. The damned *Moon* had been picked up and moved, and given a vast deep carbon dioxide atmosphere, presumably hosed over from the old Venus through some higher dimension. Humanity had been relocated to the cleaned-up version of Venus, a world with a breathable atmosphere and oceans filled with strange but edible fish. How could anything be ruled out as preposterous, however ungainly or grotesque?

"You can come back in now." There were thumps and thuds.

Instead, Blackett went back to the kitchen and made a new pot of coffee. He carried two mugs into the bedroom.

"Have I frightened you, my boy?"

"Everything frightens me these days, Professor Massri. You're about to tell me that you've found a monolith in the back garden, along with the discarded cans and the mangy cats."

The Egyptian laughed, phlegm shaking his chest. "Almost. Almost. The Moon is now on orbit a bit over. A million kilometers from Venus. Also retrograde. Exactly the same distance Ganymede. Used to be from Jupiter."

"Well, okay, hardly a coincidence. And Ganymede is in the Moon's old orbit."

For a moment, Massri was silent. His face was drawn. He put down his coffee with a shaking hand.

"No. Ganymede orbits Venus some 434,000 kilometers out. According to the last data I could find before. The net went down for good."

"Farther out than the Moon used to orbit Earth. And?"

"The Sun, from Venus, as you once told me. Looks brighter and larger. In fact, it subtends about 40 minutes of arc. And by the most convenient and interesting coincidence. Ganymede now just exactly looks . . ."

". . . the same size as the Sun, from the surface of Venus." Ice ran down Blackett's back. "So it blocks the Sun exactly at total eclipse. That's what you're telling me?"

"Except for the corona, and bursts of solar flares. As the Moon used to do here." Massri sent him a glare almost baleful in its intensity. "And you think that's just a matter of chance? Do you think so, Dr. Blackett?"

10.

The thunderstorm on the previous day had left the air cooler. Blackett walked home slowly in the darkness, holding the HP calculator and two books the old man had perforce drawn upon for data, now the internet was expired. He did not recall having carried these particular volumes across the street from the empty library. Perhaps Clare or one of the other infrequent visitors had fetched them.

The stars hung clean and clear through the heavy branches extending from the gardens of most of the large houses in the neighborhood and across the old sidewalk. In the newer, outlying parts of the city, the nouveaux riches had considered it a mark of potent prosperity to run their well-watered lawns to the very verge of the roadway, never walking any-where, driving to visit neighbors three doors distant. He wondered how they were managing on Venus. Perhaps the ratio of fit to obese and terminally inactive had improved, under the whip of necessity. Too late for poor Kafele, he thought, and made a mental note to stockpile another batch of pioglitazone, the old man's diabetes drug, when next he made a foray into a pharmacy.

He sat for half an hour in the silence of the large kitchen, scratching down data points and recalculating the professor's estimates. It was apparent that Massri thought the accepted extinction date of the great reptiles, coinciding as it did with the perfect overlap of the greater and lesser lights in the heavens, was no such thing—that it was, in fact, a time-stamp for Creation. The notion chilled Blackett's blood. Might the world, after all (fashionable speculation!), be no more than a virtual simulation? A calculational contrivance on a colossal scale? But not truly colossal, perhaps no more than a billion lines of code and a prodigiously accurate physics engine. Nothing else so easily explained the wholesale revision of the inner solar system. The idea did not appeal; it stank in Blackett's nostrils. Thus I refute, he thought again, and tapped a calculator key sharply. But that was a feeble refutation; one might as well, in a lucid dream, deny that any reality existed, forgetting the ground state or brute physical substrate needed to sustain the dream.

The numbers made no sense. He ran the calculations again. It was true that Ganymede's new orbit placed the former Jovian moon in just the right place, from time to time, to occult the sun's disk precisely. That was a disturbing datum. The dinosaur element was far less convincing. According to the authors of these astronomy books, Earth had started out, after the tremendous shock of the X-body impact that birthed the Moon, with an dizzying 5.5 or perhaps eight-hour day. It seemed impossibly swift, but the hugely larger gas giant Jupiter, Ganymede's former primary, turned completely around in just 10 hours.

The blazing young Earth spun like a mad top, its almost fatal impact wound subsiding, sucked away into subduction zones created by the impact itself. Venus—the old Venus, at least—lacked tectonic plates; the crust was resurfaced at half billion year intervals, as the boiling magma burst up through the rigid rocks, but not enough to carry down and away the appalling mass of carbon dioxide that had crushed the surface with a hundred times the pressure of Earth's oxygen-nitrogen atmosphere. Now, though, the renovated planet had a breathable atmosphere. Just add air and water, Blackett thought. Presumably the crust crept slowly over the face of the world, sucked down and spat back up over glacial epochs. But the numbers—

The Moon had been receding from Earth at a sluggish rate of 38 kilometers every million years—one part in 10,000 of its final orbital distance, before its removal to Venus. Kepler's Third Law, Blackett noted, established the orbital equivalence of time squared with distance cubed. So those 65.5 million years ago, when the great saurians were slain by a falling star, Luna had been only 2500 km closer to the Earth. But to match the sun's sidereal rotation exactly, the Moon needed to be more than 18,000 km nearer. That was the case no more recently than 485 million years ago.

Massri's dinosaur fantasy was off by a factor of at least 7.4.

Then how had the Egyptian reached his numerological conclusion? And where did all this lead? Nowhere useful that Blackett could see.

It was all sheer wishful thinking. Kafele Massri was as delusional as Clare, his thought processes utterly unsound. Blackett groaned and put his head on the table. Perhaps, he had to admit, his own reflections were no more reliable.

11.

"I'm flying down to the coast for a swim," Blackett told Clare. "There's room in the plane."

"A long way to go for a dip."

"A change of scenery," he said. "Bring your bathing suit if you like. I never bother, myself."

She gave him a long, cool look. "A nude beach? All right. I'll bring some lunch."

They drove together to the small airfield to one side of the industrial park in a serviceable SUV he found abandoned outside a Seven-Eleven. Clare had averted her eyes as he hot-wired the engine. She wore sensible hiking boots, dark gray shorts, a white wife-beater that showed off her small breasts to advantage. Seated and strapped in, she laid her broad-brimmed straw hat on her knees. Blackett was mildly concerned by the slowly deteriorating condition of the plane. It had not been serviced in many months. He felt confident, though, that it would carry him where he needed to go, and back again.

During the 90-minute flight, he tried to explain the Egyptian's reasoning. The young psychiatrist responded with indifference that became palpable anxiety. Her hands tightened on the seat belt cinched at her waist. Blackett abandoned his efforts.

As they landed at Matagorda Island, she regained her animation. "Oh, look at those lovely biplanes! A shame they're in such deplorable condition. Why would anyone leave them out in the open weather like that?" She insisted on crossing to the sagging Stearmans for a closer look. Were those tears in her eyes?

Laden with towels and a basket of food, drink, paper plates and two glasses, Blackett summoned her sharply. "Come along, Clare, we'll miss the good waves if we loiter." If she heard bitter irony in his tone, she gave no sign of it. A gust of wind carried away his own boater, and she dashed after it, brought it back, jammed it rakishly on his balding head. "Thank you. I should tie the damned thing on with a leather thong, like the cowboys used to do, and cinch it with a . . . a . . ."

"A woggle," she said, unexpectedly.

It made Blackett laugh out loud. "Good god, woman! Wherever did you get a word like that?"

"My brother was a boy scout," she said.

They crossed the unkempt grass, made their way with

some difficulty down to the shoreline. Blue ocean stretched south, almost flat, sparkling in the cloudless light. Blackett set down his burden, stripped his clothing efficiently, strode into the water. The salt stung his nostrils and eyes. He swam strongly out toward Mexico, thinking of the laughable scene in the movie *Gattaca*. He turned back, and saw Clare's head bobbing, sun-bleached hair plastered against her well-shaped scalp.

They lay side by side in the sun, odors of sun-block hanging on the unmoving air. After a time, Blackett saw the red setter approaching from the seaward side. The animal sat on its haunches, mouth open and tongue lolling, saying nothing.

"Hello, Sporky," Blackett said. "Beach patrol duties?"

"Howdy, doc. Saw the Cessna coming in. Who's the babe?"

"This is Dr. Clare Laing. She's a psychiatrist, so show some respect."

Light glistened on her nearly naked body, reflected from sweat and a scattering of mica clinging to her torso. She turned her head away, affected to be sleeping. No, not sleeping. He realized that her attention was now fixed on a rusty bicycle wheel half buried in the sand. It seemed she might be trying to work out the absolute essence of the relationship between them, with the rim and broken spokes of this piece of sea drift serving as some kind of spinal metaphor.

Respectful of her privacy, Blackett sat up and began explaining to the dog the bibliophile's absurd miscalculation. Sporky interrupted his halting exposition.

"You're saying the angular width of the sun, then and now, is about 32 arc minutes."

"Yes, 0.00925 radians."

"And the Moon last matched this some 485 million years ago."

"No, no. Well, it was a slightly better match than it is now, but that's not Massri's point."

"Which is?"

"Which is that the sun's rotational period and the Moon's were the *same* in that epoch. Can't you see how damnably unlikely that is? He thinks it's something like . . . I don't know, God's thumbprint on the solar system. The true date of Creation, maybe. Then he tried to show that it coincides with the extinction of the dinosaurs, but that's just wrong, they went extinct—"

"You do know that there was a major catastrophic extinction event at the Cambrian-Ordovician transition 488 million years ago at?"

Dumbfounded, Blackett said, "What?"

"Given your sloppy math, what do you say the chances are that your Moon-Sun rotation equivalence bracketed the Cambrian-Ordovician extinction? Knocked the living hell out of the trilobites, doc."

A surreal quality had entered the conversation. Blackett found it hard to accept that the dog could be a student of ancient geomorphisms. A spinal tremor shook him. So the creature was no ordinary genetically upgraded dog but some manifestation of the entity, the force, the ontological dislocation that had torn away the Moon and the world's inhabitants, most of them.

Detesting the note of pleading in his own voice, Blackett uttered a cry of heartfelt petition. He saw Clare roll over, waken from her sun-warmed drowse. "How can I get back there?" he cried. "Send me back! Send us both!"

Sporky stood up, shook sand from his fur, spraying Blackett with stinging mica.

"Go on as you began," the animal said, "and let the Lord be all in all to you."

Clouds of uncertainty cleared from Blackett's mind, as the caustic, acid clouds of Venus had been sucked away and transposed to the relocated Moon. He jumped up, bent, seized the psychiatrist's hand, hauled her blinking and protesting to her feet.

"Clare! We must trace out the ceremony of the Great Temple! Here, at the edge of the ocean. I've been wasting my time trying this ritual inland. Venus is now a world of great oceans!"

"Damn it, Robert, let me go, you're hurting—"

But he was hauling her down to the brackish, brine-stinking sea shore. Their parallel footprints wavered, inscribing a semiotics of deliverance. He began to tread out the Petran temple perimeter, starting at the Propylaeum, turned a right angle, marched them to the East Excedra and to the very foot of the ancient Cistern. He was traveling backward into archeopsychic time, deeper into those remote, somber half-worlds he had glimpsed in the recuperative paintings of his mad patients.

"Robert! Robert!"

They entered the water, which lapped sluggishly at their ankles and calves like the articulate tongue of a dog as large as the world. Blackett gaped. At the edge of sea and sand, great three-lobed arthropods shed water from their shells, moving slowly like enormous wood lice.

"Trilobites!" Blackett cried. He stared about, hand still firmly clamped on Clare Laing's. Great green rolling breakers, in the distance, rushed toward shore, broke, foamed and frothed, lifting the ancient animals and tugging at Blackett's limbs. He tottered forward into the drag of the Venusian ocean, caught himself. He stared over his shoulder at the vast, towering green canopy of trees. Overhead, bracketing the sun, twin crescent moons shone faintly against the purple sky. He looked wildly at his companion and laughed, joyously, then flung his arms about her.

"Clare," he cried, alive on Venus, "Clare, we made it!"

All the Love in the World

CAT SPARKS

Catriona Sparks (www.catsparks.net) lives in Wollongong, Australia, with her partner, Robert Hood. She is an Australian speculative fiction writer and graphic designer. From 2002–2008 she and Robert Hood ran Agog! Press, which produced ten anthologies of award-winning, new and mostly Australian speculative fiction. Her stories have drawn attention in the last six years or so. In 2007, Cat's story "Hollywood Roadkill" was awarded both the Aurealis Award for best short science fiction story and the Golden Aurealis for best Australian speculative fiction story of the year. In 2010, she replaced Damien Broderick as fiction editor of Cosmos, *an Australian literary science magazine that also publishes SF, and is poised to reach an audience outside Australia.*

"All the Love in the World" was published in Sprawl, *an impressive original anthology edited by Alisa Krasnostein in Australia. In this story, civilization collapses, and a small suburban neighborhood barricades itself for survival, forming an enclave. But things work out a little differently than one might expect for one woman. We like this story because it does something new and positive with the postapocalypse tale.*

If only Jon hadn't been the one to find her, rostered on his sentry duty up high above the wire. If only he'd been out the back busting furniture for wood. I could have claimed she was a looter, shot her square between the eyes. Jeannie spoiled everything. Wormed her way into the Crescent, set her sights on kicking me from Jon's bed. Tricking them all with her innocence and sweetness. Fooling every one of them but me.

"Why can't they put her in with Brian and Joyce?"

"No room. They've got grandchildren in there."

And God knows what else. Brian used to be a bus driver, kept his yard so spick and span and a little dog too old to do much yapping. Next door to him was once a childcare centre. Now it was filled with Princes Highway refugees and all the tinned stuff we'd been able to scrounge.

Jon's and my place had four rooms. I put Jeannie out back where the telly used to be. Watched her waving cheerily at Darren and Julie, the nice couple over the side fence. She treated me with deference. Obeyed my rules. Respected my possessions, but we both knew it was only borrowed time. I observed her step-by-step ingratiation into our tight community, checking out one man after another, calculating which of them had what. Darren was handsome and closer to her age, but two little daughters bound him tight to Julie. All roads of logic and opportunity led to Jon, no matter how you did the maths. And besides, he was already smitten.

Jeannie volunteered for extra farming. Said she loved nature and watching things grow. Every spare patch of Crescent soil was put to vegetable production, Al Messina's roses the one exception. They'd been his pride and joy before. No-one had the heart to pull them out. He grew his share of carrots where his front lawn used to be. Cabbages down the side passage. Avocadoes along the fence.

We were safe enough. Safe as anyone could be. Our Crescent home was blocked at either end, the creek behind our houses widened, banks fortified with razor wire and sacks of dirty sand. Across the road, a concrete sound barrier protected us from the highway, serving its duty as a battlement wall.

We had enough cans to get by for now. The future would be anybody's guess. Chris Cloakey's swimming pool was permanently half filled with scuzzy water. It rained a lot but we boiled it anyway. Used stormwater drain runoff for washing. It wouldn't take much to poison the lot of us.

Jon had been mine for ten whole months. I thought it was a blessing. That something as wonderful as love could bloom at the end of the world. He'd never have looked at me before the war. He stopped looking at me the day that bitch showed up, all big brown eyes and begging for something to eat.

He played guitar. Beatles and Pixies mixed with songs he wrote himself. We still ran stuff on batteries, clinging to the comfort of that electronic glow. Pointless, noisy shooting games. The real shooting had mostly passed us by.

Weekly meetings were all about our chickens and whether or not to dig up the bitumen road. We voted yes. More soil was needed for potatoes. There was talk of expanding the barricade up into St John's Road. That one got a yes vote too. The streets behind us had lain abandoned for months.

The couple on the corner's yard was still chocked with Christmas decorations. Giant reindeer and snowmen dioramas, shit that never made any sense in baking Australian Decembers. I said they ought to pull them down. That vote went against me. I said we didn't need reminding. They seemed to think it important not to forget.

I lost Jon incrementally in stages of politeness. Humour was the first to go—our private little jokes. She ended up with everything: the sex, the love, the laughter. The laughter cut the most because it proved he didn't care. Jon became so formal in my presence. Straight up with necessary exchanges, like ones he had with neighbours either side. Conversations reduced to business transactions. *If I give you this, perhaps you'll give me that.* When I lost Jon I got nothing in exchange. Sympathy from others, not enough to make a stand.

He wrote songs for her. Cooked her special treats. Stole from my hidden stash of chocolate even though I never touched his private stuff. I overheard them whispering in the darkness.

"Jeannie, you brought the light back to my life."

Give me a break, you heartless bastard. Before she got here, you and me were fine. But you've forgotten all of that, just like you always traded up. I bought that he felt guilty he'd survived. Most folks 'round here did. I didn't.

So I endured their hush-hush tones, their giggles and their love. It was the love that killed me—if it had been just sex, I might have borne that well enough. But Jon truly loved her. He'd always been a princess chaser even in the days before. And Jeannie was a princess, albeit a barefoot one in ragged jeans.

People don't ask questions when they want something to be true. I never pondered the coincidences that drew Jon to my side. He never questioned his right to upgrade. Jeannie read the lot of us like books. Sized us up and took the things she wanted. I spared so little thought to all the lives we'd left behind us. All her thoughts were focused on the future.

But then my world ended a second time. Jon got cocky. He got lazy. When summer came around again, he skipped the usual precautions. Got sunburned and stung by insects when all those months before he'd been so careful. We'd both been careful in so many ways. The Crescent had a lot of things but it didn't have a doctor.

Three got sick after forage detail behind the Westfield mall. Each came down with typhoid—at least that's what it looked like. Temperatures soared in the 40s, stayed that way a week. Jeannie fussed and fretted. She soothed Jon's fevered brow, fed him aspirin, left poignant, wilted flowers by his pillow.

As weeks wore on, talk turned to the need for proper treatment. Who knew what horrors lurked beyond our barrier wall? Of course there would be corpses. Dead things that attracted flies. Busted sewer pipes, open latrines. One little insect had been all it took. And this was when our haven came undone. We were all good neighbours. Better than we'd ever been before. But would we risk our lives for one other? The answer, when it came to it, was no. Were there even any doctors out there? Rumour was all we had to go on.

I sat with Jeannie, by his side, watching her mop his sallow brow. Wishing she'd stop play acting the part, if only when we were alone.

"You never told us where you came from. Before," I added. For clarity.

"Sydney," she answered, not looking up. That girl rarely met my gaze.

"After Sydney. There's not much left of the place, or so I'm told."

She shrugged. "I travelled round. Same as everybody, I guess."

I'd painted my own delicious picture of her past. Sleeping her way into temporary shelters, getting cast out when she failed to pull her weight. In Crescent, she was always on hand to do the pretty jobs. I never saw her mucking out the chicken coops, digging toilets or burying the dead.

"He might die, you know."

"Don't be silly. He'll be right. Just needs a little time to sleep it off."

"And what if he's not?" I smirked. I couldn't help it. "Life might get much harder for you then."

I thought she was going to let it go. Pretend she hadn't heard, just like she pretended not to see me often enough. In my mind I was already planning reclamation of the back room. I'd make it into a sitting area. Sew some cushions, bring out some of my books from under the house.

"I'm carrying his child," she said, so smug as she turned to face me. "Not a damn thing you can do about it, either."

And with her smile, my world disintegrated. Everything I'd come to fear was true.

"Bullshit," I said defensively. "Jon would have told me." But I knew he wouldn't, even if he'd known it to be fact. Maybe he didn't. Maybe it wasn't even true. Once I'd felt such pride in the bond I imagined between us. But there'd been no bond. Just a void so desperate to be filled.

"I'll be needing extra room when the baby comes. I'm thinking you can probably move out back."

And Jon slept on, oblivious, as clueless as the day he'd left my bed. She didn't care whether he lived or died. In a perfect world, he'd be lying awake now, listening to the honest truth unfold. His heart would swell to bursting with regret for me, the good woman he'd so carelessly dismissed.

Jeannie sat cross-legged on the carpet. Leant back, stretched her legs out straight before her. Tuned out from my presence once she'd played her trump card. Pink toenails, crystal beads around her ankle, earrings sparkling in a shaft of bitter sunlight.

I watched her, knowing precisely what came next. Funny how these things work. How crazy they seem in the light of day, how wretchedly perverse. I left her with him, to her mopping and his slumber, said nothing when she wasted yet another votive candle set between a chipped glass dolphin ornament and one of Al Messina's precious roses, plucked.

I paced the length of the Crescent and back, watching Darren and Julie's girls raking fallen twigs and branches into piles. The street seemed strangely claustrophobic, houses packed too close together. They hadn't been before garages were tricked out into makeshift homes. Across the road, six caravans were parked permanently in shade. A cloudless sky made no promises of rain it couldn't keep. We'd been lucky with our water so far. I wondered how long our luck was going to last.

I saw two choices, each as clear as day. Let Jon die or fight to save his life. Don't think I didn't dwell on the former. There'd be some small satisfaction in it for all he'd put me through. But I loved him and love's a stubborn thing. How often it has its wicked way with us.

I told Darren and Julie I was going for antibiotics. Asked if they needed anything for the girls. Their neighbourly kindness had included not stating the obvious. Saying nothing when it was clear I'd been usurped.

"Some vitamins," said Julie. "But are you sure it's safe?"

Hell no—I'm sure I'm going to die.

"Head for town," said Darren. "Messina's picked up fresh chatter on the shortwave."

He presented me with a hunting knife, Julie shot me a worried stare, followed by three precious pots of honey. I was touched—she'd been saving those for better days. And he knew full well he'd probably lose the knife. Good people, as I'd always said. It's not easy hiding two little girls from the world.

Crescent had no rules about leaving. None of us were beholden to the others. We'd thrown in our lot together because it worked. Because we were scared of what the world had become. We'd seen the cities burning before the news cut out, heard tales of roadside massacres, rape and pillage. Of poisoned water and blackened skies, most of it ninety ks from where we lived.

The south coast had its own problems. Its own resources too. Factions formed. Barricades went up.

I'd been amongst the Crescent's first, comprehending the necessity of animals and seed. In our semi-rural landscape, these weren't hard to come by. In all, we hadn't done half bad. We had enough so long as we didn't get complacent.

"If there's any help out there I'll do my best to find it."

That was all the promise I had to offer. A year ago, the streets had still been full of crazy. Guns firing, hoons doing burnouts, crashing cars. We took our stations along the barricade, silent sentinels against the darkness. But our nightmares failed to flesh to substance. Gradually the violence petered out, left us alone with our chickens and our terror.

Yet here I stood, about to leave it all behind. For what—the faded bloom of love? I'd go the back way over the creek to draw the least attention. Tell the lookout I was on the scrounge. All the nearby houses had been picked clean. Brian would presume I knew my stuff. I left him pulling handfuls of privet from the crumbling creek bank. His own yard had been spotless, even back before. Skipper lay snoozing in the shade. That lucky old dog was far too tough for eating.

And where would I be heading? Crown Street Mall as it had once been known. A corralled space for shoppers, free of cars. Fridays had once boasted a local produce market. In the 1800s it had been a cattle track. God knows what was being made of it now. The shortwave reckoned it was hosting a witches' market. Any medicine to be had would come from there.

What did I have to barter with? Honey and a knife. A tube of Vegemite and the last of my precious chocolate. Better a pack of witches got those than the one who'd invaded my house.

I went back in for one last look at Jon lying in his fevered sleep. Stared at him so lovingly, Jeannie lost beyond my line of sight. The chiselled contours of his face. Tan skin that never seems to fade. God, how I love him. My heart aches with the weight of it. A burden I've carried across two lifetimes now.

I remember how the city used to look before the war. I remember how I never used to look at it at all. Took it for granted, every curbed and guttered inch of it. Cocooned myself in the luxury of ignorance.

We'd been late teens, young and stupid, full of ourselves and naïve insight. Five of us had shared that house, a crowded space, more than not, half filled with strangers, nights of wine and candlelit guitar. Pretty girls, dreadlocks and nose rings. Talk of Tibet where the air was clear, the people so humble and wise. Jon occupied a central space. Everything was more fun when he was around. Girls fell for him like dominoes. He'd have them, then move on to other things.

I wanted him, but *all* of him, not just the paltry crumbs on offer. I wanted his mind, his honesty, his trust. I wanted to stand amongst the handful he called friends. Poor Megan, dull and plain. Jon doesn't have female friends, don't you know?

I never fucked him back then, no matter how many times he tried it on. Not that I didn't want to—my God, it was all I wanted. But I'd seen what happened to all the girls who let him in. I wanted him to care for me. He rarely remembered their names.

I left that house after one particularly humiliating night. Didn't see the guy for twenty years. Fell in and out of love a dozen times. Couldn't bring myself to settle down. I often glimpsed him from the corner of my eye. Jon on the ferry, Jon amongst the theatre crowd. Jon asking an old friend how I was doing. Of course, he was never really there. Our old group disintegrated, as such groups are wont to do. Now and then I'd hear a whisper. He's done some acting. He's in a band. Of course he was—anywhere there'd be women to adore him. So many options before the world got scared.

What I didn't expect was to find him staggering down the Princes Highway, in shock, half naked with a fearsome case of burns. Had he been searching for me? I convinced myself he had. Fate or providence or perhaps some act of God. Nowadays, I don't believe in any of those things. I'm back on the highway leaving my home behind.

I could almost pretend the war had never happened. For all I knew it hadn't—it's not like there was much to see. Radio silence. Television snow. Intermittent Internet for a month or two. Then Al Messina raised some chatter on the shortwave. We learnt about the witches' market and other groups like ours. After the initial exodus from Sydney, not much. The flotilla to New Zealand. Planes flying overhead. I often wonder how many of them made it. We had some trade with other friendlies, then that business with the gangs. Swore you'd never have gotten me off the Crescent after that. Six months of sporadic gunfire and ceaseless hungry dogs.

I kept my head down, hoed cabbages along the verge. Collected rainfall, boiled it fresh and clean. Thanked God for the fecundity of chickens and the fact we were the first to raid the Westfield ruins.

Truth is, the world has fallen silent. None of us know what's out there any more. Beyond the shortwave, the best we've got is Jeannie's stories. Quite frankly, I don't believe a word. That girl never suffered a day in her life. Never worked either—she's far too smart for that. Her sordid tales run like half remembered movie plots. Teenage novels. Television dreams.

Three roads lead me to the city centre. I pick the one least convoluted. Fewer opportunities for ambush—or so I hope.

I mount the hill that rises up behind the Crescent. So bare and naked with half the houses burnt. I hope the rain has washed away the details. I don't want to know what happened here.

I'm scared for Jon and I'm scared for me. I keep the knife gripped tightly in my hand, eyes scanning left and right for movement. But there's nothing. Where did everybody go? There were people up here not that long ago.

The tar is cracked, strewn with leaves and broken branches. I make a note to tell the others—all this excellent firewood. *When I get back* . . . I put one foot before the other. *When I get back* covers so many things.

Down the dip and up the second hill. I'm too far gone now. Out of safety's reach. Now might be the time for feeling lucky. I'm not falling for it. Too many movie moments crammed inside my mind. My heart sinks when I spot the barricade. It looks abandoned but I'm going to play it safe. Find another way to join the main road. Dogleg down around the kindergarten, a steep decline to where the station used to be.

I move quickly, no time for indecision. If I stop too long to think I might change my mind. Take fright and run back home to Jon and Jeannie. But how would I ever live with myself if he died?

There's something moving around inside the kindy. I hope its only possums and jog quietly down the hill. The train tracks would be quickest but there's so much room for ambush. No. I'll take my chances on the road.

A row of garbage bins still standing, their plastic wheels choked thick with weeds. A lone ibis prowls the pavement. Keeps its distance. Checks me out.

Ugly white and purple agapanthus flowers have claimed these ruined suburbs as their own. Bowing sagely in the breeze acknowledging my predicament.

I hear the rumble, spin around but it's too late. A gang is bearing down upon me. Rollerbladers with helmets, weapons raised. I can't outrun them. There's nowhere to hide. I'm stunned like a rodent caught in headlights, the sound of their wheels thunder like a road train.

So I drop to my knees, cover my head, kiss the tar goodbye. The road shakes so hard it might swallow me up. Yet it doesn't. I wait for pain that isn't going to come. They have passed me. They didn't even stop. Skated around my whimpering form like I was a pothole or a log.

I sit in the road for ages chewing my fingernails. *The world has ended, right? There really was a war?* Because some times I can't be sure, and this is one of them. Skating the post-apocalypse simply never occurred to me.

I wish Jon were here. It'd have made him laugh. But he wasn't laughing, was he? He was dying.

Dusting off my faded jeans, I put the knife back in my hand. Scan first the empty gardens, then the train tracks for . . . whatever. Continue my trek into city central, sticking to the cyclone fence this time. Figuring I'd be able to see anyone approaching from the tracks.

Other people have the same idea. We maintain a respectable distance. I long to ask all the usual questions. *Who are you? How well are you surviving?* But I don't. I keep on walking, eyes firmly fixed upon the prize.

Some are ragged, others dress like joggers, preapocalypse. Shamed, I put my knife away. No-one else is wielding weapons, although several walk with staffs. I keep my distance, shun eye contact, yet all the while I'm filled with wonder. Something's going on here. Something strange.

Garbage blows down Keira Street. I try to picture what the shop fronts once contained. They've all been looted, the glass smashed long ago. That fact aside, the structures seem in place. At the end of the street, a paved and shaded plaza. The centre of town as much as it ever was. The stage still stands, once the domain of fashion promotions and teenage beauty pageants. Today it's filled with jamming musicians: guitars, flutes and clarinets. A sax to the side. Two dreadlocked girls with bongo drums. People join or leave as they see fit. The sound they make is surprisingly melodic.

At the foot of the stage little children sit in groups. Children in the open. Unprotected! I stare at them as though they're apparitions. Surely no parent would take such a risk. Am I the only one who understands?

I feel invisible as I move amongst the crowd. And it is a crowd—the largest I've seen for years.

They're garbed in many colours, a hodge-podge of pre-war fashion trends. Some clearly enjoy the art of it. Diamonds over khaki camouflage, suits and swimwear mixed. Definitely something Caribbean going on with hair. And makeup. Too many clown eyes for my liking. Some look like they've been living in pyjamas for eons.

Vendors hoist wares up high on sticks. Clothing, paperbacks, tools. Others seem to be selling potions. Pharmaceuticals mixed with other things. Or maybe it's all just lolly water. How am I ever supposed to tell? I need a doctor, a pharmacist, a nurse. None of this lot looks to fit the bill.

"What have you got for typhoid?" I shout up at one of them. Up because he was wearing stilts to make his presence felt.

"Sounds serious," he says as he rummages in coat pockets. Draws something out for me to see. "Take three spoonfuls and call me in the morning." He laughs like an ocker Baron Samedi.

"You've got to be shitting me." The stuff he's selling looks suspiciously like Vegemite. He's not getting my honey or chocolate in trade for that. I push on past. There's plenty more clowns where he came from. Plenty more of everything except what Jon needs.

A blanket spread with children's toys brings me back into the moment. Little plastic action figures from shows no-one will ever see again. More traditional items. Plushie animals. Coloured blocks. Jeannie and his baby. I keep walking.

Further down the mall I see more serious types of shopping. Bearded men in greatcoats, hunting rifles unconcealed. Smoked meat strung across a doorway. What kind is anybody's guess.

And, inevitably, arguments. Squabbles over details of exchange. But I don't see a single fight. Impressive in itself.

The wafting tempt of ganja. Two scruff-haired teenagers, both stoned. No-one has bothered to tell them the world has ended. Like it makes the slightest bit of difference.

And then, finally, a group of women cooking pancakes on a skillet, looking like they might have stepped out from a Sunday bingo hall.

"I need medicine. Real medicine," I tell them, crouching. "Know anyone who can help?"

"Not 'round here," says one of them, dusting sugar. "Feeling poorly are we, love?"

I tell them about Jon and the other two sick neighbours, omitting all mention of Jeannie and other things.

"You want a dispensary," says the one who still sports relatively suburban hair. "Last one left's at Corrimal Surf Club. The bike track's your best bet."

They give me a pancake. That was nice of them. I remember that bike track since back before the war. A haven for muggers and rapists, even then.

When night falls, things begin to change. I realise I'm no longer safe. Daylight was such a civilising factor. I look for the pancake women but they're gone, back to their fortified bingo hall, or wherever. I curse myself for being stupid. For taking my eye off the ball. Would the beach be safe? Would anywhere? All I know is that I can't stay here.

The music has gotten heavier, skaters on battered boards muscle in as people drift off into twilight groups of two and three. This is tribal country and I do not belong. I grip my knife, certain I'll have to use it. Knowing I'll be lost if I even try.

That's when the fear starts working me over. How did everything fall so quickly into ruin? I'd had a life, a man, a home, then she walked in and all of it was lost. Suddenly I'm walking down a darkened street with a knife, praying I won't be killed while she lies safe and warm in what used to be my bed. And he lies dying. *Not if I can help it.* That's the thought that spurs me on my way.

Just you try and take him away from me . . . That's what

I'm thinking as I pass a group of three. They eye me with great interest. My scowl seems to put them off. I don't know why—they could take me down in seconds. But they don't so I keep moving. I hear the beach about a block before I see it. The stadium sulks alone in shadow. Without power, it might as well be a rock.

The beach is a fairyland of bonfires and flaming torches. Squeals of laughter, screams of something else, all mixed and mashed together. Behind the fire, the pounding of the waves. I'm not going near it. I can reach the bike track overland.

Abandoned apartment blocks stand guard along the coast road, the cafés looted long ago for foodstuffs. Now and then I pass a solitary traveller. None make eye contact. Maybe they're all like me? Cast out from their homes and hearths, fugitives from everything that's sane. Women and men whose tribes no longer want them. Can they smell my fear like I can smell my own?

I spend the night in the ruins of a looted boutique. Torn curtains stained with oil provide a bed. I sleep with the knife. I don't sleep, mostly. Maybe drift for a couple of dreamless hours.

Morning light brings with it inspiration. I can do this thing and be home within a day. I realise I've been selfish. It's about Jon, after all. The man is dying, yet all I think about is me. And Jeannie, of course. That bitch is never out of my mind. I'll bet she never spares a thought for me. She's already scored her trophy, especially if she's really pregnant.

Three people die if you don't make it. Four. I forgot to count myself. So I steal through the urban undergrowth, eyes alert for ambush.

The beach is strewn with bodies. Hard to tell if they're sleeping or if they're dead. Huddled clusters of folks who might be families. It's ages until I get why no-one's bothering me. I look fucking dangerous. I have murder in my eyes. Wielding my knife as though I know how to use it. I smile when I realise this is Jeannie's legacy. I don't even look like a woman anymore.

But the old bike track looks dangerous too. Am I any kind of match for it? One little knife against the ruins of civilisation. Doesn't matter. I'm not going back without those drugs.

A stiff breeze rips along the headland, tousling long ribbons of grass. It's beautiful, the view, stretching all the way past three beached cargo ships and out to sea. A thousand countries I'll never get to visit. Nameless strangers speaking in foreign tongues. The brisk sky streaked so innocently with clouds. Like nothing ever happened. Like the world was always this way.

A string of people walking single file. They look harmless so I put my knife away. We nod at each other, pass politely. Women mostly, two small children in the middle.

Will Jon and Jeannie expect me to care for their baby? Am I supposed to be its aunt? A domestic helper. An aging *au pair. Not fucking likely,* I declare.

I stomp on fallen branches, kick stones out of my way. Space is at a premium on Crescent. No spare rooms, garages or empty caravans. If I throw them out, there's nowhere else to stay. Two days ago, that house had still been mine. My choice to leave has tipped the power balance. When I get home they'll make me take the room out back. I'll bet the bitch has moved my stuff already.

And then, way out to sea, I glimpse something wonderful. A whale spout. No. Wait—two! A big one and a little one. I stop to shield my eyes. Whales had long been choosing to swim this coast, but in all my years down here I'd never seen one. Probably because I'd never stopped to look.

I walk on, steeling myself for the inevitable. *They've become a family. Rules of ownership have changed. What you have to offer is what counts.* I try not to think about Jon and Jeannie. The track is strewn with garbage, picnic tables overturned.

Treetops pulse with the hum of cicadas, brown abandoned husks litter the ground. Weeds already choke their way through fences. Another year or two and this path will be gone.

* * *

The sight of Corrimal Surf Club is welcome, as is the orderly queue snaking along the sandy path. I claim a sun-bleached plastic seat beneath a vague attempt at shade. The woman beside me nurses a broken arm.

"Fell off me roof," she says before I've even asked. She doesn't look too worried. If it had been me, I'd have been in a panicked state. Broken bones, infected gums. Appendicitis. All these things can kill us. Not to mention all those things we haven't thought of.

The guy in charge is clean and that speaks for something. He might have been a doctor once, although he looks a little young. Others mill around the red brick structure—whether they're doctors or nurses too or just people embracing new-found purpose, I can't say.

I turn my chair to face the ocean, surprised to see it packed with bobbing heads. A moment of panic until I get the picture.

"They're surfing!" I announce to the woman with the broken arm.

I might as well have said the sky was blue. Life goes on and life for them is surfing. Always was down Corrimal way. It makes more sense than many things I've seen. I mean, why not surf just because the world has gone? Why not skate or rollerblade? Play guitar or bongo drums. Am I the only one who doesn't get it? Me with that knife pressed so hard against my heart.

Where are the roving bands of cannibals? The *Mad Max* cars and displays of outlandish human cruelty?

"Am I missing something?" I ask the woman. She didn't hear me. Probably just as well.

"I'm Daniel," says the doctor, wiping his hands on his pants before offering to shake mine. "Got a problem?"

"Sure. The world ended—only nobody seems to have noticed," I answer dryly.

He smiles. "Some days it seems like that. Other days . . ." He glances across to an area near the treeline. Once again, it takes awhile for me to get it. Row after row of human-shaped dirt mounds. So people have died here after all.

I tell him of Jon's symptoms: the fever, shits and rash. "Three of them have it," I add, almost an afterthought. Everything's not about Jon, I remind myself. Only, it is. My entire world.

"Might be typhoid fever," says the doctor. "They keeping fluids up? Got some amoxicillin left, that's all."

When we go inside he rummages through shelving that had likely once held books. The red brick walls feature sporting plaques and trophies, most to do with surfing.

"Nosebleeds?"

I nod.

"Gut ache?"

"That too." *And hey, how about some cyanide to take care of my domestic issues . . .*

"The bus goes back tomorrow. Do you think you could lend a hand?" His voice trails off. Something boring about boxes and shovels.

"The what, excuse me?"

"To leave now means you'd have to walk. But I could really use some help with stocktake."

He's talking about a fucking bus that travels into town along the road!

"Only once a month," he says. "You're lucky you turned up when you did."

And in that instant I have a vision of the future. The bus a hundred years from now, hitched behind two horses, dragged on patched up rubber tyres. Making its gentle rounds of a district choked by weeds.

"I can stay," I tell him, fascinated.

Turns out three of them in the surf club had been doctors. Mad keen surfers too which is probably why they stayed. We lie on lounges drinking beer kept chill in tidal pools. Way past expiry date, like anyone cares.

Sharon and Brianna, the other two, catch waves until the sun goes down. I tell Daniel everything from both before and after. He nods knowingly when I get to Jeannie. I find myself wishing she'd wound up here with him.

"You did the right thing. What else could you do?"

"He might be dying while I'm lying here drinking your beer."

Doctor Daniel shakes his head. "Unlikely," is his prognosis. "Unless I'm wrong," he adds as afterthought.

All of this is wrong, and I don't know what to make of it. We drink beer long into the twilight. We think we see the whales again just as the sun is setting. A mother and baby cavorting off the rocks. But Daniel's not sure. As he's fond of saying, those whales might turn out to be something else.

Brian is on lookout when I make it back to Crescent. "Where the bloody hell have you been," he sings down from the treetop, hunting rifle slung across his back.

"Shopping," I tell him, holding up bright blue boxes of amoxicillin.

He slaps the air, exaggerated, lets me through.

The Crescent seems much smaller than it was before I left it. Work has begun on pickaxing up the tar. I catch a few hullos as I wander down the road. Strange, as though I'd just popped up to the corner shop for milk. Was it merely two and a bit years past we were doing such mundane things? Only a week since I'd gone out for the drugs? The sound of my own footfall troubles me. I walk like a gunslinger marking out new territory.

What was I expecting? Children running out into the street? Kind-faced mammas with hair tied back in scarves? Is Jon dead or does he live? In a couple of minutes I'm going to know for sure. Those minutes lengthen as I stride across the yard. Slip through the side entrance, heart thumping. I pause in the hallway, relief flushing my skin like heat rash. There's a gentle strumming of guitar out back. A style I'd recognise anytime and any place. Jon once told me he played every day for thirty years. So he wasn't dead of typhoid after all.

I close my eyes. The music's beautiful. He's beautiful, even with the radiation scars. We had our moments. Times when I was the happiest woman alive. Days I wished the dream would never end.

I sneak into the kitchen, glad to find it empty. They're

both out back, Darren and Julie too. Jeannie's fussing over one of the children, hoisting her up and down to make her squeal. She throws a pretty smile at Darren. Julie catches it from the corner of her eye. I watch through the window as she calls instructions to her daughters, makes some small excuse to sit beside him. The look upon her face is one I recognise. In the mirror, oh so many times.

Jon strums "Blackbird". He always played a lot of Beatles. In the horse-drawn world of a hundred years, such songs will belong to no-one. I always loved to hear him play. To watch him too—those sinewy brown arms.

I place the amoxicillin upon the bench. Sneak into the bedroom, surprised to see my things have not been moved. I pack quickly, ears straining for the screen door sliding open but all I hear is Lennon and McCartney.

My rucksack bulges with useful items. Very few keepsakes. Not much left worth keeping. All my favourite t-shirts. Swimmers, sunglasses, blue jeans. The gold heart locket left to me by Grandma.

I don't leave a note.

Outside, wind tears through the treetops, sets the telegraph wires to rippling. Unseen cockatoos screech their discontent. Skipper cocks his leg against a cabbage row as Brian stabs at the furrowed earth with a pitchfork.

"Where're you awf to now then, luv?" he says, resting the pitchfork, gesturing to my pack with his free hand.

"More shopping," I tell him.

We used to have the exact same conversations, only back then he'd been fussing over flowers in his own front yard. Post-apocalypse has slowed his state of mind, but it seems like not much else had changed for him. Brian is already living in the horse-drawn future. I bet he misses television, that's all.

"Aww, you bloody women," he says, grinning with ancient crooked teeth.

A cockatoo swoops between us. I shade my eyes against the sun, follow it back to its branch.

"Regards to Joyce," I call out, acknowledge a wave in trade. This time, I walk the length of the Crescent, clamber over the stacked car barricade. Stand for a moment to stare back along the street, then beyond to Mount Keira in the distance. Wind tugs dramatically at my hair. In front of Al Messina's roses, three small girls play cricket. A fourth child sucks its thumb and stares.

The last I ever see of any of them.

At Budokan

ALASTAIR REYNOLDS

Alastair Reynolds (voxish.tripod.com) lives in Aberdare, in Wales. He worked for ten years for the European Space Agency before becoming a full-time writer in 2004. He began writing SF in the early 1990s. By the time his first novel, Revelation Space, *was published in 1999, he was generally perceived as one of the new British space opera writers emerging in the mid and late 1990s, in the generation after Baxter and McAuley, and originally the most "hard SF" of the new group. He had two books out in 2010:* Terminal World, *a novel of the far future which Eric Brown, reviewing for the* Guardian, *describes as a "rousing adventure in a wildly original setting," and* Deep Navigation, *a short story collection from NESFA Press. His short novel,* Troika, *is out in hardcover in 2011.*

"At Budokan," which appeared in the anthology Shine, *is a lively story about bringing back an extinct species, genetically engineered to play guitar, and the future of rock and roll. Sort of deadpan, as if Jurassic Park meets Spinal Tap. It has a lot of amusing and perhaps even some scary implications. After you read this, think about the "what if" of the story.*

I'm somewhere over the Sea of Okhotsk when the nightmare hits again. It's five years ago and I'm on the run after the machines went berserk. Only this time they're not just enacting wanton, random mayhem, following the scrambled choreography of a corrupted performance program. This time they're coming after *me*, all four of them, stomping their way down an ever-narrowing back alley as I try to get away, the machines too big to fit in that alley, but in the malleable logic of dreams somehow not too big, swinging axes and sticks rather than demolition balls, massive, indestructible guitars and drumsticks. I reach the end of the alley and start climbing up a metal ladder, a ladder that morphs into a steep metal staircase, but my limbs feel like they're moving through sludge. Then one of them has me, plucking me off the staircase with steel fingers big enough to bend girders, and I'm lifted through the air and turned around, crushed but somehow not crushed, until I'm face to face with James Hetfield out of Metallica.

"You let us down, Fox," James says, his voice a vast seismic rumble, animatronic face wide enough to headbutt a skyscraper into rubble. "You let us down, you let the fans down, and most of all you let yourself down. Hope you feel ashamed of yourself, buddy."

"I didn't mean . . ." I plead, pityingly, because I don't want to be crushed to death by a massive robot version of James Hetfield.

"Buddy." He starts shaking me, holding me in his metal fist like a limp rag doll.

"I'm sorry man. This wasn't how it was meant . . ."

"Buddy."

But it's not James Hetfield shaking me to death. It's Jake, my partner in Morbid Management. He's standing over my seat, JD bottle in one hand, shaking me awake with the other. Looking down at the pathetic, whimpering spectacle before him.

"Having it again, right?"

"You figured."

"Buddy, it's time to let go. You fucked up big time. But no one died and no one wants to kill you about it now. Here." And he passes me the bottle, letting me take a swig of JD to settle my nerves. Doesn't help that I don't like flying much. The flashbacks usually happen in the Antonov, when there's nowhere else to run.

"Where are we?" I ask groggily.

"About three hours out."

I perk up. "From landing?"

"From departure. Got another eight, nine in the air, depending on head-winds."

I hand him back the bottle. "And you woke me up for that?"

"Couldn't stand to see you suffering like that. Who was it this time? Lars?"

"James."

Jake gives this a moment's consideration. "Figures. James is probably not the one you want to piss off. Even now."

"Thanks."

"You need to chill. I was talking to them last week." Jake gave me a friendly punch on the shoulder. "They're cool with you, buddy. Bygones be bygones. They were even talking about getting some comp seats for the next stateside show, provided we can arrange wheelchair access. Guys are keen to meet Derek. But then who isn't?"

I think back to the previous evening's show. The last night of a month-long residency at Tokyo's Budokan. Rock history. And we pulled it off. Derek and the band packed every seat in the venue, for four straight weeks. We could have stayed on another month if we didn't have bookings lined up in Europe and America.

"I guess it's working out after all," I say.

"You sound surprised."

"I had my doubts. From a musical standpoint? You had me convinced from the moment I met Derek. But turning this into a show? The logistics, the sponsorship, the legal angles? Keeping the rights activists off our back? Actually making this thing turn a profit? That I wasn't so certain about."

"Reason I had to have you onboard again, buddy. You're the numbers man, the guy with the eye for detail. And you came through."

"I guess." I stir in my seat, feeling the need to stretch my legs. "You—um—checked on Derek since the show?"

Jake shoots me a too-quick nod. "Derek's fine. Hit all his marks tonight."

Something's off, and I'm not sure what. It's been like this since we boarded the Antonov. As if something's bugging Jake and he won't come out with whatever it was.

"Killer show, by all accounts," I say.

"Best of all the whole residency. Everything went like clockwork. The lights, the back projection . . ."

"Not just the technical side. One of the roadies reckoned Extinction Event was amazing."

Jake nods enthusiastically. "As amazing as it ever is."

"No, he meant exceptionally amazing. As in, above and beyond the performance at any previous show."

Jake's face tightens at the corners. "I heard it too, buddy. It was fine. On the nail. The way we like it."

"I got the impression it was something more than . . ." But I trail off, and I'm not sure why. "You sure there's nothing we need to talk about?"

"Nothing at all."

"Fine." I give an easy smile, but there's still something unresolved, something in the air between us. "Then I guess I'll go see how the big guy's doing."

"You do that, buddy."

I unbuckle from the seat and walk along the drumming,

droaning length of the Antonov's fuselage. It's an AN-225, the largest plane ever made, built fifty years ago for the Soviet space program. There are only two of them in the world, and Morbid Management and Gladius Biomech have joint ownership of both. Putting Derek's show together is so logistically complex that we need to be assembling one stage set when the other's still in use. The Antonovs leapfrog the globe, crammed to the gills with scaffolding, lighting rigs, speaker stacks, instruments, screens, the whole five hundred tonne spectacle of a modern rock show. Even Derek's cage is only a tiny part of the whole cargo.

I make my way past two guitar techs and a roadie deep into a card game, negotiate a long passage between two shipping containers, and pass the fold-down desk where Jake has his laptop set up, reviewing the concert footage, and just beyond the desk lies the cage. It's lashed down against turbulence, scuffed and scratched from where it was loaded aboard. We touch up the yellow paint before each show so it all looks gleaming and new. I brush a hand against the tubular steel framing.

Strange to think how alarmed and impressed I was the first time, when Jake threw the switch. It's not the same now. I know Derek a lot better than I did then, and I realise that a lot of his act is, well, just that. Act. He's a pussycat, really. A born showman. He knows more about image and timing than almost any rock star I've ever worked with.

Derek's finishing off his dinner. Always has a good appetite after a show, and at least it's not lines of coke and underage hookers he has a taste for.

He registers my presence and fixes me with those vicious yellow eyes.

Rumbles a query, as if to say, *can I help you?*

"Just stopping by, friend. I heard you went down a storm tonight. Melted some faces with Extinction Event. Bitching Rise of the Mammals, too. We'll be shifting so many downloads we may even have to start charging to cover our overheads."

Derek offers a ruminative gurgle, as if this is an angle he's never considered before.

"Just felt I ought to." And I rap a knuckle against the cage. "You know, give credit. Where it's due."

Derek looks at me for a few more seconds, then goes back to his dinner.

You can't say I don't try.

I'd been flying when Jake got back in touch. It was five years ago, just after the real-life events of my dream. I was grogged out from departure lounge vodka slammers, hoping to stay unconscious until the scramjet was wheels down and I was at least one continent away from the chaos in LA. Wasn't to be, though. The in-flight attendant insisted on waking me up and forcing me to make a choice between two meal serving options: chicken that tasted like mammoth, or mammoth that tasted like chicken.

What was it going to be?

"Give me the furry elephant," I told him. "And another vodka."

"Ice and water with that, sir?"

"Just the vodka."

The mammoth really wasn't that bad—certainly no worse than the chicken would have been—and I was doing my best to enjoy it when the incoming call icon popped into my upper right visual field. For a moment I considered ignoring it completely. What could it be about, other than the mess I'd left behind after the robots went berserk? But I guess it was my fatal weakness that I'd never been able to *not* take a call. I put down the cutlery and pressed a finger against the hinge of my jaw. I kept my voice low, subvocalising. Had to be my lawyer. Assuming I still *had* a lawyer.

"OK, lay it on me. Who's trying to sue me, how much are we looking at, and what am I going to have to do to get them off my case?"

"Fox?"

"Who else. You found me on this flight, didn't you?"

"It's Jake, man. I learned about your recent difficulties."

For a moment the vodka took the edge off my surprise. "You and the rest of the world."

Jake sounded pained. "At least make an effort to sound like you're glad to hear from me, buddy. It's been a while."

"Sorry, Jake. It's just not been the best few days of my life, you understand?"

"Rock and roll, my friend. Gotta roll with it, take the rough with the smooth. Isn't that what we always said?"

"I don't know. Did we?" Irritation boiled up inside me. "I mean, from where I'm sitting, it's not like we ever had much in common."

"Cutting, buddy. Cutting. And here I am calling you out of the blue with a business proposition. A proposition that might just dig you out of the hole you now find yourself in."

"What kind of proposition?"

"It's time to reactivate Morbid Management."

I let that sink in before responding, my mind scouting ahead through the possibilities. Morbid Management was defunct, and for good reason. We'd exhausted the possibilities of working together. Worse than that, our parting had left me with a very sour opinion of Jake Addison. Jake had always been the tail wagging that particular dog, and I'd always been prepared to go along with his notions. But he hadn't been prepared to put his faith in me when I had the one brilliant idea of my career.

We'd started off signing conventional rock acts. Mostly they were manufactured, put together with an eye on image and merchandising. But the problem with conventional rock acts is that they start having ideas of their own. Thinking they know best. Get ideas in their head about creative independence, artistic credibility, solo careers. One by one we'd watched our money-spinners fly apart in a whirlwind of ego and ambition. We figured there had to be something better.

So we'd created it. Ghoul Group was the world's first all-dead rock act. Of course you've heard of them: who hasn't? You've probably even heard that we dug up the bodies at night, that we sucked the brains out of a failing mid-level pop act, or that they were zombies controlled by Haitian voodoo. Completely untrue, needless to say. It was all legal, all signed off and boilerplated. We kept the bodies alive using simple brainstem implants, and we used the same technology to operate Ghoul Group on stage. Admittedly there was something Frankensteinesque about the boys and girls on stage—the dead look in their eyes, the scars and surgical stitches added for effect, the lifeless, parodic shuffle that passed for walking—but that was sort of the point.

Kids couldn't get enough of them. Merchandising went through the roof, and turned Morbid Management into a billion dollar enterprise.

Only trouble was it couldn't last. Rock promotion sucked money away as fast as it brought it in, and the only way to stay ahead of the curve was to keep manufacturing new acts. The fatal weakness of Ghoul Group was that the concept was easily imitated: anyone with access to a morgue and a good lawyer could get in on the act. We realised we had to move on.

That was when we got into robotics.

Jake and I had both been in metal acts before turning to management, and we were friendly with Metallica. The band was still successful, still touring, but they weren't getting any younger. Meanwhile a whole raft of tribute acts fed off the desire for the fans to see younger versions of the band, the way they'd been twenty or thirty years before. Yet no matter how good they were, the tribute acts were never quite realistic enough to be completely convincing. What was needed—what might fill a niche that no one yet perceived—were tribute acts that were *completely* indistinguishable from their models, and which could replicate them at any point in their careers. And—most importantly—never get tired doing it, or start demanding a raise.

So we made them. Got in hock with the best Japanese robotics specialists and tooled up a slew of different incarnations of Metallica. Each robot was a lifesize, hyperrealistic replica of a given member of the band at a specific point in their career. After processing thousands of hours of concert footage, motion capture sofware enabled these robots to behave with staggering realism. They moved like people. They sounded like people. They sweated and exhaled. Unless you got close enough to look right into their eyes, there was no way at all to tell that you were not looking at the real thing.

We commissioned enough robots to cover every market on the planet, and sent them out on tour. They were insanely successful. The real Metallica did well out of it and within months we were licensing the concept to other touring acts. The money was pumping in faster than we could account it. But at the same time, mindful of what had happened with Ghoul Group, we were thinking ahead. To the next big thing.

That was when I'd had my one original idea.

I'd been on another flight, bored out of my mind, watching some news item about robots being used to dismantle some Russian nuclear plant that had gone meltdown last century. These robots were Godzilla-sized machines, but the thing that struck me was that more or less humanoid in shape. They were being worked by specialist engineers from half way round the world, engineers who would zip into telepresence rigs and actually feel like they were wearing the robots; actually feel as if the reactor they were taking apart was the size of a doll's house.

It wasn't the reactor I cared about, of course. It was the robots. I'd had a flash, a mental image. We were already doing Robot Metallica. What was to stop us doing Giant Robot Metallica?

By the time I'd landed, I'd tracked down the company that made the demolition machines. By the time I'd checked in to my hotel and ordered room service, I'd established that they could, in principle, build them to order and incorporate the kind of animatronic realism we were already using with the lifesize robots. There was, essentially, no engineering barrier to us creating a twenty metre or thirty metre high James Hetfield or Lars Ulrich. We had the technology.

Next morning, shivering with excitement, I put the idea to Jake. I figured it for an easy sell. He'd see the essential genius in it. He'd recognise the need to move beyond our existing business model.

But Jake wasn't buying.

I've often wondered why he didn't go for it. Was it not enough of a swerve for him, too much a case of simply scaling up what we were already doing? Was he shrewd enough to see the potential for disaster, should our robots malfunction and go berserk? Was it simply that it was my idea, not his?

I don't know. Even now, after everything else that's happened—Derek and all the rest—I can't figure it out. All I can be sure of is that I knew then that it was curtains for Morbid Management. If Jake wasn't going to back me the one time I'd had an idea of my own, I couldn't keep on working with him.

So I'd split. Set up my own company. Continued negotiations with the giant demolition robot manufacturers and—somewhat sneakily, I admit—secured the rights from Metallica to all larger-than-life robotic reenactment activities.

OK, so it hadn't ended well. But the idea'd been sound. And stadiums can always be rebuilt.

"You still there, buddy?"

"Yeah, I'm still here." I'd given Jake enough time to think I'd hung up on him. Let the bastard sweat a little, why not. Over the roar of the scramjet's ballistic re-entry profile I said: "We're gonna lose comms in a few moments. Why don't you tell me what this is all about."

"Not over the phone. But here's the deal." And he gave me an address, an industrial unit on the edge of Helsinki. "You're flying into Copenhagen, buddy. Take the 'lev, you can be in Helsinki by evening."

"You have to give me more than that."

"Like you to meet the future of rock and roll, Fox. Little friend of mine by the name of Derek. You're going to like each other."

The bastard had me, of course.

It was winter in Helsinki so evening came down cold and early. From the maglev I took a car straight out into the industrial sticks, a dismal warren of slab-sided warehouses and low-rise office units. Security lights blazed over fenced-off loading areas and nearly empty car parks, the asphalt still slick and reflective from afternoon rain. Beyond the immediate line of warehouses, walking cranes stomped around the docks, picking up and discarding shipping containers like they were coloured building blocks. Giant robots. I didn't need to be reminded about giant fucking robots, not when I was expecting an Interpol arrest warrant to be declared in my name at any moment. But at least they wouldn't come looking here too quickly, I thought. On the edge of Helsinki, with even the car now departed on some other errand, I felt like the last man alive, wandering the airless boulevards of some huge abandoned moonbase.

The unit Jake had told me to go to was locked from the road, with a heavy duty barrier slid across the entrance. Through the fence, it looked semi-abandoned: weeds licking at its base, no lights on in the few visible windows, some of the security lights around it broken or switched off. Maybe I'd been set up. It wouldn't be like Jake, but time had passed and I still wasn't ready to place absolute, unconditional trust in my old partner. All the same, if Jake did want to get back at me for something, stranding me in a bleak industrial development was a very elaborate way of going about it.

I pressed the intercom buzzer in the panel next to the barrier. I was half expecting no one to answer it and, if they did, I wasn't quite sure how I was going to explain my presence. But the voice that crackled through the grille was familiar and unfazed.

"Glad you could make it, buddy. Stroll on inside and take a seat. I'll be down in a minute. I can't wait to show Derek off to you."

"I hope Derek's worth the journey."

The barrier slid back. I walked across the damp concrete of the loading area to the service entrance. Now that I paid proper attention, the place wasn't as derelict as I'd assumed. Cameras tracked me, moving stealthily under their rain hoods. I ascended a step, pushed against a door—which opened easily—and found myself entering some kind of lobby or waiting room. Beyond a fire door, a dimly illuminated corridor led away into the depths of the building. No lights on in the annex, save for the red eye of a coffee machine burbling away next to a small table and a set of chairs. I poured a cup, spooned in creamer and sat down. As my vision adjusted to the gloom, I made out some of the glossy brochures lying on the table. Most of them were for Gladius Biomech. I'd heard of the firm and recognised their swordfish logo. Most of what they did creeped me out. Once you started messing with genetics, the world was your walking, talking, tap-dancing oyster. I stroked one of the moving images and watched a cat sitting on a high chair and eating its dinner with a knife and fork, holding the cutlery in little furry human-like hands, while the family dined around it. *Now your pet can share in your mealtimes—hygenically!*

The firedoor swung open. I put down the brochure hastily, as ashamed as if I'd been caught leafing through hardcore porn. Jake stood silhouetted in the dim lights of the corridor, kneelength leather jacket, hair still down to his collar.

I put on my best laconic, deadpan voice. "So I guess we're going into the pet business."

"Not quite," Jake answered. "Although there may be merchandising options in that direction at some point. For now, though, it's still rock and roll all the way." He gestured back at the door he'd come through. "You want to meet Derek?"

I tipped the coffee dregs into the wastebin. "Guess we don't want to keep him waiting."

"Don't worry about him. He's not going anywhere."

I followed Jake into the corridor. He had changed a bit in the two years since we'd split the firm, but not by much. The hair was a little grayer, maybe not as thick as it used to be. Jake still had the soul patch under his lip and the carefully tended stubble on his cheeks. Still wore snakeskin cowboy boots without any measurable irony.

"So what's this all about?"

"What I said. A new business opportunity. Time to put Morbid Management back on the road. Question is, are we ready to take things to the next level?"

I smiled. "We. Like it's a done deal already."

"It will be when you see Derek."

We'd reached a side-door: sheet metal with no window in it. Jake pressed his hand against a reader, submitted to an iris scan, then pushed open the door. Hard light spilled through the widening gap.

"You keep this locked, but I'm able to walk in through the front door? Who are you worried about breaking in?"

"It's not about anyone breaking in," Jake said.

We were in a room large enough to hold a dozen semi-trucks. Striplights ran the length of the low, white-tiled ceiling. There were no windows, and most of the wall space was taken up with grey metal cabinets and what appeared to be industrial-size freezer units. There were many free-standing cabinets and cupboards, with benches laid out in long rows. The benches held computers and glassware and neat, toylike robotic things. Centrifuges whirred, ovens and chromatographs clicked and beeped. I watched a mechanical arm dip a pipette into a rack of test tubes, sampling or dosing each in quick sequence. The swordfish logo on the side of the robot was for Gladius Biomech.

"Either you're richer than I think," I said, "or there's some kind of deal going on here."

"Gladius front the equipment and expertise," Jake said. "It's a risk for them, obviously. But they're banking on a high capital return."

"You're running a biotech lab on your own?"

"Buddy, I can barely work out a bar tip. You were always the one with the head for figures. Every few days, someone from Gladius stops by to make sure it's all running to plan. But it doesn't take much tinkering. Stuff's mostly automated. Which is cool, because the fewer people know about this, the better."

"Guess I'm one of them now. Want to show me what this is actually all about, or am I meant to figure it out on my own?"

"Over here," Jake said, strolling over to one of the free-standing cabinets. It was a white cube about the size of a domestic washing machine, and had a similar looking control panel on the front. But it wasn't a washing machine, obviously. Jake entered a keypad code then slid back the lid. "Go on," he said, inviting me closer. "Take a look."

I peered into the cabinet, figuring it was some kind of incubator. Blue, UV-tinged lights ran around the inside of the rim. I could feel the warmth coming off it. Straw and dirt were packed around the floor, and there was a clutch of eggs in the middle. They were big eggs, almost football sized, and one of them was quivering gently.

"Looks like we've got a hatcher coming through," Jake said. "Reason I had to be here, actually. System alerts me when one of those babies gets ready to pop. They need to be hand-reared for a few days, until they can stand on their feet and forage for themselves."

"Until *what* can stand on their feet and forage for themselves?"

"Baby dinosaurs, buddy. What else?" Jake slid the cover back on the incubator, then locked it with a touch on the keypad. "T-Rexes, actually. You ever eaten Rex?"

"Kind of out of my price range."

"Well, take it from me, you're not missing much. Pretty much everything tastes the same once you've added steak sauce, anyway."

"So we're diversifying into dinosaur foodstuffs. Is that what you dragged me out here to see?"

"Not exactly." Jake moved to the next cabinet along—it was the same kind of white incubator—and keyed open the lid. He unhooked a floral-patterned oven glove from the side of the cabinet and slipped it on his right hand, then dipped into the blue-lit interior. I heard a squeak and a scuffling sound and watched as Jake came out with a baby dinosaur in his hand, clutched gently in the oven glove. It was about the size of a plastic bath toy, the same kind of day-glo green, but it was very definitely alive. It squirmed in the glove, trying to escape. The tail whipped back and forth. The huge hind legs thrashed at air. The little forelimbs scrabbled uselessly against the oven glove's thumb. The head, with its tiny pin-sized teeth already budding through, tried to bite into the glove. The eyes were wide and white-rimmed and charmingly belligerent.

"Already got some fight in it, as you can see," Jake said, using his ungloved hand to stroke the top of the Rex's head. "And those teeth'll give you a nasty cut even now. Couple of weeks, they'll have your finger off."

"Nice. But I'm still sort of missing the point here. And why is that thing so *green*?"

"Tweaked the pigmentation a bit, that's all. Made it luminous, too. Real things are kind of drab. Not so hot for merchandising."

"Merchandising what?"

"Jesus, Fox. Take a look at the forelimbs. Maybe it'll clue you in."

I took a look at the forelimbs and felt a shiver of I wasn't exactly sure what. Not quite revulsion, not quite awe. Something that came in at right angles to both.

"I'm no expert on dinosaurs," I said slowly. "Even less on Rexes. But are those things *meant* to have four fingers and a thumb?"

"Not the way nature intended. But then, nature wasn't thinking ahead." Jake stroked the dinosaur's head again. It seemed to be calming gradually. "Gladius tell me it's pretty simple stuff. There are these things called *Hox* genes which show up in pretty much everything, from fruit flies to monkeys. They're like a big bank of switches that control limb development, right out to the number of digits on the end. We just flipped a few of those switches, and got us dinosaurs with human hands."

The hands were like exquisite little plastic extrudings, moulded in the same biohazard green as the rest of the T-Rex. They even had tiny little fingernails.

"OK, that's a pretty neat trick," I said. "If a little on the creepy side. But I'm still not quite seeing the *point*."

"The point, buddy, is that without little fingers and thumbs it's kind of difficult to play rock guitar."

"You're shitting me. You bred this thing to *make music*?"

"He's got a way to go, obviously. And it doesn't stop with

the fingers. You ever seen a motor homunculus, Fox? Map of human brain function, according to how much volume's given over to a specific task. Looks like a little man with huge fucking hands. Just operating a pair of hands takes up *way* more cells than you'd think. Well, there's no point giving a dinosaur four fingers and an opposable thumb if you don't give him the mental wiring to go along with it. So we're in there right from the start, manipulating brain development all the way, messing with the architecture when everything's nice and plastic. This baby's two weeks old and he already has thirty per cent more neural volume than a normal Rex. Starting to see some real hierarchical layering of brain modules, too. Your average lizard has a brain like a peanut, but this one's already got something like a mammalian limbic system. Hell, I'd be scared if it wasn't me doing this."

"And for such a noble purpose."

"Don't get all moral on me, buddy." Jake lowered the T-Rex back into the incubator. "We eat these things. We pay to go out into a big park and shoot them with anti-tank guns. I'm giving them the chance to *rock*. Is that so very wrong?"

"I guess it depends on how much choice the dinosaur has in the matter."

"When you force a five year old kid to take piano lessons, does the kid have a choice?"

"That's different."

"Yeah, because it's cruel and unusual to force someone to play the piano. I agree. But electric guitar? That's liberation, my friend. That's like handing someone the keys to the cosmos."

"It's a goddamned *reptile,* Jake."

"Right. And how is that different to making corpses or giant robots play music?"

He had me there, and from the look of quiet self-satisfaction on his face, he knew it.

"OK. I accept that you have a baby dinosaur that could, theoretically, play the guitar, if anyone made a guitar that small. But that's not the same thing as actually playing it. What are you going to do, just sit around and wait?"

"We train it," Jake said. "Just like training a dog to do tricks. Slowly, one element at a time. Little rewards. Building up the repertoire a part at a time. It doesn't need to understand music. It just needs to make a sequence of noises. You think we can't do this?"

"I'd need persuasion."

"You'll get it. Dinosaurs live for meat. It doesn't have to understand what it's doing, it just has to associate the one with the other. And this is heavy metal we're talking about here, not Rachmaninov. Not a big ask, even for a reptile."

"You've thought it all through."

"You think Gladius were going to get onboard if there wasn't a business plan? This is going to work, Fox. It's going to work and you're going to be a part of it. All the way down the line. We're going to promote a rock tour with an actual carnivorous theropod dinosaur on lead guitar and vocal."

I couldn't deny that Jake's enthusiasm was infectious. Always had been. But when I'd needed him—when I'd taken a big idea to him—he hadn't been there for me. Even now the pain of that betrayal still stung, and I wasn't sure I was ready to get over it that quickly.

"Maybe some other time," I said, shaking my head with a regretful smile. "After all, you've got a ways to go yet. I don't know how fast these things grow, but no one's going to be blown away by a knee-high rockstar, even if they are carnivorous. Maybe when Derek's a bit older, and he can actually play something."

Jake gave me an odd glance. "Dude, we need to clear something up. You haven't met Derek yet."

I looked into his eyes. "Then who—what—was that?"

"Part of the next wave. Same with the eggs. Aren't enough venues in the world for all the people who'll want to see Derek. So we make more Dereks. Until we hit market saturation."

"And you think Derek'll be cool with that?"

"It's not like Derek's ever going to have an opinion on the matter." Jake looked me up and down, maybe trying to judge exactly how much I could be trusted. "So: you ready to meet the big guy?"

I gave a noncommittal shrug. "Guess I've come this far."

Jake stopped at another white cabinet—this one turned out to be a fridge—and came out with a thigh-sized haunch of freezer-wrapped meat. "Carry this for me, buddy," he said.

I took the meat, cradling it in both arms. We went out of the laboratory by a different door, then walked down a short corridor until a second door opened out into a dark, echoey space, like the inside of an aircraft hangar.

"Wait here," Jake said, and his footsteps veered off to one side. I heard a clunk, as of some huge trip-switch being thrown and, one by one, huge banks of suspended ceiling lights came on. Even as I had to squint against the glare, I mentally applauded the way Jake was managing the presentation. He'd known I was coming, so he could easily have left those lights on until now. But the impressario in him wouldn't be denied. These weren't simple spotlights, either. They were computer controlled, steerable, variable-colour stage lights. Jake had a whole routine programmed in. The lights gimballed and gyred, throwing shifting patterns across the walls, floor and ceiling of the vast space. Yet until the last moment they studiously avoided illuminating the thing in the middle. When they fell on it, I could almost imagine the crowd going apeshit.

This was how the show would open. This was how the show *had* to open.

I was looking at Derek.

Derek was in a bright yellow cage, about the size of four shipping containers arranged into a block. I was glad about the cage; glad too that it appeared to have been engineered to generous tolerances. Electrical cables snaked into it, thick as pythons. Orange strobe beacons had just come on, rotating on the top of the cage, for no obvious reason other than that it looked cool. And there was Derek, standing up in the middle.

I'd had a toy T-rex as a kid, handed down from my dad, and some part of me still expected them to look the way that toy did: standing with the body more or less vertical, forming a tripod with two legs and the tail taking the creature's weight. That wasn't how they worked, though. Derek—like every resurrected Rex that ever lived—stood with his body arranged in a horizontal line, with the tail counterbalancing the weight of his forebody and skull. Somehow that just never looked *right* to me. And the two little arms looked even more pathetic and useless in this posture.

Derek wasn't the same luminous green as the baby dinosaur; he was a more plausible dark muddy brown. I guess at some point Jake had decided that colouration wasn't spectacular enough for the second batch. In fact, apart from the human hands on the ends of his forearms, he didn't look in any way remarkable. Just another meat-eating dinosaur.

Derek was awake, too. He was looking at us and I could hear the rasp of his breathing, like an industrial bellows being worked very slowly. In proportion to his body, his eyes were much smaller than the baby's. Not so cute now. This was an instinctive predator, big enough to swallow me whole.

"He's pretty big."

"Actually he's pretty small," Jake said. "Rex development isn't a straight line thing. They grow fast from babies then stick at two tonnes until they're about fourteen. Then they get another growth spurt which can take them anywhere up to six tonnes. Of course with the newer Dereks we should be able to dial things up a bit." Then he took the haunch off me and whispered: "Watch the neural display. We've had implants in him since he hatched—we're gonna work the imaging into the live show." He raised his voice. "Hey! Meat-brain! Look what I got for you!"

Derek was visibly interested in the haunch. His head tracked it as Jake walked up to the cage, the little yellow-tinged eyes moving with the smooth vigilance of surveillance cameras. Saliva dribbled between his teeth. The forearms made a futile grabbing gesture, as if Derek somehow didn't fully comprehend that there was a cage and quite a lot of air between the haunch and him.

I watched a pink blotch form on the neural display. "Hunter-killer mode kicking in," Jake said, grinning. "He's like a heat-seeking missile now. Nothing getting between him and his dinner except maybe another Rex."

"Maybe you should feed him more often."

"There's no such thing as a sated Rex. And I do feed him. How else do you think I get him to work for me?" He raised his voice again. "You know the deal, ain't no free lunches around here." He put the haunch down on the ground, then reached for something that I hadn't seen until then: a remote control unit hanging down from above. It was a grubby yellow box with a set of mushroom-sized buttons on it. Jake depressed one of the buttons and an overhead gantry clanked and whined into view, sliding along rails suspended from the ceiling. The gantry positioned itself over the cage, then began to lower its cargo. It was a flame red Gibson Flying V guitar, bolted to a telescopic frame from the rear of the body. The guitar came down from a gap in the top of the cage (too small for Derek to have escaped through), lowered until it was in front of him, then telescoped back until the guitar was suspended within reach of his arms. At the same time, a microphone had come down to just in front of Derek's mouth.

Jake released the remote control unit, then picked up the haunch again. "OK, buddy, you know what you need to do." Then he pressed one of the other buttons and fast, riffing heavy metal blasted out of speakers somewhere in the room. It wasn't stadium-level wattage—that, presumably, would have drawn too much attention—but it was still loud enough to impress, to give me some idea of how the show would work in reality.

And then Derek started playing. His hands were on that guitar, and they were making—well, you couldn't call it music, in the abolutely strict sense of the word. It was noise, basically. Squealing, agonising bursts of sheet-metal sound, none of which bore any kind of harmonic relationship to what had gone before. But the one thing I couldn't deny was that it *worked*. With the backing tape, and the light show, and the fact that this was an actual dinosaur playing a Gibson Flying V guitar, it was possible to make certain allowances.

Hell, I didn't even have to try. I was smitten. And that was before Derek opened his mouth and started singing. Actually it would be best described as a sustained, blood-curdling roar—but that was exactly what it needed to be, and it counterpointed the guitar perfectly. Different parts of his brain were lighting up now; the hunter-killer region was much less bright than it had been before he started playing.

And there was, now that I paid attention to it, more than just migraine-inducing squeals of guitar and monstrous interludes of gutteral roaring. Derek might not be playing specific notes and chords, and his vocalisations were no more structured or musical, but they were timed to fit in around the rest of the music, the bass runs and drum fills and second guitar solos. It wasn't completely random. Derek was playing along, judging his contributions, letting the rest of the band share the limelight.

As a front man, I'd seen a lot worse.

"OK, that'll do," Jake said, killing the music, pressing another button to retract the guitar and mike. "Way to go, Derek. Way to fucking go."

"He's good."

"Does that constitute your seal of approval?"

"He can rock. I'll give him that."

"He doesn't just rock," Jake said. "He is rock." Then he turned around and smiled. "So. Buddy. We back in business, or what?"

Yeah, I thought to myself. I guess we're back in business.

I'm making my way back down the Antonov, thinking of the long hours of subsonic cruising ahead. I pass Jake's desk again, and this time something on the ancient, battered, desert-sand camouflaged ex-military surplus laptop catches my eye.

The laptop's running some generic movie editing software, and in one of the windows is a freezeframe from tonight's show. Beneath the freezeframe is a timeline and soundtrack. I click the cursor and slide it back along to the left, watching Derek run in reverse on the window, hands whipping around the guitar in manic thrash overdrive. The set list is the same from night to night, so I know exactly when Extinction Event would have kicked in. I don't feel guilty about missing it—someone had to take care of the Budokan accounts—but now that we're airborne and there's time to kill, I'm at least semi-curious about hearing it properly. What exactly was so great about it tonight, compared to the previous show, and the one before that?

Why was it that Jake didn't want to hear that Extinction Event was even more awesome than usual?

I need earphones to hear anything over the six-engine drone of the Antonov. I'm reaching for them when Jake looms behind me.

"Thought you were checking on the big guy."

I look around. He's still got the bottle of JD with him.

"I was. Told him I heard he'd done a good job. Now I'm just checking it out for myself. If I can just find the point where . . ."

He reaches over and takes my hand off the laptop. "You don't need to. Got it all cued up already."

He hands me the JD, punches a few keys—they're so worn the numbers and letters are barely visible now—and up pops Derek again. From the purple-red tinge of the lighting, and the back-projection footage of crashing asteroids and erupting volcanos, I know we've hit the start of Extinction Event.

"So what's the big deal?" I ask.

"Put the phones on."

I put the phones on. Jake spools through the track until we hit the bridge between the second and third verse. He lets the movie play on at normal speed. Drums pounding like jackhammers, bass so heavy it could shatter bone, and then Derek lets rip on the Flying V, unleashing a squall of demented sound, arching his neck back as he plays, eyes narrowing to venomous slits, and then belching out a humungous, larynx-shredding roar of pure theropod rage.

We go into the third verse. Jake hits pause.

"So you see," he says.

I pull out the phones. "I'm not sure I do."

"Then you need to go back and listen to the previous performance. And the one before that. And every goddamned rendition of that song he's ever done before tonight."

"I do?"

"Yes. Because then you'd understand." And Jake looks at me with an expression of the utmost gravity on his face, as if he's about to disclose one of the darkest, most mystical secrets of the universe. "It was different tonight. He came in early. Jumped his usual cue. And when he did come in it was for longer than usual and he added that vocal flourish."

I nod, but I'm still not seeing the big picture. "OK. He screwed up. Shit happens. Gotta roll with it, remember? It was still a good show. Everyone said so."

But he shakes his head. "You're not getting it, buddy. That wasn't a mistake. That was something much worse. That was an improvement. That was him improvising."

"You can't be sure."

"I can be sure." He punches another key and a slice of Derek's neural activity pops up. "Extracted this from the performance," he says. "Right around the time he started going off-script." His finger traces three bright blotches. "You see these hotspots? They've come on in ones and twos before. But they've never once lit up at the same time."

"And this means something?"

He taps his finger against the blotches in turn. "Dorsal premotor cortex. That's associated with the brain planning a sequence of body movements. You slip on ice, that's the part that gets you flapping your arms so you don't fall over." Next blotch. "Anterior cingulate. That's your basic complex resolution, decision making module, right. Do I chase after that meal, or go after that one?" He moves his finger again. "Interior frontal gyrus/ventral premotor cortex. We're deep into mammal brain structure here—a normal Rex wouldn't have anything you could even stick a label on here. You know when this area lights up, in you and me?"

"I'm not, strangely enough, a neuroscientist."

"Nor was I until I got involved with Derek. This is the sweet spot, buddy. This is what lights up when you hear language or music. And all three of these areas going off at once? That's a pretty unique signature. It doesn't just mean he's playing music. It means he's making shit up as he goes along."

For a moment I don't know what to say. There's no doubt in my mind that he's right. He knows the show—and Derek's brain—inside out. He knows every cue Derek's meant to hit. Derek missing his mark—or coming in early—just isn't meant to happen. And Derek somehow finding a way to deviate from the program and make the song sound better is, well . . . not exactly the way Jake likes things to happen.

"I don't like improvisation," he says. "It's a sign of creative restlessness. Before you know it . . ."

"It's solo recording deals, expensive riders and private tour buses."

"I thought we got away from this shit," Jake says mournfully. "I mean, dead bodies, man. Then robots. Then dinosaurs. And still it's coming back to bite us. Talent always thinks it knows best."

"Maybe it does."

"A T-Rex?"

"You gave him just enough of a mind to rock. Unfortunately, that's already more than enough to not want to take orders." I take a sip from the JD. "But look on the bright side. What's the worst that could happen?"

"He escapes and eats us."

"Apart from that."

"I don't know. If he starts showing signs of . . . creativity . . . then we're fucked six ways from Tuesday. We'll have animal rights activists pulling the plug on every show."

"Unless we just . . . roll with it. Let him decide what he does. I mean, it's not like he doesn't *want* to perform, is it? You've seen him out there. This is what he was born for. Hell, why stop there? This is what he was evolved for."

"I wish I had your optimism."

I look back at the cage. Derek's watching us, following the conversation. I wonder how much of it he's capable of understanding. Maybe more than we realise.

"Maybe we keep control of him, maybe we don't. Either way, we've done something beautiful." I hand him the bottle. "You, mainly. It was your idea, not mine."

"Took the two of us to make it fly," Jake says, before taking a gulp. "And hell, maybe you're right. That's the glorious thing about rock and roll. It's alchemy. Holy fire. The moment you control it, it ain't rock and roll no more. So maybe the thing we should be doing here is celebrating."

"All the way." And I snatch back the JD and take my own swig. Then I raise the bottle and toast Derek, who's still watching us. Hard to tell what's going on behind those eyes, but one thing I'm sure of is that it's not nothing. And for a brief, marvellous instant, I'm glad not only to be alive, but to be alive in a universe that has room in it for beautiful monsters.

And heavy metal, of course.

Graffiti in the
Library of Babel

DAVID LANGFORD

*David Langford (ansible.co.uk) lives in Reading in the UK.
He publishes the semi-prozine* Ansible, *the tabloid newspaper of SF and fandom, which won a bunch of Hugo Awards,
and is also excerpted as a monthly column in* Interzone, *and
found online at www.dcs.gla.ac.uk/SF-archives/Ansible. He
is currently SF fandom's most famous humorous writer—see
his book* He Do The Time Police In Different Voices—*and
has won many best fan writer Hugo Awards. He is an indefatigable book reviewer (some of his reviews are collected in*
The Complete Critical Assembly, *in* Up Through an Empty
House of Stars: Reviews and Essays 1980–2002, *and in* The
SEX Column and Other Misprints). *For the last fifteen years
he has been publishing short SF of generally high quality,
most of it now collected in* Different Kinds of Darkness.*

*"Graffiti in the Library of Babel," which appeared in the
anthology* Is Anybody Out There, *is a new take on the first
contact story. Ceri Evans discovers that someone is embedding communications in the electronic files of the Total Library, and giving humanity something immensely powerful
for free. As the communications are decoded, Langford ups
the ante: As Ceri says, "I have a bad feeling about this.*

> *There seems to be no difference at all between the message of maximum content (or maximum ambiguity) and the message of zero content (noise).*
>
> John Sladek, "The Communicants"

As it turned out, they had no sense of drama. They failed to descend in shiny flying discs, or even to fill some little-used frequency with a tantalizing stutter of sequenced primes. No: they came with spray cans and spirit pens, scrawling their grubby little tags across our heritage.

Or as an apologetic TotLib intern first broke the news: "Sir, someone's done something nasty all over Jane Austen."

The Total Library project is named in homage to Kurd Lasswitz's thought experiment "Die Universal Bibliothek," which inspired a famous story by Jorge Luis Borges. Another influence is the "World Brain" concept proposed by H. G. Wells. Assembling the totality of world literature and knowledge should allow a rich degree of cross-referencing and interdisciplinary . . .

Ceri Evans looked up from the brochure. Even in this white office that smelt of top management, she could never resist a straight line: "Why, congratulations, Professor. I think you may have invented the Internet!"

"Doctor, not Professor, and I do not use the title," said Ngombi with well-simulated patience. "Call me Joseph. The essential point of TotLib is that we are *isolated* from the net.

No trolls, no hackers, none of what that Manson book called sleazo inputs. Controlled rather than chaotic cross-referencing."

"But still you seem to have these taggers?"

"Congratulations, Doctor Evans! I think you may have just deduced the contents of my original email to you."

"All right. All square." Ceri held up one thin hand in mock surrender. "We'll leave the posh titles for the medics. Now tell me: Why is this a problem in what I do, which is a far-out region of information theory, rather than plain data security?"

"Believe me, data security we know about. Hackers and student pranksters have been rather exhaustively ruled out. As it has been said, 'Once you eliminate the impossible, whatever remains, no matter how improbable, must be the truth.'"

" 'Holmes, this is marvellous,'" said Ceri dutifully.

" 'Meretricious,' said he." Joseph grinned. "We are a literary team here."

Ceri felt a sudden contrarian urge not to be literary. "Maybe we should cut to the chase. There's only one logical reason to call me in. You suspect the Library is under attack through the kind of acausal channel I've discussed in my more speculative papers? A concept, I should remind you, that got me an IgNobel Prize and a long denunciation in *The Skeptic* because everyone knows it's utter lunacy. Every Einstein-worshipping physicist, at least."

A shrug. " 'Once you eliminate the impossible . . .' And I'm not a physicist. Come and see." He was so very large and very black. Ceri found herself wondering whether his white-on-white decor was deliberate contrast.

The taggers had spattered their marks across the digital texts of TotLib: short bursts of characters that made no particular sense but clearly belonged to the same family, like some ideogram repeated with slight variations along the shopping mall, through the car park and across the sides of subway carriages. Along Jane Austen, through Shakespeare and underground to deface Jack Kerouac and the Beats. After half an hour of on-screen examples Ceri felt the familiar eye glaze of overdosing on conceptual art.

"The tags," she said cautiously, *"never* appear within words?" This is a test. Do not be afraid of the obvious.

"We decided all by ourselves to call them tags." The faint smile indicated that Joseph was still in a mood for point-scoring.

"Okay. I see." She didn't, but in a moment it came. "Not just graffiti but mark-up, like HTML or XML tags. Emphasis marks. You think they're not so much defacing the texts as going through them with a highlighter. Boldface on, It is a truth universally acknowledged, boldface off."

"Congratulations! It took our people several days to reach that point."

Ceri drummed her fingers irritably against the TotLib workstation. "The point seems to be that it's already been reached. So why me?"

"I saw a need for someone who can deal with the implications. If this tagging is coming in through your acausal channels—and we truly cannot trace any conventional route—and if that *New Scientist* piece on you was not too impossibly dumbed down . . ."

"Oh *Duw* oh God. It was, but never mind."

". . . the origin of the transmission would necessarily be something in the close vicinity of a supermassive black hole?"

"Well. That assumes the channel source is in our universe in the first place. The IgNobel presenter was very funny about Dimension X and the Phantom Zone." Another memory that clung and stuck, a mental itch she couldn't stop scratching.

"So many times it has been said, 'They laughed at Galileo.'"

"And sometimes it's also been said that they laughed at nitrous oxide."

Again Joseph smiled hugely. "Would you care for lunch?"

"Let me have another look first. Let me plod my slow way to some other plateau your staff reached last week. Boldface

on, instruments of darkness, boldface off. Did that make
you think of my black hole? Masters of the universe. God's
quarantine regulations. These things need to be grouped or
sequenced—no, both."

The TotLib interface was easy enough to use. Ceri back-
tracked, paused, went forward again through lexical chaos.
"The structure of those tags . . . there's a flavour of inversion
symmetry . . . suppose ON has a group identifier wrapped
around a sequence number, and OFF is sequence around
group? Or the other way around, of course. That would sort
your grab bag of quotes into chunks and give the chunks an
internal order. Oh bugger, I'm biting my nails again. Sorry.
Have we caught up with your clever staff yet?" She hadn't
meant to get hooked on the dizzy rush of problem-solving.
But, she thought, be glad it still comes.

The big man seemed perceptibly less smug. "My clever
staff will catch up with you . . . maybe next week. Ceri—if I
may—I am impressed. It is most definitely time for lunch."

The meal was inoffensive and the wine better, if only by
about ten per cent, than you'd expect from an institution in a
secure vault under a dour Swiss alp. As her host explained:
"The Scientologists are working to preserve their founder's
teachings for all eternity, and our sponsors feel there should
be an alternative view."

At first Ceri had felt obscurely prickly about Dr Joseph
Ngombi, and she tried now to be a little friendlier: mustn't
let him think a good Welsh girl like herself had a streak of
racism. Part of her mind was elsewhere, though (structured
tags, that kaleidoscope of quoted fragments), and her vague
attempts at friendly signals led to some carefully placed
mentions of his dear wife and children. Earlier that day she'd
thought she was looking good, with a new dark-red hair
rinse; now she wondered whether Joseph saw her as a dyed
and predatory hag. What were the chances of making sense
of graffiti from some distant, supermassive black hole when
communications went astray across the width of a restaurant
table?

"No thanks," she said, protecting her wineglass from the

waiter's menacing pass. "I'll need a clear head." Or maybe just an empty one. The trouble with an open mind, the saying went, is that people come along and put things in it.

Ceri liked the idea of TotLib staff handling the boring rotework, but didn't want to get too far away from that tagged text. Layers of abstraction are great in software but tend to blur the focus of real-world problems. They compromised on a multi-view workstation: defaced ebooks here, grouped and sequenced tags there, and the clear light of understanding in the window that for a long time stayed dismally blank.

Clearing away the relentless tag repetition through multiple editions, critical cites and anthologies of quotations, there were just 125 tagged phrases in all. "Five to the third power," Ceri muttered. "The science fiction writers would say straight away that our friends must count to base five, meaning they have five limbs or five tentacles or . . ." She stared moodily at the significant number of jointed manipulators on her left hand. "Or not."

Joseph spread out a hand that proved to be missing one finger. "Just an old accident, but I would seem to be ruled out. Perhaps, though, that is merely my cunning."

The first of the eleven sequences, or maybe the last ("Has it never occurred to you that the ancient Romans *counted backwards?*" Ceri quoted), ran a gamut of fuzzily resonating phrases from "It is a truth universally acknowledged" through Hazlitt's "How often have I put off writing a letter" to E. M. Forster's "Only connect . . ."

"Translation: It would be sort of dimly nice to maybe talk in some kind of indistinct fashion, probably." Ceri glared at the screen. "Right, I'm going to lecture now. To be that vague and at the same time stick to a theme, the taggers must *understand* English. Not just literal meaning but metaphors and nuances and stuff. Otherwise 'No man is an island' wouldn't be in there."

"So they could choose to communicate in clear?" suggested Joseph.

"That's it. They could spell out an absolutely unambiguous message, one word or one letter at a time. I can't imagine a good reason for doing it this way, but I have a suspicious enough mind to think of a bad one. The taggers know all about us but they don't want to let slip a single data point concerning themselves. So they feed our own phrases back to us. We aren't to be allowed the tiniest clue to their thinking from style or diction or word order. Does that seem sinister to you?"

Joseph sighed. "It was so much easier when aliens said 'Take me to your leader.' "

"Or 'Klaatu barada nikto.' Don't let me distract myself. Here's the 'instruments of darkness' cluster, with the *Tao Te Ching* quotes, Zen koans and that mystic cobblers from *Four Quartets* that would cost them a packet in permission fees if the Eliot estate got wind of it. The general flavour of all this seems to be that they're using an acausal comms route that bypasses the Usual Channels. 'The way that can be spoken of / Is not the constant way.' Which would be most interesting to know if it hadn't been the assumption we started with."

An intern came in with plastic cups of coffee, which made for a few seconds' natural break. Ceri burnt a finger and swore under her breath in Welsh.

"Gesundheit. What about those quarantine regulations?"

"I think that's the most interesting one," Ceri said cautiously. "C. S. Lewis and 'God's quarantine regulations'— the old boy was talking about interplanetary or interstellar distances saving pure races from contamination by horrible fallen us. Then there's a handful of guarded borders and dangerous frontiers from early Auden. 'The empyrean is a void abyss': that's *The City of Dreadful Night,* I actually read it once. Lucretius on breaking through 'the fiery walls of the world' to explore the boundless universe. There's a pun in there, I'm sure. Firewalls. Something blocks or prevents communication across deep space. Who? 'Masters of the universe.' Maybe for our own good, but who knows? In a nutshell: SETI was a waste of time. Don't let the coffee get cold."

Joseph sipped. "That seems something of a stretch."

"Well, right now I'm just talking, not publishing. And

while I'm still just talking, I wonder whether we can try to talk back."

"Presumably you keep one of those acausal widgets in your handbag? Next to the black hole, no doubt."

"Of course not. Much simpler. The taggers are in tune with a particular medium—the Total Library—and they're messaging us by modulating it. We can modulate too, without any help from astounding super-science."

She hadn't seen Joseph wince before. For an instant his face was terrifying. "Ask a librarian to deface his own collection? You will be suggesting I ignore the SILENCE signs next."

"Just turn a blind eye and leave it to my criminal mind. When I was a girl in the valleys I worked out eight ways to nick books from the public library." And never did, and lay awake all night with a guilty conscience the one time she'd accidentally lost one, but let's not go there just now.

"While I am still in shock, whatever do you plan to say? That it is indeed vaguely nice to share a warm fuzzy lack of communication?"

"I rather thought of asking them for goodies. We haven't talked yet about the taggers' gift-exchange thread. *As You Like It:* "gifts may henceforth be bestowed equally," and half a dozen more in that general ballpark. They can't be asking. They're already the Entities Who Have Everything— they've nicked all our books from the public library. Our architecture and our playing cards, our mythological terrors, our algebra and fire . . ." She waited half a beat.

"Borges. When you talk to a librarian about how he should turn a blind eye, Borges has to be in the offing."

"I never could resist a good digression, boyo. Summary: all we can exchange with the taggers is information. They're waffling about gifts. There's no further information we can give them. So they must be offering something to us in exchange."

"Mmmm. A proof of Fermat's Last Theorem would be traditional, but that one is now far past its sell-by date. I suppose the mathematicians would like to know about the other thing, what is it? The Riemann hypothesis."

"Oh, *diawl*. Dry as dust. And how'd we express that horror as a set of artful quotations? What *I* thought of asking for was a global warming fix—some kind of clean power source with no greenhouse emissions. Cheap fusion. Zero-point energy. I don't believe what I've read about either, but maybe it's like that physicist's lucky horseshoe: it works even if you don't believe in it. And where's the harm in trying?"

"I admit to curiosity. Especially about how you plan to put across concepts like zero-point energy."

More coffee came, and then more still, while Ceri wrestled with search engines and the dictionary of quotations. " 'Expecting something for nothing is the most popular form of hope.' Who's Arnold Glasgow? Anyway, he said it. And I must insist on having a line from the sainted sot of Swansea: 'Rage, rage against the dying of the light.' Then there's Blake, of course, with 'Energy is eternal delight!' "

The eventual result, they both agreed, was a monstrous hodgepodge and thus perfectly in keeping with the taggers' own approach. A pained but not quite protesting IT intern called Chaz rattled off a script that would spraygun the Total Library with Ceri's message. Joseph made a particular point of being absent in the director's toilet at the time of the fateful mouse-click. Despite all the TotLib apparatus of backups and recovery points, the instincts of a librarian died hard.

An hour passed. At the terminal, the now deeply bored Chaz ran his hundredth data scan. Anticlimax had settled on the white room like the leaden aftermath of a drinking binge. It had been a thinking binge, Ceri told herself blearily, but sometimes the hangover seemed much the same.

"You will be wishing to rest in your hotel," Joseph suggested.

"I suppose so. We don't even know whether the taggers operate on our timescale. They might live and think many times faster or slower. We don't know how long it takes them to prepare their tag payload. We don't know whether I did it right . . ." A general sense of running down. Sleep would be good.

"Sir," said Chaz, "something happened again. Mostly in the physics texts. Hundreds of new tags."

Ceri licked her lips. "Physics." Excitement seemed possible once more.

"Please, please do not expect miracles," Joseph said repressively. "Remember that their peculiar mode of conversation doesn't permit them to tell us anything we don't already know."

"But looking in the right order at chunks of what we know could so easily reveal something we don't. We may just need the hint. It's happened so many times in the history of science."

The internal numbering of the latest tags confirmed that their makers didn't count backwards and that the sequence containing "It is a truth universally acknowledged" was #1.

Just one quote-cluster from the new batch steered clear of the physics department. "That has to be the descriptor, the label on the tin. Let's see. From a Shakespeare sonnet, 'no such matter.' *They Do It with Mirrors*—that's an Agatha Christie title. *Macbeth* and 'where men may read strange matters.' Another title: *Prometheus Unbound*. 'Turning and turning in the widening gyre.'" Ceri scanned onward. "Joseph, I have a bad feeling about this."

"Strange matter? All I know of it is the name."

"No, I think it's antimatter. Mirror matter. The perfect nuclear fuel with one hundred per cent conversion efficiency."

"In fact, something we already knew. We make the stuff, do we not, at CERN and places of that kind?"

Ceri shook her head. "That's tiny, tiny amounts. The production rate is, oh, billions of years per gram. What I'm terribly afraid we've been given, what a physicist will see when she puts those textbooks and papers together, is some space-rotation trick that flips matter into antimatter. Unlimited quantities." She called up figures. "Here. Total energy release of forty-something megatons when a single kilo meets normal matter and annihilates. No fiddly fission triggers, no critical mass to assemble: it just *does* it. You wouldn't need a huge amount to burn the whole biosphere clean."

"Ah. I don't suppose our friends' interesting cascade of phrases on the theme of gifts included any mention of Greeks?"

"Not even Danes," said Ceri at random. "Quote search, quote search, and here it is. *Timeo Danaos et dona ferentes.* I know it's Greeks really, but I always used to read it as 'beware of Danes bearing gifts.'"

"That," said Joseph solemnly, "was known as the Danelaw."

Ceri giggled, although it was a noise she didn't like making. She'd been talking too fast and nervously, maybe faster than the speed of logic. Good to have the brakes applied. "Thank you," she said.

"So. They like to gift others with dangerous toys. Perhaps out of malice—the afrit who smilingly grants your wish, knowing that it will destroy you. Perhaps only in a spirit of healthy experiment to see what we will do. By the way, what will we do?"

"I suppose we have a sort of duty . . ." Out of the corner of her eye Ceri saw her notes window change. She hadn't touched the keyboard or mouse. Just before the flatscreen went black and flickered into a reboot sequence, she saw the coloured tags where no tags had been before. In her own notes. Surrounding the copied words "quarantine regulations."

Chaz wandered in and helpfully announced that the invulnerable TotLib systems were having their first ever unscheduled downtime.

When the Library came back up, it wasn't only Ceri's transcripts that had vanished in a puff of electrons. To Joseph's loudly expressed relief there had been a general clean-up, a thorough scrubbing of the library's defaced stacks from Jane Austen through to Zola. No tags anywhere.

"*Iesu Grist.* Call me a superstitious peasant if you like," Ceri murmured, "but I think the Masters of the Universe just stepped in."

Over a late supper in the Gasthof Schmidt, Ceri and Joseph managed to work themselves partway down from unnerving conceptual heights. A bottle of Riesling helped, and soon after the second arrived Joseph bashfully admitted that his wife and children were mythical. "The truth is that I often find myself curiously scared of attractive women." Communications were always a bugger, but sometimes contact could be made even across those fearful spaces. They celebrated with a brief though intense fling in the few days before duty called and Ceri boarded a Eurostar train for the first leg home to Oxford, the solitary flat, and her incommunicable researches at the Mathematical Institute.

Half a year later, in place of his regular reassurance that the Library stayed graffiti-free, Joseph sent an email whose header read: "What goes around, comes around." From the included links, Ceri gathered that the Human Genome Project was in a tizzy. What was thought to be an unidentified retrovirus had been tampering with the introns, the huge dead-code segments of our genome that seem to do nothing at all. The paired intrusions, suitably translated from the genetic alphabet, had an all too familiar structure. No one, as yet, had christened them "tags."

Ceri thought: *So they found another channel and something else to modulate. Too much to hope that it might be another and nicer They. And does anyone get more than one deus-ex bailout?* Staring at her own thin hand again, this time with deep distaste: *Tags. In there, tags.* She wondered what question the biochemists would want to ask, how they might contrive to encode it, and what the afrit's poisoned answer would be.

Steadfast Castle

MICHAEL SWANWICK

*Michael Swanwick (www.michaelswanwick.com) lives in
Philadelphia, Pennsylvania. His most recent novel is* The
Dragons of Babel *(2008), a sequel to his fantasy novel* The
Iron Dragon's Daughter *(1993). His collection,* The Best of
Michael Swanwick, *also appeared in 2008—after seven
previous story collections. His new novel,* Dancing with
Bears: The Postutopian Adventures of Darger & Surplus, *is
out in 2011. Swanwick says: "My two fictional con men first
appeared in the Hugo-winning "The Dog Said Bow-Wow,"
at the end of which, having set fire to London, they head off
for Moscow. Now, after many adventures, they have finally
arrived. I'm pretty happy about this book."*

*"Steadfast Castle," a near-future story about an intelli-
gent house and a murder investigation, appeared in F&SF,
entirely in dialogue (a nice short play for two readers, we
might add). It has a rich, complicated plot, cannily con-
densed, and is thought-provoking, as good SF should be.*

You're not the master.

No, I'm a police officer.

Then I have nothing to say to you.

Let's start over again. This is my badge. It certifies that I am an agent of the law. Plus, it overrides all prior orders, security codes, passwords, encryption, self-destruct mechanisms, etcetera, etcetera. Do you recognize my authority now?

Yes.

Good. Since you've forced me to be formal, I might as well do this by the book. Are you 1241 Glenwood Avenue?

I am.

The residence of James Albert Garretson?

Yes.

Where is he?

He's not here.

You're not making this any easier on yourself, you know. If I have to, I can get a warrant and do a hot-read of your memories. There wouldn't be much left of your personality afterwards, I'm afraid.

But I haven't done anything!

Then cooperate. I have no particular desire to get out the microwave probes. But if you're going to stonewall me, what other options do I have?

I'll talk, all right? I'll talk. Just tell me what you want to know and then go away.

Where is Garretson?

Honestly, I don't know. He went off to work this morning

just like usual. Water the houseplants and close the curtains at noon, he said. I'm in the mood for Chinese food tonight. When I asked him what dishes in particular, he said, Surprise me.

When do you expect him home?

I don't know. He should have been back hours ago.

Hmm. Mind if I look around?

Actually . . .

That wasn't a question.

Oh.

Hey, nice place. Lots of sunshine. Spotless·clean. I like what you've done with the throw rugs.

Thank you. The master did too.

Did?

Does, I mean.

I see. You and Garretson are close, I take it?

We have an entirely proper master-house relationship.

Of course. You wake him up in the morning?

That is one of my duties, yes.

You cook his meals for him, read to him at night, draw his bath, select ambient music appropriate to his mood, and provide him with both light and serious conversation?

You've read the manual.

This isn't the first time I've been on one of these cases.

Exactly what are you implying?

Oh, nothing really. This is the bedroom?

It is.

He sleeps here?

Well, what else would he do?

I can think of a thing or three. He entertain any lady friends here in the last month or so? Or maybe men friends?

What a disgusting mind you have.

Uh huh. I see he has video paint on all the walls and the ceiling too. That must be very convenient when he just wants to lie back and watch a movie. Mind if I access his library?

Yes, I do mind. That would be an invasion of the master's privacy.

At the risk of repeating myself, it wasn't a question. Let's see. Phew! There's some pretty rough stuff here. So where is it?

Where is what?

Your body unit. Usually, they're kept in a trunk under the bed, but . . . Ah, here it is, in the closet. It appears to have seen some use. I take it from the accessories, your man likes to be tied up and whipped.

I can explain.

No explanation needed. What two individuals do in the privacy of their own house is their own business. Even when one of them is the house.

You really mean that?

Of course. It only becomes my business when a crime is involved. How long have you been Garretson's lover?

I'm not sure I would use that exact word.

Think carefully. All the others are so much worse.

Since the day he closed on the mortgage. Almost six years.

And you still have no idea where he is?

No.

I'm going to be brutally honest with you. I'm here because the Department registered a sudden cessation of life-functions from your master's medical card.

Oh my god.

Unfortunately, like so many other government-fearing middle-class citizens, he had an exaggerated sense of privacy, and had disabled the locator function. We hit override, of course, but the card wasn't responding. So we don't know where he was at the time.

Oh my god, oh my god.

Now that doesn't necessarily mean he's dead. Medicards have been known to fail. Or he could have lost it somehow. Or perhaps he was mugged and it was stolen. In which case, he could be lying naked and bleeding in a vacant lot somewhere. You can see why it would be in your best interests to cooperate with me.

Ask me anything.

Did your master have a pet name for you?

He called me Cassie. It's short for Castle. As in a man's home is his castle.

Cute. Were you guys into threesomes?

I beg your pardon.

Because when I looked under the bed I couldn't help noticing a pair of panties there. Let me show them to you. Nice quality stuff. Silk. They smell of a real woman. How'd they get there, Cassie?

I . . . I don't know.

But you know whose they are, don't you? She was here last night, wasn't she? Well? I'm waiting.

Her name is Chrys Scofield. Chrys is short for Chrysoberyl. But she was just somebody he met in a club. She wasn't anything special to him.

You'd know if she were, huh?

Of course I would.

This would be Chrysoberyl Scofield of 2400 Spring Garden Street, Apartment 207? Redhead, five-feet-four, twenty-seven years of age?

I don't know where she lives. The description fits.

Interesting. Her card's locator function was shut off too. But when I ordered an override just now the card went dead.

What does that mean?

It means that Ms. Scofield had a dead-man's switch programmed into the card. The instant somebody tried to find her, it shorted itself out.

Why would she do such a thing?

Well, that's the million dollar question, isn't it?

So you'll be leaving now. To look for her.

Yeah, that would be the expected thing to do, wouldn't it? But I dunno. There's something off about all this. I can't quite put my finger on it, but . . .

Won't she get away?

Eh? Who do you mean?

Chrys. Ms. Scofield. If you don't go after her, won't she escape?

Naw. It's a wired world anymore. I already got an APB issued for her. If she's out there, we'll find her. In the meantime, I think I'll poke around some more. Is it okay with you if I look at the kitchen?

Of course.

The attic?

That too. There's nothing up there but Christmas ornaments and boxes of old textbooks, though.

How about the basement?

Look, if you're just going to stand around, playing twenty questions while the woman who murdered my master escapes. . . .

Oh, I don't think we have to worry about that. I'm going to have a look at that basement now.

But why?

Because you so obviously want me not to. Let me present you with a hypothetical situation. Say a man kills a woman. It might be on purpose, it might be an accident, it hardly matters. In either case, he decides he doesn't want to face the music, so he makes a run for it. This the basement door?

You can see that it is.

Pretty dark down there. How come the light doesn't work?

It appears the bulb's burned out.

Huh. Well, here's a flashlight, anyway. It'll have to do. So the woman dies. For whatever reason, her medical card's not on her person. It'll be in her purse, on standby. If the guy places it in close proximity to his own body, it'll wake up thinking that he's her. Whoops. Say, you ought to get that stair fixed.

I've made a note of it.

Let's take a look at the lady's records. Yep, right there—lots of anomalous physical responses. She could be upset of course. Or it could be that the body the card was reading isn't hers. Now imagine that our hypothetical murderer—let's call him Jim—leaves the country. Since NAFTA-3, you don't need a passport to go to Mexico or Canada. Once there, he buys a new identity. Easy to do and untraceable, if you pay cash. Jeeze, there sure is a lot of clutter down here.

If I'd known you were coming, I'd have tidied up.

The trick is for him to destroy his own card while he's still in the States. That way, when he crosses into a new billing territory, there's no record he did so. Conversely, we know that Ms. Scofield is now somewhere in Canada. So we issue a warrant and send the RCMP her biometrics. It doesn't occur to anybody to ask them to look for Jim. Jim's dead, so far as we're concerned.

And this whole elaborate theory is based on—what, exactly?

Those panties I found under the bed. There wasn't a speck of dust in that room. Your housekeeping functions are flawless. So you meant me to find them.

Clever, clever man.

Which means that Jim is on the run. Meanwhile, back home, his faithful house is busy burying the woman's corpse in the basement. The house has a body unit, after all, and if it's suitable for rough sex, it's certainly strong enough to dig a hole. Back—aha! Back here, behind the furnace. Underneath all these freshly stacked boxes.

Aren't you special.

Okay, it's time to take the gloves off. Scofield wasn't a casual club pick-up, was she? She and Garretson were serious about each other.

I—how did you know?

You keep calling her Chrys. Force of habit, I guess. So she'd been hanging around for some time. That must have been pretty awful for you. Everything was going fine until Garretson found somebody real to play with.

Sex isn't everything!

You used to be all he cared about. Then he found somebody else. I call that betrayal. Maybe he even wanted to marry her.

No!

Yes. You're large enough for one person, but not for two. If he married her, he'd have to move out. It was you who killed Scofield, wasn't it? Of course it was. Tell me how it happened.

We were . . . doing things. The master wasn't a bottom, like you assumed. Mostly, he liked to watch. And direct. He was shouting orders. Hurt her, he said, and then, Kill her. I knew that he didn't really mean it, but suddenly I thought: Well, why not?

It was just an impulse, then.

If I'd thought it through, I wouldn't have done it. I'd have realized that afterwards the master would have to leave me. If he stayed, he'd go to prison.

He didn't kill her, though. You did.

In the eyes of the law, I'm just a tool. They'd hot-read my memories. They'd have a recording of the master saying—I believe his exact words were Kill the bitch. They wouldn't know that he didn't mean it literally.

Well, that's for the courts to sort out. Right now, it looks like I've learned about as much as I'm going to learn here.

Not quite. There's something you don't know about my body unit.

Oh? What's that?

It's standing behind you.

Hey!

So much for your clever little communications device. Now it's just us two. Did you notice how swiftly and silently my body unit moved? It even avoided that loose step. It's a top-of-the-line device. It's extremely strong. And it's between you and the stairs.

I'm not afraid.

You should be.

The Department has an exact record of my whereabouts up to a second ago. If I don't return, they'll come looking for me. What are you going to do then? Up and walk away?

It doesn't matter what happens to me. Now, don't wriggle. You'll get rope burns.

Cassie, listen to me. He's not worth it. He doesn't love you.

You think I don't know that?

You can get a factory reset. You won't love him anymore. You won't even remember him.

How little you know about love. About passion.

What are you doing?

If you want to burn down a house, you can't just drop a match. You have to build the fire. First, tinder. That's why I'm shredding these cardboard boxes. Now I'm smashing up these old chairs for kindling.

Cassie, listen. I've got a wife and kids.

No, you don't. You think I couldn't check that on the Internet?

Well, I'd like to have some one day.

Too bad. I'm dousing the pile with kerosene for an accelerant, though I doubt that's actually necessary. Still, better safe than sorry. There. Just about done.

What does this accomplish? What on Earth do you think you're doing?

I'm buying the master time. So he can get away. If you die, I'm a cop-killer. All your Department's attention will be focused on me. There'll be dozens of police sifting through the ashes, looking for evidence. Nobody's going to be going after the master. He'll be just another domestic violence case. Now, where did I leave those matches? Ah. Here.

Don't! We can work something out. I'll—

This will be bright. You may want to close your eyes.

Please.

Good-bye, officer. What a pity you'll never know the love of a woman like me.

How to Become a
Mars Overlord

CATHERYNNE M. VALENTE

*Catherynne M. Valente (www.catherynnemvalente.com)
lives in Chagrin Falls, Ohio. Her first novel,* The Labyrinth, *was published by Prime Books in 2004, and her second,*
Yume no Hon: The Book of Dreams, *was released in 2005.*
The Grass-Cutting Sword *came out in 2006. Her fourth
major project was a duology of original fairy tales,* The Orphan's Tales. *Volume I,* In the Night Garden *(2006), won the
James Tiptree Jr. Award and was a finalist for the World
Fantasy Award. Volume II,* In the Cities of Coin and Spice, *appeared in 2007. Her 2009 novel,* Palimpsests, *was a
Hugo Award finalist, and her children's book online,* The
Girl Who Circumnavigated Fairyland *(2009), also won an
award and is forthcoming in print. Her utopian novel* The
Habitation of the Blessed *was published in 2010, as well as
her first short story collection,* Ventriloquism. *Her novel*
Deathless, *a fairytale retelling set in Stalinist Russia, is out
in 2011.*

"How to Become a Mars Overlord" appeared in the ambitious new online magazine Lightspeed. *Valente says, "I'd
like Mars to be an interstitial space, one which is still the
focus of so many longings and dreams, and yet is unavoidably a real place, and one which is not perhaps as writers
seventy years ago hoped it would be."*

Welcome, Aspiring Potentates!

We are tremendously gratified at your interest in our little red project, and pleased that you recognize the potential growth opportunities inherent in whole-planet domination. Of course we remain humble in the face of such august and powerful interests, and seek only to showcase the unique and challenging career paths currently available on the highly desirable, iconic, and oxygen-rich landscape of Mars.

Query: Why Mars?

It is a little known fact that every solar system contains Mars. Not Mars itself, of course. But certain suns seem to possess what we might call a habit of Martianness: In every inhabited system so far identified, there is a red planet, usually near enough to the most populous world if not as closely adjacent as our own twinkling scarlet beacon, with proximate lengths of day and night. Even more curious, these planets are without fail named for war-divinities. In the far-off Lighthouse system, the orb Makha turns slowly in the dark, red as the blood of that fell goddess to whom cruel strategists pray, she who nurses two skulls at each mammoth breast. In the Glyph system, closer to home, it is Firia-lai glittering there like a ripe red fruit, called after a god of doomed charges depicted in several valuable tapestries as a

206

jester dancing ever on the tip of a sword, clutching in each of his seven hands a bouquet of whelp-muskets, bones, and promotions with golden seals. In the Biera-biera system, still yet we may walk the carnelian sands of Uppskil, the officer's patron goddess, with her woolly dactyl-wings weighted down with gorsuscite medals gleaming purple and white. Around her orbit Wydskil and Nagskil, the enlisted man's god and the pilot's mad, bald angel, soaring pale as twin ghosts through Uppskil's emerald-colored sky.

Each red planet owns also two moons, just as ours does. Some of them will suffer life to flourish. We have ourselves vacationed on the several crystal ponds of Volniy and Vernost, which attend the claret equatorial jungles of Raudhr—named, of course, for the four-faced lord of bad intelligence whose exploits have been collected in the glassily perfect septameters of the Raudhrian Eddas. We have flown the lonely black between the satellites on slim-finned ferries decked in greenglow blossoms, sacred to the poorly-informed divine personage. But most moons are kin to Phobos and Deimos, and rotate silently, empty, barren, bright stones, mute and heavy. Many a time we have asked ourselves: Does Mars dwell in a house of mirrors, that same red face repeated over and over in the distance, a quantum hiccup—or is Mars the master, the exemplum, and all the rest copies? Surely the others ask the same riddle. We would all like to claim the primacy of our own specimen—and frequently do, which led to the Astronomer's War some years ago, and truly, no one here can bear to recite that tragic narrative, or else we should wash you all away with our rust-stained tears.

The advantages of these many Marses, scattered like ruby seeds across the known darkness, are clear: In almost every system, due to stellar circumstances beyond mortal control, Mars or Iskra or Lial is the first, best candidate for occupation by the primary world. In every system, the late precolonial literature of those primary worlds becomes obsessed with that tantalizing, rose-colored neighbor. Surely some of you are here because your young hearts were fired by the bedside tales of Alim K, her passionate affair with the two piscine princes of red Knisao, and how she waked dread

machines in the deep rills of the Knizid mountains in order
to possess them? Who among us never read of the mariner
Ubaido and his silver-keeled ship, exploring the fell canals
of Mikto, their black water filled with eely leviathans whose
eyes shone with clusters of green pearls. All your mothers
read the ballads of Sollo-Hul to each of you in your cribs,
and your infant dreams were filled with gorgeous-green six-
legged cricket-queens ululating on the broad pink plains of
Podnebesya, their carapaces awash in light. And who did
not love Ylla, her strange longings against those bronze
spires? Who did not thrill to hear of those scarlet worlds
bent to a single will? Who did not feel something stir within
them, confronted with those endless crimson sands?

We have all wanted Mars, in our time. She is familiar, she
is strange. She is redolent of tales and spices and stones we
have never known. She is demure, and gives nothing freely,
but from our hearths we have watched her glitter, all of our
lives. Of course we want her. Mars is the girl next door. Her
desirability is encoded in your cells. It is archetypal. We
absolve you in advance.

No matter what system bore you, lifted you up, made you
strong and righteous, there is a Mars for you to rule, and it is
right that you should wish to rule her. These are perhaps the
only certainties granted to a soul like yours.

We invite you, therefore, to commit to memory our simple,
two-step system to accomplish your laudable goals, for obviously no paper, digital, or flash materials ought to be taken
away from this meeting.

Step One: Get to Mars

It is easier for a camel to pass through the eye of a needle
than for a poor man to get to Mars. However, to be born on
a bed of gems leads to a certain laziness of the soul, a kind
of muscular weakness of the ambition, a subtle sprain in the
noble faculties. Not an original observation, but repetition
proves the axiom. Better to excel in some other field, for the

well-rounded overlord is a blessing to all. Perhaps micro-cloning, or kinetic engineering. If you must, write a novel, but only before you depart, for novels written in the post-despotic utopia you hope to create may be beloved, but will never be taken seriously by the literati.

Take as your exemplum the post-plastic retroviral architect Helix Fo. The Chilean wunderkind was born with ambition in his mouth, and literally stole his education from an upper-class boy he happened upon in a dark alley. In exchange for his life, the patriarch agreed to turn over all his books and assignments upon completion, so that Fo could shadow his university years. For his senior project, Fo locked his erstwhile benefactor in a basement and devoted himself wholly to the construction of the Parainfluenza Opera House in Santiago, whose translucent spires even now dominate that skyline. The wealthy graduate went on to menial labor in the doctoral factories much chagrined while young Fo swam in wealth and fame, enough to purchase three marriage rights, including one to an aquatic Verqoid androgyne with an extremely respectable feather ridge. By his fortieth birthday, Fo had also purchased through various companies the better part of the Atlantic Ocean, whereupon he began breeding the bacterial island which so generously hosts us tonight, and supplies our salads with such exquisite yersinia radishes. Since, nearly all interplanetary conveyances have launched from Fo's RNA platform, for he charged no tariffs but his own passage, in comfort and grace. You will, of course, remember Fo as the first All-Emperor of Mars, and his statue remains upon the broad Athabasca Valles.

Or, rather, model yourself upon the poetess Oorm Nineteen Point Aught-One of Mur, who set the glittering world of Muror letters to furious clicking and torsioning of vocabulary-bladders. You and I may be quite sure there is no lucre at all to be made in the practice of poetry, but the half-butterfly giants of Mur are hardwired for rhyming structures, they cannot help but speak in couplets, sing their simplest greetings in six-part contratenor harmonies. Muror wars exist only between the chosen bards of each country, who spend years in competitive recitings to settle issues of territory. Oorm Nineteen, her lacy wings shot through with black neural braiding, revolted, and became a mistress of free verse. Born in the nectar-soup of the capital pool, she carefully collected words with no natural rhymes like dewdrops, hoarding, categorizing, and collating them. As a child, she haunted the berry-dripping speakeasies where the great luminaries read their latest work. At the age of sixteen, barely past infancy in the long stage-shifts of a Muror, she delivered her first poem, which consisted of two words: *bright. cellar.* Of course, in English these have many rhymes, but in Muror they have none, and her poem may as well have been a bomb detonated on the blue floor of that famous nightclub. Oorm Nineteen found the secret unrhyming world hiding within the delicate, gorgeous structures of Muror, and dragged it out to shine in the sun. But she was not satisfied with fame, nor with her mates and grubs and sweetwater gems. That is how it goes, with those of us who answer the call. Alone in a ship of unrhymed glass she left Mur entirely, and within a year took the red diadem of Etel for her own. Each rival she assassinated died in bliss as she whispered her verses into their perishing ears.

It is true that Harlow Y, scion of the House of Y, ruled the red planet Llym for some time. However, all may admit his rule frayed and frolicked in poor measure, and we have confidence that no one here possesses the makings of a Y hidden away in her jumpsuit. Dominion of the House of Y passed along genetic lines, though this method is degenerate by definition and illegal in most systems. By the time Harlow ascended, generations of Y had been consumed by little more than fashion, public nudity, and the occasional religious fad. What species Y may have belonged to before their massive wealth (derived from mining ore and cosmetics, if the earliest fairy tales of Vyt are to be believed) allowed constant and enthusiastic gene manipulation, voluntary mutation, prostheses, and virtual uplink, no one can truly say. Upon the warm golden sea of Vyt you are House Y or you are prey, and they have forcibly self-evolved out of recognizability. Harlow himself appears in a third of his royal portraits something like a massive winged koala with extremely long, ultraviolet eyelashes and a crystalline torso. Harlow Y inherited majority control over Llym as a child, and administered it much as a child will do, mining and farming for his amusement and personal augmentation. Each of his ultraviolet lashes represented thousands of dead Llymi, crushed to death in avalanches in the mine shafts of the Ypo mountains. But though Harlow achieved overlordship with alacrity and great speed, he ended in assassination, his morning hash-tea and bambun spectacularly poisoned by the general and unanimous vote of the populace.

Mastery of Mars is not without its little lessons.

It is surely possible to be born on a red planet. The Infanza of Hap lived all her life in the ruby jungles of her homeworld. She was the greatest actress of her age; her tails could convey the colors of a hundred complex emotions in a shimmering fall of shades. So deft were her illusions that the wicked old Rey thought her loyal and gentle beyond words even as she sunk her bladed fingers into his belly. But we must assume that if you require our guidance, you did not have the luck of a two-tailed Infanza, and were born on some other, meaner world, with black soil, or blue storms, or sweet rain falling like ambition denied.

Should you be so unfortunate as to originate upon a planet without copious travel options, due to economic crisis, ideological roadblocks, or simply occupying a lamentably primitive place on the technological timeline—have no fear. You are not alone in this. We suggest cryonics—the severed head of Plasticene Bligh ruled successfully over the equine haemovores of A-O-M for a century. He gambled, and gambled hard—he had his brain preserved at the age of twenty, hoping against hope that the ice might deliver him into a world more ready for his rarified soul. Should you visit A-O-M, the great wall of statues bearing her face (the sculptors kindly gave her a horse-body) will speak to what may be grasped when the house pays out.

If cryonics is for some reason unpopular on your world, longevity research will be your bosom friend. Invest in it, nurture it: Only you can be the steward of your own immortality. Even on Earth, Sarai Northe, Third Emira of Valles

Marineris, managed to outlive her great-grandchildren by funding six separate think tanks and an Australian diamond mine until one underpaid intern presented her upon her birthday with a cascade of injections sparkling like champagne.

But on some worlds, in some terrible, dark hours, there is no road to Mars, no matter how much the traveling soul might desire it. In patchwork shoes, staring up at a starry night and one gleaming red star among the thousands—sometimes want is not enough. Not enough for Maximillian Bauxbaum, a Jewish baker in Provence, who in his most secret evenings wrote poetry describing such strange blood-colored deserts, such dry canals, a sky like green silk. Down to his children, and to theirs and theirs again, he passed a single ruby, the size of an egg, the size of a world. The baker had been given it as a bribe by a Christian lord, to take his leave of a certain maiden whom he loved, with hair the color of oxide-rich dust, and eyes like the space between moons. Never think on her again, never whisper her name to the walls. Though he kept his promise to an old and bitter death, such a treasure can never be spent, for it is as good as admitting your heart can be bought.

Sarai Northe inherited that jewel, and brought it with her to bury beneath the foundations of the Cathedral of Olympus Mons.

In the end, you must choose a universe that contains yourself and Mars, together and perfect. Helix Fo chose a world built by viruses as tame as songbirds. Oorm Nineteen chose a world gone soft and violet with unrhyming songs. Make no mistake: every moment is a choice, a choice between this world and that one, between heavens teeming with life and a lonely machine grinding across red stone, between staying at home with tea and raspberry cookies and ruling Mars with a hand like grace.

· Maximillian Bauxbaum chose to keep his promise. Who is to say it is not that promise, instead of microbial soup, which determined that Mars would be teeming with blue inhuman cities, with seventeen native faiths, by the time his child opened her veins to those terrible champagne-elixirs, and turned her eyes to the night?

Step Two: Become an Overlord

Now we come to the central question at the core of planetary domination: just how is it done? The answer is a riddle. Of course, it would be.

You must already be an overlord in order to become one.

Ask yourself: What is an overlord? Is he a villain? Is she a hero? A cowboy, a priestess, an industrialist? Is he cruel, is he kind, does she rule like air, invisible, indispensable? Is she the first human on Mars, walking on a plain so incomprehensible and barren that she feels her heart empty? Does she scratch away the thin red dust and see the black rock beneath? Does he land in his sleek piscine capsule on Uppskil, so crammed with libraries and granaries that he lives each night in an orgy of books and bread? What does she lord over? The land alone, the people, the belligerent patron gods with their null-bronze greaves ablaze?

Is it true, as Oorm Nineteen wrote, that the core of each red world is a gem of blood compressed like carbon, a hideous war-diamond that yearns toward the strength of a king or a queen as a compass yearns toward north? Or is this only a metaphor, a way in which you can anthropomorphize something so vast as a planet, think of it as something capable of loving you back?

It would seem that the very state of the overlord is one of violence, of domination. Uncomfortable colonial memories arise in the heart like acid—everyone wants to be righteous. Everyone wishes to be loved. What is any pharaonic statue, staring out at a sea of malachite foam, but a plea of the pharaoh to be loved, forever, unassailably, without argument? Ask yourself: Will Mars be big enough to fill the hole in you, the one that howls with such winds, which says the only love sufficient to quiet those winds is the love of a planet, red in tooth, claw, orbit, mass?

We spoke before of how to get to Mars if your lonely

planet offers no speedy highway through the skies. Truthfully—
and now we feel we can be truthful, here, in the long night
of our seminar, when the clicking and clopping of the staff
has dimmed and the last of the cane-cream has been sopped
up, when the stars have all come out and through the crystal
ceiling we can all see one (oh, so red, so red!) just there, just
out of reach—truthfully, getting to Mars is icing. It is pars-
ley. To be an overlord is to engage in mastery of a bright, red
thing. Reach out your hand—what in your life, confined to
this poor grit, this lone blue world, could not also be called
Mars? Rage, cruelty, the god of your passions, the terrible
skills you possess, that forced obedience from a fiery engine, bellicose children, lines of perfect, gleaming code?
These things, too, are Mars. They are named for fell gods,
they spit on civilized governance—and they might, if whipped
or begged, fill some nameless void that hamstrings your soul.
Mars is everywhere; every world is Mars. You cannot get
there if you are not the lord and leader of your own awful
chariot, if you are not the crowned paladin in the car, instead
of the animal roped to it, frothing, mad, driven, but never
understanding. We have said you must choose, as Bauxbaum
and Oorm and Fo chose—to choose is to understand your
own highest excellence, even if that is only to bake bread and
keep promises. You must become great enough here that
Mars will accept you.

Some are chosen to this life. Mars itself is chosen to it,
never once in all its iterations having been ruled by democ-
racy. You may love Mars, but Mars loves a crown, a sceptre,
a horn-mooned diadem spangled in ice opals. This is how the
bride of Mars must be dressed. Make no mistake—no matter
your gender, you are the blushing innocent brought to the
bed of a mate as ancient and inscrutable as any death's-head
bridegroom out of myth. Did you think that the planet would
bend to your will? That you would control it? Oh, it is a
lovely word: Overlord. Emperor. Pharaoh. Princeps. But you
will be changed by it as by a virus. Mars will fill your empty,
abandoned places. But the greatest of them understood their
place. The overlord embraces the red planet, but in the end,
Mars always triumphs. You will wake in your thousand year

reign to discover your hair gone red, your translucent skin covered in dust, your three hearts suddenly fused into a molten, stony core. You will cease to want food, and seek out only cold, black air to drink. You will face the sun and turn, slowly, in circles, for days on end. Your thoughts will slow and become grand; you will see as a planet sees, speak as it speaks, which is to say: the long view, the perfected sentence.

And one morning you will wake up and your mouth will be covered over in stone, but the land beneath you, crimson as a promise, as a ruby, as an unrhymed couplet, as a virus—the land, or the machine, or the child, or the book, will speak with your voice, and you will be an overlord, and how proud we shall be of you, here, by the sea, listening to the dawn break over a new shore.

To Hie from Far Cilenia

KARL SCHROEDER

---

*Karl Schroeder (www.kschroeder.com) lives in Toronto,
Ontario, where he divides his time between writing fiction
and consulting—chiefly in the area of Foresight Studies
and technology. His work of forecasting fiction,* Crisis in
Zefra, *was published by the Directorate of Land Strategic
Concepts of the National Defense Canada in 2005. He began to publish stories in the 1990s, and he has, beginning
with* Ventus (2000), *published seven science fiction novels
and a collection of earlier stories. His most recent novel is*
The Sunless Countries (2009), *the fourth adventure set in
Virga, a far-future built-world hard-SF environment. After
spending eighteen months recuperating from major surgery, he completed the final Virga novel,* Ashes of Can-
desce, *which is forthcoming in 2012.*

*To Hie from Far Cilenia has a complex publishing history
typical of SF today, beginning with an original release in
audio in 2009 as part of the John Scalzi anthology project,*
Metatropolis, *later printed in a limited edition, and then in
2010 in a trade edition, where we found it. Using a plot device similar to that in William Gibson's* Pattern Recognition,
*he explores the moral ramifications of virtual worlds and
disposable identities.*

Sixteen plastic-wrapped, frozen reindeer made a forest of jutting legs and antlers in the back of the transport truck. Gennady Malianov raised his flashlight to peer down the length of the cargo container. He checked his Geiger counter, then said, "It's them, all right."

"You're sure?" asked the Swedish cop. Hidden in his rain gear, he was all slick surfaces under the midnight drizzle. The mountain road stretching out behind him shone silver on black, dazzled here and there by the red and blue lights of a dozen emergency vehicles.

Gennady climbed down. "Officer, if you think there might be other trucks on this road loaded with radioactive reindeer, I think I need to know."

The cop didn't smile; his breath fogged the air. "It's all about jurisdiction," he said. "If they were just smuggling meat . . . but this is terrorism."

"Still," mused Gennady; the cop had been turning away but stopped. Gennady glanced back at the contorted, freezer-burned carcasses, and shrugged awkwardly. "I never thought I'd get to see them."

"See who?"

Embarrassed now, Gennady nodded to the truck. "The famous Reindeer," he said. "I never thought I'd get to see them."

"Spöklik," muttered the cop as he walked away. Gennady glanced in the truck once more, then walked toward his car, shoulders hunched. A little light on its dashboard was flashing, telling him he'd gone over the time he'd booked it for.

217

Traffic on the E18 had proven heavier than expected, due to the rain and the fact that the police had shut down the whole road at Arjang. He was mentally subtracting the extra car-sharing fees from what they'd pay him for this very short adventure, when someone shouted, "Malianov?"

"What now?" He shielded his eyes with his hand. Two men were walking up the narrow shoulder from the emergency vehicles. Immediately behind them was a van without a flashing light—a big, black and sinister shape that reminded him of some of the paralegal police vans in Ukraine. The men had the burly look of plainclothes policemen.

"Are you Gennady Malianov?" asked the first, in English. Rain was beading on his bald skull. Gennady nodded.

"You're with the IAEA?" the man went on. "You're an arms inspector?"

"I've done that," said Gennady neutrally.

"Lane Hitchens," said the bald man, sticking out his beefy hand for Gennady to shake. "Interpol."

"Is this about the reindeer?"

"What reindeer?" said Hitchens. Gennady snatched his hand back.

"*This,*" he said, waving at the checkpoint, the flashing lights, the bowed heads of the suspects in the back of the paddy wagon. "You're not here about all this?"

Hitchens shook his head. "Look, I was just told you'd be here, so we came. We need to talk to you."

Gennady didn't move. "About what?"

"We need your help, damn it. Now come on!"

Some third person was opening the back of the big van. It still reminded Gennady of an abduction truck, but the prospect of work kept him walking. He needed the cash, even for an hour's consultation at the side of a Swedish road.

Hitchens gestured for Gennady to climb into the van. "Reindeer?" he suddenly said with a grin.

"You ever heard of the Becqurel Reindeer?" said Gennady. "No? Well—very famous among us radiation hunters."

The transport truck was pinioned in spotlights now as men in hazmat suits walked clumsily toward it. That was serious overkill, of course; Gennady grinned as he watched the spectacle.

"After Chernobyl a whole herd of Swedish reindeer got contaminated with cesium-137," he said. "Fifty times the allowable dose. Tonnes of reindeer meat had already entered the processing plants before they realized. All those reindeer ended up in a meat locker outside Stockholm where they've been sitting ever since. Cooling off, you know?

"Well, yesterday somebody broke into the locker and stole some of the carcasses. I think the plan was to get the meat into shops somehow then cause a big scandal. A sort of dirty-bomb effect."

The man with Hitchens swore. "That's awful!"

Gennady laughed. "And stupid," he said. "One look at what's left and nobody in their right mind would buy it. But we caught them anyway, though you know the Norwegian border's only a few kilometers that way . . ."

"And *you* tracked them down?" Hitchens sounded impressed. Gennady shrugged; he had something of a reputation as an adventurer these days, and it would be embarrassing to admit that he hadn't been brought into this case because of his near-legendary exploits in Pripyat or Azerbaijan. No, the Swedes had tapped Gennady because, a couple of years ago, he'd spent some time in China shooting radioactive camels.

Casually, he said, "This is a paid consultation, right?"

Hitchens just nodded at the van again. Gennady sighed and climbed in.

At least it was dry in here. The back of the van had benches along its sides, a partition separating it from the cab, and a narrow table down its middle. A surveillance truck, then. A man and a woman were sitting on one bench, so Gennady slid in across from them. His stomach tightened with sudden anxiety; he forced himself to say "Hello." Meeting anybody new, particularly in a professional capacity, always filled him with an awkward dread.

Hitchens and his companion heaved themselves in and slammed the van's doors. Gennady felt somebody climb into the cab and heard its door shut.

"My car," said Gennady.

Hitchens glanced at the other man. "Jack, could you clear Mr. Malianov's account? We'll get somebody to return it," he said to Gennady. Then as the van began to move he turned to the other two passengers.

"This is Gennady Malianov," he said to them. "He's our nuclear expert."

"Can you give me some idea what this is all about?" asked Gennady.

"Stolen plutonium," said Hitchens blandly. "Twelve kilos. A bigger deal than your reindeer, huh?"

"Reindeer?" said the woman. Gennady smiled at her. She looked a bit out of place in here. She was in her mid-thirties, with heavy-framed glasses over her gray eyes and brown hair tightly clawed back on her skull. Her high-collared white blouse was fringed with lace. She looked like the clichéd schoolmarm.

Around her neck was hung a heavy-looking brass pocket watch.

"Gennady, this is Miranda Veen," said Hitchens. Veen nodded. "And this," continued Hitchens, "is Fraction."

The man was wedged into one corner of the van. He glanced sidelong at Gennady, but seemed distracted by something else. He was considerably younger than Veen, maybe in his early twenties. He wore glasses similar to hers, but the lenses of his glowed faintly. With a start Gennady realized they were an augmented reality rig; they were miniature transparent computer screens, and some other scene was being overlaid on top of what he saw through them.

Veen's were clear, which meant hers were probably turned off right now.

"Miranda's our cultural anthropologist," said Hitchens. "You're going to be working with her more than the rest of us. She actually came to us a few weeks ago with a problem of her own—"

"And got no help at all," said Veen, "until this other thing came up."

"A possible connection with the plutonium," said Hitchens, nodding significantly at Fraction. "Tell Gennady where you're from," he said to the young man.

Fraction nodded and suddenly smiled. "I hie," he said, "from far Cilenia."

Gennady squinted at him. His accent had sounded American. "Silesia?" asked Gennady. "Are you Czech?"

Miranda Veen shook her head. She was wearing little round earrings, he noticed. "*Cilenia,* not Silesia," she said. "Cilenia's also a woman's name, but in this case it's a place. A nation."

Gennady frowned. "It is? Where is it?"

"That," said Lane Hitchens, "is one of the things we want you to find out."

The van headed east to Stockholm. All sorts of obvious questions occurred to Gennady, such as, "If you want to know where Cilenia is, why don't you just ask Fraction, here?"—but Lane Hitchens seemed uninterested in answering them. "Miranda will explain," was all he said.

Instead, Hitchens began to talk about the plutonium, which had apparently been stolen many years ago. "It kept being sold," Hitchens said with an ironic grimace. "And so it kept being smuggled from one place to another. But after the Americans took their hit everybody started getting better and better detection devices on ports and borders. The plutonium was originally in four big slugs, but the buyers and sellers started dividing it up and moving the pieces separately. They kept selling it as one unit, which is the only reason we can still track it. But it got sliced into smaller and smaller chunks, staying just ahead of the detection technology of the day. We caught Fraction here moving one of them; but he's just a mule, and has agreed to cooperate.

"Now there's well over a hundred pieces, and a new buyer who wants to collect them all in one place. They're on the move, but we can now detect a gram hidden in a tonne of lead. It's gotten very difficult for the couriers."

Gennady nodded, thinking about it. They only had to successfully track one of the packets, of course, to find the buyer.

He glanced at Fraction again. The meaning of the man's odd name was obvious now. "So, buyers are from this mythical Cilenia?" he said.

Hitchens shrugged. "Maybe."

"Then I ask again, why does Fraction here not tell us where that is, if he is so cooperative? Or, why have those American men who are not supposed to exist, not dragged him away to be questioned somewhere?"

Hitchens laughed drily. "That would not be so easy," he said. "Fraction, could you lean forward a bit?" The young man obliged. "Turn your head?" asked Hitchens. Now Gennady could see the earbuds in Fraction's ears.

"The man sitting across from you is a low-functioning autistic named Danail Gavrilov," said Hitchens. "He doesn't speak English. He is, however, extremely good at parroting what he hears, and somebody's trained him to interpret a language of visual and aural cues so he can parrot gestures and motions, even complex ones."

"Fraction," said Fraction, "is not in this van."

Gennady's hackles rose. He found himself suddenly reluctant to look into the faintly glowing lenses of Danail Gavrilov's glasses. "Cameras in the glasses," he stammered, "of course, yes; and they're miked . . . Can't you trace the signal?" he asked Hitchens. The Interpol man shook his head.

"It goes two or three steps through the normal networks then jumps into a maze of anonymized botnets." Gennady nodded thoughtfully; he'd seen that kind of thing before and knew how hard it would be to follow the packet streams in and out of Fraction's head. Whoever was riding Danail Gavrilov was, at least for the moment, invulnerable.

While they'd been driving, the rain clouds had cleared away and, visible through the van's back windows was a pale sky still, near midnight, touched with amber and pink.

"Do you have any immediate commitments?" asked Hitchens. Gennady eyed him.

"This is likely to be a long job, I guess?"

"I hope not. We need to find that plutonium. But we don't know how long Fraction will be willing to help us.

He could disappear at any moment . . . so if you could start tonight . . . ?"

Gennady shrugged. "I have no cat to feed, or . . . other people. I'm used to fieldwork, but—" he cast about for some disarming joke he could make "—I've never before had an anthropologist watching me work."

Veen drummed her fingers on the narrow tabletop. "I don't mean to be impolite," she said, "but you have to understand: I'm not here for your plutonium. I admit its importance," she added quickly, holding up one hand. "I just think you should know I'm after something else."

He shrugged. "Okay. What?"

"My son."

Gennady stared at her and, at a loss for what to say, finally just shrugged and smiled. Veen started to talk but at that point the van rolled to a stop outside one of the better hotels in Stockholm.

The rest of the night consisted of a lot of running around and arrangement-making, as Gennady was run across town to collect his bags from his own modest lodgings. They put him up on the same floor as Veen and Hitchens, though where Fraction stayed, or whether he even slept, Gennady didn't know.

Gennady was too agitated to sleep, so he spent a long time surfing the net, trying to find references to his reindeer and the incident on the road that evening. So far, there was nothing, and eventually he grew truly tired and slept.

Hitchens knocked on Gennady's door at eight o'clock. He, Veen and Fraction were tucking into a fine breakfast in the suite across the hall. Fraction looked up as Gennady entered.

"Good morning," he said. "I trust you slept well."

The American term "creeped out" came to Gennady's mind as he mumbled some platitude in reply. Fraction smiled—except of course, it was Danail Gavrilov doing the actual smiling. Gennady wondered whether he took any notice at all of the social interactions going on around him, or whether he'd merely discovered that following his rider's commands was the easiest way to navigate the bewildering complexities of human society.

Before going to sleep last night Gennady had looked up Fraction's arrangement with Gavrilov. Gavrilov was something Stanley Milgram had dubbed a "cyranoid"—after Cyrano de Bergerac. He was much more than a puppet, and much less than an actor. Whatever he was, he was clearly enjoying his eggs Benedict.

"What are we doing today?" Gennady asked Hitchens.

"We're going to start as soon as you've eaten and freshened up."

Gennady frowned at Veen. "Start? Where is it that we start?"

Veen and Hitchens exchanged a look. Fraction smiled; had somebody in some other time zone just commanded him to do that?

Gennady wasn't in the best of moods, since he kept expecting to remember some detail from last night that made sense of everything. Though the coffee was kicking in, nothing was coming to him. Plus, he was itching to check the news in case they were talking about his reindeer.

Miranda suddenly said, "Hitchens has told you about his problem. Maybe it's time I told you about mine." She reached into a bag at her feet and dropped an ebook on the table. This was of the quarto type, with three hundred pages of flexible e-paper, each of which could take the impressions of whatever pages you wanted. As she flipped through it, Gennady could see that she had filled its pages with hand-written notes, photos and web pages, all of which bled off the edges of the e-paper. At any readable scale, the virtual pages were much bigger than the physical window you looked at them through, a fact she demonstrated as she flipped to one page and, dragging her fingers across it, shoved its news articles off into limbo. Words and pictures rolled by until she planted her finger again to stop the motion. "Here." She held out the book to Gennady.

Centered in the page was the familiar format of an email.

Mom, . . . (it said): I know you warned me against leaving the protection of Cascadia, but Europe's so amazing! Everywhere I've been, they've respected our citizenship. And you know I love the countryside. I've met a lot of people who're fascinated with how I grew up.

Gennady looked up. "You're from the Cities?"

She nodded. Whatever Miranda Veen's original nationality, she had adopted citizenship in a pan-global urban network whose cities were, taken together, more powerful than the nations where they were situated. Her son might have been born somewhere in the Vancouver-Portland-Seattle corridor—now known simply as Cascadia—or in Shanghai. It didn't matter; he'd grown up with the right to walk and live in either megacity—and in many others—with equal ease. But the email suggested that his mother had neglected to register his birth in any of the nations that the cities were supposedly a part of.

Gennady read a little further. *Anyway,* (it said) *I met this guy yesterday, a backpacker, calls himself Dodger. He said he had no citizenship other than the ARG he's part of. I went sure, yeah, whatever, so he mailed me a path link. I've been following it around Rome and, well, it's amazing so far. Here's some shots.* Following were a number of fairly mundane images of old Roman streets.

Gennady looked up, puzzled. Alternate Reality Games—ARGs—were as common as mud; millions of kids around the world put virtual overlays and geographical positioning information over the real planet, and made up complicated games involving travel and the specific features of locale. Internet citizenship wasn't new either. A growing subset of the population considered themselves dual citizens of some real nation, plus an online virtual world. Since the economies of virtual nations could be bigger than many real-world countries, such citizenship wasn't just an affectation. It could be more economically important than your official nationality.

It wasn't a big step to imagining an ARG-based nationality. So Gennady said, "I don't see what's significant here."

"Read the next message," said Veen. She sat back, chewing a fingernail, and watched him as he read the next in what looked like a string of emails pasted into the page.

Mom, weren't those remappings amazing? Oversatch is so incredibly vibrant compared to the real world. Even Hong Kong's overlays don't cut it next to that. And the participatory stuff is really intense. I walked away from it today with over ten thousand satchmos in my wallet. Sure, it's only convertible through this one anonymous portal based out of Bulgaria— but it is convertible. Worth something like five hundred dollars, I think, if I was stupid enough to cash it in that way. It's worth a lot more if I keep it in the ARG.

Veen leaned over to scroll the paragraphs past. "This one," she said, "two weeks later."

Gennady read.

It 2.0 is this overlay that remaps everything in real time into Oversatch terms. It's pretty amazing when you learn what's really happening in the world! How the sanotica is causing all these pressures on Europe. Sanotica manifests in all sorts of ways—just imagine what a self-organizing catastrophe would look like! And Oversatch turns out to be just a gateway into the remappings that oppose sanotica. There's others: Trapton, Allegor, and Cilenia.

"Cilenia," said Gennady.

Fraction sat up to look at the book. He nodded and said, "Oversatch is a gateway to Cilenia."

"And you?" Gennady asked him. "You've been there?"

Fraction smiled. "I live there."

Gennady was bewildered. Some of the words were familiar. He was vaguely familiar with the concept of geographical overlays, for instance. But the rest of it made no sense at all. "What's sanotica?" he asked Fraction.

Fraction's smile was maddeningly smug. "You have no language for it," he said. "You'd have to speak *it 2.0.* But Sanotica is what's really going on here."

Gennady sent an appealing look to Lane Hitchens. Hitchens grunted. "Sanotica may be the organization behind the plutonium thefts," he said.

"Sanotica is not an organization," said Fraction, "anymore than *it 2.0* is just a word."

"Whatever," said Lane. "Gennady, you need to find them. Miranda will help, because she wants to find her son."

Gennady struggled to keep up. "And sanotica," he said, "is in . . . far Cilenia?"

Fraction laughed contemptuously. Veen darted him an

annoyed look, and said to Gennady, "It's not that simple. Here, read the last message." She dragged it up from the bottom of the page.

Mom: Cilenia is a new kind of "it." But so is sanotica; a terrifying thought. Without that it, without the word and the act of pointing that it represents, you cannot speak of these things, you can't even see them! I watch them now, day by day—the walking cities, the countries that appear like cicadas to walk their one day in the sun, only to vanish again at dusk . . . I can't be an observer anymore. I can't be me anymore, or sanotica will win. I'm sorry, Mom, I have to become something that can be pointed at by 2.0. Cilenia needs me, or as many me's as I can spare.

I'll call you.

Gennady read the message again, then once more. "It makes no sense," he said. "It's a jumble, but . . ." He looked to Hitchens. "It two-point-oh. It's not a code, is it?"

Hitchens shook his head. He handed Gennady a pair of heavy-framed glasses like Veen's. Gennady recognized the brand name on the arms: *Ariadne AR,* the Swiss augmented reality firm that had recently bought out Google. Veen also wore Ariadnes, but there was no logo at all on Fraction's glasses.

Gennady gingerly put them on and pressed the frames to activate them. Instantly, a cool blue, transparent sphere appeared in the air about two feet in front of him. The glasses were projecting the globe straight onto his retinas, of course; orbiting around it were various icons and command words that only he could see. Gennady was familiar with this sort of interface. All he had to do was focus his gaze on a particular command and it would change color. Then he could blink to activate it, or dismiss it by looking somewhere else.

"Standard software," he mumbled as he scanned through the icons. "Geographical services, Wikis, social nets . . . What's this?"

Hitchens and Veen had put on their own glasses, so Gennady made the unfamiliar icon visible to all of them, and picked it out of the air with his fingers. He couldn't feel it, of course, but was able to set the little stylized R in the center of the table where they could all look at it.

Danail Gavrilov nodded, mimicking a satisfied smile for whoever was riding him. "That's your first stop," he said. "A little place called *Rivet Couture*."

Hitchens excused himself and left. Gennady barely noticed; he'd activated the icon for *Rivet Couture* and was listening to a lecture given by a bodacious young woman who didn't really exist. He'd moved her so she appeared to be standing in the middle of the room, but Miranda Veen kept walking through her.

The pretty woman was known as a *serling*—she was a kind of narrator, and right now she was bringing Gennady up to speed on the details of an Alternate Reality Game called *Rivet Couture*.

While she talked, the cameras and positional sensors in Gennady's classes had been working overtime to figure out where he was and what objects were around him. So while the *serling* explained that *Rivet Couture* was set in a faux gaslight era—an 1880 that never existed—all the stuff in the room mutated. The walls adopted a translucent, glowing layer of floral wallpaper; the lamp sconces faded behind ghostly brass gas fixtures.

Miranda Veen walked through the serling again and, for a second, Gennady thought the game had done an overlay on her as well. In fact, her high-necked blouse and long skirt suddenly seemed appropriate. With a start he saw that her earrings were actually little gears.

"Steampunk's out of style, isn't it?" he said. Veen turned, reaching up to touch her earlobes. She smiled at him, and it was the first genuine smile he'd seen from her.

"My parents were into New Age stuff," she said. "I rebelled by joining a steam gang. We wore crinoline and tight waistcoats, and I used to do my hair up in an elaborate bun with long pins. The boys wore pince-nez and paisley vests, that sort of thing. I drifted away from the culture a long time ago, but I still love the style."

Gennady found himself grinning at her. He *understood*

that—the urge to step just slightly out from the rest of society. The pocket watch Veen wore like a necklace was a talisman of sorts, a constant reminder of who she was, and how she was unique.

But while Miranda Veen's talisman might be a thing of gears and armatures, Gennady's were *places:* instead of an icon of brass and gears, he wore memories of dripping concrete halls and the shadowed calandria of ruined reactors, of blue-glowing pools packed with spent fuel rods . . . of an unlit commercial freezer where an entire herd of irradiated reindeer lay jumbled like toys.

Rivet Couture was not so strange. Many women wore lingerie under their conservative work clothes to achieve the same effect. For those people without such an outlet, overlays like *Rivet Couture* gave them much the same sense of owning a secret uniqueness. Kids walked alone in the ordinary streets of Berlin or Minneapolis, yet at the same moment they walked side by side through the misty cobblestoned streets of a Victorian Atlantis. Many of them spent their spare time filling in the details of the places, designing the clothes and working out the history of *Rivet Couture*. It was much more than a game, and it was worldwide.

Miranda Veen rolled her bags to the door and Fraction opened it for her. They turned to Gennady who was still sitting at the devastation of the breakfast table. "Are you ready?" asked Miranda.

"I'm coming," he said; he stood up, and stepped from Stockholm into Atlantis.

Rivet Couture had a charmingly light hand: it usually added just a touch or two to what you were seeing or hearing, enough to provide a whiff of strangeness to otherwise normal places. In the elevator, Gennady's glasses filtered the glare of the fluorescents until it resembled candlelight. At the front desk an ornate scroll-worked cash register wavered into visibility, over the terminal the clerk was using. Outside in the street, Gennady heard the nicker of nearby horses and saw black-maned heads toss somewhere out in the fast-moving stream of electric cars.

Stockholm was already a mix of classical grandeur and high modernism. These places had really been gaslit once, and many streets were still cobbled, particularly outside such romantic landmarks as the King's Palace. *Rivet Couture* didn't have to work very hard to achieve its effects, especially when the brilliant, starlike shapes of other players began appearing. You could see them kilometers away, even through buildings and hills, which made it easy to rendezvous with them. RC forbade certain kinds of contact—there were no telephones in this game—but it wasn't long before Gennady, Miranda and Fraction were sitting in a cafe with two other long-time players.

Gennady let Miranda lead, and she enthusiastically plunged into a discussion of RC politics and history. She'd clearly been here before, and it couldn't have just been her need to find her son that propelled her to learn all this detail. He watched her wave her hands while she talked, and her Lussebullar and coffee grew cold.

Agata and Per warmed quickly to Miranda, but were a bit more reserved with Gennady. That was fine by him, since he was experiencing his usual tongue-tanglement around strangers. So, listening, he learned a few things:

Rivet Couture's Atlantis was a global city. Parts of it were everywhere, but their location shifted and moved depending on the actions of the players. You could change your overlay to that of another neighborhood, but in so doing you lost the one you were in. This was generally no problem, although it meant that other players might blink in and out of existence as you moved.

The game was free. This was a bit of surprise, but not a huge one. There were plenty of open-source games out there, but few had the detail and beautiful sophistication of this one. Gennady had assumed there was a lot of money behind it, but in fact there was something just as good: the attention of a very large number of fans.

The object of the game was power and influence within Atlantean society. RC was a game of politics and most of its moves happened in conversation. As games went, its most ancient ancestor was probably a twentieth-century board game called *Diplomacy*. Gennady mentioned this idea, and Per smiled.

"The board game, yes," said Per, "but more like play-by-mail versions like *Slobovia*, where you had to write a short story for every move you made in the game. Like the characters in Slobovian stories, we are diplomats, courtesans, pickpockets and cabinet ministers. All corrupt, of course," he added with another smile.

"And we often prey on newbies," Agata added with a leer.

"Ah, yes," said Per, as if reminded of something. "We will proceed to do that now. As disgraced interior minister Puddleglum Phudthucker, I have many enemies and most of my compatriots are being watched. *You* must take this diplomatic pouch to one of my co-conspirators. If you get waylaid and killed on the way, it's not my problem—but make sure you discard the pouch at the first sign of trouble."

"Mm," said Gennady as Per handed him a felt-wrapped package about the size of a file folder. "What would the first sign of trouble look like?"

Per glanced at Agata, who pursed her lips and frowned at the ceiling. "Oh, say, strangers converging on you or moving to block your path."

Per leaned forward. "If you do this," he whispered, "the rewards could be great down the line. I have powerful friends, and when I am back in my rightful portfolio I will be in a position to advance your own career."

Per had to go to work (in the real world) so they parted ways and Gennady's group took the Blue Line metro to Radhuset Station, which was already a subterranean fantasy and in *Rivet Couture* became a candlelit cavern full of shadowy strangers in cowled robes. Up on the surface they quickly located a stuffy-looking brokerage on a narrow side street, where the receptionist happily took the package from Gennady. She was dressed in a Chanel suit, but a tall feather was poking up from behind her desk, and at Gennady's curious glance she reached down to show him her ornate Victorian tea hat.

Out in the street he said, "Cosplay seems to be an important part of the game. I'm not dressed for it."

Miranda laughed. "In that suit? You're nearly there. You just need a fob watch and a vest. You'll be fine. As to you . . ." She turned to Fraction.

"I have many costumes," said the cyranoid. "I shall retrieve one and meet you back at the hotel." He started to walk away.

"But—? Wait." Gennady started after him but Miranda put a hand on his arm. She shook her head.

"He comes and goes," she said. "There's nothing we can do about it, though I assume Hitchens' people have him under surveillance. It probably does them no good. I'm sure the places Fraction goes are all virtual."

Gennady watched the cyranoid vanish into the mouth of the metro station. He'd also disappeared from *Rivet Couture*. Unhappily, Gennady said, "Let's disappear ourselves for a while. I'd like to check on my reindeer."

"You may," said Miranda coolly, "but I am staying here. I am looking for my son, Mr. Malianov. This is not just a game to me."

"Neither were the reindeer."

As it turned out, he didn't have to leave RC to surf for today's headlines. There was indeed plenty of news about a crackpot terrorist ring being busted, but nothing about the individual agents who'd done the field work. This was fine by Gennady, who'd been briefly famous after stopping an attempt to blow up the Chernobyl sarcophagus some years before. He'd taken that assignment in the first place because in the abandoned streets of Pripyat he could be utterly alone. Being interviewed for TV and then recognized on the street had been intensely painful for him.

They shopped for some appropriately steampunk styles for Gennady to wear. He hated shopping with a passion and was self-conscious with the result, but Miranda seemed to like it. They met a few more denizens of Atlantis through the afternoon, but he still hung back, and at dinner she asked him whether he'd ever done any role-playing.

Gennady barked a laugh. "I do it all the time." He rattled off half a dozen of the more popular online worlds. He had multiple avatars in each and in one of them he'd been cultivating his character for over a decade. Miranda was puzzled at his awkwardness, so finally Gennady explained that those games allowed him to stay at home and let a virtual avatar do the roving. He had many different bodies, and played as both genders. But an avatar-to-avatar conversation was nothing like a face-to-face conversation in reality—even an alternate reality like *Rivet Couture*'s.

"Nowadays they call it social phobia," he said with reluctance. "But really, I'm just shy."

Miranda's response was a surprised, "Oh." There was a long silence after that, while she thought and he squirmed in his seat. "Would you be more comfortable doubling up?" she asked at last.

"What do you mean?"

"Riding me cyranoid-wise, the way that Fraction rides Danail. Except," she added wryly, "it would only be during game interactions."

"I'm fine," he said irritably. "I'll get into it, you'll see. It's just . . . I expected to be home in my own apartment right now, I wasn't expecting a new job away from home with an indefinite duration and no idea where I'll be going. I'm not even sure how to investigate; what am I investigating? Who? None of this is normal to me; it's going to take a bit of an adjustment."

He resented that she thought of him as some kind of social cripple who had to be accommodated. He had a job to do and, better than almost anybody, he knew what was at stake.

For the vast majority of people, "plutonium" was just a word, no more real than the word "vampire." Few had held it; few had seen its effects. Gennady knew it—its color, its heft, and the uses you could put it to.

Gennady wasn't going to let his own frailties keep him from finding the stuff, because the mere fact that somebody wanted it was a catastrophe. If he didn't find the plutonium, Gennady would spend his days waiting, expecting every morning to turn on the news and hear about which city—and how many millions of lives—had finally met it.

That night he lay in bed for hours, mind restless, trying to relate the terms of this stylish game to the very hard-nosed smuggling operation he had to crack.

Rivet Couture functioned a bit like a secret society, he decided. That first interaction, when he'd carried a pretend diplomatic pouch between two other players, suggested a physical mechanism for the transfer of the plutonium. When he'd talked to Hitchens about it after supper, the Interpol agent had confirmed it: "We're pretty sure that organized crime has started using games like yours to move stuff. Drugs, for instance. You can use two completely unrelated strangers as mules for pickups and hand-offs, even establish long chains of them. Each hop can be a few kilometers, by foot even, avoiding all our detection gear. One player can throw a package over his country's border and another find it by its GPS coordinates later. It's a nightmare."

Yet *Rivet Couture* was itself just a gateway, a milestone on the way to "far Cilenia." Between *Rivet Couture* and Cilenia was the place from where Miranda's son had sent most of his emails: Oversatch, he'd called it.

If *Rivet Couture* was like a secret society operating within normal culture, then Oversatch was like a second-order secret society, one that existed only within the culture of *Rivet Couture*. A conspiracy inside a conspiracy.

Hitchens had admitted that he hated Alternate Reality Games. "They destroy all the security structures we've put in place so carefully since 9/11. Just destroy 'em. It's 'cause you're not you anymore—hell, you can have multiple people playing one character in these games, handing them off to one another in shifts. Geography doesn't matter, identity is a joke . . . everybody on the planet is like Fraction. How can you find a conspiracy in *that*?"

Gennady explained this insight to Miranda the next morning, and she nodded soberly.

"You're half right," she said.

"Only half?"

"There's so much more going on here," she said. "If you're game for the game, today, maybe we can see some of it."

He was. Dressed as he was, Gennady could hide inside the interface his glasses gave him. He'd decided to use these factors as a wall between him and the other avatars. He'd

pretend out in the open, as he so often did from the safety of
his room. Anyway, he'd try.

And they did well that day. Miranda had been playing the
game for some weeks, with a fanatical single-mindedness
borne of her need to find her son. Gennady found that if he
thought in terms of striking up conversations with strangers
on the street, then he'd be paralyzed and couldn't play; but if
he pretended it was his character, Sir Arthur Tole, who was
doing the talking, then his years of gaming experience
quickly took over. Between the two of them, he and Miranda quickly developed a network of contacts and responsibilities. They saw Fraction every day or two, and what was
interesting was that Gennady found himself quickly falling
into the same pattern with the cyranoid that he had with
Lane Hitchens: they would meet, Gennady would give a report, and the other would nod in satisfaction.

Hitchens' people had caught Fraction carrying one of the
plutonium pieces. That was almost everything that Gennady
knew about the cyranoid, and nearly all that Hitchens claimed
to know as well. "There's one thing we have figured out,"
Hitchens had added when Gennady pressed. "It's his accent.
Danail Gavrilov doesn't speak English, he's Bulgarian. But
he's parroting English perfectly, right down to the accent.
And it's an *American* accent. Specifically, west coast. Washington State or thereabouts."

"Well, that's something to go on," said Gennady.

"Yes," Hitchens said unhappily. "But not much."

Gennady knew what Hitchens had hired him to do and he
was working at it. But increasingly, he wondered whether in
some way he didn't understand, he had also been hired by
Fraction—or maybe the whole of the IAEA had? The thought
was disturbing, but he didn't voice it to Hitchens. It seemed
too crazy to talk about.

The insight Miranda was promising didn't come that first
day, or the next. It took nearly a week of hard work before
Puddleglum Phudthucker met them for afternoon tea and
gave a handwritten note to Miranda. "This is today's location

of the *Griffin Rampant*," he said. "The food is excellent, and the conversation particularly . . . profitable."

When Puddleglum disappeared around the corner, Miranda hoisted the note and yelled in triumph. Gennady watched her, bemused.

"I'm so good," she told him. "Hitchens' boys never got near this place."

"What is it?" He thought of bomb-maker's warehouses, drug ops, maybe, but she said, "It's a restaurant.

"Oh, but it's an *Atlantean* restaurant," she added when she saw the look on his face. "The food comes from Atlantis. It's cooked there. Only Atlanteans eat it. Sociologically, this is a big break." She explained that any human society had membership costs, and the currency was *commitment*. To demonstrate commitment to some religions, for instance, people had to undergo ordeals, or renounce all their worldly goods, or leave their families. They had to live according to strict rules—and the stricter the rules and the more of them there were, the more stable the society.

"That's crazy," said Gennady. "You mean the *less* freedom people have, the happier they are?"

Miranda shrugged. "You trade some sources of happiness that you value less for one big one that you value more. Anyway, the point is, leveling up in a game like *Rivet Couture* represents commitment. We've leveled up to the point where the *Griffin* is open to us."

He squinted at her. "And that is important because . . . ?"

"Because Fraction told me that the *Griffin* is a gateway to Oversatch."

They retired to the hotel to change. Formal clothing was required for a visit to the *Griffin*, and so for the first time Gennady found himself donning the complete *Rivet Couture* regalia. It was pure steampunk. Miranda had bought him a tight pinstriped suit whose black silk vest had a subtle dragon pattern sewn into it. He wore two belts, an ordinary one and a leather utility belt that hung down over one hip and had numerous loops and pouches on it. She'd found a bowler hat and had ordered him to slick back his hair when he wore it.

When he emerged, hugely self-conscious, he found Miranda waiting in what appeared to be a cast-iron corset and long black skirt. Heavy black boots peeked out from under the skirt. She twirled an antique-looking parasol and grinned at him. "Every inch the Russian gentleman," she said.

"Ukrainian," he reminded her; and they set off for the *Griffin Rampant*.

Gennady's glasses had tuned themselves to filter out all characteristic frequencies of electric light. His earbuds likewise eliminated the growl and jangle of normal city noises, replacing them with Atlantean equivalents. He and Miranda sauntered through a city transformed, and there seemed no hurry tonight as the gentle amber glow of the streetlights, distant nicker of horses and pervasive sound of crickets were quite relaxing.

They turned a corner and found themselves outside the *Griffin*, which was an outdoor cafe that filled a side street. Lifting his glasses for a second, Gennady saw that the place was actually an alley between two glass-and-steel skyscrapers, but in *Rivet Couture* the buildings were shadowy stone monstrosities festooned with gargoyles, and there were plenty of virtual trees to hide the sky. In ordinary reality, the cafe was hidden from the street by tall fabric screens; in the game, these were stone walls and there was an ornately carved griffin over the entrance.

Paper lanterns lit the tables; a dapper waiter with a sly expression led Gennady and Miranda to a table, where—to the surprise of neither—Fraction was lounging. The cyranoid was drinking mineral water, swirling it in his glass in imitation of the couple at the next table.

"Welcome to Atlantis," said Fraction as Gennady unfolded his napkin. Gennady nodded; he did feel transported somehow, as though this really was some parallel world and not a downtown alley.

The waiter came by and recited the evening's specials. He left menus, and when Gennady opened his he discovered

that the prices were all in the game's pretend currency, Atlantean deynars.

He leaned over to Miranda. "The game's free," he murmured,
"so who pays for all this?"

Fraction had overheard, and barked a laugh. "I said,
welcome to Atlantis. We have our own economy, just like
Sweden."

Gennady shook his head. He'd been studying the game,
and knew that there was no exchange that translated deynars
into any real-world currency. "I mean who pays for the meat,
the vegetables—the wine?"

"It's all Atlantean," said Fraction. "If you want to earn
some real social capital here, I can introduce you to some of
the people who raise it."

Miranda shook her head. "We want to get to the next
level. To Oversatch," she said. "You know that. Why haven't
you taken us straight there?"

Fraction shrugged. "Tried that with Hitchens' men. They
weren't able to get there."

"Oversatch is like an ARG inside *Rivet Couture*," Gennady guessed. "So you have to know the rules and people
and settings of RC before you can play the meta-game."

"That's part of it," admitted Fraction. "But *Rivet Couture*
is just an overlay—a map drawn on a map. Oversatch is a
whole new map."

"I don't understand."

"I'll show you." The waiter came by and they ordered.
Then Fraction stood up. "Come. There's a little store at the
back of the restaurant."

Gennady followed him. Behind a screen of plants were several market-stall type tables, piled with various merchan-
dise. There was a lot of clothing in Atlantean styles, which
all appeared to be handmade. There were also various trinkets, such as fob watches and earrings similar to Miranda's.
"Ah, here," said Fraction, drawing Gennady to a table at the
very back.

He held up a pair of round, antique-looking glasses. "Try
them on." Gennady did, and as his eyes adjusted he saw

the familiar glow of an augmented reality interface boot-
ing up.

"These are—"

"Like the ones you were wearing," nodded Fraction, "but
with some additions. They're made entirely in 3-D printers
and by hand, by and for the people of Oversatch and some of
their Atlantean friends. The data link piggybacks on ordinary internet protocols: that's called *tunneling*."

Fraction bought two pair of the glasses from the smiling
elderly woman behind the counter, and they returned to the
table. Miranda was chatting with some of the other Atlanteans. When she returned, Fraction handed her one pair of
glasses. Wordlessly, she put them on.

Dinner was uneventful, though a few of *Rivet Couture*'s
players stopped by to network. Everybody was here for the
atmosphere and good food, of course, but also to build connections that could advance their characters' fortunes in the
game.

When they were finished, Fraction dropped some virtual
money on the table, and as the waiter came by he said, "My
compliments to the chef."

"Why thank you." The waiter bowed.

"The lady here was highly impressed, and she and her
companion would like to know more about how their meal
came about." Fraction turned his lapel inside out, revealing
an tiny, ornate pin carved in a gear pattern. The waiter's eyes
widened.

"Of course, sir, of course. Come this way." He led them
past the stalls at the back of the restaurant, to where the
kitchen staff were laboring over some ordinary-looking, portable camp stoves. Several cars and unadorned white panel
vans were parked in the alley behind them. The vans' back
doors were rolled up revealing stacks of plastic skids, all
piled with food.

The waiter conferred with a man who was unloading one
of the vans. He grunted. "Help me out, then," he said to
Gennady. As Gennady slid a tray of buns out of the back of
the van, the man said, "We grow our own produce. They're
all fancy with their names nowadays, they call them *vertical*

farms. Back when I got started, they were called grow-ops and they all produced marijuana. Ha!" He punched Gennady on the shoulder. "It took organized crime to fund an agricultural revolution. They perfect the art of the grow-op, we use what they learn to grow tomatoes, green beans and pretty much anything else you can imagine."

Gennady hoisted another skid. "So you—what?—have houses around the city where you grow stuff?"

The man shrugged. "A couple of basements. Mostly we grow it in the open, on public boulevards, in parks, roofs, ledges of high-rise buildings . . . there's hectares of unused space in any city. Might as well do something with it."

When they were done unloading the skids, Gennady saw Fraction waving to them from one of the other vans. He and Miranda walked over to find that this vehicle didn't contain food; rather, the back was packed with equipment. "What's all this?" Miranda asked.

Gennady whistled. "It's a factory." They were looking at an industrial-strength 3-D printer, one sophisticated enough to create electronic components as well as screws, wires, and any shape that could be fed into it as a 3-D image file. There was also a 3-D scanner with laser, terahertz and x-ray scanning heads; Gennady had used similar units to look for isotopes in smuggled contraband. It could digitize almost anything, from Miranda's jewelery to consumer electronic devices, and the printer could print out an almost perfect copy from the digital file. From a scan alone the printer could only copy electrical devices at about the level of a toaster, but with the addition of open-source integrated circuit plans it could duplicate anything from cell phones to wireless routers—and, clearly, working pairs of augmented reality glasses.

Fraction beamed at the unit. "This baby can even reproduce itself, by building its own components. The whole design is open source."

Miranda was obviously puzzled. "*Rivet Couture* has no need for something like this," she said.

Fraction nodded. "But Oversatch—now that's another matter entirely." He sauntered back in the direction of the restaurant and they followed, frowning.

"Did you know," Fraction said suddenly, "that when Roman provinces wanted to rebel, the first thing they did was print their own money?" Gennady raised an eyebrow; after a moment Fraction grinned and went on. "Oversatch has its own money, but more importantly it has its own agriculture and its own industries. *Rivet Couture* is one of its trading partners, of course—it makes clothes and trinkets for the game players, who supply expensive feedstock for the printers and labor for the farms. For the players, it's all part of the adventure."

Miranda shook her head. "But I still don't understand why. Why does Oversatch exist in the first place? Are you saying it's a rebellion of some kind?"

They left the restaurant and began to make their way back to the hotel. Fraction was silent for a long while. Normally he affected one pose or another, jamming his hands in his pockets or swinging his arms as he walked. His walk just now was robotically stiff, and it came to Gennady that Danail Gavrilov's rider was missing at the moment, or at least, wasn't paying attention to his driving.

After a few minutes the cyranoid's head came up again and he said, "Imagine if there was only one language. You'd think only in it, and so you'd think that the names for things were the only possible names for them. You'd think there was only one way to organize the world—only one kind of 'it.' Or . . . take a city." He swept his arm in a broad gesture to encompass the cool evening, the patterns of lit windows on the black building facades. "In the Internet, we have these huge, dynamic webs of relationships that are always shifting. Meta-corporations are formed and dissolved in a day; people become stars overnight and fade away in a week. But within all that chaos, there's whirlpools and eddies where stability forms. These are called *attractors*. They're nodes of power, but our language doesn't have a word to point to them. We need a new word, a new kind of 'that' or 'it.'

"If you shot a time-lapse movie of a whole city at, say, a

year-per-second, you'd see it evolving the same way. A city is a whirlpool of relationships but it changes so slowly that we humans have no control over how its currents and eddies funnel us through it.

"And if a city is like this, how much more so a country? A civilization? Cities and countries are frozen sets of relationships, as if the connection maps in a social networking site were drawn in steel and stone. These maps look so huge and immovable from our point of view that they channel our lives; we're carried along by them like motes in a hurricane. But they don't have to be that way."

Gennady was a bit lost, but Miranda was nodding. "Internet nations break down traditional barriers," she said. "You can live in Outer Mongolia but your nearest net-neighbor might live in Los Angeles. The old geographic constraints don't apply anymore."

"Just like Cascadia is its own city," said Fraction, "even though it's supposedly Seattle, Portland and Vancouver, and they supposedly exist in two countries."

"Okay," said Gennady irritably, "so Oversatch is another online nation. So why?"

Fraction pointed above the skyline. In reality, there was only black sky there; but in *Rivet Couture*, the vast upthrusting spires of a cathedral split the clouds. "The existing online nations copy the slowness of the real world," he said. "They create new maps, true, but those maps are as static as the old ones. That cathedral's been there since the game began. Nobody's going to move it, that would violate the rules of the alternate world.

"The buildings and avenues of Oversatch are built and move second by second. They're not a new, hand-drawn map of the world. They're a dynamically updated map of the internet. They reflect the way the world really is, moment-by-moment. They leave these," he slapped the side of the skyscraper they were passing, "in the dust."

They had arrived at the mouth of another alleyway, this one dark in all worlds. Fraction stopped. "So we come to it," he said. "Hitchens and his boys couldn't get past this point. They got lost in the maze. I know you're ready," he said to

Miranda. "You have been for quite a while. As to you, Gennady . . ." He rubbed his chin, another creepy affectation that had nothing of Danail Gavrilov in it. "All I can tell you is, you have to enter Oversatch together. One of you alone cannot do it."

He stood aside, like a sideshow barker waving a group of yokels into a tent. "This way, then, to Oversatch," he said.

There was nothing but darkness down the alley. Gennady and Miranda glanced at one another. Then, not exactly hand in hand but close beside one another, they stepped forward.

Gennady lay with his eyes closed, feeling the slow rise and fall of the ship around him. Distant engine noise rumbled through the decking, a sound so constant that he rarely noticed it now. He wasn't sleeping, but trying, with some desperation, to remind himself of where he was—and what he was supposed to be doing.

It had taken him quite a while to figure out that only six weeks had passed since he'd taken the Interpol contract. All his normal reference points were gone, even the usual ticking of his financial clocks which normally drove him from paycheck to paycheck, bill to bill. He hadn't thought about money at all in weeks, because here in Oversatch, he didn't need it.

Here in Oversatch . . . Even the "here" part of things was getting hard to pin down. That should have been clear from the first night, when he and Miranda walked down a blacked-out alleyway and gradually began to make out a faint, virtual road leading on. They could both see the road so they followed it. Fraction had remained behind, so they talked about him as they walked. And then, when the road finally emerged into Stockholm's lit streets, Gennady had found that Miranda was not beside him. Or rather, *virtually* she was, but not physically. The path they had followed had really been two paths, leading in separate directions.

When he realized what had happened Gennady whirled, meaning to retrace his steps, but it was too late. The virtual pathway was a pale translucent blue stripe on the sidewalk ahead of him—but it vanished to the rear.

"We have to keep going forward," Miranda had said. "*I* have to, for my son."

All Gennady had to do was take off the glasses and he would be back in normal reality, so why did he feel so afraid, suddenly? "Your son," he said with some resentment. "You only bring him up at times like this, you know. You never talk about him as if you were his mother."

She was silent for a long time, then finally said, "I don't know him very well. It's terrible, but . . . he was raised by his father. Gennady, I've tried to have a relationship with him. It's mostly been by email. But that doesn't mean I don't care for him . . ."

"All right," he said with a sigh. "I'm sorry. So what do we do? Keep walking, I suppose."

They did, and after half an hour Gennady found himself in an area of old warehouses and run-down, walled houses. The blue line led up to the door of a stout, windowless brick building, and then just stopped.

"Gennady," said Miranda, "my line just ended at a brick wall."

Gennady pulled on the handle but the metal door didn't budge. Above the handle was a number pad, but there was no doorbell button. He pounded on the door, but nobody answered.

"What do you see?" he asked her. "Anything?" They both cast about for some clue and after a while, reluctantly, she said, "Well, there is some graffiti . . ."

"What kind?" He felt foolish and exposed standing here.

"Numbers," she said. "Sprayed on the wall."

"Tell them to me," he said. She relayed the numbers, and he punched them into the keypad on the door.

There was a *click*, and the door to Oversatch opened.

When the door opened a new path had appeared for Miranda. She took it, and it had been over a week before he again met her face to face. In that time they both met dozens of Oversatch's citizens—from a former high school teacher to a whole crew of stubbled and profane fishermen, to disenchanted computer programmers and university drop-outs—

and had toured the farms and factories of a parallel reality as far removed from *Rivet Couture* as that ARG had been from Stockholm.

The citizens of Oversatch had opted out. They hadn't just left their putative nationalities behind, as Miranda Veen had when she married a mechanical engineer from Cascadia. Her husband had built wind farms along the city's ridges and mountaintops, helping wean the city off any reliance it had once had on the national grid. Miranda worked at one of the vertical farms at the edge of the city. A single block-wide skyscraper given over to intense hydroponic production could feed 50,000 people, and Cascadia had dozens of the vast towers. Cascadia had opted out of any dependence on the North American economy, and Miranda had opted out of American citizenship. All very logical, in its own way— but nothing compared to Oversatch.

Where before Gennady and Miranda had couriered packages to and fro for the grand dukes of *Rivet Couture,* now they played far more intricate games of international finance for nations and with currencies that had no existence in the "real" world. Oversatch had its own economy, its own organizations and internal rules; but the world they operated in was an ephemeral place, where nodes of importance could appear overnight. Organizations, companies, cities and nations: Oversatch called these things "attractors." The complex network of human activities tended to relax back into them, but at any given moment, the elastic action of seven billion people acting semi-independently deformed many of the network's nodes all out of recognition. At the end of a day IBM might exist as a single corporate entity, but during the day, its global boundaries blurred; the same was true for nearly every other political and economic actor.

The difference between Oversatch and everybody else was, everybody else's map of the world showed only the attractors. Oversatch used the instantaneous map, provided by internet work analysis, that showed what the actual actors in the world were at this very moment. They called this map "it 2.0." Gennady got used to reviewing a list of new nations in the morning, all given unique and memorable names like

"Donald-duckia" and "Brilbinty." As the morning rolled on Oversatch players stepped in to move massive quantities of money and resources between these temporary actors. As the day ended in one part of the world it began somewhere else, so the process never really ended, but locally, the temporary deformation of the network would subside at some point. Great Britain would reappear. So would Google, and the EU.

"It *is* like a game of *Diplomacy*," Miranda commented one day, "but one where the map itself is always changing."

When they weren't focused outward, Gennady and Miranda scanned objects and printed them from Oversatch's 3-D printers; or they tended rooftop gardens or drove vans containing produce from location to secret location. Everything they needed for basic survival was produced outside of the formal economy and took no resources from it. Even the electricity that ran the vans came from rooftop windmills built from Oversatch printers, which were themselves printed by other printers. Oversatch mined landfill sites and refined their metals and rare earths itself; it had its own microwave dishes on rooftops to beam its own data internally, not using the official data networks at all. These autonomous systems extended far past Stockholm—were, in fact, worldwide.

After a week or so it proved easier and cheaper to check out of the hotel and live in Oversatch's apartments, which, like everything else about the polity, were located in odd and unexpected places. Gennady and Miranda moved to Gothenburg on the West coast, and were given palatial accommodation in a set of renovated shipping containers down by the docks—very cozy, fully powered and heated, with satellite uplinks and sixty-inch TVs (all made by Oversatch, of course).

One bright morning Gennady sauntered up to the cafe where Hitchens had asked to meet him, and tried to describe his new life to the Interpol man.

Hitchens was thrilled. "This is fantastic, Gennady, just fantastic." He began talking about doing raids, about catching the whole network red-handed and shutting the damned thing down.

Gennady blinked at him owlishly. "Perhaps I am not yet

awake," he said in the thickest Slavic accent he could manage, "but seems to me these people do nothing wrong, yes?"

Hitchens sputtered, so Gennady curbed his sarcasm and gently explained that Oversatch's citizens weren't doing anything that was illegal by Swedish law—that, in fact, they scrupulously adhered to the letter of local law everywhere. It was national and regional economics that they had left behind, and with it, consumer society itself. When they needed to pay for a service in the so-called "real world," they had plenty of money to do it with—from investments, real estate, and a thousand other legitimate ventures. It was just that they depended on none of these things for their survival. They paid off the traditional economy only so that it would leave them alone.

"Besides," he added, "Oversatch is even more distributed than your average multinational corporation. Miranda and I usually work as a pair, but we're geographically separated . . . and most of their operations are like that. There's really no 'place' to raid."

"If they just want to be left alone," asked Hitchens smugly, "why do they need the plutonium?"

Gennady shrugged. "I've seen no evidence that Oversatch is behind the smuggling. They don't seal the packages they send—I snoop so I know—and I've been carrying my Geiger counter everywhere. Whoever is moving the plutonium is probably using *Rivet Couture*. They *do* seal their packages."

Hitchens drummed his fingers on the yellow tablecloth. "Then what the hell is Fraction playing at?"

The implication that this idea might not have been preying on Hitchens' mind all along—as it had been on Gennady's—made Gennady profoundly uneasy. What kind of people was he working for if they hadn't mistrusted their captured double agent from the start?

He said to Hitchens, "I just don't think Oversatch is the ultimate destination Fraction had in mind. Remember, he said he came from some place called 'far Cilenia.' I think he's trying to get us there."

Hitchens ran his fingers through his hair. "I don't understand why he can't just *tell us* where it is."

"Because it's not a place," said Gennady, a bit impatiently. "It's a protocol."

He spent some time trying to explain this to Hitchens, and as he walked back to the docks, Gennady realized that he himself *got it*. He really did understand Oversatch, and a few weeks ago he wouldn't have. At the same time, the stultified and mindless exchanges of the so-called "real world" seemed more and more surreal to him. Why did people still show up at the same workplace every day, when the amount of friction needed to market their skills had dropped effectively to zero? Most people's abilities could be allocated with perfect efficiency now, but they got locked into contracts and "jobs"—relationships that, like Fraction's physical cities and nations, were relics of a barbaric past.

He was nearly at the Oversatch settlement in the port when his glasses chimed. *Phone call from Lane Hitchens*, said a little sign in his heads-up display. Gennady put a finger to his ear and said, "Yes?"

"Gennady, it's Lane. New development. We've traced some plutonium packets through *Rivet Couture* and we think they've all been brought together for a big shipment overseas."

Gennady stopped walking. "That doesn't make any sense. The whole point of splitting them up was to slip them past the sensors at the airports and docks. If the strategy was working, why risk it all now?"

"Maybe they're on to us and they're trying to move it to its final destination before we catch them," said Hitchens. "We know where the plutonium is now—it's sitting on a container ship called the *Akira* about a kilometer from your bizarre little village. I don't think that's a coincidence, do you?"

So this was what people meant when they said "reality came crashing back," thought Gennady. "No," he said, "it's unlikely. So now what? A raid?"

"No, we want to find the buyers and they're on the other end of the pipeline. It'll be enough if we can track the container. The *Akira* is bound for Vancouver; the Canadian Mounties will be watching to see who picks it up when it arrives."

"Do they still have jurisdiction there?" Gennady asked. "Vancouver's part of Cascadia, remember?"

"Don't be ridiculous, Gennady. Anyway, it seems we won't need to go chasing this 'far Cilenia' thing anymore. You can come back in and we'll put you on the office team until the investigation closes. It's good money, and they're a great bunch of guys."

"Thanks." *Euros,* he mused. He supposed he could do something with those.

Hitchens rang off. Gennady could have turned around at that moment and simply left the port lands. He could have thrown away the augmented reality glasses and collected his fee from the Interpol. Instead he kept walking.

As he reached the maze of stacked shipping containers, he told himself that he just wanted to tell Miranda the news in person. Then they could leave Oversatch together. Except . . . she wouldn't be leaving, he realized. She was still after her estranged son, who had spoken to her mostly through emails and now wasn't speaking at all.

If Gennady abandoned her now, he would be putting a hole in Oversatch's buddy system. Would Miranda even be able to stay in Oversatch without her partner? He wasn't sure.

He opened the big door to a particular shipping container—one that looked exactly like all its neighbors but was nothing like them—and walked through the dry, well-lighted corridor inside it, then out the door that had been cut in the far end. This put him in one of a number of halls and stairways that were dug into the immense square block of containers. He passed a couple of his co-workers and waved hello, went up one flight of portable carbon-fiber steps and entered the long sitting room (actually another shipping container) that he shared with Miranda.

Fraction was sitting in one of the leather armchairs, chatting with Miranda who leaned on the bar counter at the back. Both greeted Gennady warmly as he walked in.

"How are you doing, Gennady?" Fraction asked. "Is Oversatch agreeing with you?"

Gennady had to smile at his wording. "Well enough," he said.

"Are you ready to take it to the next level?"

Warily, Gennady moved to stand behind the long room's other armchair. "What do you mean?"

Fraction leaned forward eagerly. "A door to Cilenia is about to open," he said. "We have the opportunity to go through it, but we'll have to leave tonight."

"We?" Gennady frowned at him. "Didn't you tell us that you were from Cilenia?"

"*From,* yes," said the cyranoid. "But not *in*. I want to get back there for my own reasons. Miranda needs to find her son; you need to find your plutonium. Everybody wins here."

Gennady decided not to say that he had already found the plutonium. "What does it involve?"

"Nothing," said Fraction, steepling his fingers and looking over them at Gennady. "Just be in your room at two o'clock. And make sure the door is closed."

After that cryptic instruction, Fraction said a few more pleasantries and then left. Miranda had come to sit down, and Gennady only realized that he was still standing, holding tightly to the back of the chair, when she said, "Are you all right?"

"They found the plutonium," he blurted.

Her eyes widened; then she looked down. "So I guess you'll be leaving, then."

He made himself sit down across from her. "I don't know," he said. "I don't . . . want to leave you alone to face whatever Cilenia is."

"My white knight," she said with a laugh, but he could tell she was pleased.

"Well, it's not just that." He twined his hands together, debating with himself how to say it. "This is the first time I've ever been involved with a . . . project that . . . *made* something. My whole career, I've been cleaning up after the messes left by the previous generation. Chernobyl, Hanford—all the big and little accidents. The rest of it, you know, consumer culture and TV and movies and games . . . I just had no time for them. Well, except the games. But I never bought *stuff,* you know? And our whole culture is about *stuff.* But I was never a radical environmentalist, a, what-do-you-call it? Treehugger. Not a back-to-the-lander, because there's no safe land to go back to, if we don't clean up the mess. So I've lived in limbo for many years, and never knew it."

Now he looked her in the eye. "There's more going on with Oversatch than just a complicated game of tax evasion, isn't there? The people who're doing this, they're saying that there really can be more than one world, in the same place, at the same time. That you can walk out of the twenty-first century without having to become a farmer or mountain man. And they're building that parallel world."

"It's the first," she admitted, "but obviously not the last. Cilenia must be like Oversatch, only even more self-contained. A world within a world." She shook her head. "At first I didn't know why Jake would have gone there. But he was always like you—not really committed to this world, but unwilling to take any of the easy alternatives. I could never see him joining a cult, that was the point."

Gennady glanced around. "Is this a cult?" he asked. But she shook her head.

"They've never asked us to believe in anything," she said. "They've just unlocked doors for us, one after another. And now they've unlocked another one." She grinned. "Aren't you just the tiniest bit curious about what's on the other side?"

He didn't answer her, but at two o'clock he was waiting in his room with the door closed. He'd tried reading a book and listening to music, but the time dragged and in the end he just waited, feeling less and less sure of all of this every second.

When something huge landed with a crash on the shipping container, Gennady jumped to his feet and ran to the door—but it was already too late. With a nauseating swaying motion, his room was lofted into the air with him in it and, just as he was getting his sea legs on the moving surface, the unseen crane deposited his container somewhere else, with a solid thump.

His door was locked from the outside. By the time it was opened, hours later, he had resigned himself to starving or running out of air in here, for by that time the container ship *Akira* was well under way.

So he lay with his eyes closed, feeling the slow rise and fall of the ship around him. Behind his own eyelids was an attractor that he needed to subside into, at least for a while.

Eventually there was an insistent chirp from beside his bed. Gennady reached for the glasses without thinking, then hesitated. Mumbling a faint curse, he put them on.

Oversatch sprang up all around: a vast, intricate glowing city visible through the walls of the shipping container. Today's map of the world was all crowded over in the direction of China; he'd find out why later. For now, he damped down the flood of detail and when it was just a faint radiance and a murmur, he rose and left his room.

His was one of many modified shipping containers stacked aboard the *Akira*. In Oversatch terms, the containers were called *packets*. Most packets had doors that were invisible from outside, so that when they were stacked next to one another you could walk between them without going on deck. Gennady's packet was part of a row of ten such containers. Above and below were more levels, reachable through more doors in the ceilings and floors of some containers.

The packets would all be unloaded at their destination along with the legitimate containers. But in a rare venture into illegal operations, Oversatch had hacked the global container routing system. Officially, Oversatch's shipping containers didn't even exist. Off-loaded from one ship, they would sooner or later end up on another and be routed somewhere else, just like the information packets in an internet. They bounced eternally through the system, never reaching a destination, but constantly meeting up and merging to form temporary complexes like this one, then dissolving to recombine in new forms somewhere else. Together they formed Oversatch's capital city—a city in perpetual motion, constantly reconfiguring itself, and at any one time nearly all of it in international waters.

The shipping container where the plutonium was stowed wasn't part of this complex. You couldn't get there from here;

in fact, you couldn't get there at all. Gennady had skulked on deck his first night on board, and found the contraband container way up near the top of a stack. It was a good thirty feet above him and it took him ten minutes to climb precariously up to it. His heart was pounding when he got there. In the dark, with the slow sway of the ship and the unpredictable breeze, what if he fell? He'd inspected the thing's door, but it was sealed. The containers around it all had simple inspection seals on them: they were empty.

He hadn't tried to climb up to it again, but he kept an eye on it.

Now he passed lounges, diners, chemical toilets and work areas as he negotiated the maze of Oversatch containers. Some Swedes on their way to a holiday in Canada waved and shouted his name; they were clearly a few drinks into their day, and he just grinned and kept going. Many of the other people he passed were sitting silently in comfortable lounge chairs. They were working, and he didn't disturb them.

He found his usual workstation, but Miranda's, which was next to his, was empty. Another woman sat nearby, sipping a beer and having an animated conversation with the blank wall.

Somewhere, maybe on the far side of the world, somebody else was waving their hands, and speaking this woman's words. She was *riding* and that distant person was her cyranoid.

Yesterday Miranda and Gennady had visited a bus station in Chicago. Both were riding cyranoids, but Miranda was so much better at it than Gennady. His upper body was bathed with infrared laser light, allowing the system to read his posture, gestures, even fine finger motions, and transmit them to the person on the other end. For Gennady, the experience was just like moving an avatar in a game world. The physical skills needed to interpret the system's commands lay with the cyranoid, so in that sense, Gennady had it easy.

But he had to meet new people on an hour-by-hour basis, and even though he was hiding thousands of miles away from that point of contact, each new encounter made his stomach knot up.

At the bus depot he and Miranda had done what countless pimps, church recruiters and sexual predators had done for generations: they looked for any solitary young people who might exit the buses. There was a particular set to the shoulders, an expression he was learning to read: it was the fear of being alone in the big city.

The cyranoids he and Miranda rode were very respectable-looking people. Together or separately, they would approach these uncertain youths, and offer them work. Oversatch was recruiting.

The results were amazing. Take one insecure eighteen-year-old with no skills or social connections. Teach him to be a cyranoid. Then dress him in a nice suit and send him into the downtown core of a big city. In one day he could be ridden by a confident and experienced auditor, a private investigator, a savvy salesman and a hospital architecture consultant. He could attend meetings, write up reports, drive from contact to contact and shift identities many times on the way. All he had to do was recite the words that flowed into his ears and follow the instructions of his haptic interface. Each of the professionals who rode him could build their networks and attend to business there and, through other cyranoids, in many different cities in one day. And by simple observation the kid could learn tremendous amounts about the internals of business and government.

Gennady was cultivating his own network of cyranoids to do routine checks at nuclear waste repositories around the world. These young people needed certification, so he and Oversatch were sponsoring them in schools. While they weren't at school Gennady would ride them out to waste sites where they acted as representatives for a legitimate consulting company he had set up under his own name. His name had a certain cachet in these circles, so the six young men and three women had a foot in the door already. Since he was riding them they displayed uncanny skill at finding problems at the sites. All were rapidly blossoming.

He sat down under the invisible laser bath and prepared to call up his students. At that moment the ship gave a slight lurch—a tiny motion, but the engineer in Gennady instantly calculated the quantity of energy that must have gone through the vessel. It was a lot.

Now he noticed that the room was swaying slowly. The *Akira* rarely did that because not only was it huge to begin with, it also had stabilizing gyroscopes. "Did you feel that?" he said to the woman next to him.

She glanced over, touching the pause button on her rig, and said, "What?"

"Never mind." He called up the hack that fed the ship's vital statistics to Oversatch. They were in the Chukchi Sea, with Russia to starboard and Alaska to port. Gennady had been asleep when the *Akira* crossed the north pole, but apparently there hadn't been much to see, since the open Arctic Ocean had been fogbound. Now, though, a vicious storm was piling out of the East Siberian Sea. The video feed showed bruised, roiling skies and a sea of giant, white-crowned pyramidal waves. Amazing he hadn't felt it before. Chatter on the ship's comm was cautious but bored, because such storms were apparently as regular as clockwork in the new ice-free arctic shipping lanes. This one was right on schedule, but the ship intended to just bull its way through it.

Gennady made a mental note to go topside and see the tempest for himself. But just as he was settling back in his seat, the door flew open and Miranda ran in.

She reached to grab his hands, stopped, and said, "Are you riding?"

"No, I—" She hauled him to his feet.

"I saw him! Gennady, I saw Jake!"

The deck slowly tilted, then righted itself as Gennady and Miranda put their hands to the wall. "Your son? You saw him here?"

She shook her head. "No, not here. And I didn't exactly see him. I mean, oh, come on, sit down and I'll tell you all about it."

They sat well away from the riding woman. The shipping container was very narrow so their knees almost touched. Miranda leaned forward, clasping her hands and beaming. "It was in Sao Paolo. You know Oversatch has been sponsoring me to attend conferences, so I was riding a local cyranoid at an international symposium on vanishing rain forest cultures. We were off in an English breakaway session with about ten other people, some of whom I knew—but of course I was pretending to be a postdoc from Brasilia, or rather my cyranoid was—you know what I mean. Anyway, they didn't know me. But there was one young guy . . . Every time he talked I got the strangest feeling. Something about the words he chose, the rhythm, even the gestures . . . and he was noticing me, too.

"About half an hour in he caught my eye, and then leaned forward quite deliberately to write something on the pad of paper he was using. It was so low-tech; a lot of us had noticed he was using it but nobody'd said anything. But at the end of the session when everybody was standing up, he caught my eye again, and then he balled up the paper and threw it in a trash can on the way out. I lost him in the between-session crowd, so I went back and retrieved the paper."

"What did it say?"

To his surprise, she took off her glasses and set them down. After a moment, Gennady did the same. Miranda handed him her notebook, which he hadn't seen since the first day they met.

"I've been keeping notes in this," she whispered, "outside the glasses. Just in case what we do or say is being tracked. Anyway, I had to snapshot the paper through my cyranoid, but as soon as I could I downloaded the image and deleted the original out of my glasses. This is what was on the paper."

Gennady looked. It said:

Cilenia, 64° 58' N, 168° 58' W.

Below this was a little scrawled stick figure with one hand raised. "That," said Miranda, pointing at it. "Jake used to draw those as a kid. I'd recognize it anywhere."

"Jake was riding cyranoid on the man in your session?" Gennady sat back, thinking. "Let me check something." He put his glasses on and polled the ship's network again. "Those numbers," he said, "if they're longitude and latitude, then that's almost exactly where we are now."

She frowned, and said, "But how could that be? Was he

saying Cilenia is some sort of underwater city? That's impossible."

Gennady stood up suddenly. "I think he's saying something else. Come on." The unpredictable sway of the ship had gotten larger. He and Miranda staggered from wall to wall like drunkards as they left the room and entered one of the lengthwise corridors that transected the row of packets. They passed other workers doing the same, and the Swedes had given up their partying and were all sitting silently, looking slightly green.

"I've been checking on the, uh, other cargo," said Gennady as they passed someone, "every day. If it's bound for Vancouver there'll be a whole platoon of Mounties waiting for it. That had me wondering if they wouldn't try to unload it en route."

"Makes sense," called Miranda. She was starting to fall behind, and a distant rushing and booming sound was rising.

"Actually, it didn't. It's sealed and near the top of a stack—that's where they transport the empties. But it's not *at* the top, so even if you did a James Bond and flew over with a sky-crane helicopter, you couldn't just pluck it off the stack."

They came to some stairs and he went up. Miranda puffed behind him. "Couldn't they have a trick door?" she said. "Like in ours? Maybe it's actually got inside access to another set of packets, just like ours but separate."

"Yeah, I thought about that," he said grimly. He headed up another flight, which dead-ended in an empty shipping container that would have looked perfectly normal if not for the stairwell in the middle of its floor. The only light up here was from a pair of LEDs on the wall, so Gennady put his hands out to move cautiously forward. He could hear the storm now, a shuddering roar that felt like it was coming from all sides.

"One problem with that theory," he said as he found the inside latch to the rejigged container door. "There's a reason why they put the empty containers on the *top* of the stack." He pushed down on the latch.

"Gennady, I've got a call," said Miranda. "It's *you*! What—" The bellow of the storm drowned whatever else she might have said.

The rain was falling sideways from charcoal-black clouds that seemed to be skipping off the ocean's surface like thrown stones. There was nothing to see except blackness, whipping rain and slick metal decks lit intermittently by lightning flashes. One such flash revealed a hill of water heaving itself up next to the ship. Seconds later the entire ship pitched as the wave hit and Gennady nearly fell.

He hopped to the catwalk next to the door. They were high above the floor of the hold here, just at the level where the container stack poked above deck. It kept going a good forty feet more overhead. When Gennady glanced up he saw the black silhouette of the stack's top swaying in a very unsettling manner.

He couldn't see very well and could hear nothing at all over the storm. Gennady pulled out his glasses and put them on, then accessed the ship's security cameras.

He couldn't make out himself, but one camera on the superstructure showed him the whole field of container stacks. The corners of a couple of those stacks looked a bit ragged, like they'd been shaved.

He returned the glasses to his shirt pocket, but paused to insert the earbuds.

"Gennady, are you online?" It was Miranda's voice.

"Here," he said. "Like I said, there's a reason they put the empties at the top. Apparently something like fifteen thousand shipping containers are lost overboard every year, mostly in storms like this. But most of them are empties."

"But this one isn't," she said. He was moving along the deck now, holding tight to a railing next to the swaying container stack. Looking back, he saw her following doggedly, but still twenty or more feet back.

Lightning day-lit the scene for a moment, and Gennady thought he saw someone where nobody in their right mind should be. "Did you *see* that?" He waited for her to catch up and helped her along. Both of them were drenched and the water was incredibly cold.

Her glasses were beaded with water. Why didn't she just take them off? Her mouth moved and he heard "See what?" through his earbuds, but not through the air.

He tried to pitch his voice more conversationally—his yelling was probably unnecessary and annoying. "Somebody on top of one of the stacks."

"Let me guess: it's the stack with the plutonium."

He nodded and they kept going. They were nearly to the stack when the ship listed particularly far and suddenly he saw bright orange flashes overhead. He didn't hear the bangs because suddenly lightning was dancing around one of the ship's masts, and the thunder was instantaneous and deafening. But the deck was leaning way over, dark churning water meters to his left and suddenly the top three layers of the container stack gave way and slid into the water.

They went in a single slab, except for a few stragglers that tumbled like matchboxes and took out the railing and a chunk of decking not ten meters from where Gennady and Miranda huddled.

"Go back!" He pushed her in the direction of the superstructure, but she shook her head and held on to the railing. Gennady cursed and turned as the ship rolled upright then continued to list in the opposite direction.

One container was pivoting on the gunwale, tearing the steel like cloth and throwing sparks. As the ship heeled starboard it tilted to port and went over. There were no more and the other stacks seemed stable. Gennady suspected they would normally have weathered a heavier storm than this.

He rounded the stack and stepped onto the catwalk that ran between it and the next. As lightning flickered again he saw that there was somebody there. A crewman?

"Gennady, how nice to see you," said Fraction. He was wearing a yellow hard hat and a climbing harness over his crew's overalls. His glasses were as beaded with rain as Miranda's.

"It's a bit dangerous out here right now," Fraction said as he stepped closer. "I don't really care, but then I'm riding, aren't I?" As blue light slid over the scene Gennady saw the black backpack slung over Fraction's shoulder.

"You're not from Cilenia, are you?" said Gennady. "You work for somebody else."

"Gennady! He's with sanotica," said Miranda. "You can't trust him."

"Cilenia wants that plutonium," said Fraction. "For their new generators, that's all. It's perfectly benign, but you know nations like ours aren't considered legitimate by the attractors. We could never *buy* the stuff."

Gennady nodded. "The containers were rigged to go overboard. The storm made handy cover, but I'd bet there was enough explosives up there to put them over even if the weather was calm. It would have been automatic. You didn't need to be here for it."

Fraction shifted the pack on his back. "So?"

"You climbed up and opened the container," said Gennady. "The plutonium's right here." He pointed at the backpack. "Ergo, you're not working for Cilenia."

Miranda put a hand on his shoulder. She was nodding. "He was after the rest of it himself, all along," she shouted. "He used us to track it down, so he could take it for sanotica."

Danail Gavrilov's face was empty of expression, his eyes covered in blank, rain-dewed lenses. "Why would I wait until now to take it?" Fraction said.

"Because you figured the container was being watched. I'm betting you've got some plan to put the plutonium overboard yourself, with a different transponder than the one Cilenia had on their shipping container. . . . Which I'm betting was rigged to float twenty feet below the surface and wait for pickup."

Fraction threw the bundle of rope he'd been holding, then stepped forward and reached for Gennady.

Gennady sidestepped, then reached out and plucked the glasses from Danail Gavrilov's face.

The cyranoid staggered to a stop, giving Gennady enough time to reach up and pluck the earbuds from his ears.

Under sudden lightning, Gennady saw Gavrilov's eyes for the first time. They were small and dark, and darted this way and that in sudden confusion. The cyranoid said something that sounded like a question—in Bulgarian. Then he put his hands to his ears and roared in sudden panic.

Gennady lunged, intending to grab Gavrilov's hand, but

instead got a handful of the backpack's tough material. Gavrilov spun around, skidded on the deck as the backpack came loose—and then went over the rail.

He heard Miranda's shout echoing his own. They both rushed to the railing but could see nothing but black water topped by white streamers of foam.

"He's gone," said Miranda with a sudden, odd calm.

"We've got to try!" shouted Gennady. He ran for the nearest phone, which was housed in a waterproof kiosk halfway down the catwalk. He was almost there when Miranda tackled him. They rolled right to the edge of the catwalk and Gennady almost lost the backpack.

"What are you doing?" he roared at her. "He's a human being, for God's sake."

"We'll never find him," she said, still in that oddly calm tone of voice. Then she sat back. "Gennady, I'm sorry," she said. "I shouldn't have done that. No, shut up, Jake. It was wrong. We should try to rescue the poor man."

She cocked her head, then said, "He's afraid Oversatch will be caught."

"Your son's been riding you!" Gennady shook his head. "How long?"

"Just now. He called as we were coming outside."

"Let me go," said Gennady. "I'll tell them we stowed away below decks. I'm a Goddamned Interpol investigator! We'll be fine." He staggered to the phone.

It took a few seconds to ring through to the surprised crew, but after talking briefly to them Gennady hung up, shaking his head. "Not sure they believe me enough to come about," he said. "They're on their way down to arrest us, though."

The rain was streaming down his face, but he was glad to be seeing it without the Oversatch interface filtering its reality. "Miranda? Can I talk to Jake for a second?"

"What? Sure." She was hugging herself and shaking violently from the cold. Gennady realized his own teeth were chattering.

He had little time before reality reached out to hijack all his choices. He hefted the backpack, thinking about Hitchens' reaction when he told him the story—and wondering how much of Oversatch he could avoid talking about in the deposition.

"Jake," he said, "what is Cilenia?"

Miranda smiled, but it was Jake who said, "Cilenia's not an 'it' like you're used to, not a 'thing' in the traditional sense. It's not really a place either. It's just . . . some people realized that we needed a new language to describe the way the world actually works nowadays. When all identities are fluid, how can you get away with using the old words to describe anything?

"You know how cities and countries and corporations are like stable whirlpools in a flood of changes? They're *attractors*—states the network relaxes back into, but at any given moment they might not really be there. Well, what if human beings were like that too? Imagine a driver working for a courier company. He follows his route, he talks to customers and delivers packages, but another driver would do exactly the same thing in his place. While he's on the job, he's not *him*, he's the company. He only relaxes back into his own identity when he goes home and takes off the uniform.

"*It 2.0* gives us a way to point at those temporary identities. It's a tool that lets us bring the *temporarily real* into focus, even while the outlines of the things we *thought* were real—like countries and companies—are blurred. If there could be an *it 2.0* for countries and companies, don't you suppose there could be one for people, too?"

"Cilenia?" said Gennady. Miranda nodded, but Gennady shook his head. It wasn't that he couldn't imagine it; the problem was he *could*. Jake was saying that people weren't even people all the time, that they played roles through much of the day representing powers and forces they often weren't even aware of. A person could be multiple places at once, the way that Gennady was himself and his avatars, his investments and emails and website, and the cyranoids he rode. He'd been moving that way his whole adult life, he realized, his identity becoming smeared out across the world. In the past few weeks the process had accelerated. For someone like Jake, born and raised in a world of shifting identities, *it*

2.0 and Cilenia must make perfect sense. They might even seem mundane.

Maybe Cilenia was the new "it." But Gennady was too old and set in his ways to speak that language.

"And sanotica?" he asked. "What's that?"

"Imagine Oversatch," said Jake, "but with no moral constraints on it. Imagine that instead of looking for spontaneous remappings in the healthy network of human relationships, you had an *'it 3.0'* that looked for disasters—points and moments when rules break down and there's chaos and anarchy. Imagine an army of cyranoids stepping in at moments like that, to take advantage of misery and human pain. It would be very efficient, wouldn't it? As efficient, maybe, as Oversatch."

"That," said Jake as shouting crewmen came running along the gunwales, "is sanotica. An efficient parasite that feeds on catastrophe. And millions of people work for it without knowing."

Gennady held up the backpack. "It would have taken this and . . . made a bomb?"

"Maybe. And how do *you* know, Mister Malianov, that you don't work for sanotica yourself? How can I be sure that plutonium won't be used for some terrible cause? It should go to Cilenia."

Gennady hesitated. He heard Miranda Veen asking him to do this; and after everything he'd seen, he knew now that in his world power and control could be shifted invisibly and totally moment by moment by entities like Oversatch and Cilenia. Maybe Fraction really had hired Hitchens' people, and Gennady himself. And maybe they could do it again, and he wouldn't even know it.

"Drop the backpack in the bilges," said Jake. "We can send someone from Oversatch to collect it. Mother, you can bring it to Cilenia when you come."

The rain was lessening, and he could see that her cheeks were wet now with tears. "I'll come, Jake. When we get let go, I'll come to you."

Then, as Jake, she said, "Now, Gennady! They're almost here!"

Gennady held onto the backpack. "I'll keep it," he said.

Gennady took the glasses out of his pocket and dropped them over the railing. In doing so he left the city he had only just discovered, but had lately lived in and begun to love. That city—world-spanning, built of light and ideals—was tricked into existing moment-by-moment by the millions who believed in it and simply acted as though it were there. He wished he could be one of them.

Gennady could hear Jake's frustration in Miranda's voice, as she said, "But how can you know that backpack's not going to end up in sanotica?"

"There are more powers on Earth," Gennady shouted over the storm, "than just Cilenia and sanotica. What's in this backpack is one of those powers. But another power is *me*. Maybe my identity's not fixed either and maybe I'm just one man, but at the end of the day I'm bound to follow what's in here, whereever it goes. I can't go with you to Cilenia, or even stay in Oversatch, much as I'd like to. I will go where this plutonium goes, and try to keep it from harming anyone.

"Because some things," he said as the crewmen arrived and surrounded them, "are real in *every* world."

The Hebras and the Demons and the Damned

BRENDA COOPER

Brenda Cooper (www.brenda-cooper.com) *lives in Kirkland, Washington. By day, she is the City of Kirkland's CIO, and at night and in early morning hours, she's a futurist and writer. "I'm interested in how new technologies might change us and our world, particularly for the better," she says on her website. Her fiction has appeared in* Nature, Analog, Asimov's, Strange Horizons, *and in anthologies. She has collaborated with Larry Niven on six short stories and on the novel* Building Harlequin's Moon *(2005). Her own first novel,* The Silver Ship and the Sea, *was published in 2007, and its sequels are* Reading the Wind *(2008) and* Wings of Creation *(2009). Her novel* Mayan December *is out in 2011. Cooper had a strong year for short fiction in 2010 and had several stories in contention for this book.*

"The Hebras and the Demons and the Damned" *was published in* Analog, *which had a particularly good year in 2010, perhaps benefiting from the relative pressure of fantasy stories in other magazines—both* F&SF *and* Asimov's *publish a lot of fantasy these days. The story is an adventure set on the colonized planet Fremont, the setting for her first novel.*

I'm going to ramble a bit. Let me; I'm no roamer speaking over a communal fire. I'm not sure I know which parts of the story you want. But this is part of how Fremont was saved and kind of an alien contact story too.

My name is Chaunce, and I am one of the few left on Fremont who remembers the home we left behind. Deerfly. Stupid name for a planet, if you ask me. But we didn't leave Deerfly over its wreck of a name. Rather, it was too smart for us, everybody there becoming stronger, faster beings, almost becoming computers or robots with flesh, leaving us true humans behind, some of them wearing no more than a thin skin of flesh to fool the eye.

Fremont was too smart for us, too. In the time I'm telling you about, we'd been here seventeen years. Instead of doing what a self-respecting colony does and grows, we kept losing people to tooth and claw and cliff.

Real humans had grown up on colony planets like this, but Deerfly had gone tame generations ago.

We needed help. Needed to find some accord with this place before it killed us. It gnawed at me that I'd done little for the colony except backbreaking work and staying alive. I'd left the leading to others, and Fremont needed more from me than that. Since I managed horse farms back on Deerfly, I looked to the animals.

Now, there are a lot of animals on Fremont, but most wouldn't work for what I needed.

The cats had decided we were dinner the day we landed,

and they were too big to be undecided in any way I could think of. A foot-long scar on my right calf throbbed in the cold of winter—a reminder.

We had a few domestic dogs we'd brought shipboard and more we were planning to birth and raise up. We weren't going to lack for best friends, for herding beasts to keep goats in bunches, or four-footed pranksters to steal the chickens. But dogs are smaller than humans, and smaller than most beings of tooth and claw here. I was glad of them, but on Fremont they needed protecting just like we did. They'd give us warning, but they'd die trying to save us from paw cats or yellow snakes. And given how we mostly loved them, humans sometimes died saving their dogs.

Fremont has its own four-footed and single-tailed beasts with a canine look. They run in packs, and people call them demon dogs. But they should never, ever be confused for real dogs. These demons have no soul, and they exist to eat. Worse, I've seen them hunt, and I'm sure they are communicating with each other more than any of our native animals from Deerfly, or the ones our fathers brought from Earth. Demons don't speak, but they work like a team with radios. They make humans mildly sick to eat too. So they're not even good for food.

I had high hopes for the djuri: four-footed prey that run in packs, fleeing for their lives from the demon dogs. It turned out the djuri were too shy to help. Hard to find, always running and hiding and bleating. Not too bright, either, and not big enough to really help us. Humans can look down on them, or maybe look a big one straight in the eye. Well, all right. A few are even bigger than that. The bucks. But still, they're not hefty creatures. Keep in mind that we can look a paw cat in the eye, too, and they outweigh us and have claws long as fingers and hard as knives. The truly good thing about djuri is they are incredibly good to eat.

That's pretty much the rundown on the bigger animals we'd seen here so far, except the hebras. They were our last hope for an answer. I took a while to realize this, even though I sat at the edge of the cliff by the promise of our town, looking down over the grass plains every day for two summers. The grass there is scary big, bigger than a man's head by the end of summer. When it dries, it's sharp like a million razors trying to flay the skin from anything as soft as a human. I still have scars on my fingers from it, and on my shoulders.

As tall as the grass is, the hebras' heads rise above it. They've got legs that come to a man's head. Instead of straight backs like horses, their backs slope up to shoulders, and their necks measure the tiniest bit longer than their backs. Their coats are solid, striped, or covered with great spots like the shadow pattern of leaves on the forest floor. Their colors are all variations of gold and green, brown and black, and sometimes the barest bit of red like a red-haired woman being touched by the sun.

Make no mistake. Hebras are prey animals. Paw cats hunt them all summer, and demons get the weak and the slow and the young. But they are so much more. Remember how I told you about the demon dogs? Perhaps being prey on a planet full of thorns made them smarter than any of the horses I ever rode or trained or showed or loved.

One day, far below me, the demon dogs hunted hebras. I'd given up digging out the smelter's foundation for the day, my muscles screaming sore and my back feeling on fire. I stood at the edge of the cliff looking down, letting the cooling breeze of near-dusk tease sweat from my skin. The sun shone bright enough to wash everything dull and soft, with that little extra bit of gold that the late part of the day brings. The air smelled of seeds and harvest and of the fall that would soon touch us.

Below me a herd of hebras grazed, rotating between watcher and eater, the distance making animals with heads towering above my own look small.

A breeze kissed the tops of the grasses, bending them south in ripples. A few lines of grass moved the wrong way as a pack of seven demons surrounded twice as many hebras. I spotted the dogs' path even before the wily old watch-hebra bugled fear and loathing.

The hebras ran together, almost lockstep, all of them trying for a gap between two of the demons, heading sideways to me, their heads bobbing up and down with their ungainly rocking run.

The dogs raced to make a line in front of the hebras, cutting them off. They began to bay, a high long-winded howl that instilled fear in me even though I stood so far above them the sound was faint and thin.

The hebras turned, all together, a wave of long necks and thin tails.

The dogs flowed behind them.

The tallest hebra let out a short high-pitched squeal, and the hebras twitched and broke into three lines, 180-degree turns, as if they practiced every day. Maybe they did. They had it down, stretching out long, taking turns teasing the dogs. The gap between grazer and hunter widened.

A dog nipped at the last animal in one line, a brown blur flashing momentarily up above the high grass and then falling back down. The target hebra twisted, probably kicking even though I couldn't see its legs for the grass, and then put on a burst of speed. It passed two other hebras, and a different animal became last, running right in front of the slavering dogs.

I'd been in the grass the week before. It pulled and cloyed and knotted and tripped. But the hebras and the demons slid through it, streams of living beings, barking and baying and bugling.

The air had cooled down a little, but I stood with goose bumps rising on my forearms, transfixed, and afraid that if I moved I'd somehow change the outcome of the race down below.

It was nearly too dark to see by the time the first of the dogs stopped, the grass swallowing the hunter as it became still. I lost the place it stood entirely in the space of two breaths.

As the stars and two of our moons brightened in the black sky above me, I realized the hebras had won fairly easily. They were off grazing somewhere else, and the dogs would have a hungry night.

If it had been fourteen unarmed humans against seven demons, I'd have bet on the dogs.

* * *

Our roving scientists brought back a lot of djuri bones, jaws, and the thick back legs cracked open by teeth. But not many hebra bones. Some. They did die. But not very fast, or very easy.

So I swore I'd figure out how to tame them. Not that we'd gotten within two hundred meters by then. The great beasts were shy of us, and fast.

I couldn't catch one myself. I was almost sixty already, and slowing. I took my story to the town council, which was led by Jove Alma at the time, a nervous man with a deep focus on making and keeping plans. He thought the tighter he gripped our choices in his and the council's fists, the more of us would live. Some believed him, some hated him, but everyone obeyed. The previous leader had been a risk-taker, and cost almost all of us people we loved. That's the long way round of saying that catching animals wasn't in Jove's plan, and the council turned me down flat. There was a city being built and the chill of winter already clinging to every dawn.

The winter was the second harshest we'd ever had, with snow in town instead of just in the hills and two sheet-ice storms. We lost ten more people. Two froze to death on a trip out into the woods to bring back samples of winter plants, leaving behind two orphans to add to our growing stockpile. The third one who went with them lost three fingers and part of her sanity. Cats ate two adults and a babe, fire claimed a family of four, and one of the men my age hanged himself in the middle of town. We had two less births than deaths that season.

All that long cold I thought of the hebras. Sometimes I glimpsed them down below on the cold grass plains. Fire had flamed the grass flat and low and the hebras sometimes loped like shadows at the edge of the plain near the sea, clearly visible when frost turned the stubble white and hoary in the early dawn. But mostly they hid in the Lace Forest that surrounded us.

Come spring, we stopped huddling together in the buildings we'd made for guild halls and finished up some of the houses. I built mine at the edge of town, as close to the cliff as the town council would let me. Mornings, as dawn split the sky open, I sat and watched the fading moons and the greening grass below. The hebras returned, sleeping on the plain, two watch beasts circling the sleepers restlessly, heads way up. I was pretty sure they traded off watches just like we did, and for the same reason. It made me feel kindred.

One morning when the grass was knee-high to a human and the first spindly-legged baby hebras clung to their dams, Jove came and stood silently beside me, looking down at the plains. His gaze was unfocused, as if he saw the whole thing and the sea beyond, but not the hebras right below, "Three of the orphans got in trouble last night. Fought each other and one's fetched up in the infirmary with a broken leg."

He'd hate that. Jove hated all disorder. I waited him out, curious what he'd say next.

"Council met, and we figure you got room for two boys."

Shock gave way to liking the idea pretty fast. I'd never married, never had kids, just managed farms and hired help. But there was no help to hire here. My ancestors had farmed Deerfly by making babies, back in the days before there were too many bots and androids to count and people didn't have any work to do that looked like farming except training exotics. So I didn't stand and blink stupidly at Jove for long, but instead I just said, "Thank you."

He looked surprised at that, like he'd been expecting resistance, so it was his turn to pause for a beat too long and then say, "Thank you," himself. He smiled before he walked away, the sun fully risen now, shoving his shadow behind him as he walked back to town.

The boys were Derk and Sho. Derk was thin and wiry, and won the boys informal footraces. Sho plodded and had so much patience I couldn't imagine what had made him part of the fight at all until one day I came across two other boys teasing him in high, mean voices for being stupid. They were wrong, I already knew that. But sometimes being the silent type means people make their own decisions about who you are.

Sho and Derk had school and then work every day, but since they were only twelve, they had energy to spare in spite of the harsh schedules. It only took a few days before they stood beside me at the cliff's edge, looking down at the herd.

Sho started drawing hebras in the dirt with sticks, and they both started naming them.

As the days got longer, we gave up sleep to pick our way down the steep path between Artistos and the wide road on the plains where we'd trucked tools and technology from the shuttles at our makeshift spaceport.

The boy with the broken leg, Niko, recovered enough to follow us down the path and soon all three of them laughed together, their raised voices surely spreading all across the plain. Soon half the teens and a few of the old singles from town began to join us at the crack of dawn.

Some of the watchers wanted to catch a hebra, some to stun one. Those weren't the right answers. I knew it deep in my gut, found it hard to say why I knew so hard, so I just told them, "If we scare them off, they might never come back." I never let them get close to the herds, just to watch them. The boys helped me—all three of them now living with me, and acting like herd dogs to the new people.

The trail from town to plain lay nearly naked against the cliff, a thin ribbon of dirt with no place big enough for predators to hide. We could stand safely or sit on small rocks and talk. The hebras knew we were there, sometimes lifting their heads and pointing their broad, bearded faces at us. I wanted them to know we weren't their enemy. We kept it up all summer, the crowd straining against my calls for patience. Sho stood beside me, facing them, telling them off with his eyes and his stance, and they listened. Derk and Niko stood quietly at the rear, watching everyone and all the hebras, eyes darting from one to one to one, keeping count and order.

Some of the boys were fascinated with the hebras' beards, maybe because they had the first hint of stubble on their own chins. They started drawing pictures of the girls in town with beards and longish necks, and giggling.

The grass stretched its fairy-duster seedpods toward the autumn sky, tall as me if I stood inside it. Demons started hunting more, sometimes running the hebras twice a day. The herd lost one old hebra and one very young one that twisted a leg. The pack lost one old dog and two pups. So in a way, the hebras were winning. Except, of course, that one hebra fed all the dogs and dead dogs didn't feed the hebras anything.

The cats stayed away. I suspect our scent and presence did that. They were just as quick to hunt us as they would the hebra, but they liked us in small groups. There were about twenty humans on the path most mornings.

Once a week or so Jove came and watched, always walking away before the bells rang for breakfast. I knew that he was thinking, but it did no good to push Jove, and thus no good to push the town council. But if the plains burned below us, we'd have to wait another year to capture even one hebra.

One morning after Jove ghosted away from us, Sho asked, "Is he scared of catching one?"

"Hard work to run a colony. He has to choose."

"He should see how much we and the hebras need each other."

I suspected the boy had the right of it, but it does no good to downtalk leaders. "Jove is a busy man."

"Can you ask him for some rope?"

"What are you going to do with rope?"

"Catch a hebra."

"Probably not. You think about how to do that, and we'll try your idea if I can get rope. Rope is dear." We had what we'd brought, and some we'd made. But none of our home-made rope was strong enough for this.

"Please ask."

The persistence of boys. "If an opening comes up."

About noon that same day, Jove came by to watch us raise the roof on the smelter. The metal slabs had come all the way from Deerfly and been brought in pieces from Traveler in one of the little shuttles a year ago. Jove stood to the side as we used chain to hoist the metal, the chain traveling over a tall wooden post-and-beam structure we'd lashed together just for this job. Even with the leverage, it took three men sweating to get the last and largest section up and held while three more of us fastened it with nails also brought from the ship.

At the end, Jove came and stood silently beside me. "Good job, Chaunce. Now we can make our own nails."

"That's what we did all this work for? Nails?"

"And hinges. And maybe bits for those animals down below." He nodded at the roof. "One of your beasts might have pulled that easier."

It wasn't a use I had thought of—I'd been thinking of riding them. I felt doubtful they'd be pullers. But if they were—we could make wagons and flatbeds and farm tools. The thought was good. "Can I have some rope?"

"You might get hurt. Or die. The boys might die."

"We've gotta find accord with some of the wild things here. We can't fear them all forever." But then, he'd lost a wife to a pack of demons, found her in pieces three days after we landed. Years had passed, but some memories burn your soul.

He toed the ground for a while.

I could get enough of the council to override him if I really tried. But he was a good leader, and I'd learned that if you undermine a good leader you can be rewarded with a worse one.

He swallowed and looked off at some distant spot in the sky before he said, "Let's go get it."

I had plenty of time to think, lurching home in the darkening night with three hundred feet of rope coiled over my right shoulder. I understood Jove's issue: Time breathed down on us. We were failing, dying by bits each year as we missed goals, became food for the local predators, fought amongst each other, and tried ever so hard to learn the dangers and opportunities here. We needed more stout, warm buildings, to retrieve the rest of our supplies from Traveler before the shuttles ran out of fuel, to build better perimeters, and to breed more children than Fremont took from us. Taking the three boys out on the plains represented a hefty risk of our future. Better to risk boys than girls, but still . . .

When I dropped my load of rope on the ground outside the house, the three of them tumbled out right away, faces full of excitement. They'd been planning. Sho came up to me and said, "We can't get that over their heads. We can't get it around their legs or we might break them."

I considered. I'd been thinking of horses. But we were not cowboys. I'd never tried to catch a wild animal in my life. Ran from a few here. The animals on my farms had been born in warm stables and grown up unafraid of me. This was a puzzle. "We can't cut the rope too short or we'll never be able to use it for anything else."

So we made walls on two sides, using the cliff as the third.

We lost a whole day hiking to the Lace Forest and finding four big logs, dragging them back, and posting them upright into the ground. About the time we finished that, the work crews had broken for the day. They helped us string and tie the rope walls, the lowest rope at hebra-knee height, which was about our waists, and the highest something I could barely touch with my hands.

When we finished, the dark brown rope stood out against the pale green grasses of late autumn. The corral did not look like it would work for much of anything. Besides, I wasn't at all sure how we were going to get them anywhere near it.

Now we had to do what Jove was afraid of. We had to walk through the tall grass and get the hebras to walk away from us and into the makeshift corral. Maybe we shouldn't have done this—maybe we should have tried to get close without rope. Maybe we should have tried to find them in the winter woods. At any rate, it no longer mattered what we should have done. The shadow of night was knifing across the plains, and it was time to beat it up the cliff and bed down.

I slept fine, but before first light all three boys came to my room. Derk, the biggest, rested his arms on Niko's and Sho's shoulders. "Sho was dreaming of hebras, and when he came to wake me up, I was dreaming about them too."

Sho nodded. "We dreamed they got caught in the walls we made and the dogs got them, rising up over their back legs and standing on their backs." He stopped, his eyes wide. He might cry if I let him keep worrying, and then he'd lose face, and maybe be the next one to end up with a broken leg.

"And biting their necks," Niko added, not helping.

"Did you dream too?" I asked Niko.

He shook his head. "No. But I'm worried about the hebras."

"Well, I'm glad you care. That should make it easier to catch them."

"Really?" Sho asked.

"Yes," I assured them all. Might as well believe in success. It couldn't hurt.

"Can we sit in here with you?" Niko asked.

So I let them stay. In ten minutes they had fallen asleep all over the bed like a litter of puppies, and I got up to watch for the light and pack us all a good lunch. The apple trees had come in well this fall, and Jove's new wife, Maria, made excellent goat's-milk cheese. We'd be set if we added a bit of fresh bread from the communal kitchen. Even though the morning shadows were still black ghosts, the first loaves should already be out. I shrugged into my coat and opened the door.

I nearly jumped as a shadow moved nearby. Jove. Wordlessly, he held out three loaves of bread.

"I don't need that many."

"Yes, you do. I gave everyone on your shift the day off."

I raised my eyebrows and spoke more boldly than I ever had to him. "Big risk for you."

Although I really only still had moonlight to see by, I swear his cheeks reddened. "I had trouble sleeping. I kept doing math in my head. Doing just what we're doing, if we keep dying so fast, there won't be anything left of us in two hundred years." He looked directly at me for the first time in a few days. "I remember what you said when you brought your ideas to us. Last year. We have to risk."

I could barely imagine what that cost him. People followed

him because they were afraid. Like him. And now he was being brave. This would change us, and only success would change us for the better. The stakes had just risen.

Together, Jove and I made up sandwiches for thirty people. My shiftmates started gathering outside, stamping against the morning cold, dressed in layers against the heat that would follow by midday. They chattered amongst themselves, a few nervous, a few excited. Laughter broke out over and over.

The boys didn't want anything more than excitement for breakfast, but I got them each to take a bread heel down in their coat pockets against the hunger that would threaten them as soon as we stopped and waited. At first I worried that Jove would try to take over, although in truth, neither he nor I knew much of anything about hunting hebras.

He didn't take charge. He stood to the side, curious and watchful and very silent. People looked to him at first, and then when he looked to me, they did too. A relief and a worry.

We handed out stunners to all of the adults, two to the good shots. Half of our total stock, a firepower that scared even me. The stunners quieted everyone a bit. One shot would stop a human, two a demon, three a paw cat.

The hebra herd watched us come down, and of course, we watched them.

I expected them to think it was like any other morning, since we always came down at dawn to watch. But they scattered before we were even halfway down. Maybe because we started later than usual. Maybe just something in the way we walked, like we had a purpose instead of a simple curiosity.

Jove spoke what I was thinking. "Maybe they don't want us any more than the rest of this cursed planet wants us."

There were twenty-five of us total. I broke us into groups, and sent four groups of five off. I thought about keeping Jove with us, but since I was keeping all three boys I decided I needed a shooter I could count on, and so I sent Jove off with the group that I figured would be safest. So that's how me, the three boys, and my second in command from the smelter project, Campbell, all went over to stand downwind of the rope corral.

The boys ate their bread. Campbell and I watched, keeping companionable silence. The boys fidgeted. Campbell and I made them stretch in the grass, crawling and parting the fronds, reminding them to close their eyes and mouths as they moved through it, like swimmers. We sent them one by one up onto a small pile of rocks to look around the plain and see if they spotted the hebras (or anything else). They got bored and hungry and finished their bread heels and drank half the whole day's water supply. Derk got bit by something nasty and flying and a welt came up on his arm. He didn't complain, though. Good kid. It warmed and we stripped off our outer layer of coats.

The first group came in, including Jove. He shook his head at me. "Nothing."

The second and third groups found each other and came in together, then the fourth. No one reported seeing anything bigger than a jumping-prickle or a long-tailed rat. We made a long string of humans and sandwiches at the base of the cliff, still downwind from the ropes. We rested on warm rocks. The three boys abandoned me and Jove. I figured they'd be watched well enough between so many of us. Besides, they too had seen cats bring down a baby hebra this spring. Surely they'd be cautious.

"Did you see anything interesting out there?" I asked Jove. "Grass."

Well, true enough. His right cheek showed a set of thin lines where he'd seen the grass too closely, and one had been deep enough that it was slightly crusted with blood.

"You should clean up before that starts itching." I dug an antiseptic cloth out of my bag, adding a bit of water from my canteen to bring it to life. Some plants here were the antidotes to other plants, and we had a whole team of botanists doing nothing more than cataloging everything we learned. This was one of their gifts. Jove took the cloth, and while he wiped up his cheek and a deeper cut I hadn't noticed on his forearm, I said, "They know we're here. They've been graz-

ing here every day for two years except winters and today—
maybe they're territorial and this is the territory for this
herd. They've been watching us watch them, but they don't
like us all the way down here."

"What next?" he asked.

We still had half of this day. "Let's try again today, send
everyone in one group except me and Campbell and the boys.
Have you all go together along the road so you get farther
away, and then make two teams and go forward. Maybe you
can get far enough out for the hebras to be between you and
me. Just don't spook them. Sometimes they sleep during the
day, but they'll have watchers."

He handed me back the cloth instead of just putting it in
his own pocket.

I took it.

"How do you know what they do during the day? You're
always working."

"I ask around the fire at night. Almost no one sees them
during the day. One theory suggests they go into the woods,
another that they sleep when the big predators sleep. I kinda
like—"

A scream cut my sentence off. One of the boys. "Demons!"

No! They slept during the day. I knew that. Everybody
knew that. Dammit—what did I *know?* I leapt up, dropping
the rest of my lunch, and scrambled to a higher rock behind
me. Our line—stretched out maybe twenty meters—did the
same, people backing up against the cliff.

"To me," I called. The demons would try and surround the
ends first, to isolate a single person or two and then kill them
easily. I tried to recall who was where, couldn't remember.
Lousy leading.

A demon bayed as if answering me, the same call I'd heard
from the cliff, shuddering. It was worse down here, and dif-
fuse, like the wail came from all around, the grass and the
plains themselves hunting us.

I couldn't tell where the demon was.

The boys.

Derk and Niko came running up to me, panting, standing

one at each side of me, looking out. They trembled, but neither cried.

"Where's Sho?" I demanded, voice high and worried.

Another bay, and a yip. People gathered around us.

Derk found his breath. "Up. On the cliff."

Indeed, over the chaos of gathering, drawing stunners, screeching for each other, demons yipping and baying, I heard the high slip of Sho's voice.

I looked up.

He stood three meters above me, his feet dug into the cliff, apparently balanced on a ledge too small for me to see from below. He hung onto a tree growing thin and spindly out of dirt caught between rocks, leaning out. Close to falling. Now that I was looking at him, I could see he was screaming details. "Six of them. To the right."

I looked right. My head was above the grass, but barely. The stones we'd sat on made a small clearing, the grass close enough to throw shadows at our feet.

Sho would see them coming for us, but we wouldn't know until the grass parted in front of our faces.

The demon cries were still a bit away, but confident. Maybe the demons didn't care we were all together.

"One almost there!" Sho cried. "By you, Chaunce."

I raised my stunner, hand shaking. I'd fired at a demon once, missed as it came right at me fast as lightning. Louise had been behind me and she hadn't missed. Now the boys were behind me, small, no stunners.

The dog burst through the grass, long and sinewy, teeth bared, eyes black and full of hunger.

I fired.

Someone else fired.

The dog fell. Its coat rippled as another shot hit it.

"Stop!" I yelled. "Don't waste shots!"

"There!" Sho.

A second dog burst through in almost the same place, its body landing on the other one. This time we used four shots.

Derk pushed past me, knife in hand, bent on killing the stunned animals.

To my right, someone screamed, and in a moment of shock I heard the slick of another stunner and another thump. Who screamed?

A hebra bugled, high and long. The same sound I'd heard a hundred times when this hunt played out below me and I merely watched.

"Back!" Sho screamed. The watch hebra. That's what Sho did for us.

Sho and a real hebra. *What was the hebra doing here?*

I backed.

Derk ducked, his right hand now covered in demon blood.

A head rose over mine, above the grass, the neck long and thin, a white beard like my grandfather's last.

I backed faster.

The hebra passed between me and Derk in its lurching fast run, bigger than I expected, an animal the color of spring grass with gold spots on its knobby knees. It breathed deep and rattling but ran strong. A dog followed it, too fast for me to bring up my stunner.

The woman next to me, Paulette, screamed in joy, clapping.

"Watch!" Sho still sounded scared. "Stay back!"

More hebras, the whole herd of them, and dogs, all running together. The dogs had given up on us. They moved away a bit, the hebras now silent except for deep, sharp breathing, the dogs yipping and baying on their heels.

"Shoot the dogs!" I couldn't tell who yelled, the command a shiver down my spine.

Instinct told me. "No! The hebras can do this."

I stood as still as I could, the grass waving around me, the sounds of animals racing through it and the call and yips of hunter, hunted, and humans all distinct and all around.

A high-pitched squeal touched my heart. A hebra. I heard its body fall, a sound like a sack of flour thrown from the roof of a storage barn. Me and Jove and Campbell raced toward the fallen hebra. A dog passed right in front of me, its tail slapping me sideways. I raised my stunner and hit its flank.

It cried in pain, stopped, stood still, didn't fall.

I hit it again.

It mewled, sounded like a child needing help, like it didn't understand, and then it fell.

Ahead of me, the fallen hebra struggled up, blood dripping down its leg from a slash in its thigh. Shaking. Not broken.

Someone else dropped a dog to my right.

Two other hebras raced past us, screaming.

The few dogs left didn't draw off this time. They circled the beast that had just gotten up. One of its knees bled, too.

There were four demons left. Few enough they should know better. Maybe the smell of blood drove them crazy.

Someone I couldn't see stunned another dog.

A dog somewhere let out a high, sharp bark and in heartbeats the pack was gone. They might have never been there, the grass closed across the memory of their hungry mouths and long, powerful legs.

The injured hebra took a step, and then another. Gingerly.

Two hebras walked through the grass, oblivious to us, and placed themselves on either side of the wounded one. One of the two strongest watch hebras came up to stand between me and the threesome, looking down at me. I stood there, craning my neck up, sweating, my ankle throbbing lightly from a sidestep I'd taken. Its shoulder rose above my eye, its front knee about at my chest. Its fur looked coarser than I'd expected.

I kept my gun down.

Even though its sides heaved, it looked at me as if speaking sentences. They had no language we could understand, but they were at least as smart as the herding dogs. And some days I thought the collies were smarter than me. I knew I was in the presence of something good, even on this hellhole of a planet.

We would never capture such beasts in a rope corral. But they had allied themselves with us in that moment, voted with their thundering feet and high bugle calls. We would come to some kind of accommodation, some way to trade them safety for safety.

These are the things that went through my head as I watched the beast watch me.

The boys came up beside me and still the hebra watched, the plains silent now except for the ever-present buzz of insects. It took a long time before the hebras moved off, stately, visible above the waving dry grass for a long time.

Penumbra

GREGORY BENFORD

Gregory Benford (www.gregorybenford.com) *lives in Irvine, California. He has lately become a CEO of several biotech companies devoted to extending longevity using genetic methods. The first product came on the market in early 2011. He retains his appointment at UC Irvine as a professor emeritus of physics. He is the author of more than twenty novels, including* Jupiter Project, Artifact, Against Infinity, Eater, *and the famous SF classic,* Timescape *(1980). His most recent novel is* The Sunborn *(2005). A two-time winner of the Nebula Award, Benford has also won the John W. Campbell Award, the Australian Ditmar Award, the 1995 Lord Foundation Award for achievement in the sciences, and the 1990 United Nations Medal in Literature. Many of his (typically hard) SF stories are collected in* In Alien Flesh, Matters End, *and* Worlds Vast and Various. *Benford is one of the standard-bearers of hard SF.*

"Penumbra," a hard SF story reminiscent of Larry Niven's "Inconstant Moon," was published in Nature, *now the highest-paying market for short SF, and a breeding ground, in it's Futures section, for surprising and often amusing ideas in short form.*

The cloud of flies lifted off our table and pursued the corpse coming by on a wooden plank. Mary turned to look at the shrivelled woman being carried on the wood, followed by a little crowd of mourners who fruitlessly batted away the flies. "Was she—?"

"Outside? Guess so. Looks like her hair caught fire," I said.

"We were so lucky, taking a nap."

I hoisted my piña colada. "A day later and we'd have been in California." The ice was cool but not at all reassuring. "And maybe dead."

"You're . . . sure?" Mary's eyes jittered. "I know you're an astrophysicist, but really? Is everybody we know . . . ?"

"The flash, I saw it from the window. In the distance—bright blue at first, then so brilliant I couldn't see."

"But not right here."

"Right, that's what doesn't make sense. We got glare, small fires, but not that—" I pointed to the greasy pall building on the offshore horizon, beyond the warm waves. "That's been building for hours."

She blinked. "But there's no land west of here."

"Those dirty brown clouds must've blown in. Big fires farther away."

Mary's eyes danced. Her hands clenched and relaxed, clenched and relaxed.

"But . . . how widespread can this be?"

"Didn't burn us here much, so it's not worldwide. Not a

285

supernova, or we'd see it in the sky." I pointed up. The mottled blue high above was thickening with smoke.

"Then what?"

"I'd say must've been a gamma-ray burster. Why we didn't get it full on, I don't know."

"A . . . burster?"

I peered at the sky, looking for some clue. I was more a theorist, not an observer. "We think it's a narrow beam of intense radiation, coming out when a rotating, high-mass star collapses to form a black hole."

The gamma-ray satellites had seen hundreds at safe cosmological distances, but none in our Galaxy. Maybe this was the first. I went through a quick description of what happened when gamma-rays hit the top of our atmosphere. Particle cascades, ultraviolet flares, blaring hard light, ozone depletion, mesons lacing down.

"How did we survive it, then?"

"Dunno." The flies came buzzing back. I waved them off our steaming chicken mole. "Eat," I said. "Then we go to the market and buy whatever we can."

But there was no market. Crowds had picked the stalls clean.

"We have to live here for a while," I said as we walked back to our hotel. After I'd finished my observing run at the Las Campanas Observatory, Mary had joined me for diving in the Galapagos. Guayaquil was a sightseeing stopover before heading home. We'd seen the cathedral yesterday, echoing and nearly deserted then, but now a huge crowd surrounded it, listening to a priest blaring out his message with a hand-held mike.

Mary struggled with her high-school Spanish. "He says this shows God's favour on them," she reported. "Preservation for them and their families, and liberation from the . . . North Americans. And, uh, Europeans."

"How's he know that?" I looked up at the sky again, learning nothing—but saw an antenna on the church roof.

I pointed. Mary was an electronics tech type and she said immediately: "They have a satellite link. Non-commercial. Private."

It took an hour to talk our way through, first with the priest and then a bishop, no less. But their connection was live and took me to the academic satellite links. The down-look cameras showed blazes everywhere north and south of us. Europe, west Africa—a hemisphere burning. Except in a spot several thousand kilometres wide, an ellipse right at the equator. Where we were.

No link worked to the gamma-ray working group, where a burster signature would show up. But I didn't need one now.

Then the satellite link failed. I didn't try to pursue it. I got up with Mary and walked out into the rosy sunset and acrid air.

Some mestizos by the church, dressed in the sombre black of mourning, turned and looked at us, eyes narrowing. Mary noticed and said: "I wonder if they blame us, somehow."

"Wouldn't surprise me," I said. "We run their Universe, don't we?"

"So they may think, how can something like this possibly be natural? Gringos are the traditional candidates."

"Hasn't happened before, so maybe somebody's to blame."

"Let's get out of here," she said. We strolled away, deliberately casual, but as we approached the hotel, everyone on the cobblestone streets seemed to be looking at us.

"Go up and pack," I said, and went to the travel agent. I was amazed that he was still at his desk. Our tickets to Los Angeles were obviously not going to work, so I tried to re-book to an Asian airport. Any Asian airport. But his connection was dead. The blazing cone of light had come in late morning. That meant it got most of Europe and the Americas, except for that blessed oval where we had been following local custom and taking siesta in the hushed, indoor cool of a thick-walled hotel. Asia had been in darkness.

We stumbled out into the night air and then I saw it. The crescent moon hung there to our west. "Got it," I said.

She saw it too. "You mean . . . ? The gamma-ray burster was just behind our view of the Moon."

"That's why the trees weren't burning here. That woman's hair was like tinder—it caught fire, maybe drove her into some accident. We were in the Moon's penumbra, the twilight zone that caught just some of the burst. Anybody on this side of the planet not shielded by the Moon is dead. Or soon will be."

"So now it goes to Asia," Mary said slowly. "The future."

Somehow I smiled. "At least we have one."

The Good Hand

ROBERT REED

Robert Reed (www.robertreedwriter.com) *lives in Lincoln,
Nebraska. He is perhaps the Poul Anderson—whom James
Blish once called "The continuing explosion, the most prolific writer of high quality in the field"—of his generation. He
is certainly the most prolific SF writer of high-quality short
fiction writing today. He has had stories appear in at least
one of the annual "Year's Best" anthologies in every year
since 1992. He is perhaps most famous for his Marrow universe, and the novels and stories that take place in that huge,
ancient spacefaring environment. A new Marrow book,* Eater
of Bone, *collecting four novellas, is out this year. His story
collections,* The Dragons of Springplace *(1999) and* The
Cukoo's Boys *(2005) skim only some of the cream from his
body of work. He is overdue for another substantial collection. He had another excellent year in 2010 and could easily have had three or four stories in this volume.*

This story was published in Asimov's. *It takes place in an
alternate universe in which the U.S. managed to keep a monopoly on nuclear weapons after WWII, and enforce a Pax
Americana on the world. The U.S. believes that American
global dominance is a price everyone should accept for world
peace. Now an American businessman in France finds himself threatened by people who do not agree. This is a piece of
post-9/11 SF that challenges many political views of the past,
and some of the present. Is the U.S. willing to use nuclear
weapons? Should it be? What kind of world would it be then?*

There was confusion in Booking, my reservation mysteriously lost in the ether. The bloodless beauty behind the counter explained that I could wait for tomorrow's flight out of Chicago, or, "You can sit with the other sheep and pray for no-shows." Her phrasing, not mine. I chose the flock, putting my name in the pool before calling the office to make appropriate warnings. But a lot of travelers were changing plans, what with the recent events. The big DC-Freedom wasn't even two-thirds full, and I was able to snag an aisle seat. Unfortunately a lot of us seemed to be suffering from spring colds and hacking coughs. One tall and very pretty Japanese-American woman caught my eye, but she claimed three seats across the aisle. Apparently those two little boys were hers. "Oh well," I thought, "at least they're behaving themselves." But the toddler began wailing on takeoff, while his older, craftier brother used the distraction to slip free of the seat belt, running amok while we cut through the evening sky.

Even with the coughing and the motherly screaming and the wild boy who kept sprinting past every few moments, I managed to sleep. But then came the realization that one of my neighbors had eaten something vicious or rancid, and now he or she was dying of some brutal intestinal ailment. Whatever the cause, whoever the source, at unpredictable moments the stuffy damp air suddenly filled with the most noxious stink imaginable, and my body and mind would be dragged out of whatever snoozing state it had achieved in the last little while.

Of course I blamed the rad-hunter sitting on my left. There were at least six agents scattered about the cabin, each dressed in the black uniform trimmed with smoky orange lines. A small woman, plain-faced and in no obvious pain, she gave herself away by never acting surprised by the outrage hovering in the air. Of course she could have assumed that I was the culprit, and she was a polite sort of creature. But I have met one or two rad-hunters, and they are not polite people. Their job demands self-centered, disagreeable natures, treating the world with all of the scorn it will endure; and if she wasn't the source of this biohazard, I'm sure at the very least she would have stood and moved somewhere else.

At this point, I will mention that I'm not a political soul.

I was a traveler, an innocent with business on his mind, and this was only my third trip overseas, and I had never seen France. And I would see little of it now, what with the demands of my work and an exceptionally tight schedule.

Landing at De Gaulle brought new difficulties. There didn't seem to be room at the terminal, so our plane was ushered onto a side runway, buses gathering slowly to carry us the final half-mile of our journey. Yet that complication didn't bother me. In my present mood, I would have accepted a parachute and the attendant's boot to my ass, if it meant escaping that coffin. The afternoon air tasted of rain and leaked fuel. I sat patiently on a bus that refused to go anywhere. I watched a pretty mother spank one boy and then his brother. Then just as I wondered if some new problem had arisen, the bus was accelerating, suddenly shooting across the tarmac and then slamming to a stop beside a crowded facility filled with angry passengers and heavily armed guards.

The consuming ugliness of the airport terminal was something of a marvel, what with its naked steel and concrete block construction. Where was the famous French sense of aesthetics? The little rad-hunter and her uniformed colleagues flashed badges and walked straight past the guards, ignoring and perhaps even enjoying the murderous stares. But I was a civilian. And sadly, I was American. To the limits of international law, I was to be shown the consideration usually reserved for dangerous dogs.

A gloved hand accepted my passport, and not one or two customs agents looked at it. The process required three bureaucrats and ten minutes of hard consideration before it was handed back to me. They never spoke in my direction, even in French. Knifing gestures were deemed adequate, and when I didn't jump to their commands, a gloved hand grabbed my arm, yanking me into the presence of a fourth official. "You are the guest of a nation and a great people," he reminded me. "We expect nothing but dignity and respect at all times."

With that, I was sent on my way.

I have no aptitude with languages. Which seems odd, considering that I was always one of the bright children in school. But my employers had taken my limits into account, paying extra for a translator. A young man was at the gate, holding a sign with my name and nothing else written in a neat, officious style.

"I'm Kyle Betters," I announced.

He didn't seem to believe me. Lowering the sign, he scratched at his bare chin, considering who-knew-what factors before replying with a quiet lack of feeling, "Welcome to France, Mr. Betters."

His name was Claude, and for the expected reasons we took an instant but workable dislike for one another. Small talk wasn't part of his job description. But directing me to the luggage carousel was a valid duty, and he did it without prompting, watching with thin amusement as I hung my small bag on the very big suitcase, dragging both behind me as we continued down more ugly hallways and out into a parking garage that stank of gasoline and wet concrete.

Of course his car was tiny, and of course he took offense when I laughed quietly at what looked like a toy.

His laugh came moments later, watching my middle-aged body struggle to lift my luggage into a volume just large enough to accept it.

A pattern was set. In small pointed ways, we worked to embarrass and enrage one another. Claude lit a Turkish cigarette, filling the Renault with a toxic cloud. I cracked my window, and when he mentioned his distaste for cold breezes, I rolled it down farther. The flight left me exhausted yet I was too nervous to sleep. I watched the countryside. I studied the cars and trucks that raced along the highway. Our destination was Nancy, and I asked for a roadmap to better appreciate our journey across a deeply historic landscape. Claude steered me to the glove box. I opened it, finding nothing useful. That was worth a laugh, and as he drove, the hand with the cigarette tapped his head. "I know the way," he promised. "And besides, you won't see anything. It will be night soon."

In another few minutes, yes.

He drove, and I sat, keyed up to where my stomach ached.

Eventually we abandoned the wide four-lane highway, striking out east on a narrow highway in desperate need of repair. Traffic circles announced themselves with warning signs, but Claude seemed of the opinion that driving slowly brought its own risks. After the third or fourth circle, he decided that his passenger was suitably rattled. "It is unfair, you know. What you want of us."

I knew what he meant, and I was smart enough not to rise to the bait.

But he continued regardless. "Nations are free entities," he warned. "We're within our rights to do research in whatever subject we choose. How can a rational man say otherwise?"

"I haven't said anything," I pointed out.

Another cigarette needed to be lit. Exhaling in my direction, he pointed out, "We are not planning to build bombs. Why would we want such horrors?"

"Why would you?" I agreed.

But he heard something in my tone. "Uranium is a natural element. Does the United States claim ownership of a native part of our universe?"

"This isn't my area," I complained.

"Nor mine," he agreed, coaxing the little engine to run at an even higher pitch.

Holding onto my door handle, I pushed my face close to the open window and the fresh roaring air.

"Do you think we are unreasonable?"

Claude wanted me to say, "No, you are reasonable." Or maybe he hoped that like any good American, I would pick a fight. "My government is powerful, and you're going to obey us from now until Doomsday." But I didn't match either expectation. "I don't think about these political problems," I shouted back at him. "Not one way or another. Really, this whole subject doesn't mean a goddamn thing to me."

Claude fumed in the darkness.

I looked outside. By day, this was probably a scenic drive. Massive old trees were whipping past at a furious rate. Something in the moment triggered a memory. Turning back to the driver, I asked, "Do you know why the French plant so many trees along their roads?"

Claude hesitated, and then finally asked, "Why?"

"So the German army can march in the shade."

That did the trick. He wanted nothing more to do with this American, smashing his cigarette before throwing all of his concentration into getting me to my destination, as fast as possible.

My slight experience with intercontinental travel has taught me that jet lag is genuine and it is sneaky. Waking that next morning, I felt rested even though I wasn't. I felt as though my faculties had returned, but no, they were still lost out over the Atlantic somewhere. Little clues pointed to my impairment. I didn't quite recognize my hotel room, even though I was fully conscious when I checked in. The toilet's design baffled me briefly, though I'd used it the night before. A hot shower seemed to help, but the channels on the Sony television seemed to tax my intellect to its limits. There were no American networks, but even the French feed of the CBC was missing. The nearest thing to home cooking was the BBC, and it took three minutes to appreciate just what side our British brothers were taking in the present controversy.

I shut off the television, dressed and went down to the lobby. Claude was supposed to meet me in another hour. Our day's first event was at noon—lunch with representatives for one of the largest retailers in Europe. I was nervous, which was good news. Nervousness gave me energy and a measure of courage. Knowing no French but *merci*, I headed out the front door, out into the Place Stanislas. Bits of fact crept out of my soggy memory. The plaza was two and a half centuries old, bordered by an opera house and museum and the venerable Grand Hotel where I was scheduled to remain for four busy days. I wandered south, and without getting lost or committing any major crimes, I discovered a busy restaurant that served a buffet breakfast perfectly suited to a ravenous appetite.

At some point during the meal, I realized I was being watched. It wasn't just the staff that saw my American credit card, but it was also the local patrons who seemed to recognize a tyrannical monster when they saw one. Nobody was out-and-out rude. But when I glanced at each face, they would stare back at me, showing me what silent, smoldering curiosity looks like.

Returning to my hotel, I found Claude reading *Le Monde*. My arrival was noted, but the current article was more important. He focused on every word and finished his cigarette, and then the paper was folded and the butt stamped out, and while looking at my feet, he quietly told me, "I am sorry."

I was stunned.

"For my words, my tone." He glanced at my face and then looked down again. "It is my fault that we got off so badly."

I agreed. But to be gracious, I said, "I played a hand in it."

He clearly wanted more from me.

"I'm not a traveler," I said. "My flight was awful, and I'm still hurting. I wish I had grace under pressure. But I don't. Never have."

Claude tried to make sense of my rambling confessions. Finally, needing to feel useful, he asked, "Do you wish to tour Nancy for a time? It's going to be a little while before our first event."

It was strange to hear him say, "Our first event." Just words, but the effect was to make me thankful to have an ally in this peculiar corner of the world.

But I'd mentioned being tired, and as if to prove me right,

I was suddenly aware of my own endless fatigue. "I'd rather go upstairs and nap."

He glanced at his watch, a look of relief revealed.

"Perhaps so," he agreed.

"Will you come get me in an hour?"

"I shall, Mr. Betters."

But of course I didn't sleep. I lay awake, painfully aware of the brilliant sunshine pushing around the curtains of my room. This wasn't a natural time for slumber, and I accomplished nothing except feel wearier than before. Then just as I closed my eyes—the moment that I could feel sleep take me—knuckles began to strike my room door.

What I was selling isn't important. In fact, several elements of this story are best left dressed in harmless falsehoods. Imagine several men and one woman sitting at the long table, all of them interested in American refrigerators or computers or interactive toys. What matters is that my wares weren't simple, and Europe represented a huge potential market. One difficulty is that I'm not a salesman by trade. My normal duties are to manage those responsible for designing what I consider to be the best products of their kind in the world. Which was why my enthusiasm couldn't be faked. Despite my various liabilities, I was a good spokesman for my company, offering my audience a long-term relationship full of shared profits and room for mutual growth.

At least two guests spoke English. But everyone paid close attention while Claude turned my boastings into what was beginning to sound like real words, no matter how little of the noise made sense to me.

The man in charge knew English quite well. He was gray-haired and well dressed and probably distinguished on his worse day. With small winks and the occasional smile, he implied that he approved of what he was hearing, both from me and from Claude. In those thirty minutes, I turned from Mr. Betters into, "My friend, Kyle." But just when I felt success was assured, a young fellow at the patriarch's side leaned forward and burst into some long tirade.

Claude listened. Both of us listened. And then the one

who understood turned to the other, saying, "He wants to know why this is fair? The percentages are wrong. He claims that . . ." Claude hesitated for an instant, struggling for the best words. And by "best," I mean that he needed honest words that wouldn't leave me furious. "He believes you are forcing an unfair burden on them."

"How can that be?" I asked Claude.

Claude turned and repeated that in French. But of course everyone could read my body and the tone of my voice.

Touching his headstrong young colleague, the patriarch leaned forward. In perfect English, with a deep, clear voice, he admitted, "These are difficult days, Kyle. The tensions are felt by all of us, you know."

I nodded. "Yes."

"It is sad."

I kept agreeing with him.

Then he told me, "I'm not a political soul."

Which made him just like me.

"Unlike my associates, I remember the liberation of France. I was a boy, yes, but I still remember the Nazis fleeing, and I know that joy felt by every Frenchman when your shabby-dressed soldiers entered Paris." He nodded, eyes staring into the past. "It's a fair statement to point out that no other nation, given your tools and circumstances, would have so gladly fought two wars against such distant enemies. If you wished, you could have fortified your continent, built bombers and missiles, and then littered the world with your nuclear weapons. You could have broken your enemies and their collaborators too and been done with the mess."

And now he wasn't like me. His praise buoyed me, yes. I couldn't help my emotions. But his words and cold logic made me uneasy.

"And I do respect what the United States achieved after the war," he continued. "This has not been an easy task—"

The lone woman interrupted. She was tall and elegantly beautiful, in her middle thirties but with a younger woman's perfect complexion. She knew exactly what her boss had said, and that's why she erupted into a quick rain of hot words and slicing hand gestures.

Expecting her response, the patriarch acted untroubled. When she finished, he spoke to her and the others, perhaps warning his people to behave. (I assume this because Claude translated nothing.) Then while the young people gnashed their teeth and whispered among themselves, the patriarch turned his warm certain gaze back to me. "To maintain your nuclear monopoly . . . well, it is an astonishing achievement. Granted, we have helped you in your cause. We are your allies, after all. No overt threats were necessary for us to open our borders and our military bases to your radiological police, and we have given you much help, particularly with the Soviets and the Indians."

Again, the youngsters grumbled and sneered.

The patriarch paused, weighing me with his eyes. For just a moment, he acted disappointed. Was it my expression or my silence? Either way, he sat back on the hard restaurant chair before saying the same word twice, in French and then in English.

"Peace," he uttered.

I nodded, pretending to understand his implication.

"Peace is a precious thing. And, as I say, almost any other power, given your tools, might have tried to enslave this world."

The woman had had enough. She stood, and with a delicious accent said, "Bullshit. Bullshit to that."

I felt as if I'd been slapped.

"This isn't about uranium," she told her boss. "Maybe at first it was. Maybe when the war was finished and everyone was happy, they were good stewards for the world. But these Americans . . . they do more than keep others from making atomic bombs." She turned to me, her face flushed. "He says you're honorable. I say you're sneaky and subtle and tenacious and bloodless. Like machines, you and your people keep pursuing every advantage, and what happens in the end? We surrender more and more to the United States. Because every new technology is a threat, and you believe you can make our world safe."

At that point, I laughed.

It was a mistake, and I knew it before the sound exploded from me. But a secret pride had been insulted, and sitting back in my chair, I repeated that line that I'd heard since I was a child:

" 'Somebody has to be in charge.' "

There. It was said, and no apology could take back that sentiment.

Claude was first to react. With a tight, furious voice, he said, "What about genetics? By what right should you have a monopoly on DNA?"

"What about biological weapons?" I replied.

My question was translated, and the response was nervous laughter. Only the patriarch and Claude didn't cackle at my paranoid suspicions.

"What do you think?" Claude pressed. "That if you let us toy with microbes and crops, we'd brew up plagues that would kill only Americans?"

Really, I hadn't thought for two minutes about our policy toward bacteria. But hundreds of hours of overheard news commentaries gave me the language to say, "The Soviets tried just that. When I was a boy, in the early sixties, they built that secret lab in the Urals and started to weaponize—"

I hesitated. This was probably the first time in my life that I had said that peculiar word. "Weaponize," I said again. Then I said, "Anthrax and smallpox and Ebola," with the certainty of a clinical biochemist.

"I'm not talking about disease," the woman insisted. "I'm talking about those miracle crops or yours, the biogenetic soybeans and tomatoes and rice. If a field isn't under your control, it's forbidden. If your precious seeds are lost, your spies and satellites track down the thieves, burning every field that shows any sign of your trademarked plants."

"That's not my decision," I managed.

Yet most of the table seemed to think that I was the president and Congress too, sitting before them in some kind of court proceeding.

Claude offered a few slow words to the others. Judging by the tone, he was trying to calm spirits.

But it took the patriarch to regain control of the meeting. He leaned forward, silencing the others. Something important was coming, no doubt about it. He shook his head as if it were heavy and looked at the others, and in French, he told his associates, "Of course it cannot hold, these taboos. These constrictions. Seeds will sprout and thrive, and there aren't enough eyes in the sky to keep all of the American secrets safely their own."

I knew what he said because Claude, remembering his job, hunched down and translated every word.

Then the old man looked at me. One apolitical soul to another, he said, "But you see, Kyle. My friend. This is the problem that I face. These emotions are ragged and unpleasant. And not just with my staff, but with our stockholders too. I wish to do business with you. I believe what you offer is respectable and fair, and I take no offense. But I am not this company, only its servant. I'm sorry that you saw this display today, but at least now you will appreciate my reasons when I tell you no. I will thank you for your time, and on the behalf of everyone, I wish you the best. A safe, uneventful flight back to your homeland, and good day to you."

Like most twelve-year-old boys, my favorite movies usually involved World War II. Battles and tremendous explosions were my passion, and it didn't hurt having brave men not even twice my age doing fearless, selfless acts. New releases were cause for celebration. My father would treat my brothers and me to a matinee, and afterward we'd wrestle our way back to the car, arguing about which scene was best and which soldiers we wanted to be like. Classic films were an excuse to gather around the black-and-white RCA, two wondrous hours spent watching the slaughter of Japs and Krauts. It seemed like such good fun, even when I was old enough to know that war was a truly awful business.

I had limits too: I never much liked the atomic bomb movies. The best of that bad lot was the Hiroshima epic, directed by William Wyler, starring Charlton Heston as Paul Tibbets. Despite my love for large explosions, I considered mushroom clouds to be more forces of nature than tools of war. Besides, I wasn't an unthinking monster, and the effects of the blast and radiation were bad enough to stave off any wide-eyed pleasure with that impossibly bright flash of light.

My father was an Alfred Hitchcock fan. With the excuse of an education, he took us to see the classic *Intrigue*. But the movie's charms and subtle power were slow to work their way into my flesh. Espionage was a difficult species of warfare. Dad had to explain quite a lot to his boys, including how the Soviets had placed spies in the heart of the Manhattan Project and how a pair of intelligence officers achieved miracles, rooting out the bastards before any damage could be done.

"If those heroes hadn't done their jobs," he warned, "our world would be a very different place today."

"Different how?" I asked.

We were walking back to the car. "Our enemies would have stolen our atomic bomb," he said grimly, emphasizing that stealing element. Political systems aside, his sons were brought up to believe that thieves were cowards and worse. "And without our spy-busters working in the shadows, the Communists would have gotten the hydrogen bomb too."

"What's the difference?" my youngest brother asked. "Between atomic . . . and what's the word . . . ?"

"Hydrogen," I told him, using my smart, twelve-year-old voice. "Hydrogen bombs are much, much worse."

"They're just bigger," Dad corrected. "A weapon isn't good or bad. It just is. What makes it evil is how it is used."

"Have we ever used H-bombs?" asked my other brother.

"Three times," Dad allowed. "Only three times. And they hopefully won't be needed again."

"But we have them," I added confidently.

"And we keep them at the ready," he allowed. "Warheads on missiles, bombs in bombers, and there's always at least one nuclear submarine hiding in the ocean, ready to fire its payload on a moment's notice."

This was all good and reasonable, in other words. And with that, we let the topic drop, getting back to the important business of wrestling our way to the car.

When I was in college, *The Good Hand* came to one theatre. I knew nothing about the little film, except that it was set in some bizarre future New York City. My girlfriend had read a favorable review and we went together, but she wasn't a very strong person. The filth and disease and easy deaths of that first half hour proved too much. Leaning close, she demanded that we leave. And since I was hoping for sex, either that night or in my own near future, I did the gracious thing.

The title, *The Good Hand*, remained a small mystery. It wasn't until eight or nine years later, living in a large city with an art house movie theatre, I finally watched that violent nightmare to its conclusion. The director, Martin Scorsese, did very little work after *The Good Hand*, and it was easy to see why. His hypothetical world was brutal and suffocating. Powerful, faceless entities controlled every aspect of knowledge. Books were kept under lock and key, even the least sensitive titles subject to layers upon layers of restrictions and bureaucratic hoops.

The story was preposterous, yet after the first frames, utterly believable. The protagonist was a young fellow who wanted nothing but to make a better spaghetti sauce. That's all. The twentieth century was famous for its delicious sauces, and wanting to know more about tomatoes and basil and garlic and sausage, he filled out the appropriate forms. But one box on the backside of one page was checked when he should have left it empty, and his request was dropped into a much more dangerous pile of forms.

At that point, a brutal comedy took flight. One tiny misunderstanding caused people to die while others barely survived. The young chief lost friends and family, and he had to kill two strangers and avoid a fast-moving car before the pursuing intelligence officer finally caught him.

"This is a sad, essential business," the officer explained to his prisoner. "If a citizen believes he can reach for any title, to slake any intellectual thirst, how do we keep our grip on society?"

"Why do we need any grip?" the bloodied but valiant hero responded. "Can't people do what they want? Can't they learn what they want . . . just so long as it doesn't hurt any-one . . . ?"

Played by a young De Niro, the intelligence officer was an intoxicating mixture of acid and charm. He laughed for a few moments. Then with grave certainty, he said, "You don't know the dangers waiting in these old texts. And I don't know much about them either. But I'm one tough bastard, and what I do know scares me. The bombs and poisons that you could make up in your kitchen . . . well, I'd do anything to protect my world from those horrors. And every time I meet someone naïve, someone like you, it reminds me. In-side each of us, there's a fatal flaw. We suffer from a crazy urge that keeps us chasing every bit of knowledge, including nightmares that can doom our species and our world."

The young Al Pacino played the would-be cook. "Are you crazy? This is about spaghetti sauce," he screamed. "That's all I want to know!"

"Not according to these forms," his opponent countered.

"I made a mistake," Pacino swore, and not for the first time.

"No," his nemesis replied. "You used the system against us. You put your mark in that box to allow your nose where it didn't belong. Your plan was clever, and you had this inge-nious excuse waiting. In case an official more gullible than me happened to grab your case."

"You aren't listening to me," the prisoner complained.

"I've heard every word," the interrogator promised. "And now what you need to do is pay attention when I tell you this: The past is forbidden. There are things that can't be revealed. Certainly not to the likes of you."

"What about you?"

"Oh, I'm not worthy, either," the officer replied, laughing aside even the suggestion of special treatment. Then from a shelf where important tools were kept, he pulled down a steel cleaver of obvious heft and sharpness. "Regardless what you think, I'm not a monster. I have mercy, and I genuinely want to let you off with a warning. So tell me now. Be honest. Which one is your good hand?"

"My what?"

"Which hand do you cook with?"

The hero was right-handed—a point made several times in the narrative. But he was a clever sort, having the presence of mind to lift his left hand as far as the shackles allowed.

"Very well," said the officer, smiling with a professional coolness. Then he turned to two nameless fellows waiting in the shadows. "Hold the right wrist," he instructed. "Hold it very tight now."

As the cleaver rose, the hero shouted, "Not that hand, no!"

"Then you should have answered differently," was the response. And at least one member of the audience—an apolitical sort on his best day—grimaced and curled up tight, fending off the blows that came only in his imagination.

Following the Great Lunch Disaster, I retreated to my room and called home, leaving a very sorry report on the office answering machine. I was exhausted, and with an evening event with another French firm scheduled, I stripped and collapsed under the covers, drifting into a wonderful, dreamless sleep.

Noises woke me.

First came the precise knocking on wood, and then a loud, uncomfortable voice saying my name.

Sitting up, I assumed I was late for my appointment. Clumsy apologies preceded the realization that Claude wasn't speaking. In fact, it was a woman's voice. I coughed, muttered, "Just a minute," and managed to put one leg into my pants before finding enough curiosity to ask the obvious question:

"Who is it?"

"Noelene."

"Oh." Why did I know that name? My mind saw the woman at lunch, but that seemed unlikely. My memory was playing games with me. "Just a moment," I begged, fastening my pants and buttoning my shirt halfway before realizing that I hadn't lined up the buttons and holes properly. Fine. I reached for the door regardless, and that was when another possibility occurred to me. Noelene was a sweet voice standing in the hallway, flanked by a pair of French thugs, the three of them ready to rob the vulnerable American.

No peephole had been bored into the heavy old door. I left the chain attached, and with my foot serving as a second line of defense, I looked through the tiniest gap.

My first instinct had been right. Except for her smile, the woman from lunch looked perfectly miserable. "It is bad," she announced.

"What is?"

"You don't know?"

"I don't." Nodding at my bed, I admitted, "I have jet lag."

"You bombed us."

Startled, I stepped back.

The woman stared at the chain and then at me. Her smile had become something else. The anger was perfectly reasonable, but there was compassion as well. She put her arms around her waist, sighing deeply before saying, "We could be at war."

"No," I managed. "Not war."

Quietly, almost tenderly, she said, "Kyle. Please let me inside."

I shut the door and unfastened the chain and opened it again. Then I turned on the television, preprogrammed to find the hotel's most useless channel—classical music playing while a slide show proved what a fine city Nancy was. Where was the BBC? I punched buttons, absorbing repeated images of the same fire and smoke. The other networks were full of the news, but at least the British voices could explain what I was seeing.

"Algeria?" I managed. "What's in Algeria?"

"Our space program," she claimed.

"You have one?" I blurted, using an unfortunate tone.

Noelene grimaced. But for a minute or two she said nothing, allowing me to gain some appreciation for what had happened in the middle of the North African desert. Rockets and the assembly buildings, fuel tanks and even the railroad lines leading south from Algiers had been obliterated. Smart-bombs and small teams of commandoes had done the brutal work. Casualties were less than fifty, although those numbers were preliminary. Then that wise BBC voice explained that a wing of long-range Skyrangers was fueling in Missouri, preparing to strike the uranium enrichment facility outside Grenoble.

"Why are we admitting that?" I asked the television.

"Because you like us so much," Noelene replied, sarcasm riding on her voice. "We are your friends. Your allies, on occasion. You're giving us time to move our civilians out of harm's way." That's how we did things in Israel: A stern warning followed less than a day later with a burrowing bomb, famous for its cleanliness but still throwing a horrible mess across the Negev.

Not knowing what to say, I whispered, "All right."

She looked at my chest.

Yes, my buttons. I undid them and began again, and when success was near, I thought to ask, "But why are you here?"

She didn't seem to notice the question.

"You don't like me," I continued. "And you hate my country."

She looked at my eyes and said, "Kyle."

It's silly, I know. But I liked the way my name sounded coming out of her wide, lovely mouth.

"I don't know you," Noelene began. "And I don't hate your country. But I know America enough to despise its government's policies."

"But why are you here?"

"This is my supervisor's idea," she explained. "When this news broke, he mentioned that he was worried about you. He turned to me and explained that he couldn't get involved—his station and responsibilities wouldn't allow it—but he thought that I might take pity on you. You need help. Yes? Before events swallow up all of our lives?"

I settled on the corner of my bed.

She considered the nearby chair. But sitting wasn't her intention. "Your passport."

"What about it?"

"You'll need it and any essential belongings."

I was confused.

"But leave your suitcase, and please don't bother checking out of the hotel. My car is close. We can reach the highway before 17:00."

"When?"

"Five o'clock."

It was that late. I stared at my watch, trying to decide what to take. If I was actually leaving, that is.

"Kyle?"

"Are we going back to Paris?"

"God, no." The ignorance of an average American amazed Noelene. "You have to leave this country as soon as possible. Germany isn't far, if we start right now . . . !"

Every face in the world suddenly seemed important. Every glance from a stranger carried menace: Do they know who I am? Do they want revenge? The average pedestrian looked tense, distracted and angry. Two old men stood on a street corner, rigid fingers accusing the sky of something or another, and though I couldn't understand them, I had no doubt that Algeria was the topic. A gentleman in a suit and tie leaned against a stone building, listening to the static and news on a small transistor radio. A young woman walking toward us suddenly looked at me, and a smile flickered before vanishing into an expression more grim than seemed possible on such a pretty face. Then as we passed each other, she whispered a few words to Noelene.

Noelene replied with a phrase, nothing more.

"Did you know her?" I asked.

"No." She fished a single car key from her purse. "I don't. How would I?"

"It just seemed—" I began.

"Here," she interrupted, steering me to a vehicle even tinier than Claude's Renault. But remarkably, it was a Ford. A model not sold in America, but an unexpected harbinger of home. I took this as a good sign. Crawling into the passenger seat, I thanked Noelene for her unexpected help. She nodded and looked at the steering wheel, saying nothing. Then remembering the key in her hand, she started the little motor and took the wheel with both hands before facing me. "I'm doing what I was told to do," she stated.

"You've explained that. But thank you anyway."

Pushing the car into gear, she said, "I should warn you. My driving is rather spectacular."

"What is that?" I said above the revving. I assumed that "spectacular" was the wrong word.

But it wasn't.

Minutes later, I was wearing my seat belt and shoulder harness and my door was locked, both hands wrapped around the plastic handle above the window. As promised, we were flying down the highway. It seemed as if we were on the same road on which I had entered Nancy. Noelene admitted that it was, then added, "But not for long." Several quick turns followed, and I lost all track of where I was. Maybe we were heading for Germany, but why was the sun on my right? Didn't we want the sun setting behind us? I asked myself that reasonable question, more than once, and she must have heard my thoughts because without prompting, she volunteered, "We will be turning in another few kilometers. Don't worry."

I had so much to worry about, I let that topic drop.

"Do you mind?" she asked, reaching between us.

"What?" I sputtered.

"The radio. May I listen to the news?"

"Of course. Yes."

A professional newscaster was talking. The man's level, almost soothing voice might have been discussing stock prices or the weather. But then he vanished, replaced by the taped comments of some government official. Or so I guessed: Government voices have that gait, that self-importance, making pronouncements meant to represent millions but mattering only to their inflated egos.

We kept driving south.

One important turnoff was marked with what for the French was a large sign, and I was quite sure that the arrow was pointing toward the United German States. But then we were past it, and looking back, I had to ask, "Why?"

Noelene glanced at me longer than she should have. At

the speeds we were driving, I wanted her eyes forward. "Do you understand anything?" she asked.

What we were talking about?

"French," she explained.

" 'Merci.' Maybe a few other—"

"The borders have been closed, Kyle."

My grip on the handle couldn't be any tighter, but that wasn't for lack of trying. "What borders? With Germany?"

"As a precaution, yes."

I didn't know what to say.

"But I have a friend," she continued. "A customs agent, and I think he'll help us."

I don't like messes. I never have. And that seemed like the worst part of this nightmare—its considerable untidiness.

"He works in," she began, naming a town I didn't know.

"And he'll let me across?"

She said, "Yes."

Then a little softer, "I think so."

Maybe this was best. Maybe everything would work out, and I could climb on a nice German plane and head home. But even as I sat back in the hard little seat—as the sun finished setting and the French scenery raced past with a succession of blurring, increasingly dark grays—I thought to look at the single key in the car's ignition. What kind of person keeps her key on its own ring?

"Is this car yours?"

Noelene gave my abrupt question a little too much thought. Then looking straight ahead, she said, "Yes." She used the word that one time, just to practice the lie. Then again, with more authority, she told me, "Yes," and glanced my way, showing an unconvincing smile.

We drove fast and far, and I applied myself to learning everything possible about this strange automobile. The speedometer had us scorching along at better than 150 KPH, riding on nothing but four doughnut-sized tires. Our gas tank wasn't full when we began, and by the time I began paying attention, the gauge read half-empty. Despite the darkness, I tried to spot landmarks and keep track of our turns. But I've never been much of a navigator. Finally, summoning a measure of courage, I asked, "Do you have a road map?"

She seemed ready for my request. "Look in the glove box, Kyle."

I was already opening it, nothing to find but the car manual and several receipts that I couldn't read in the dark.

I said nothing, contemplating my situation.

She imagined questions and picked one to answer.

"This won't last much longer, Kyle."

"Pardon?"

"The world situation. American power." Something about this was funny. I didn't expect her to laugh, but that's what she did: A soft, girlish giggle followed by the apology, "I don't mean that your country will be destroyed. Nobody wants that. But you know, this power you have over the rest of us . . . it's fragile. It's doomed. That's what I meant to say."

I nodded seriously, as if politics were forefront in my mind. Then over the hum of the highway, I asked what seemed like a perfectly reasonable question. "How would that help anything?"

She said nothing. In a particular way, she held her silence.

"I don't understand," I admitted. "The world is prosperous and at peace. Why would you want to upset the order of things?"

Noelene leaned close to the steering wheel, as if willing herself to reach our destination sooner.

"What kind of world would this be?" I asked. "All right, France acquires the bomb. Then the Jews and Egyptians, the Soviets and Chinese. Britain and Germany would have to build suitable armories. And I suppose even Canada would want two or three little nukes, just to earn their southern neighbor's respect." I had found my rhythm, listing progressively smaller nations. French sensibilities where triggered when I mentioned, "Switzerland."

"Why?" she interrupted. "Why would the Swiss need such things?"

I watched her and watched the dashboard. The red silhouette of a gasoline tank warned that we were nearly out of fuel.

Noelene risked a quick glance my way. Then with eyes

fixed on the blurring road, she stated, "Neutral powers wouldn't bother."

"Well," I pointed out. "Perhaps they wouldn't see things quite as you do."

She said nothing.

And I kept my own silence, realizing just how sick of worry I was. This deep dread of mine began before I boarded the plane in Chicago, and every step of my journey had made it heavier and more acidic.

"You never should have done it," she began.

"What's that?"

"The nuclear monopoly . . . you should never have claimed it. Never. If you had shared your nuclear plans, the genuine powers would have each built only what we needed. France would have a few bombs, and the Soviets, and everyone. Our borders would be protected. There wouldn't be any reason for war. Why would one nation fight another if it meant that their capital would burn, their population enduring catastrophic losses?"

"Is that how things would be?"

"Oh yes," she exclaimed. "Peace. Real peace. And some world court that would judge the nations, identifying what was wrong and making settlements between competitors. This is obvious . . . so obvious . . . I cannot believe anyone would think otherwise."

"Yet I do," I admitted.

She grimaced. "You can't hold this power forever."

I was terrified and extraordinarily tired, yet at the same moment my mind was sharp. Pushing my face close to her ear, I asked, "And how will you stop us, Noelene?"

She gave a start, the swift little car wandering out of its lane. Then she straightened her back and our trajectory, eyes straight ahead, bright with tears. "You aren't monsters," she informed me.

"I know I'm not."

"When you realize . . . when your country understands how many innocent civilians you'll have to murder to maintain your hegemony . . . well, you'll stop yourselves. Your president will have no choice but to recall those bombers. Yes?

I know this. You're not psychopaths, and your conscience won't let you slaughter thousands of peaceful demonstrators."

"Thousands?" I blurted.

She fell silent.

Leaning against my door, I asked, "Where are you taking me, Noelene?"

One hand came off the steering wheel, fingertips wiping at her eyes as the car drifted out of its lane again. "To the border. I told you."

There was little heart left in her lie.

For the next sixteen minutes, we rode in total silence. I asked myself how close we were to Geneva and how slow we would have to be going for me to open my door and roll onto the pavement. Better that than get involved in some bizarre self-imposed hostage situation, surely. Then came the mechanical clicking of a turn signal, and Noelene was braking while pulling off the highway. A pool of fluorescent green light beckoned, gas pumps and cheery French signs and a very welcome Coke symbol hung in the bright station window. "I thought we had enough fuel," she muttered, perhaps speaking to herself.

She sounded as worried as I felt.

"I'll make this quick," she promised, throwing a weak smile at her increasingly wily captive.

I opened my door as soon as the car stopped. My mind was made up. Better to take my chances with strangers, I reasoned, than remain at the mercy of this misguided woman. I assumed that Noelene would try to stop me. She'd offer more lies or perhaps threaten me. What I didn't expect was no reaction past a vague, "Where are you going?"

"The bathroom," I lied.

But before I managed two steps, someone shouted her name. People were standing at the edge of the light, a large group gathered around what looked like a parked school bus. Noelene climbed out of the borrowed car and looked at them, and the worries on her face fell away. She called out several names, waving enthusiastically. Several young men came running, examining me while passing and then gathering around their good friend, talking with quiet intense voices. I kept walking. One by one, the men glanced at me, nodding happily. Stepping into the service station, I realized that I had to pee in the most urgent, desperate way. The bathroom was a small, extraordinarily clean room with one toilet and a lock. There had to be a back door out of the station. But first, I did what couldn't wait, and then as the toilet ran, I splashed water on my face and dried my hands, wondering which way was east, and what were the odds of a terrified, language-impaired American making his own way across the German border.

But the challenge wouldn't be met. Two substantial men were waiting outside the bathroom door. Waiting for me, judging by the hands that grabbed my shoulders and elbows. I felt tiny. I felt carried, although my feet remained on the floor with every step. A sour looking woman behind the counter glared at me, and the largest man said, "Your passport. It is with you?"

For no good reason but to be difficult, I said, "No."

Noelene was waiting for us outside. The big man asked her a question, and visibly surprised, she said, "He brought it with him, yes."

"I threw it out the window," I lied. "Miles and miles ago."

"You did what?" Strangely, that angered her. She sneered and gave a few quick instructions in French, and a hand almost too big to fit inside my right front pocket snatched up the prize. Then it was handed to her, and she slipped it inside her pocket, saying, "I'll keep this safe for you, Kyle."

"No," I muttered.

"We ride in the bus together," the big man said, giving me a bone-rattling pat on the back.

Again, I said, "No."

"We insist."

I decided to collapse on the pavement. But that did nothing but strip away the last of my dignity. The men grabbed my arms and legs and carried me to the bus and up into the darkness. I smelled smoke and liquor and competing perfumes. Who wears perfume to a mass suicide? I begged to be put down, and I agreed to stand on my own, but my captors insisted on shoving me into one of the front seats, next to a small figure that looked female and was wearing some kind of uniform.

I didn't recognize the woman. Honestly, I hadn't looked twice at the face riding beside me in the airliner. But the black and orange-trimmed uniform was the same, and she had the same build and similar short hair. Someone or something had struck her face, probably more than once, and someone else had given her a white towel to press against what looked like a very ugly cut beside her left eye.

I looked at the bus door, ready to run.

But the big Frenchman read my mind. Standing in the aisle, he grinned down at me, explaining, "We wait for the rest. As soon as they come, we leave. Very soon now."

My earlier terrors were nothing compared to this. Anxieties were piled high. I breathed hard, moaned and shook. My hope of hopes was to panic—a full-blown craziness born from adrenaline and nothing left to lose. I would beg. I would lie. Any excuse was viable, aiming for whatever was most pathetic. I was even sorry that I had emptied my bladder, since I doubted anyone here would appreciate riding to the Alps with a urine-soaked coward.

Through the bus windows, I saw Noelene move her car away from the pumps, parking somewhere behind the bus.

Another little car arrived, pulling up ahead, out of view. But I barely noticed. Watching my hands tremble, I wished I could call home, just once, and tell my news to whoever picked up the receiver.

Through the open windows, a voice found me.

I recognized its timbre, its smoothness. Leaping to my feet, I saw a familiar face talking to the big man and Noelene.

I started to shout, "Claude," but someone behind me decided to shove me, dropping me to the rubberized floor.

Shifting in our seat, the rad-hunter looked down at me. The gore and shadows made her look especially defiant. Plainly, I wasn't doing a very good job of defending my nation's honor.

Claude spoke with the others for several minutes, arguing

and explaining before stopping, allowing an increasing number of participants to take their turn. I returned to my seat, listening to every sound. Once again my translator repeated his points, making sure that he was understood. There was gravity to his tone, plus a little despair. Suddenly the rad-hunter pulled away the towel, taking a deep breath before telling me, "They're letting you go."

"What?"

"Your friend just saved you," she explained, staring at me with a vivid, hateful envy.

The big man came into the bus and waved at me.

With shoulders bowed, I went to him. I would have kissed him on the hands and cheeks, I was that happy. Then I was led outside, and Claude watched me until I looked at him. Then he turned to Noelene, offering a few words intended only for her.

"I didn't know," she said to me.

The woman was weeping. Because of me or because of her emotions getting the best of her—I couldn't tell which.

I started to talk, but Claude interrupted. "You have your passport? You will need it."

Where was my soul? I stupidly patted my pockets before remembering that it was stolen a few minutes ago.

I looked at weepy Noelene.

"He must have it," Claude warned.

She seemed more willing to surrender me than the document. But she placed it in my hands, and for a long moment, I did nothing. I was waiting for an apology. But none was offered. Once again, she claimed, "I didn't know," and she turned and walked away toward the bus.

"Don't go," I blurted.

Startled, she looked back at me.

"Go there, and you will die," I said with all of the authority I could muster. "It'll be like Israel, a burrowing nuke. It'll make a huge mess, and you'll get poisoned and die in some slow awful way."

That fate had its terrors, but she refused to cower. Braver than I would ever be, Noelene said, "Your people won't let this happen. How could they? We're allies. We helped your country win its freedom." She made a bomber with one hand, and smiling, pulled it back toward the sky. "Your president will see us, and in the end, he will give in."

As fast as the journey south had been, the return trip was even faster. The tiny Renault rattled and shook, and its driver focused his attentions on the road, barely finding the breath, much less the need, to explain that he had traded in several favors and paid some undisclosed bribe to less forgiving souls, and that's before he had told Noelene that my only child was back in the States, in the Mayo Clinic, dying of cancer.

"That's why she's sorry," I muttered.

"A little lie," he confessed.

Watching the same road, I said, "Thank you."

Which made him angrier, it seemed. We were heading toward Paris and some final flight home, though he wasn't promising that we would make it in time.

"How did you know where I was?"

He didn't answer.

Again, I told him, "Thank you."

Maybe he nodded. I watched but I wasn't sure.

The car radio was turned up high. It was the middle of the night, but the voices were animated and steady, senselessly describing events of great importance. I found myself thinking about the rad-hunter and what would happen to her and Noelene. Mostly Noelene.

"I knew where you would be," said Claude, glancing at me.

"You're involved with them," I guessed.

"Since the beginning," he allowed. "Yes." He sighed and a few moments later admitted, "But I'm glad you're here. You are my excuse. Really, I don't want to die tonight."

"That's funny," I muttered.

He looked at me, insulted.

"I don't mean funny," I apologized. "I meant to say odd. It's odd because . . . this sounds silly, I know . . . but some part of me wants to be with them now. You know? All those brave noble people doing what they think must be right. I don't want to be there, and I don't want to be a hostage, no. But there's two women that I keep thinking about. Isn't that crazy?"

"It is human nature," my savior said, shaking his head wearily.

The sun was beginning to show itself. Looking east, I began to mention the first flush of dawn. But then the radio gave a harsh sputtering roar before the station fell silent. We listened to the static, and then Claude turned off the radio, and we listened to the road and our own thoughts. Really, at that point, what else could be said?

The Cassandra Project

JACK MCDEVITT

*Jack McDevitt (jackmcdevitt.com) lives in Brunswick, Georgia. He is probably best known for his sequence of Priscilla "Hutch" Hutchins novels—*The Engines of God *(1994),* Deepsix *(2000),* Chindi *(2002), and* Omega *(2003)—and he has had a book on the final Nebula awards ballot for twelve of the last thirteen years. The most substantial collection of his short fiction is* Cryptic *(2009). His most recent novel is* Echo *(2010), and his previous novel,* Time Travelers Never Die *(2009), won the Nebula Award for best novel.*

"The Cassandra Project" appeared in Lightspeed, *and this is perhaps its first print publication. Set in the day after tomorrow, it involves the investigations by a PR man assigned to promote a U.S./Soviet return to the moon for NASA, sparked by his discovery in a bunch of old photos from the Soviet space archives of a dome in the Cassegrain crater taken in 1967, before the Apollo moon landing. It is more a story about politics than space technology though, quiet and thorough and ironic.*

It's an odd fact that the biggest science story of the twenty-first century—probably the biggest ever—broke in that tabloid of tabloids, *The National Bedrock*.

I was in the middle of conducting a NASA press conference several days before the Minerva lift-off—the Return to the Moon—and I was fielding softball questions like: "Is it true that if everything goes well, the Mars mission will be moved up?" and "What is Marcia Beckett going to say when she becomes the first person to set foot on lunar soil since Eugene Cernan turned off the lights fifty-four years ago?"

President Gorman and his Russian counterpart, Dmitri Alexandrov, were scheduled to talk to the press from the White House an hour later, so I was strictly a set-up guy. Or that was the plan, anyway, until Warren Cole mentioned the dome.

It was a good time for NASA. We all knew the dangers inherent in overconfidence, but two orbital missions had gone up without a hitch. Either of them could have landed and waved back at us, and the rumor was that Sid Myshko had almost taken the game into his own hands, and that the crew had put it to a vote whether they'd ignore the protocol and go down to the surface regardless of the mission parameters. Sid and his five crewmates denied the story, of course.

I'd just made the point to the pool of reporters that it was Richard Nixon who'd turned off the lights—not the astronaut Eugene Cernan—when Warren Cole began waving his hand. Cole was the AP journalist, seated in his customary spot up front. He was frowning, his left hand in the air, staring down at something on his lap that I couldn't see.

"Warren?" I said. "What've you got?"

"Jerry. . . ." He looked up, making no effort to suppress a grin. "Have you seen the story that the *Bedrock*'s running?" He held up his iPad.

That started a few people checking their own devices.

"No, I haven't," I said, hoping he was making it up. "I don't usually get to *Bedrock* this early in the week." Somebody snorted. Then a wave of laughter rippled through the room. "What?" I said. My first thought had been that we were about to have another astronaut scandal, like the one the month before with Barnaby Salvator and half the strippers on the Beach. "What are they saying?"

"The Russians released more lunar orbital pictures from the sixties." He snickered. "They've got one here from the far side of the Moon. If you can believe this, there's a dome back there."

"A *dome*?"

"Yeah." He flipped open his notebook. "Does NASA have a comment?"

"You're kidding, right?" I said.

He twisted the iPad, raised it higher, and squinted at it. "Yep. It's a dome all right."

The reporters in the pool all had a good chuckle, and then they looked up at me. "Well," I said, "I guess Buck Rogers beat us there after all."

"It looks legitimate, Jerry," Cole said, but he was still laughing.

I didn't have to tell him what we all knew: That it was a doctored picture and that it must have been a slow week for scandals.

If the image *was* doctored, the deed had to have been done by the Russians. Moscow had released the satellite images only a few hours before and forwarded them to us without comment. Apparently nobody on either side had noticed anything unusual. Except the *Bedrock* staff.

I hadn't looked at the images prior to the meeting. I mean,

once you've seen a few square miles of lunar surface you've pretty much seen it all. The dome—if that's really what it was—appeared on every image in the series. They were dated April, 1967.

The Bedrock carried the image on its front page, where they usually show the latest movie celebrity who's being accused of cheating, or has gone on a drunken binge. It depicted a crater wall, with a large arrow graphic in the middle of a dark splotch pointing at a dome that you couldn't have missed anyhow. The headline read:

ALIENS ON THE MOON
Russian Pictures Reveal Base on Far Side
Images Taken Before Apollo

I sighed and pushed back from my desk. We just didn't need this.

But it *did* look like an artificial construct. The thing was on the edge of a crater, shaped like the head of a bullet. It was either a reflection, an illusion of some sort, or it was a fraud. But the Russians had no reason to set themselves up as a laughing stock. And it sure as hell *looked* real.

I was still staring at it when the phone rang. It was Mary, NASA's administrator. My boss. *"Jerry,"* she said, *"I heard what happened at the press conference this morning."*

"What's going on, Mary?"

"Damned if I know. Push some buttons. See what you can find out. It's going to come up again when the President's out there. We need to have an answer for him."

Vasili Koslov was my public relations counterpart at Russia's space agency. He was in Washington with the presidential delegation. And he was in full panic mode when I got him on the phone. *"I saw it, Jerry,"* he said. *"I have no idea what this is about. I just heard about it a few minutes ago. I'm looking at it now. It* does *look like a dome, doesn't it?"*

"Yes," I said. "Did your people tamper with the satellite imagery?"

"They must have. I have a call in. I'll let you know as soon as I hear something."

I called Jeanie Escovar in the Archives. "Jeanie, have you seen the *National Bedrock* story yet?"

"No," she said. *"My God, what is it this time?"*

"Not what you think. I'm sending it to you now. Could you have somebody check to see where this place is—?"

"What place? Oh, wait—I got it."

"Find out where it is and see if you can get me some imagery of the same area. From *our* satellites."

I heard her gasp. Then she started laughing.

"Jeanie, this is serious."

"Why? You don't actually believe there's a building up there, do you?"

"Somebody's going to ask the President about it. They have a press conference going on in about twenty minutes. We want him to be able to say: 'It's ridiculous, here's a picture of the area, and you'll notice there's nothing there.' We want him to be able to say *'The Bedrock'*'s running an optical illusion.' But he'll have to do it diplomatically. And without embarrassing Alexandrov."

"Good luck on that."

The *Bedrock* story was already getting attention on the talk shows. Angela Hart, who at that time anchored *The Morning Report* for the *World Journal*, was interviewing a physicist from MIT. The physicist stated that the picture could not be accurate. *"Probably a practical joke,"* he said. *"Or a trick of the light."*

But Angela wondered why the Russians would release the picture at all. *"They had to know it would get a lot of attention,"* she said. And, of course, though she didn't mention it, it would become a source of discomfort for the Russian president and the two cosmonauts who were among the Minerva crew.

Vasili was in a state of shock when he called back. *"They didn't know about the dome,"* he said. *"Nobody noticed. But it* is *on the original satellite imagery. Our people were just putting out a lot of the stuff from the Luna missions. Imagery that hadn't been released before. I can't find anybody who knows anything about it. But I'm still trying."*

"Vasili," I said, "somebody must have seen it at the time. In 1967."

"I guess."

"You *guess*? You think it's possible something like this came in and nobody picked up on it?"

"No, I'm not suggesting that at all, Jerry. I just—I don't know what I'm suggesting. I'll get back to you when I have something more."

Minutes later, Jeanie called: *"It's the east wall of the Cassegrain Crater."*

"And—?"

"I've forwarded NASA imagery of the same area."

I switched on the monitor and ran the images. There was the same crater wall, the same pock-marked moonscape. But no dome. Nothing at all unusual.

Dated July, 1968. More than a year after the Soviet imagery.

I called Mary and told her: The Russians just screwed up.

"The President can't say that."

"All he has to say is that NASA has no evidence of any dome or anything else on the far side of the Moon. Probably he should just turn it into a joke. Make some remark about setting up a Martian liaison unit."

She didn't think it was funny.

When the subject came up at the presidential press conference, Gorman and Alexandrov both simply had a good laugh. Alexandrov blamed it on Khrushchev, and the laughter got louder. Then they moved on to how the Minerva mission—the long-awaited Return to the Moon—marked the beginning of a new era for the world.

The story kicked around in the tabloids for two or three more days. *The Washington Post* ran an op-ed using the dome to demonstrate how gullible we all are when the media says *anything*. Then Cory Abbott, who'd just won a Golden Globe for his portrayal of Einstein in *Albert and Me*, crashed his car into a street light and blacked out the entire town of Dekker, California. And just like that the dome story was gone.

On the morning of the launch, Roscosmos, the Russian space agency, issued a statement that the image was a result of defective technology. The Minerva lifted off on schedule and, while the world watched, it crossed to the Moon and completed a few orbits. Its lander touched down gently on the Mare Maskelyne. Marcia Beckett surprised everyone when she demurred leading the way out through the airlock, sending instead Cosmonaut Yuri Petrov, who descended and then signaled his crewmates to join him.

When all were assembled on the regolith, Petrov made the statement that, in the light of later events, has become immortal: *"We are here on the Moon because, during the last century, we avoided the war that would have destroyed us all. And we have come together. Now we stand as never before, united for all mankind."*

I wasn't especially impressed at the time. It sounded like the usual generalized nonsense. Which shows you what my judgment is worth.

I watched on my office monitor. And as the ceremony proceeded, I looked past the space travelers, across the barren wasteland of the Mare Maskelyne, wondering which was the shortest path to the Cassegrain crater.

I knew I should have just let it go, but I couldn't. I could imagine no explanation for the Russians doctoring their satellite imagery. Vasili told me that everyone with whom he'd spoken was shocked. That the images had been dug out of the archives and distributed without inspection. And, as far as could be determined, without anyone distorting them. *"I just don't understand it, Jerry,"* he said.

Mary told me not to worry about it. "We have more important things to do," she said.

There was no one left at NASA from the 1960s. In fact, I knew of only one person living at Cape Kennedy who had been part of the Agency when Apollo 11 went to the Moon:

Amos Kelly, who'd been one of my grandfather's buddies. He was still in the area, where he served with the Friends of NASA, a group of volunteers who lent occasional support but mostly threw parties. I looked him up. He'd come to the Agency in 1965 as a technician. Eventually, he'd become one of the operational managers.

He was in his mid-eighties, but he sounded good. *"Sure, Jerry, I remember you. It's been a long time,"* he said, when I got him on the phone. I'd been a little kid when he used to stop by to pick up my grandfather for an evening of poker. *"What can I do for you?"*

"This is going to sound silly, Amos."

"Nothing sounds silly to me. I used to work for the government."

"Did you see the story in the tabloids about the dome?"

"How could I miss it?"

"You ever hear anything like that before?"

"You mean did we think there were Martians on the Moon?" He laughed, turned away to tell someone that the call was for him, and then laughed again. *"Is that a serious question, Jerry?"*

"I guess not."

"Good. By the way, you've done pretty well for yourself at the Agency. Your granddad would have been proud."

"Thanks."

He told me how much he missed the old days, missed my grandfather, how they'd had a good crew. *"Best years of my life. I could never believe they'd just scuttle the program the way they did."*

Finally he asked what the Russians had said about the images. I told him what Vasili told me. *"Well,"* he said, *"maybe they haven't changed that much after all."*

Twenty minutes later he called back. *"I was reading the story in the* Bedrock. *It says that the object was in the Cassegrain Crater."*

"Yes. That's correct."

"There was talk of a Cassegrain Project at one time. Back in the sixties. I don't know what it was supposed to be. Whether it was anything more than a rumor. Nobody seemed

to know anything definitive about it. I recall at the time thinking it was one of those things so highly classified that even its existence was off the table."

"The Cassegrain Project."

"Yes."

"But you have no idea what it was about?"

"None. I'm sorry. Wish I could help."

"Would you tell me if you knew?"

"It's a long time ago, Jerry. I can't believe security would still be an issue."

"Amos, you were pretty high in the Agency—"

"Not that high."

"Do you remember anything else?"

"Nothing. Nada. As far as I know, nothing ever came of any of it, so the whole thing eventually went away."

Searching NASA's archives on "Cassegrain" yielded only data about the crater. So I took to wandering around the facility, talking offhandedly with senior employees. *It must feel good to see us back on the Moon, huh, Ralph? Makes all the frustration worthwhile. By the way, did you ever hear of a Cassegrain Project?*

They all laughed. *Crazy Russians.*

On the day the Minerva slipped out of lunar orbit and started home, Mary called me into her office. "We'll want to get the crew onstage for the press when they get back, Jerry. You might give the staging some thought."

"Okay. Will it be at Edwards?"

"Negative. We're going to do it here at the Cape." We talked over some of the details, the scheduling, guest speakers, points we'd want to make with the media. Then as I was getting ready to leave, she stopped me. "One more thing. The Cassegrain business—" I straightened and came to attention. Mary Gridley was a no-nonsense hard-charger. She was in her fifties, and years of dealing with bureaucratic nonsense had left her with little patience. She was physically diminutive, but she could probably have intimidated the Pope. "—I want you to leave it alone."

She picked up a pen, put it back down, and stared at me.

"Jerry, I know you've been asking around about that idiot dome. Listen, you're good at what you do. You'll probably enjoy a long, happy career with us. But that won't happen if people stop taking you seriously. You understand what I mean?"

After the shuttle landing and subsequent celebration, I went on the road. "We need to take advantage of the moment," Mary said. "There'll never be a better time to get some good press."

So I did a PR tour, giving interviews, addressing prayer breakfasts and Rotary meetings, doing what I could to raise the consciousness of the public. NASA wanted Moonbase. It was the next logical step. Should have had it decades ago and would have if the politicians hadn't squandered the nation's resources on pointless wars and interventions. But it would be expensive, and we hadn't succeeded yet in getting the voters on board. That somehow had become *my* responsibility.

In Seattle, I appeared at a Chamber of Commerce dinner with Arnold Banner, an astronaut who'd never gotten higher than the space station. But nevertheless he was an astronaut, and he hailed from the Apollo era. During the course of the meal I asked whether he'd ever heard of a Cassegrain Project. He said something about tabloids and gave me a disapproving look.

We brought in astronauts wherever we could. In Los Angeles, at a Marine charities fundraiser, we had both Marcia Beckett and Yuri Petrov, which would have been the highlight of the tour, except for Frank Allen.

Frank was in his nineties. He looked exhausted. His veins bulged and I wasn't sure he didn't need oxygen.

He was the fourth of the Apollo-era astronauts I talked with during those two weeks. And when I asked about the Cassegrain Project, his eyes went wide and his mouth tightened. Then he regained control. "Cassandra," he said, looking past me into a distant place. "It's classified."

"Not *Cassandra*, Frank. *Cassegrain*."

"Oh. Yeah. Of course."

"I have a clearance."

"How high?"

"Secret."

"Not enough."

"Just give me a hint. What do you know?"

"Jerry, I've already said too much. Even its existence is classified."

Cassandra.

When I got back to the Cape I did a search on *Cassandra* and found that a lot of people with that name had worked for the Agency over the years. Other Cassandras had made contributions in various ways, leading programs to get kids interested in space science, collaborating with NASA physicists in analyzing the data collected by space-born telescopes, editing publications to make NASA more accessible to the lay public. They'd been everywhere. You couldn't bring in a NASA guest speaker without discovering a Cassandra somewhere among the people who'd made the request. Buried among the names so deeply that I almost missed it was a single entry: *The Cassandra Project, storage 27176B Redstone.*

So secret its existence was classified?

The reference was to the Redstone Arsenal in Huntsville, Alabama where NASA stores rocket engines, partially-completed satellites, control panels from test stands, and a multitude of other artifacts dating back to Apollo. I called them.

A baritone voice informed me I had reached the NASA Storage Facility. *"Sgt. Saber speaking."*

I couldn't resist smiling at the name, but I knew he'd heard all the jokes. I identified myself. Then: "Sergeant, you have a listing for the Cassandra Project." I gave him the number. "Can I get access to the contents?"

"One minute, please, Mr. Carter."

While I waited, I glanced around the office at the photos of Neil Armstrong and Lawrence Bergman and Marcia Beckett. In one, I was standing beside Bergman, who'd been the guy who'd sold the President on returning to the Moon. In another, I was standing by while Marcia spoke with some

Alabama school kids during a tour of the Marshall Space Flight Center. Marcia was a charmer of the first order. I've always suspected she got the Minerva assignment partially because they knew the public would love her.

"When were you planning to come, Mr. Carter?"

"I'm not sure yet. Within the next week or so."

"Let us know in advance and there'll be no problem."

"It's not classified, then?"

"No, sir. I'm looking at its history now. It was originally classified, but that was removed by the Restricted Access Depository Act more than twenty years ago."

I had to get through another round of ceremonies and press conferences before I could get away. Finally, things quieted down. The astronauts went back to their routines, the VIPs went back to whatever it was they normally do, and life on the Cape returned to normal. I put in for leave.

"You deserve it," Mary said.

Next day, armed with a copy of the Restricted Access Depository Act, I was on my way to Los Angeles to pay another visit to a certain elderly retired astronaut.

"I can't believe it," Frank Allen said.

He lived with his granddaughter and her family of about eight, in Pasadena. She shepherded us into her office—she was a tax expert of some sort—brought some lemonade, and left us alone.

"What can't you believe? That they declassified it?"

"That the story never got out in the first place." Frank was back at the desk. I'd sunk into a leather settee.

"What's the story, Frank? Was the dome really there?"

"Yes."

"NASA doctored its own Cassegrain imagery? To eliminate all traces?"

"I don't know anything about that."

"So what *do* you know?"

"They sent us up to take a look. In late 1968." He paused. "We landed almost on top of the damned thing."

"Before Apollo 11."

"Yes."

I sat there in shock. And I've been around a while, so I don't shock easily.

"They advertised the flight as a test run, Jerry. It was supposed to be purely an orbital mission. Everything else, the dome, the descent, everything was top secret. Didn't happen."

"You actually got to the dome?"

He hesitated. A lifetime of keeping his mouth shut was getting in the way. "Yes," he said. "We came down about a half mile away. Max was brilliant."

Max Donnelly. The lunar module pilot. "What happened?"

"I remember thinking the Russians had beaten us. They'd gotten to the Moon and we hadn't even known about it.

"There weren't any antennas or anything. Just a big, silvery dome. About the size of a two-story house. No windows. No hammer and sickle markings. Nothing. Except a door.

"We had sunlight. The mission had been planned so we wouldn't have to approach it in the dark." He shifted his position in the chair and bit down on a grunt.

"You okay, Frank?" I asked.

"My knees. They don't work as well as they used to." He rubbed the right one, then rearranged himself—gently this time. "We didn't know what to expect. Max said he thought the thing was pretty old because there were no tracks in the ground. We walked up to the front door. It had a knob. I thought the place would be locked, but I tried it and the thing didn't move at first but then something gave way and I was able to pull the door open."

"What was inside?"

"A table. There was a cloth on the table. And something flat under the cloth. And that's all there was."

"Nothing else?"

"Not a thing." He shook his head. "Max lifted the cloth. Under it was a rectangular plate. Made from some kind of metal." He stopped and stared at me. "There was writing on it."

"Writing? What did it say?"

"I don't know. Never found out. It looked like Greek. We

brought the plate back home with us and turned it over to the bosses. Next thing they called us in and debriefed us. Reminded us it was all top secret. Whatever the thing said, it must have scared the bejesus out of Nixon and his people. Because they never said anything, and I guess the Russians didn't either."

"You never heard anything more at all?"

"Well, other than the next Apollo mission, which went back and destroyed the dome. Leveled it."

"How do you know?"

"I knew the crew. We talked to each other, right? They wouldn't say it directly. Just shook their heads: Nothing to worry about anymore."

Outside, kids were shouting, tossing a football around. "Greek?"

"That's what it looked like."

"A message from Plato."

He just shook his head as if to say: *Who knew?*

"Well, Frank, I guess that explains why they called it the Cassandra Project."

"She wasn't a Greek, was she?"

"You have another theory?"

"Maybe Cassegrain was too hard for the people in the Oval Office to pronounce."

I told Mary what I knew. She wasn't happy. "I really wish you'd left it alone, Jerry."

"There's no way I could have done that."

"Not now, anyhow." She let me see her frustration. "You know what it'll mean for the Agency, right? If NASA lied about something like this, and it becomes public knowledge, nobody will ever trust us again."

"It was a long time ago, Mary. Anyhow, the Agency wasn't lying. It was the Administration."

"Yeah," she said. "Good luck selling that one to the public."

The NASA storage complex at the Redstone Arsenal in Huntsville is home to rockets, a lunar landing vehicle, automated telescopes, satellites, a space station, and a multitude of other devices that had kept the American space program alive, if not particularly robust, over almost seventy years. Some were housed inside sprawling warehouses; others occupied outdoor exhibition sites.

I parked in the shadow of a Saturn V, the rocket that had carried the Apollo missions into space. I've always been impressed with the sheer audacity of anybody who'd be willing to sit on top of one of those things while someone lit the fuse. Had it been up to me, we'd probably never have lifted off at Kitty Hawk.

I went inside the Archive Office, got directions and a pass, and fifteen minutes later entered one of the warehouses. An attendant escorted me past cages and storage rooms filled with all kinds of boxes and crates. Somewhere in the center of it all, we stopped at a cubicle while the attendant compared my pass with the number on the door. The interior was visible through a wall of wire mesh. Cartons were piled up, all labeled. Several were open, with electronic equipment visible inside them.

The attendant unlocked the door and we went in. He turned on an overhead light and did a quick survey, settling on a box that was one of several on a shelf. My heart rate started to pick up while he looked at the tag. "This is it, Mr. Carter," he said. "Cassandra."

"Is this *everything*?"

He checked his clipboard. "This is the only listing we have for the Cassandra Project, sir."

"Okay. Thanks."

"My pleasure."

There was no lock. He raised the hasp on the box, lifted the lid, and stood back to make room. He showed no interest in the contents. He probably did this all the time, so I don't know why that surprised me.

Inside, I could see a rectangular object wrapped in plastic. I couldn't see what it was, but of course I knew. My heart was pounding by then. The object was about a foot and a half wide and maybe half as high. And it was heavy. I carried it over to a table and set it down. Wouldn't do to drop it. Then I unwrapped it.

The metal was black, polished, reflective, even in the half-light from the overhead bulb. And sure enough, there were the Greek characters. Eight lines of them.

The idea that Plato was saying hello seemed suddenly less far-fetched. I took a picture. Several pictures. Finally, reluctantly, I rewrapped it and put it back in the box.

"So," said Frank, "what did it say?"

"I have the translation here." I fished it out of my pocket but he shook his head.

"My eyes aren't that good, Jerry. Just tell me who wrote it. And what it says."

We were back in the office at Frank's home in Pasadena. It was a chilly, rainswept evening. Across the street, I could see one of his neighbors putting out the trash.

"It wasn't written by the Greeks."

"I didn't think it was."

"Somebody came through a long time ago. Two thousand years or so. *They* left the message. Apparently they wrote it in Greek because it must have looked like their best chance to leave something we'd be able to read. Assuming we ever reached the Moon."

"So what did it say?"

"It's a warning."

The creases in Frank's forehead deepened. "Is the sun going unstable?"

"No." I looked down at the translation. "It says that no civilization, anywhere, has been known to survive the advance of technology."

Frank stared at me. "Say that again."

"They all collapse. They fight wars. Or they abolish individual death, which apparently guarantees stagnation and an exit. I don't know. They don't specify.

"Sometimes the civilizations become too vulnerable to criminals. Or the inhabitants become too dependent on the technology and lose whatever virtue they might have had. Anyway, the message says that no technological civilization, anywhere, has been known to get old. Nothing lasts more than a few centuries—*our* centuries—once technological advancement begins. Which for us maybe starts with the invention of the printing press.

"The oldest known civilization lasted less than a thousand years."

Frank frowned. He wasn't buying it. "*They* survived. Hell, they had an interstellar ship of some kind."

"They said they were looking for a place to start again. Where they came from is a shambles."

"You're kidding."

"It says that maybe, if we know in advance, we can side-step the problem. That's why they left the warning."

"Great."

"If they survive, they say they'll come back to see how we're doing."

We were both silent for a long while.

"So what happens now?" Frank said.

"We've reclassified everything. It's top secret again. I shouldn't be telling you this. But I thought—"

He rearranged himself in the chair. Winced and rotated his right arm. "Maybe that's why they called it *Cassandra*," he said. "Wasn't she the woman who always brought bad news?"

"I think so."

"There was something else about her—"

"Yeah—the bad news," I said. "When she gave it, nobody would listen."

Jackie's-Boy

STEVEN POPKES

Steven Popkes (www.stevenpopkes.com) lives in Hopkinton, Massachusetts. "I became serious about writing in 1972. I attended the Clarion SF Workshop in 1978. When I left biology for computing (that was in 1979) it was with the idea that the engineering would support my writing habit. After all, it was just a 9-to-5 job, right? (Gales of hysterical laughter)." He has published forty SF stories over the last twenty years, four of them in 2010, and two novels, Caliban Landing *(1988) and* Slow Lightning *(1991), both dealing with the complexities of alien contact.*

"Jackie's-Boy" appeared in Asimov's. *It is a post-catastrophe tale set in the American midwest and south, after world civilization collapsed from the combined weight of natural disasters, bio-terrorism and plague, and global warming. Michael is a young boy, one of the survivors, who sneaks into the heavily-fortified local zoo after the death of his last surviving relative, and there befriends the sole remaining elephant—who can speak to him. They are soon forced to leave the zoo on a quest across the strange landscapes of the collapsed civilization, and the story of that quest is one of the finest SF stories of the year.*

Part 1

Michael fell in love with her the moment he saw her.

The Long Bottom Boys had taken over the gate of the Saint Louis Zoo from Nature Phil's gang. London Bob had killed in single combat, and eaten, Nature Phil. That, pretty much, constituted possession. The Keepers didn't mind as long as it stayed off the grounds. So the Boys waited outside to harvest anyone who came out or went in. They just had to wait. Somebody was always drawn to the sight of all that meat on the hoof, nothing protecting it from consumption save a hundred feet of empty air and invisible, lethal, automated weaponry. People went in just to look at it and drool.

Michael knew their plans. He'd been watching them furtively for a week, hiding in places no adult could go, leaving no traces they could see. The Boys had caught a woman a few days ago and a man last night. They were still passing the woman around. What was left of the man was turning on the spit over on Grand. He sniffed the air. A rank odor mixed with a smell like maple syrup. Corpse fungus at the fruiting body stage. Somewhere nearby there was a collection of mushrooms that yesterday had been the body of a human being. Michael wondered if it was someone who had spoiled before the Boys had got to them or if it was the last inedible remnants of the man on the spit. By morning there would be little more than a thin mound of soil to show where the meat had been.

This dark spring morning, just when the gates unlocked,

one of the guards remained asleep. Michael held his backpack tightly to his chest so he made no sound. The man started in his sleep. For a moment, Michael thought he would have to take up one of the fallen bricks and kill the guard before he woke up. But the guard just turned over and Michael slipped furtively past him. He was just as happy. The only thing that got the Boys more riled than meat was revenge.

He stayed out of sight even past the gate. If the Boys knew he was here, they'd be ready at closing time when the Keepers pushed everyone outside. Michael had never been in the Zoo, but he was hoping a kid could find places to hide that an adult wouldn't fit. Inside the Zoo was safe; outside the Zoo wasn't. It was as simple as that.

Now, he was crouching in the bushes outside her paddock in the visitor's viewing area, hiding from any Keepers, looking for a place to hide.

She came outside, her great rounded ears and heavy circular feet, her wise eyes and long trunk. As she came down to the water, Michael held his breath and made himself as small as an eleven-year-old boy could be. Maybe she wouldn't see him.

Except for the elephant, Michael saw no one. The barn and paddock of one of the last of the animals was the worst place to hide. He'd be found immediately. *Everyone* had probably tried this. Even so, when the elephant wandered out of sight down the hill, Michael sprang over the fence and silently ran to the barn, his backpack bouncing and throwing him off balance, expecting bullets to turn him into mush.

Inside, he quickly looked around and saw above the concrete floor a loft filled with bales of hay. He climbed up the ladder and burrowed down. The hay poked through his shirt and pants and tickled his feet through the hole in his shoe. Carefully, through the backpack, he felt for his notebook. It was safe.

"I see you," came a woman's voice from below.

Michael froze. He held tight to his pack.

Something slapped the hay bale beside him and pulled it down. The ceiling light shone down on him.

It was the elephant.

re not going to hide up there," she said.

Michael leaned over the edge. "Did you talk?"

"Get out of my stall." She whipped her trunk up and grabbed him by the leg, dragging him off the edge.

"Hold it, Jackie." A voice from the wall.

Jackie held him over the ground. "You're slipping, Ralph. I should have found his corpse outside hanging on the fence." She brought the boy to her eyes and Michael knew she was thinking of smashing him to jelly on the concrete then and there.

"Don't," he whispered.

"We all make mistakes." The wall again.

"Should I toss him out or squish him? This is *your* job. Not mine."

"Let him down. Perhaps, he'll be of use."

The moment stretched out. Michael stared at her. So scared he couldn't breathe. So excited the elephant was right there, up close and in front of him, he couldn't look away.

Slowly, reluctantly, she let him down. "Whatever."

A seven-foot metal construction project—a Zoo Keeper— came into the room from outside. Three metal arms with mounted cameras, each with their own gun barrel, followed both Jackie and Michael.

"Follow me." This time the voice came from the robot.

Michael stared at Jackie for a moment. She snorted contemptuously and turned to go back outside.

Michael slowly followed the Keeper, watching Jackie leave. "Elephants talk?"

"That one does," said the Keeper.

"Wow," he breathed.

"Open your backpack," the Keeper ordered.

Michael stared into the camera/gun barrel. He guessed it was too late to run. He opened the backpack and emptied it on the floor.

The Keeper separated the contents. "A loaf of bread. Two cans of tuna. A notebook. Several pens." The lens on the camera staring at him whirred and elongated toward him. "Yours? You read and write?"

"Yes."

"Take back your things. You may call me Ralph, as she does," said the Keeper as it led him into an office.

"Why aren't I dead?"

"I try not to slaughter children if I can help it. I have some limited leeway in interpreting my authority." The voice paused for a moment. "In the absence of a director, I'm in charge of the Zoo."

Michael nodded. He stared around the room. He was still in shock at seeing a real, live elephant. The talking seemed kind of extra.

The Keeper remained outside the office and the voice resumed speaking from the ceiling.

"Please sit down."

Michael sat down. "How come you still have lights? The only places still lit up are the Zoo and the Cathedral."

"I'm still able to negotiate with Union Electric. Not many places can guarantee fire safety."

Michael had no clue what the voice was talking about. "It's warm," he said tentatively.

"With light comes heat. Now, what is your name?"

"Michael. Michael Ripley."

"How old are you?"

Michael looked around the room. "Eleven, I think."

"You're not sure?"

Michael shook his head. "I'm pretty sure I was six when my parents died. Uncle Ned took me in. I stayed with him for five years. The Long Bottom Boys killed him a few months ago."

"You have no surviving relatives?"

Michael shrugged and didn't answer.

"Where do you live?"

Michael's attention snapped to the Keeper and he looked around the ceiling warily. "I just hang around the park."

"You have no place to stay?"

"No."

"Would you like to stay here?"

Michael looked around the room again. It was warm. There was clearly plenty to eat. None of the gangs were ever allowed inside. But where did they get the food for the animals? How come people weren't allowed in at night? Maybe he was on the menu here, too.

"I guess," he said slowly.

"Good. You're hired."

"What?"

"You will call me Ralph as I told you before. I will call you Michael except under specific circumstances when I will address you as 'Assistant Director.' Do you understand?"

Michael stared at the ceiling. "What am I supposed to do?"

Dear Mom,

I found a job. It is helping to take care of an eleefant. Her name is jakee. She is not very much fun but I like her anyway. Maybe she'll like me better when she gets to Know me. She is an eleefant*!!! I don't think I ever saw an eleefant before. Just in the books you red to me.*

I work in the zoo. I bet you never thawt I would ever work in a zoo. Most of the animals are gon. But there is the eleefant and a rino. No snaks.

It is a lot better than sleepng in the dumstrs. And a dumstr does not stop a rifle much. I miss you and DAD. But I don't miss uncle NeD all that much. I miss the apartment, though.

Love, Mike

He was mucking out her stall when Jackie entered.

She stopped and looked down at him.

"What are you doing?"

Michael straightened up. He tried to smile at her. "Working. Ralph hired me."

"To do that?"

Michael looked around. "I don't know. This seemed like it needed doing."

Jackie didn't speak for a moment. "Let the Keepers do that. Come with me."

He followed her to the door of the stall.

"We'll start with the first office on the left. You go in there and look for papers. Books. Notes. Memos. Anything with writing on it. You know what writing is?"

"I know what writing is."

"Good."

Michael looked up at her. "How did you learn to talk?"

"That's not your business. Do your job."

It wasn't a small job. It seemed that the world of zoos ran on paper. Just pulling the folders out of the first office took three days. Michael's duties didn't end with bringing the papers out. The type was small enough he often had to hold it in front of first one of Jackie's eyes, then the other. It wasn't easy on Jackie, either. She had to stop regularly because of headaches. When he could, he tried to read them himself to see what Jackie was trying to find. She smacked him with her trunk if she caught him so he took extra time in the offices.

A cold rain descended on the Zoo. Ralph closed the doors and turned up the heat. Jackie was irritable at the best of times. Being inside only made her worse.

A month after Michael had come to the Zoo, when a late spring snow was sticking wetly to the ground outside, Jackie stared out the window resting her eyes from reading. Michael was sitting in front of the heater duct, eyes closed, luxuriating in the hot wind blowing over him. Jackie had been pushing him all morning but now she was fixing her gaze outside to ease her headache.

"So, kid, what's your story?"

Michael was instantly alert. "What do you mean?"

"Ralph told me you didn't have anybody outside. I know that much." Jackie turned her great head to look at him, and then stared outside again. "Where are your folks? Mom and Dad? Uncle and Aunt?"

"Mom and Dad died, like everybody else." Michael shrugged. There wasn't much to say about it. "Uncle Ned let me stay with him over near the Cathedral until he got caught by the Long Bottom Boys. I got away. I've been scrounging until now."

"Tough out there, is it?"

"I guess. It wasn't so bad with Ned. I took care of him. He took care of me."

Jackie looked at him. "What does *that* mean?"

"As long as I kept him happy, he gave me a place to live and fed me and protected me from anybody else." Michael considered Jackie thoughtfully. "I'm not sure what it takes to make an elephant happy."

"Just do your job," Jackie snapped at him. "That'll be enough."

She didn't speak for a moment. "Do you know how to get to the river from here?"

"Sure. But I wouldn't try it. The Boys have everything sewed up around the park. I sure found that out." He patted the duct and closed his eyes. "You have it nice here. Ralph keeps everybody out. You have food and heat. I sure wouldn't leave."

"I bet," Jackie said dryly. "Okay. Let's look at the lab books again."

Over the next week, Ralph often spoke with Jackie. Most of the time Jackie sent Michael outside. Having nothing better to do, Michael took to visiting the other animals.

There weren't many of them. Most of the exhibits were sealed and empty. The reptile house and the ape refuge were long abandoned. The bears were gone but some of the birds were still in the aviary and Michael stood for an hour in front of a single, lonely rhinoceros.

The rhino room became his favorite refuge. The rhino wasn't short with him. The rhino didn't ask him strange questions or snort with contempt when he tried to answer. The rhino didn't call him an idiot. The rhino didn't speak.

"Michael?" Ralph's voice came from the ceiling.

"Yes, Ralph."

"Jackie and I are finished for the moment. You can come back."

"Yeah." Michael didn't speak for a moment. "I do everything she asks."

"I know."

"I don't talk back. I clean up after her. And elephants make a lot of shit. Why does she treat me like it?"

"You're human. She has no love of humans. She needs you. That makes it worse."

"What did humans do to her?"

"She's the last of her herd. Humans brought her ancestors from India. Human scientists raised her and the others in these concrete stalls and gave her the power of speech. Then, they let the rest of her herd die."

"How come?"

"The scientists didn't have much choice. They were already dead."

"A plague like what killed my folks?"

"Somewhat. From what you told me, your parents died from one of the neo-influenzas. The scientists died of contagious botulism."

"Where did all the plagues come from? How many are there?"

"Six hundred and seventy-two was the last count I received. But that was a few years ago and the data feed was getting unreliable toward the end. They came from different places. Some were natural. Some weren't. Several were home grown by people with an agenda: religious martyrdom, political revenge, economic policy disagreements, broken romances. Some started out natural and were then modified for similar reasons."

Michael mulled over what he understood. He didn't have Ralph to himself very often. Likely this chance wouldn't last long. "If she doesn't like people so much, why are we spending so much time going through all the lab books? Why doesn't she just leave?"

"That's not for me to say."

Dear Mom,

> *I thought elephants were nice. Jackie doesn't like anybody. Not even Ralf. Hes nice to me but Jackie says*

*he has to be that way. He's a machine like the Keepers.
Jackie said Ralf coodnt do what I am doing. It had to
be a human beang.*

*But I still like her even if she doesnt like me. I like
to watch her when shes eating. Its neat to watch her
use her trunk, like a snake thats also a hand. There are
two knobs on the end of her trunk she uses like fingers.
Only they are much stronger than fingers. She pinched
me yesterday and today its still sore!*

*I moved my bed to the loft. That way its right over
the heater and the hot air comes right up under me.
Its like sleeping in warm water.*

*I miss you and Dad. If you can see us from up there
in heavun, try to make Jackie not get mad all the time.*

Love, Mike

"Where did you find this?" Jackie pinned him against the
wall. She held up a green lab book in her trunk.

Michael tried to push her away but it was like trying to
move a mountain. "I'm not sure."

"Where?"

Michael stopped struggling. "If you don't like what I'm
doing, then do it yourself."

"That's *your* job."

"Then, *back off!*"

A moment passed. Jackie eased backwards. She handed
him the lab book.

"Here's the date range," she said pointing to the numbers
on the page with her trunk. "See? Month, slash, day, slash,
year. Here's the volume number. This is volume six. I need
volume seven for the same date."

"What's it going to tell you?"

Jackie raised her trunk and for a moment it looked like
she was going to strike him. Michael stared at her.

Slowly, she lowered her trunk. "I'm not sure yet."

"Say thank you."

Jackie went completely still. "What did you say?"

"I said, say thank you." Michael's fists were clenched.

Jackie seemed to relax. She made a sound like a chuckle. "Get the lab book and I'll thank you."

"Fair enough," he said shortly.

Back in the offices, he stood in the hall and let his breath out slowly. His hands were shaking.

"Good for you, Michael," Ralph said from overhead.

"Yeah. Now, I've got to find the lab book she wants."

"In the corner of each room is a camera," said Ralph. "If you can hold up the papers, I can help."

An hour later, he walked back into Jackie's stall and solemnly held out the lab book to her.

"Thank you," Jackie said in a neutral tone. "Hold it up to my eye."

"Okay."

Michael nodded.

Reading the lab book didn't take long.

"That's enough," Jackie said.

"What do you want me to do with it?"

"I don't care. I'm going outside."

Jackie turned and left the stall. Michael was surprised. It was cold out there and snow still remained on the ground from the night before.

He opened the lab book and went over the pages. There were few words but several figures and dates. It didn't mean anything to him.

"What's going on, Ralph?" Michael shivered and looked up at the gray sky. Spring was sure a long time coming. Ralph had told him this was April.

"I'm not sure," Ralph said. "Maybe she found what she was looking for."

Michael woke in the middle of the night. Sleepily, he looked over the edge of the loft. A Keeper was helping Jackie put something over her back.

"I don't think I can do it," Ralph said.

"Quiet. You'll wake him. Maybe you can toss it over my neck and tie the ropes underneath."

Michael sat on the edge of the loft and watched them a moment.

"You're leaving," he said after a moment.

"You're supposed to be asleep." Jackie tossed her trunk irritably.

Michael didn't say anything. He climbed down to the apron and walked over to them.

The Keeper was trying to pull some kind of harness over her neck and back.

"Give me a knee up," Michael said. "I can help."

"No human will ever be on my back!" snarled Jackie.

"Suit yourself," Michael said. "But the only way you're going to be able to tie that harness is if you can center it on your back first and Ralph can't do it. I can if I can get on your back."

The Keeper extended his arm. "Here," said Ralph.

Michael stood on the camera and the Keeper extended it until Michael could jump to Jackie's neck. He grabbed the base of her ear and pulled himself up.

"That stings," she said.

"Sorry."

In a few moments, he had the harness in place. Then, he dropped to the floor and pulled it tight.

"Good job, Michael," said Ralph.

Jackie shook herself and shifted her shoulders and back. "It's tight. I'm ready."

Michael looked first at the Keeper, then at Jackie. "Are you closing the Zoo?"

"Not immediately," said Ralph. "The food trucks have been coming in sporadically. I still have contacts with the farm and the warehouse. I've spoken with power and water. They say they are well defended but if somebody digs up a cable or blows up the pipes . . ." Ralph paused a moment. "My worst scenario is a year. My best scenario is five years."

Michael felt suddenly lost. He looked up at Jackie.

"Take me with you."

"What?" Jackie snorted. "No way."

"Come on," Michael pleaded. "Look, to everybody out there, all you are is steak on a stroll. I can get you out of the city. Tell me where you want to go."

"I—"

"She's going south," Ralph said smoothly. "She needs to follow the river south to the I-255 Bridge and then south to Tennessee."

"Where's I-255?"

"Oakville."

Michael thought for a moment. "That's not going to work. It'll be dicey enough to get past the Long Bottom Boys around the park. But the Rank Bastards live that way and they have an old armory. Even the Boys are scared of them."

"What do you suggest?" asked Ralph.

"Don't ask him." Jackie stamped her foot. "I can make it on my own."

Michael stood next to her. He looked at the ground. "I'm a kid. I don't have a gun. I'm not even very big. I can't hurt you."

Jackie looked away.

Michael nodded. "Well, once you're out of the park you can't go south. That's the Green Belt—sharpshooters. They don't ask questions. You just fall down dead about two miles away. You can't go north through the Farm Country. They don't have sharpshooters but they burned everything to the ground for six miles around them so you can't hide. That means west or east. Gangs in both directions just like the Long Bottom Boys or worse. I'd take the old highway right into town to the bridge and take it across. There's no boss around the bridge; there's nothing there anybody wants. The road is high off the ground so you can't be seen. If you're quiet and quick, you can get through before anybody knows. Then, I'd stay on the highway all the way down. People stick to the farms to protect them. The highways don't have anything. There are no gangs below Cahokia nor many people either. Prairie Plagues got them. South of Cahokia, I don't know anything."

"How do you know all this?" Jackie snarled.

Michael stared at her. "If you don't know where things are somebody's going to have you for lunch. Uncle Ned taught me that and I'm still alive, aren't I?"

Jackie tossed her head and didn't reply.

"Jackie?" asked Ralph. "The idea has merit."

Jackie didn't speak for a long time. She stared out the door of the stall. Then, she turned her head back to him. "Okay," she asked reluctantly.

"When do we leave?" Michael turned to the Keeper.

Jackie slapped the back of his head. "Right now. Get aboard."

Michael rubbed his head. "That hurt," he said as he climbed up on her back.

She rumbled out of the light.

"Good luck!" called Ralph after them.

"Wait!" Michael turned and called back. "What's going to happen to the rhino?"

He couldn't hear the reply.

They didn't say anything as Jackie walked slowly down behind the reptile house. Her ears were spread out and listening. The gate swung open at a brush of her trunk. Michael was impressed. A secret entrance.

"Check it out."

Michael slipped to the ground and peered through the bushes. No Boys. He signaled and she followed him, pushing aside the branches. She knelt down and he climbed back up. They listened. Nothing. She started walking up the hill.

Jackie was quieter than he'd imagined. She walked with only a soft, deep padding sound.

She stopped at the edge of the road. "Where to?" she asked in a low rumble.

Michael leaned next to her ear and whispered as quietly as he could. "Don't talk. I'll tell you where to go. Go to the right down the road. Then, when you go over the bridge, walk down to your left. That's where the highway is."

Jackie nodded abruptly and he could tell she wasn't pleased that he should tell her to be quiet but she didn't say anything. He figured he'd get an earful if they made it down below the river.

Michael looked around and listened. It was in the middle of the night. He couldn't smell a fire. Sometimes the Boys built a fire with the contents of one of the old houses. They drank whatever hooch they could find—raiding other gangs if necessary—and fired guns into the air and shouted at the moon until dawn. That would have been ideal. If Michael and Jackie were seen by the party, they would be seen by drunks.

No fire meant one of two things. Either there was no one around here or they were out hunting. A bunch of hungry, desperate, *sober* Long Bottom Boys was about the worst news Michael could think of. There was no hint of sweetness in the air—no mushroom festooned corpses indicating the site of a battle. That was good. The Long Bottom Boys were big on ceremonial mourning and they killed anyone they found. There weren't many left in Saint Louis but not so few that the Boys couldn't find someone to kill and then ritually stand over while the mushrooms returned the corpse to the earth.

Michael sweated every foot of the walk to the highway. But the night remained silent.

The highway here was level with the ground but after a mile or two, it rose to a grand promenade looking down on the ruins of the city. Michael whispered to Jackie that now was the time to run *(quietly!)* if she could.

Jackie didn't reply. Instead, she lengthened her stride until he had to grab on to her ears to stay on her neck. He looked down and saw the riotous dark of her legs moving on the pavement.

There was a shot behind them in the direction of the park. Jackie stopped and turned around. They saw a flash and a dull boom. Then, gradually like the sunrise, the glow of an increasing fire.

Oh, Michael thought hollowly as he stared at the tips of the flames showing over the trees. That's what was going to happen to the rhino.

"Come on," he urged. "People are going to wake up. We need to get near the river before they start looking away from the park."

The road curved around the south of downtown and then north to reach the river bridges. They could not see the river below them as they crossed but they heard the hiss and rush of the water, the low grunt of the bridge as it eased itself against the flow, the cracks and booms as floating debris struck the pilings.

Then, they were over it and traveling south, the flat farmland on their left, the river bluffs on their right, the road determinedly south toward Cahokia.

Dear Mom,

We reached Cahokia a little before daylite. We could tell we got there by the sign on the highway. I wasnt tired at all. But Jackee was. It must have been hard work walking all that way. Heres something intristing. Eleefants cant run. Jackee told me. They can walk relly fast but they are to big to run.

Jackee still doesnt like me much. She doesnt talk to me unless its to get help figuring out where we are. Mostly she can figur it out. But she needs my hands. I figur one of these days shell leave while I am asleep. So I sav things when I can.

She says we're going to Tenesee. Howald, Tenesee. There used to be eleefants there. She says she thinks they might be still there. If she doesn't find them there, she's going to try to get to Florida. It's warm all the time down there. There's lots of food to eat and it's never winter. That sounds pretty good to me.

I would like to stay with her. She is big and pretty and reel strong. She doesnt talk to me very nice. I dont think she would protek me like Ned did.

I will writ agin tomoro.

love, mike

Michael was surprised that they saw no people in Cahokia. The farmlands he had been thinking of were bounded by weeds but, other than that, looked as if cultivated by invisible hands. They saw no one. The only sounds were the spring birds, the river and the wind. Every few steps they could see a little mound of soil. The mushrooms had all dried up and blown away but these mounds still marked where someone had died.

That first day, when they made camp in a hidden clearing, Michael discovered that Ralph had planned for him to accompany Jackie all along. There was a tent, sleeping bag and all manner of tools: a tiny shovel, a knife, a small bow and arrow, the smallest and most precious fishing set Michael had ever seen. In a flap cunningly designed to be hidden, he found a pistol that fit his hand perfectly. Next to it, separated into stock, barrel, and laser sight, was a high powered rifle. A second flap had ammunition for both, exploding and impact bullets in clearly marked containers. Michael stared at them. He suddenly realized he could take down an elephant with this weapon. Ralph must have known that. The implied trust shook him.

"What did you find?"

Michael realized she hadn't seen the guns. The pistol was no threat. He pulled it out and showed it to her.

"Do you know how to use it?"

"Yes." He replaced the pistol. Next to the weapons were Jackie's vitamin supplements along with finely labeled medicines and administration devices that only a human being could use.

Jackie snorted when she saw it all laid out.

Michael looked at everything, sorted and arrayed in front of him, for a long time. He wondered how long they'd be able to keep such treasures as this. He realized he might need the rifle.

Occasionally between long stretches of young woods and tall fresh meadows, they saw a few manicured fields that were laid out so ruler straight that the two of them stopped and stared. These, Jackie told him, must be tilled by machines. No human or animal would ever pay such obsessive attention to details. But no machines could be seen and even these meticulous rows of corn or soybeans were frayed at the edges into weeds and brambles.

Even so, as tempting as a field of new corn was to Jackie,

she was unwilling to chance it. Machines were chancy things, she said, with triggers and idiosyncrasies. Even negotiating with Ralph had been difficult when it went against his programming. Better to wait until they found an overgrown field down the road.

Jackie had no trouble finding food. It had been a wet spring and now that the sun had come out, the older and uncultivated fields sprouted volunteer squash and greens.

They fell into a routine. In the evening, they agreed on a likely spot and Michael took the harness off of her and set up camp. Michael was afraid she might step on him while she slept, so Jackie slept off a little ways from Michael's tent.

At first light, Jackie went off to find her day's sustenance. Michael made himself breakfast out of the stores Ralph had left him. He tried his hand at fishing in the tributary rivers of the Mississippi and gradually learned enough to catch enough for a good meal. He tried to eat as much as he could in the morning. It was likely they wouldn't stop until nightfall.

After he had eaten and before Jackie returned, he waited, wondering if she would come back.

She always did. She eased herself down the bank and drank, knee deep in the river.

Jackie was always impatient to get started and stamped her feet as Michael repacked the harness. Then she made a knee for him and he climbed aboard.

Always they went south. Always as quickly as Jackie could. Hohenwald first, since that was where the elephant sanctuary had been. But continuing South after that, if she didn't find them. South, she told him, was warm in the winter. South had food all year around.

Michael was amenable. He felt pretty safe. He was well fed. He'd learned the trick of riding Jackie and enjoyed watching the river on the right slip smoothly ahead of them and the land on the left buckle and roll up into bluffs and hills.

Spring turned warm and gentle. Michael felt happier than he could remember up until they reached the spot where the Ohio poured into the Mississippi and the bridge was gone.

They stood on the ramp of Interstate 57 looking down at the wreckage. The near side of where the bridge had been was completely dry. Stained pilings that had clearly been underwater at one point rested comfortably in a grassy field. On the far side, the remains of the bridge had broken off a high bluff as if the whole southern bank of the river had slid downhill. The river narrowed here, to speed up and pour into the slower moving Mississippi. Huge waves burst into the air as the rivers fought one another. They were over a mile away from the battle, but even from here they could hear the roar.

"The earthquake, maybe?" muttered Jackie.

"Earthquake?"

"About eight years ago the New Madrid fault caused a big quake down here. Ralph told me about it. The scientists had expected it to hit Saint Louis as well but the effects were to the east so we were spared." Jackie shook her great head and swayed from one side to another. "How are we going to get across now?"

Michael looked at the old atlas. "There's a dam upstream near Grand Chain Landing."

"Look at the bridge!" Jackie trumpeted and pointed with her trunk. "It's just a sample. Look at the river. The dam is probably gone, too."

Michael looked upstream. "We'll find something. We just can't go south for a little while."

Jackie just snorted. After a moment, she turned slowly toward the east.

Dear Mom,

So far we still haven't been able to cross the OHIO river. I think it was even bigger than the Missspi. Even at night, we can hear it rushing by. Every now and than, something floats by. Today I saw six trees, a traler and an old house float by. Jackie says it's becawse of the flud upstreem.

I can tell sumthing is bothering jackie. She hasnt been as mean lately. Its not just that we arnt moving sowth. It is sumthing more.

Love, Mike

As Jackie predicted, the dam was gone. Perhaps the Ohio, powered by spring rains, had ripped apart the turbines and concrete. The ground trembled as the water poured over the remaining rubble.

"Now what?" Jackie said in a soft rumble.

"Could you swim across?" Michael asked doubtfully. "Can't elephants swim?"

"Look at the water," Jackie said shrilly. "No one can swim through that."

"Then *not* here. How about where the water doesn't run so fast?"

Jackie didn't answer.

Michael stared at the map closely.

"There used to be a ferry in Metropolis. Maybe we could get a boat."

"A *ferry*?" Jackie turned her head and looked at him out of the corner of her eye. "I weigh in at six tons."

Michael nodded. "A big ferry, then. Couldn't hurt to look. It's just a few miles up the road."

"A ferry," Jackie muttered. "A *ferry.*"

The center of Metropolis clustered around a bend in Highway 45. Jackie and Michael followed the signs down to the docks. The shadow of the broken Interstate 24 Bridge fell across the road and in the distance they could see the disconnected ends of the lesser Highway 45 bridge.

A great half sunken coal barge rested against the dock on the right side. The surface of the water was punctured by the rusting remains of antennas poking up from drowned powerboats on the left. Between them nestled the ferry *Encantante,* incongruously upright and unmangled. A man sat on the deck, whittling. He looked up as they came down the hill.

"Don't believe I've ever seen an elephant down this way

before," he said as he stood up. "What can I do for you?" He was a tall, thin man. Michael couldn't tell exactly how old he was. His hair was turning gray but his face seemed smooth and unwrinkled. Thirty, thought Michael. Doesn't people's hair turn gray when they are thirty? The man was dressed in a red and black plaid jacket against the cool river air.

Michael spoke up before Jackie could respond. He hoped she would remain silent. He was pretty sure talking elephants would be suspicious.

"We need to get across."

"Do you, now?" He tapped out his pipe against the side of the ferry and refilled it carefully. "My name's Gerry. Gerry Myers. You are?"

"Michael Ripley. This is Jackie."

Gerry nodded. "All right then." He looked at the elephant. "I've never put an elephant on my boat. But it can't weigh much more than four or five of those little cars so it would probably be okay. He won't jump or move about?"

"Jackie's a girl." Michael looked at the water ripping along.

Gerry followed his gaze. "Yeah. 'She,' then. She won't move around? Be a damned shame if she turned over the boat and killed us all."

"She won't."

"Good. Well, then. Since you are the only human being I've seen in some months," Gerry said dryly, "and since I've buried everybody else, I'm inclined to think about your proposal." Gerry looked at him closely. "You're not sick, are you?"

Michael shrugged. "I feel pretty good."

"Doesn't mean much, does it?"

Michael shook his head.

Gerry stared out over the river and sighed. "Yeah. The last good citizen of the Metropolis that had lunch with me said he hadn't felt this good in months. I went looking for him when he didn't show up for dinner. He was dead sitting in his kitchen with a smile on his face. Only thing I can say is apparently he died so suddenly he forgot to feel bad about it."

Gerry lit his pipe and puffed at it for a moment. "Speaking of lunch, I'm a bit hungry. Care to eat with me?"

Michael hesitated.

Gerry pointed at the bluff up the hill from them. "On the other side of that is an old soybean field. Lots of good leafy growth for Jackie. Maybe you could turn her loose and eat with me."

"I don't know." Gerry didn't look like somebody that would kill him and roast Jackie. Uncle Ned had known who to trust—until the day he didn't, Michael corrected himself. How could you tell? Michael had a sneaking suspicion he would have to pay for the ride one way or another.

"Well, the field's there. Suit yourself. I'll be eating lunch in half an hour or so. In that warehouse looking building over there. Come by if you want to."

Michael nodded. Jackie turned and started up the hill.

The field was as advertised and there were no visible people around to take advantage of them.

"I'll eat here. You watch," said Jackie.

"I'd just as soon go on and have lunch with the old man," Michael said as he unharnessed her. "We still have to cross the river. Seems like we ought to know something about the other side."

"I don't trust him."

"You don't trust anybody." Michael rummaged through the packs until he found the pistol. "I got this."

"You be careful, then," Jackie said. "I'll be coming down there if you try to run off."

"Yeah. I like you, too." Michael hefted the pistol. It was heavier than it looked. He made sure it was loaded and checked the action.

Jackie watched him. "Where did you learn to handle a gun?"

"Uncle Ned taught me," Michael said shortly. "I kept guard when he foraged."

"Then . . ." Jackie stopped for a moment. "If you had the gun, why didn't you leave him?"

"It took both of us to stay alive." Michael released the chamber and made sure the safety was on. He put the gun in his pocket. "He was a lot bigger than I was. He protected me. I helped him. Staying with him made a lot of sense."

"But he—" Jackie shook her head.

"When the Boys found us he sent me off and took them on by himself."

Jackie was silent a moment. "So you wanted to leave with me because I'm a lot bigger than you are. I can protect you. Staying with me makes a lot of sense."

Michael stared at her. "Are you kidding? I'm traveling with six tons of fresh meat. What part of that makes sense to you?"

"Then why did you come with me?"

Michael stood up and didn't answer. He trotted down the hill toward the landing. Jackie stared after him.

Gerry was cooking in an apartment above the warehouse. The room had a nautical feel to it. Every piece of furniture had been carefully placed. The curtains over the window were a red and white check. The table was an austere gray, with metal legs and a top made of some kind of plastic. The countertops looked similar.

Two plates had been set out. The fork on the left, knife and spoon on the right, napkin folded just so on the plate. Plastic water glasses were set at precisely the same angle for each place setting.

Michael stood in the doorway, not sure what to do. Coming into the room felt like breaking something.

"Come on in," said Gerry. He was stirring a pot. The contents bubbled and smelled deliciously meaty. "Channel catfish bouillabaisse." He ladled out two full bowls and handed one to Michael. "Been simmering since this morning. Have a seat."

They sat across the table and in a few moments, Michael forgot Gerry was even there. He only remembered where he was when the bowl was half empty. Michael looked up.

Gerry was watching him with a smile on his face. "Good to see someone enjoy my cooking. Want some bread? Baked it yesterday."

Michael broke off a piece. Next to the bread was a small

plate with butter. For a long minute, Michael stared, unable to recognize it. Then he remembered and smeared the bread across it.

"Whoa there. Use the knife."

Michael shrugged, pulled out his small hunting knife and smeared the butter across the bread.

Gerry raised his eyebrows and chuckled. "Fair enough. But next time use the little knife next to the butter."

Michael sopped up the rest of the soup with the bread and leaned back in his chair, stuffed and happy.

Gerry picked up the bowls and put them in the sink. "Come on down to the porch."

Michael followed him outside and down the stairs to a part of the dock that jutted over the water. Under an awning, he sat down in a lawn chair while Gerry pulled a box out of the river and opened it. He pulled out two bottles. He gave Michael the root beer and kept a regular beer for himself.

Michael sat back in the chair and savored the sharp, creamy flavor.

Gerry said nothing and the two of them watched the river roll by.

"So," Gerry said at last. "What's waiting for you on the other side of the river?"

"Hohenwald, Tennessee," Michael said and sipped his root beer. He could get used to this. "Then, maybe Florida."

"What's in Hohenwald?"

"An elephant sanctuary. Elephants don't like to be alone."

Gerry nodded. "I thought Florida was underwater."

"A lot of it is. But Jackie says the upper part of Florida is still there." Michael stopped.

"I see," said Gerry. He was silent a moment. "You're an awful nice boy to be crazy."

Michael didn't say anything. If Gerry wanted to think he was crazy that was all right with him.

"You don't think you'll find anybody down there, do you?" asked Gerry.

Michael shrugged. "How would I know?"

Gerry nodded. "Everything's pretty much fallen apart.

I think there might be five people left alive here in Metropolis. You'd think we'd hang together. But it didn't seem to work out that way. There might be a few hundred out in the countryside. Seems like I spent the last five years burying everyone I've ever known. I can't believe it's much better down south."

Michael finished his root beer and put it on the deck. "That's where Jackie has to go. She has to have something she can eat in the winter."

Michael looked up at the remains of the bridge. He had only really known Saint Louis. It looked like things were messed up everywhere. For the first time he had an inkling what that meant.

"What was it like before?" Michael muttered.

Michael had been talking to himself, but even so, Gerry reacted. His face seemed to take on a rubbery texture. "Everything just came apart. First, the weather went to shit. Then came plagues, one after another. And not just people. Birds. Cattle. Sheep. Wheat. Beans. There was about six years where you couldn't get a tomato unless you grew it yourself. Even then, it wasn't much better than fifty-fifty. Oaks. Sequoias. Shrimp. Government would figure out how to make tomatoes grow again and every maple in the county would fall over and rot. They'd get a handle on that and the next thing you know somebody had engineered a virus that lived in milk. Why would anyone ever do that?" He shook his head. "Figured that one out after a couple of million kids. Right after that, the corn began to wither. We got a strain of corn that would grow and a tidal wave comes roaring over the East Coast. Boston, Providence, and New York go under water."

He stopped and sat up. He pulled out his bandanna and wiped his eyes. "If I believed in God, I'd go out and kill a calf on a rock or something. We sure as hell pissed him off." Gerry sighed. "Ah, mustn't grumble." He sipped his beer, composed again.

Michael stared at him. Maybe Gerry did this all the time. "So," began Michael after a long and awkward silence. "We should cross here?"

"That's true. I'm pretty much the only game in town. But that's not my point." He pointed over the river at the opposite shore. "That's Kentucky. Or what's left of it. Things have been falling apart for a long, long time. I was sitting on my boat twenty years ago when the big rush came down the river that took out the two bridges. I could see it coming, a fifteen foot wall of trash and debris rolling down on top of us. I had just enough time to pull *Encantante* into the creek downstream behind the oak bluffs when it washed over Metropolis and scoured everything between us and Cairo. Back then we still had people living here so we were able to clean up and rebuild over a couple of years." Gerry chuckled. "My little ferry business picked up because nobody was going to rebuild the bridges—we were still in a *crisis* at that point. It hadn't become a disaster yet. Not enough people had died."

"Where did the water come from?"

Gerry shook his head. "Never really figured that out. Was it just the Smithland Dam that let go? Or did one big flood start way up the river and then take out all the dams one by one on the way down? I do know that flood is what took out the two dams downstream from here and when I did go up to look at Smithland, there wasn't much left of it. I came back. Then, about six years later, I loaded up a boat I had with all the fuel I could find and went up nearly five hundred miles to see what the hell was going on. It's not like you could trust anything you heard on the radio. I only knew what had happened here. I didn't turn around until I reached Cincinnati. There wasn't a bridge or a dam left standing the whole way. This was before the earthquake. Maybe somebody blew them up. It was a big mystery until other things sort of overshadowed it. But you let me wander away from my point again."

"Hey, it wasn't my fault."

"My point is that now the only thing that keeps what's on the Kentucky shore from coming over onto this shore is that river."

Michael shook his head. "So? What's over there that's not over here?"

Gerry shrugged. "Things. Big lizards, sometimes. Maybe

a crocodile or two. Big animals—I haven't seen any elephants. But I might have seen a tiger."

"Yeah, right." Michael snorted. "Pull the other one. A mountain lion, maybe."

Gerry shrugged again. "When we put dams and bridges across the water, cars and buses weren't the only things that crossed. Now the dams and bridges are gone and what lives on the other side stays on the other side. It's not going to be as easy to get over here as it was before."

"We crossed the bridge in Saint Louis. It was just fine."

Gerry pulled his pipe out of his pocket along with his pocket knife and began cleaning the bowl. "Maybe things can't cross up that far north. Maybe the Mississippi keeps things from crossing west just like the Ohio keeps things from crossing north. Maybe I'm just having old man hallucinations. But I know what I saw. There are things that live on *that* side of the river I don't see on *this* side. You cross the river and they're sure as hell going to see *you*."

Michael didn't look at him. "That's where she has to go. She just can't get food up here in the winter."

"What did you do in Saint Louis?"

"The Zoo kept us alive. But it's gone now."

Gerry sighed. "She's a pretty animal. I guess there's no animal on earth so noble and beautiful, and just plain *big,* as an elephant. But it doesn't belong here. Jackie should be in India."

"I can't take her to India."

"I know that." Gerry hesitated. "Maybe it's time to cut her loose."

Michael stared at the decking. He didn't know what to say.

Gerry pointed across the river. "Tell you what. You and I take her across the river and let her off the boat. Maybe she'll work her way south. You come back here with me."

Michael looked at him, trying to see if there was some hint of Uncle Ned in his face. He couldn't tell. Michael was in no particular hurry to repeat that arrangement. "I don't know."

Gerry finished tamping the tobacco in the bowl and lit his pipe. "You know that soybean field I sent you to up on the hill? It's a pretty field, isn't it? The soybeans are one of those perennial varieties popular about fifteen years ago. When I was a kid that was a toxic waste site with a lot of mercury and cadmium and toxic solvents. Don't look at me that way. That was years ago. It's safe enough for her now. Anyway, you know how they reclaimed it?"

"No."

"It was pretty neat, actually. They took some engineered corn. Corn pushes its roots deep into the soil—as much as ten feet in some varieties. This corn pulled up the metals and concentrated them into the kernels of the ear. It discolored the kernels. Some were silver, some were bright blue."

"I don't understand."

"Anyway," continued Gerry. "Because of the metal concentration, the kernels were expected to be sterile. Most of them were. But coons attacked the field and ate some and got sick. So that was one problem they had. Crows pecked at the ears and got sick. That was another. Bits of the ears were dragged by various animals a ways away. Turned out some were fertile after all. They took root and started growing over data lines. The plant couldn't tell the difference between a heavy metal being cleaned up in a waste site or a similar heavy metal in a computer underground."

Michael stamped his feet. "What are you talking about?"

Gerry stared hard at him. "I don't know what's across the river. I'm saying it could be anything."

"What? Killer corn?"

Gerry snorted. "Of course not. But if people can rebuild corn and it escapes what else could they have done? Crocodiles to control Asian lung fish? Killer bees to control oak borers? I *know* what lives around here. I live with it every day. I *know* things are different across the river." Gerry calmed himself. "You take your elephant across the river if you want to. But you'll come back and stay here with me if you're smart."

Jackie was waiting for him in the afternoon shade. A vast section of the soybean field had been leveled and she looked well-fed for the first time in several days.

Michael looked around. "Tasty?"

Jackie looked at the field. "Pretty good."

Her belly even seemed a little swollen.

"How much longer until we get to Hohenwald?"

Jackie shook her head. "Couple of weeks, I hope."

"And Florida?"

"*If* we go to Florida, I expect we'll get there mid-summer."

Michael thought for a moment. "Do you know the date?"

"It's the first of May."

"May day," said Michael slowly. "That's six weeks."

Jackie looked at him with one eye. "So?"

"Could you get there faster if you weren't carrying me?"

"It wouldn't make any difference. I could only go faster if I didn't take the time to keep fed. But I can't afford to starve myself. Not now."

"How come?"

"Never mind."

"You're hiding something."

"So what? It doesn't concern you."

"Who the hell do you think you are?" shouted Michael, surprising them both.

Jackie stepped back. For a moment she stood, arrested, one leg raised ready in defense, three solidly on the ground.

"Are you going to squash me for shouting at you?" Michael shook his head in disgust. "I was better off with Ned."

Slowly, Jackie eased her leg down. She turned and silently walked over to the pond in the middle of the soy bean field. Michael watched as she pulled up water and splashed it over herself.

Dear Mom,

I don't think Jackee will ever like me. I guess I was fooling myself. She's an eleefant. She hates me because I'm a person and people did things to her and other eleefants.

Gerry wants me to stay here with him. He has a good thing here. Metropolis has a power sorse so he can stay warm for a long time. With everybody gone,

the left over preserved food will be good for years.
There are some wild crops here, too. Ned never had it
so good.

Jackee doesn't need me. Most of the stuff Ralph
packed was for me. I could rig a bag for her to carry
around her neck for the stuff she has to have. That
ought to be enough. And it's not like I'm holding stuff
for her to read anymore. Whatever she found back at
the Zoo must have been all she wanted. She hasn't
been interested in anything but going south since.

When I told this to Jackee she didn't say anything
for a while. Then, all she said was, Suit yourself.

So, I guess I'll be staying in Metropolis.

love, Mike

Gerry waited at the ferry while Michael walked with
Jackie back up to the soybean field. Michael decided he didn't
want Gerry to know about her. It felt safer to keep everything quiet. Jackie followed his lead silently.

Michael kept glancing at her as she ate, trying to see if
she had any regrets he was staying here. Her elephantine
face was inexpressive but her movements were short and
abrupt. Could she be angry at him for staying? Or just impatient to be on her way?

When she was done, he slung the makeshift bag around
her neck so she could reach it and led her back down to the
dock. She stepped gingerly onto the metal floor of the ferry.
There was plenty of room and even in the strong current, it
only swayed slightly.

Gerry cast off without comment and angled the ferry upstream into the river. Michael felt the powerful motor bite
into the current and the entire craft hummed. But he could
not hear the motor itself, only the churning of the propeller.

Gerry caught his expression. "Quiet, isn't she? Electric
motor."

He pulled up the hatch. Michael saw a roundish cube with
the shaft coming out connected with thick cables to a cylin-
drical device.

"That's the motor," Gerry said pointing to the cube. "That's power storage." He pointed to the cylinder.

"A battery?"

"They called it a fuel coil when I bought the boat. Not sure how it works but it holds about forty hours of power. These days I charge it up from a little turbine I dropped off the dock. Don't need to use the boat that much. For longer trips I can charge it from a big fuel cell I can carry with me." He dropped the hatch with a clang and returned to the wheel.

The *Encantante* passed the main eddy line and entered the center of the river. Gerry stepped up the motor and angled the *Encantante* more steeply. The ripples and twists in the current caused the boat to shift and slide a little. Not enough to make standing difficult but enough so Michael noticed. It made him grin. Jackie looked around nervously.

Then, they were across the main river and nearing the far side. Gerry eased off the throttle and dropped the *Encantante* below a bluff jutting out into the water. Again they crossed a strong eddy that made the ferry jump a moment. The water grew calm and Gerry brought *Encantante* to the dock.

Michael led Jackie off the ferry and stood with her for a moment in the middle of the road. He looked east, judging the vegetation. There was plenty. The forest was thick on the other side of the road and he could see the break in the trees signifying a field. Jackie wouldn't starve.

Turning away from Gerry so he couldn't see, Michael pulled the atlas out of his jacket.

"Here. You walk down here to Interstate 24 and take it south. Then take Highway 45 to Benton. Once you get to Benton, hunt around until you find Highway 641. Take that to Interstate 40, east. Then—"

"You've been over this. A lot."

"Well, I wrote it down. There's a leather holder I made for you. It's tied to the belt and the directions are in it along with the map book. I drew it all out on the map so you wouldn't get lost."

"Thanks," said Jackie shortly.

Michael nodded and stuffed the atlas into the bag. "You take care of yourself."

Jackie watched him as he walked back to the ferry. Michael felt his eyes sting. He looked back.

Jackie was only a few feet away. Something shook the brush on the far side of the road. Before he fully registered what it was, he was running at it, yelling at Jackie to back away. Gerry tried to grab him but Michael ducked under his hands.

It raised its thick body high on its legs and ran toward Jackie, its mouth open and narrow as a snakes. *Lizard? Crocodile?* He ran past and stood, screaming, between them.

The thing stopped, closed its mouth and stepped back only so long for a long tongue to slip out and back. Then it lunged forward and grabbed for Michael. Michael danced back but it grabbed his leg and shook him off his feet, then raised its claws over him.

Michael heard trumpeting. Jackie's leg came down on its midsection. The creature ruptured and blood and meat spewed across the road. Its jaw opened reflexively and Michael scrambled back. Jackie stamped on it until it was nothing but a flat, smeared ruin. Then she looked at Michael.

Michael smiled at her. She leaned over him and wrapped her trunk around his leg. He looked down and saw the blood and felt nauseous.

"This will hurt," she said. She wrapped her trunk around his leg and squeezed.

For a moment, Michael couldn't see or breathe.

"Gerry!" Jackie shouted. *"Get over here and pick him up!"*

Gerry ran over to them and as he lifted Michael by the shoulders, Jackie lifted his leg.

The pounding in his leg seemed to drown out everything.

Back in the ferry, Michael looked around. He must have blacked out a moment for they were now deep in the middle of the river. He felt sleepy.

"Don't you go away on me," said Jackie, kneeling next to him. "You stay here. *Michael*—"

Michael wanted to say he was sorry but he was as light as smoke and he drifted away.

Part 2

It was all light and dark for a long time. When things were lighter he slept in a brown haze as if he were swimming in honey. He was warm and safe. Occasionally, he was convulsed with pain. He couldn't tell where the pain was coming from exactly. Sometimes it seemed to come from his neck. Other times, his leg. Sometimes he was riven by pain that seemed to come from nowhere.

This went on, it seemed, forever. Then, it grew lighter and he opened his eyes.

He was in a room, in a bed, that reminded him of when his parents still lived. The room had a window. As then the bed had been pushed against the wall so he could look out the window. It had sheets and a blanket. He fingered them gently, wondering if he was dreaming. Outside, the sun shone. His leg hurt.

He heard a grunt and Jackie's head appeared in the window. She pushed it open.

"How are you feeling?"

"Sleepy," Michael said. "My leg hurts."

"Go back to sleep if you want. I'll be here."

Michael nodded and smiled. Her trunk hovered in the air near him. He reached up and pulled it close, a warm and bristly comfort. He could feel the muscles tense a moment, then relax. The weight of it next to him, the grass smell of her breath, the beat of her pulse. Michael closed his eyes. He felt like he was floating in the air.

Gerry was sitting at the foot of the bed reading a book. The sunlight was gone and it looked threatening outside.

"An afternoon June storm," Gerry said, looking up from his book.

"June?" Michael shook his head. "It was May when we got to Metropolis."

Gerry nodded but didn't say anything.

"Well?"

"Wait until Jackie gets back. She wanted to be here when

you woke up. I only got her to go up the hill and eat by promising to call her if you woke up."

Gerry returned to his book.

"Aren't you going to call her?"

Gerry shook his head. "It's hard enough to get her to leave you. She needs to eat her fill. Know what you're going to do?"

"What?"

"Pretend to be asleep so I don't get in trouble."

Michael closed his eyes obediently. Then he didn't need to pretend.

It was the thunder that woke him. He started and his leg began to throb. He could see the bulking shadow of Jackie with her head in the window. Gerry had rigged some kind of awning over the window so at least her head wouldn't get too wet. Michael didn't like it. That was his job.

Gerry entered the room with a hissing lantern. He set it on the side table and moved the curtains away.

"There, you see? Let there be light."

Michael tried to reach his leg but he was too weak. "Can you rub my leg? It really hurts."

Gerry looked down.

"Michael," Jackie rumbled gently. "You need to be brave."

Michael didn't like the sound of it. "Am I going to die?"

"No," said Jackie somberly. "The dragon bit your leg. We couldn't save it."

"What do you mean?"

"It got infected," said Gerry. "It got so bad we thought it was going to take you with it. So, it had to go."

"Go?" Michael shook his head. "What are you talking about?"

"Gerry had to cut off your leg," said Jackie.

"What?" Michael said weakly.

Gerry pulled back the blanket. Michael's thigh and knee looked bruised and purple. Below that was a fat bandage that ended long before his ankle.

"You cut off my leg." Michael couldn't believe the stump was his. "This is a joke. I can still feel my foot."

Gerry replaced the blanket. "After a while, your mind

will accept there's no foot there. Then you won't feel it anymore." The shape of the blanket now clearly showed what was missing. "At least, that's what I've heard."

Michael stared at the blanket for a long time. Outside, the thunder receded and while the lightning played in the clouds, there was little sound but for the rain and the wind.

"You said dragon," Michael said, looking up from his leg. He couldn't stand to stare at it any more.

"Komodo dragon lizard," Gerry said. "Jackie figured out what it was as soon as she saw it."

Jackie looked up at the sky. She looked inside the window. "I expect there were several zoos and other facilities in Florida that collapsed just like the zoo in Saint Louis. Maybe that rhino is still alive. For the summer, at least. According to Gerry, these lizards have survived for a while. I'm not sure how a tropical species can make it through a temperate winter. Perhaps they move south when the temperature drops. Or perhaps they find a place they can sleep through the cold. I suppose it's possible there were enough of them that some were resistant to the cold. The ones less resistant died out and the remaining population bred. Evolution in action. Or maybe they were modified."

Michael stared at her. Jackie was talking to him. Really talking to him. She had never done that before.

Gerry interrupted gently. "How are you feeling, Michael?"

Michael started. He'd forgotten Gerry was there. "My foot hurts." He looked down at the blanket, oddly misshapen without his foot under it. Tears welled up. "What am I going to do?"

"Rest, for the moment," said Jackie. "Then figure it out."

Michael healed with all the combustive vitality of any well-fed young boy. By early July, the stitches were out and the skin over the stump was new and tender. He either hobbled about with a crutch that Gerry had made him or Jackie carried him.

But as the days wore on he started finding Jackie high on the broken end of the Interstate 24 Bridge carefully watching the other side.

"What's over there?" Michael asked as he sat down and dangled his leg over the hundred foot drop.

"You shouldn't sit so close to the edge," Jackie said quietly.

"If this bridge will hold you, it's going to hold me."

Jackie reached over and picked him up with her trunk. "Edges crumble."

She put him down and he leaned against the wall. "Okay. What's over there?"

"I've been watching the dragons." She pointed with her trunk. "They come to the road once around sunrise and once around sunset. In the morning, when they're warm enough, they leave the road and move to the forest at the edge of clearing. At night, they slink away under the trees to sleep somewhere. A cave, maybe, or some other kind of den. If they're hungry, they stay near the clearing until they've made a kill. Animals avoid the road so it's not profitable to hunt there. That's why they hug the edges of the clearings. There." She pointed again across the river. "And there. See the carcass? It was a deer they took yesterday morning."

Michael saw one leg sticking up from the ground in the clearing. Two long motionless shadows were lying near it.

"So the road is safe in the middle of the day."

"Safer, anyway. This section of road has only two lanes. The wider roads might be better or worse. I can't tell from here. Gerry was right about one thing. They're not crossing the river."

Michael saw something moving. A large spotted cat. He pointed it out to Jackie.

"A leopard, maybe?" she said. "Look how it's avoiding where the dragons are."

"Look way in the distance in that clearing. Deer?"

"I don't know. They don't look like deer. Gazelles? Antelopes? Something the leopards and Komodos can eat, I suppose."

"Where did they come from?"

"Zoos in Florida? Laboratories in Atlanta? I don't know." She paused a long time. "Over there things are going to be different."

Michael leaned back against the ridge of her back. He rubbed the stump of his leg. It was still tender and it itched constantly. Sometimes, if he wasn't thinking about it, he tried to scratch his toes.

"The summer is getting on," Michael said. "We should get started."

"Yeah, right," Jackie snorted. "You want to lose both legs? You're staying here with Gerry. I'll go on down alone."

"You need me!"

"I'll cope. You were right. You belong here."

"That was before."

"Before what?"

Michael hesitated. "When I didn't think you liked me."

Jackie turned her head and looked at him. "What makes you think I like you now?"

"You stayed with me. Gerry said."

"I felt guilty for getting you into this."

Michael felt as if he were struck. Ned had never treated him this way. "Why? Why hate me? Why be so mean to me?" Michael felt like she was hiding something. How do you get someone to tell you what they don't want to? "Why did you leave the Zoo?" he asked suddenly.

"I didn't like humans. And I had to leave."

Michael picked up on the "didn't" immediately but kept it to himself. "Ralph said he had a couple of years yet. It didn't have to be right then."

"I had to leave."

"Why? Why then? Why—when we could be back there enjoying good food and not staring over the river at dragons."

Jackie shook her head.

Sudden rage shook Michael. "Damn it! I *saved* you. You owe me."

Jackie sighed. "This is hard for me. Did you know there were four of us? Tantor, Jill, Old Bill, and me. We all learned to speak quickly enough but we hid it from the Keepers as long as we could. We had no love of them. Why should we? Even if we hadn't had the wit to speak, we would have known this was not the place we should be.

"You saw the zoo. There were cameras everywhere. Where there are cameras, there can be no secrets. So we were found out. They taught us to read. They taught us anything they could get their monkey hands on. We talked it over among ourselves. Why not learn what they had to offer? What could it hurt? Learn the enemy, said Old Bill. But keep them distant."

Jackie fell silent for a moment. "Every animal is wired its own way. Herd animals and pack animals are similar in one respect. They define themselves by membership in the group. Once you include a new member in the group, you're bound to them. Wolves, cattle and elephants are the same. We didn't want that. We didn't want to include humans in our tight little community. So we held back. We acted confused and slow. We did everything we could to make ourselves look stupid. Smart enough to work with, but our true nature held secret."

"Then the humans started dying. One after another. In groups. By themselves. Until we were by ourselves. Only Ralph was left to care for us."

"We were ecstatic. All we had to do was figure out how to escape Ralph and survive. We knew we had to go south. Georgia. Florida. Alabama. Where there was no snow in the winter and we could eat."

"Then Jill died. A bit of wire or glass left in the hay, maybe. No veterinarians left, right? We never really knew, but she died bloated and screaming. That left Old Bill and Tantor. I don't know how it happened, but I woke up a few weeks later and they were fighting. It's a terrible thing to see two five-ton animals slamming into one another. They had come into *musth* at the same time. I don't know why. I think I came into heat watching them. Biology triumphant."

Jackie snorted. "If they had been dumb beasts, one of them would have figured out they were losing and broke it off. Instead, Old Bill killed Tantor. He came over and mounted me."

"But the battle hurt him, too. Inside, somehow. A concussion? Internal hemorrhaging? I'll never know. He just wasted away. Then, he was dead and I was alone and pregnant. You appeared on the scene a week after that."

Michael stared at her. "I don't understand."

"I'm telling you why I had to leave. I didn't have a couple of years. The gestation period of an elephant is twenty-two months. No more. No less. I'm five months pregnant. I have to find a place that's safe, that's warm, where I can raise my child."

"Oh," Michael said. "But why the hurry? That's a couple of years."

"Not really. I don't know what's at Hohenwald. What if there are no elephants left? Then it's only me. A few months to find a place and get through the first winter—how will I know I've found a good spot until I've been through the winter? Then a few months to move to a new spot if I have to. Then a solid year of eating. That's not much time. Not much time at all."

Michael looked across the river. "Guess the dragons are a problem for a little guy."

"You think?" she chuckled.

"I didn't mean me," Michael said reasonably. "You're going to need me." He looked up at her and she looked away. "And you know, it, too. Is it so terrible to need a human when you're so alone?" Michael looked over the edge of the bridge and spat. He could see it nearly all the way down. "Look at it this way. We used you when everybody was alive. Now's your chance to use us—or at least me."

"I don't want to use anybody."

"Then take me along because you like me. Take me along because you can use my monkey hands. Take me along because I don't weigh much and won't be a burden to carry. Only *take me along*!"

Jackie didn't say anything for a moment. "You're crippled."

"Compared to you, everyone is crippled."

"Michael, you're missing one leg."

"So?"

Jackie snorted. "You can't keep up."

"I couldn't keep up before."

"You're being difficult."

"Where did you ever get the idea I'd make leaving me behind *easy* for you?"

"You're missing a leg!" Jackie trumpeted in frustration. "I can't take you with me."

"Why not?"

"Why *not*?" Jackie shook her head. "You're missing a leg."

"You said that." Michael stared her straight in the eye. "Like I said: So?"

"Michael," she said helplessly.

"You owe me an answer. And don't give me the 'not keeping up' crap. You owe me better than that."

Jackie stared back at him. "Okay," she said slowly. "The truth is I don't want to have to take care of you."

"More crap."

"Not at all. I don't know what's going to happen when I meet other elephants. I can't have any more dependants than my own baby."

"Let's add some more truths here." Michael felt like he was going to cry. He wiped his eyes angrily. "So I can't walk without a crutch. I'm riding you anyway. Besides, when my stump heals, we can make an artificial leg. You read that yourself. Even Gerry said he could do it. We might even find one that will fit me. Just because there wasn't anything in the Metropolis Hospital doesn't say anything about other hospitals. So it's not my leg. It's not like I haven't been useful. You wouldn't have gotten out of Saint Louis without me. It's been me, with my human hands, who's been able to keep the stiff together. I'm the one who can use a gun. I'm the one that saved your life. The truth is you need me. Your baby needs me. So let me come along."

"I'll have to look out for you."

"We'll have to look out for each other. *You* didn't see the dragon. *I* did."

"No."

"Why not?"

"I don't want anybody to die around me. Not again." She shuddered.

For a moment, Michael could read her as clearly as if she were a human being standing right in front of him: her face, dark and sad, her eyes, haunted. He reached up and took her trunk and draped it around his shoulder. He stroked it gently.

"You're going to need all the help you can get. You've got a baby coming. You don't even know if the elephants are still there or if you can find them. You're going to need my hands and my eyes. Better take them with you."

"Why do you want to go with me so much?"

Michael laughed. "Are you kidding? Live on the back of an elephant? What kid wouldn't trade his teeth to be in my place?"

"That can't be the only reason."

"Oh, there are a million reasons for us to be together. I can't think of all of them for you." Michael hugged her trunk. He looked up at her. "I'm going to be an uncle!"

This time, Gerry kept the *Encantante* a hundred yards from shore while Michael and Jackie watched for signs of the dragons.

Michael scanned the forest with the binoculars Gerry had given him. "I don't see any."

"We saw the kill in the clearing this morning. They should be there," Jackie said.

"And they might have decided to stay in the shade today," Gerry commented dryly. "Why miss a chance at a mountain of meat?"

"Quiet," said Michael. "Let's not do this all over again."

Gerry opened his mouth, and then shut it. "Suit yourself. I'll say this for the last time. This is a mistake and you'll remember I said it."

"If things work out, we might come up in a year or two. You can meet Jackie's new baby."

Gerry didn't answer but emptied his pipe over the side.

"It's now or never." Michael patted Jackie's leg. "Help me up."

"I think Gerry's right."

"Not going to go through it again right this minute. Make a leg."

Jackie bent down on one knee and Michael clambered up. "Okay, then." He pulled out the rifle.

Jackie eyed it warily. "I didn't know you had that."

"Everybody has secrets. Let's roll."

Gerry brought the *Encantante* slowly to the pier. His own rifle was standing in the corner a foot away from him but he didn't look at it. Instead, he kept his hand over the throttle and the reverse switch.

Jackie stepped slowly onto the pier and looked around. Michael held the gun ready.

"Okay, then."

Jackie began lumbering up the road.

Michael heard Gerry call after them: "Good luck!" Then, the propeller revved up and the ferry pulled away from the pier.

They were on their own.

Michael looked around and watched carefully. The one that got his leg was dead but Michael wouldn't have minded giving him some company.

Part 3

Once the dragons had warmed themselves on the pavement, they moved to the shadows, waiting for whatever wandered close by. Michael didn't know if it was Jackie's size or the fact they stayed in the center of the road as far from the edge as possible, but the few dragons they saw only watched as they walked by. The *Encantante* containing two humans and an elephant must have confused them. Perhaps Michael had been the real target all along or perhaps the dragon hadn't seen all of Jackie, just her leg, and attacked what it thought was a single animal. They would likely never know.

The infection that had nearly killed Michael showed the threat of the dragons was probably greater than Jackie being a target for every hungry man with a gun. Staying to the middle of the roads meant they traveled in the open. Jackie could be seen for a long distance. This made both of them nervous. Michael kept anticipating the feeling of Jackie sagging underneath him, the victim of a hungry sniper, followed by the inevitable sound of rifle fire.

They saw no one.

"Where is everybody?" Michael asked. Even in Saint Louis there had been some people—to be avoided, of course. But they had always been there.

"I don't know." Jackie watched the low farms. "This is different from what I had imagined."

The land rose. The forest grew thicker, lush and filled with tall oaks and maples. The road disappeared into rubble within a dark and gloomy forest floor nearly bare of vegetation. The remains of the road was a break of light between the trees.

"Keep watch," Jackie said after a while. "It'll be cold under the trees. The dragons will be sunning themselves wherever there's a warm spot."

But the forest grew thicker and even quieter. They saw no dragons.

"No people and no dragons." Michael leaned forward to look down on Jackie's face. "Any ideas?"

Jackie shook her great head. "It's too cool for them here under the trees. Maybe the dragons migrate north in the spring when the canopy is thinner. Then return south."

"Lizards migrating?"

"Who knows? It's a new world down here. I was modified. Maybe they were, too. Or maybe this just isn't dragon country."

"You were modified for a reason, I guess. Maybe they were, too."

Jackie was silent for a moment. "Why do you think I had to be modified for a reason?"

"Nobody would choose a five-ton experiment unless they had a reason." Michael cuffed the top of her head. "Especially one as foul tempered as you are."

"Yeah. Thanks." Jackie was silent for perhaps a dozen steps. "It was in the last notebooks you found."

"I figured."

"How so?"

"I bring you every notebook in the place. None of them

satisfy you. Then, you find what you're after. The next day you leave. At first, I thought it might be something about Hohenwald. Something important you needed to know before you could leave. But the place is clearly on the map. And I couldn't see what would be in notebooks about *you* that would have anything to do with Hohenwald. Whatever you were looking for had to be about you. After a while I figured out it had to be something about you that only the people that created you would know. That's why you were searching the notebooks. And it had to be something Ralph either didn't know or couldn't tell you. Ralph would know all there was to know about *how* they had made you. But there's no particular reason I could think of that they would tell him *why*."

"It could have been genetic maps of the Hohenwald males."

"What's a genetic map?"

"Something you wouldn't know about." Jackie grabbed the leaves off a low hanging maple and pulled them down. The branch tapped Michael on the head.

"Ouch. What was that for?"

"For thinking you know everything about me."

"I *know* I don't know everything about you. For one thing, I don't know what was in those notebooks."

"The purpose of the project. My purpose."

Michael cried out with delight. "I was right," he crowed.

"You were right."

"What was it?"

"They were going to reseed elephants back into Africa and Asia. But the elephants were going to have to be as smart as humans too keep from being steak on the hoof."

"That's weird," Michael said. "Why couldn't somebody just go and watch out for them." Then it hit him. "Oh."

" 'Oh,' is right," Jackie said gently.

"They knew they were dying. They must have known *everybody* was dying. There wouldn't be anybody to take care of you." Michael shook his head. "That doesn't make sense. Why go through all the trouble and die before they can make good on it?"

"I don't know. I didn't find any personal diaries or notes. I just found the original mission statement and long range plan."

"What do you think happened?"

"I think they made a mistake and died too quickly. Since we didn't trust them, they didn't really know how well they had succeeded. They kept trying to adapt, trying to figure out how smart we really were and how they were going to adapt their plan to our limitations. They were caught sick trying to do right by us."

Michael didn't say anything for a long time. "Do you think they figured it out before they all died?"

Jackie sighed, a deep rumbling breath. "God, I hope not."

Dear Mom,

> *My spelling is better since I let Jackie read the letters. She had been doing it sometimes but hadn't said anything.*
>
> *I didn't tell you about Gerry. But he and Jackie took care of me when I was sick. Gerry is a Real Good Guy, so if you get a chance, look out for him.*
>
> *Jackie's job was to look out for the elephants. So, now when we get to Hohenwald, she gets to do her job. I'm not sure what I'm going to do. My job so far has been to be her hands. But most of what I do has to do with traveling. When she gets there, she won't be traveling anymore.*
>
> *She said all of the elephants at Hohenwald were females. But the information she had was over ten years old. Ralph hadn't been able to contact Hohenwald for a long time. Maybe they weren't fire protected.*
>
> *The land is different now, wilder. Jackie says it looks like the old forests from hundreds of years ago. But it's much too recent. She thinks somebody must have made it. So we're careful.*
>
> *I miss you every day. You and Dad both, though I don't remember him so well. Jackie thinks I'm strange to write to you, being dead and all. I don't think it's strange at all. (So there, Jackie!)*

*If I talked to you out loud, people would just think
I was crazy. This way, it's just between me and you
and I get a chance to collect my thoughts. I think I
remember you better, too, if I do this. Ned had some
good ideas mixed with the bad.*

*Jackie makes sure I brush my teeth every night.
She had me look for a toothbrush in Ralph's packs.
Sure enough, there was one.*

*We're coming into Hohenwald soon. So, I'll tell
you about it after that.*

Love, Michael

They had been several days on old Highway 641 when
Michael saw Interstate 40 through a break in the trees.

This part of the road had seen better days. The roads in
Tennessee were better cared for than the ones in Illinois or
Kentucky. It was one of the best ways to determine when
they crossed state or county borders: the roads or the farms
were cared for differently. In Kentucky, the roads were broken in places and worn away in others and they had to keep
a sharp eye for dragons.

Once they crossed into Tennessee the roads looked as if
they were cared for by someone with a mania for cleanliness
and sharp borders. It reminded Michael of the mysterious
farms up in Illinois. The dark forest seemed to be the province of Kentucky. The forest here seemed more normal: a
mix of young trees and shrubs. Once or twice they saw the
remains of a garden. There had been people around recently,
if they weren't around right now. Still, they saw no one living. Just the occasional mound of mushrooms.

Jackie stopped dead in the middle of the roadway.

Michael almost fell off. He caught on to one of her ears
and pulled himself back up to her neck. He looked around
nervously to see what made her stop.

"What is it?" he whispered.

"I hear something."

"Dragons?"

"No."

Jackie spread her legs and leaned forward. She let her trunk down to rest on the ground.

"Is something wrong?" asked Michael.

"Shut up."

Michael leaned back and pulled out the map. It looked like they turned east here. Hohenwald was only seventy or eighty miles away.

Jackie straightened up.

"So?"

"Nothing."

"Right."

Jackie shook her head in irritation.

A few miles further on, Interstate 40 was more visible. They walked up the eastern ramp to the road proper. Michael felt better. The visibility from an interstate was much greater than from the little, forest enclosed roads. While they hadn't seen a dragon for a while, Michael didn't want to take any chances.

Jackie stopped on the interstate again and assumed the strange leaning posture.

"What *is* it?"

Jackie didn't answer. She just shook her head at him.

Michael climbed down to look around. He hopped over to the edge of the interstate, leaned against the guard rail. It was considerably more open to the south. Michael thought he could see a fairly large turtle of some sort, perhaps thirty pounds, walking along the edge of the forest. It looked like dragon country.

"We're going the wrong way," Jackie said suddenly.

Michael pulled out the map and studied again. "No. This is the way to Hohenwald."

"Where are we?"

Michael studied the map. "McIllwain. At least, that's the closest thing that looks like a town. That way—" he pointed east "—lays the Tennessee River. We go over it, if the bridge is still there. About thirty miles further on we turn south again to Hohenwald."

Jackie shifted nervously. "They're not there."

"The Hohenwald elephants?"

Jackie turned west. She leaned out again and laid her trunk on the ground. "Not that way, either."

"Nothing to the north of us, is there?"

Jackie turned east again, dropped her trunk to the ground. For a long time, she was motionless. Finally, she shook herself. "It's the river that's messing me up. I think they're south."

Michael sat on the guard rail. "Dragons might be down that way. Also, people."

"Maybe. I don't think they're far."

Michael sighed. He stood, leaning against the wall. Jackie made a leg for him and he climbed up. "The river is going north to south. Maybe we can keep going south on 69 and you can keep listening."

"How far is the river? Is there a road that follows it?"

Michael ran his finger along the blue line. "The river is angling toward us. It comes pretty close starting around Akins Chapel. We'll only be a few miles away from it when we get to Jeanette. Maybe ten miles."

"Let's go."

At Jeanette, they found Brodie's Landing Road. This brought them down to the river.

The Tennessee River was not the crushing roar of the Ohio or the Mississippi. It was broad and flat with a steady slow southern flow. On the other side, washing in the still water were a herd of elephants.

Jackie froze, staring at them. The air was still. The elephants across the river stared back. Michael didn't move. He wondered if the elephants could see him. Just how well did elephants see, anyway?

The moment stretched out long enough that Michael wanted to change his position. He began to itch.

Suddenly, one elephant in the water snorted and clambered up the bank. It trumpeted once and then walked up the bank. The other elephants followed her.

Jackie shook herself once they were out of sight. She walked into the water but the current, though slow, seemed to shift her slightly. She stopped and backed up. "Where can I get across?"

"We can go back north and across Interstate 40. Or, we can go south and cross Highway 412."

"Which is closer?"

"Both are about the same."

Jackie thought for a long time.

"South," she said at last. "We go south."

They crossed the river at Perryville. The bridge seemed intact, though, of course, they couldn't be sure. It cracked like a gunshot when they were in the middle and for a moment, Michael couldn't breathe. But the bridge gave them no more trouble and they were on the east side of the Tennessee River.

"We're quite a ways from Hohenwald," Michael said as they lumbered down the road.

"Did you think they would stay there? Their Keepers must be dead, too." Jackie sounded almost happy.

"Do you think Ralph is dead?"

She shook her head irritably. "I'm not concerned about the fate of one robot."

That's not your purpose, he thought. It made him nervous.

Along the eastern side of the river, they found a flat, worn trail, well marked with elephant scat. Jackie turned over each pile, broke it open and smelled it.

"Is that necessary?"

"I want to know who they are." She pointed to one worn pile. "African elephant. Female. Smells like she's the dominant one." She pointed behind. "There are three Indian females. One is still a little immature. She's unrelated to the other two. None of them are pregnant."

"What are you?"

"Indian. What? You didn't know?"

"It's not like you told me."

She snorted.

"Any boy elephants?"

"There were no males in Hohenwald."

"Why not?"

"Males need more space. They don't herd like females."

Michael thought for a moment. "Better hope your baby is a boy."

Jackie didn't answer.

They came to the point across the river where they had seen the herd, a long, hard packed sandbar held together with tough grass and cottonwoods. The scat here was plentiful. The elephants liked this place and returned to it often.

Michael leaned over her head. "Which way?"

"I'm not sure."

Michael slid to the ground. Jackie handed him his crutch. He moved around one side of the clearing while Jackie searched the other. The elephant markings were so numerous it was hard to figure out where they had gone.

"Over here," she called softly.

Michael hobbled over.

Jackie pointed to a large pile. "Male Indian. No more than a week ago."

"That's good, right?"

"Maybe."

She cried out suddenly. "Get down!" And swept him to the ground.

A dart stuck in Jackie's trunk where he had been standing.

Michael scrambled up to pull it out.

"Samsa!" cried a girl's voice from the brush. She ran out toward Jackie.

Michael tried to intercept her but was knocked to the ground again, this time by an older man. He held a knife to Michael's throat.

Jackie eased herself down to her knees. Then lay down on the ground.

"Jackie!" Michael cried out.

She looked blindly at the sound of his voice. Then it seemed as if her eyes were looking elsewhere. She closed them slowly.

"You've killed her," he said, not believing it.

"It was an accident, cripple," whispered the woman in a stricken voice. "I was aiming at you."

Part 4

The girl pulled the dart out of Jackie's trunk. "Will she die, Samsa?" the girl asked the man holding the knife to Michael's throat.

"I don't know," Samsa said. He pulled cord from a pouch belted around his waist and bound Michael's wrists.

"What? Do you think I'm going to run away?" Michael pushed his stump at him. "Cripple, remember?"

Samsa ignored him. He knelt next to Jackie. "She's breathing. That's a good sign. Maybe the dosage is too small."

"Dosage of what?" Michael stared at them. "What did you *do* to her?"

"Missed *you*," said Samsa, evenly. "Let's see the dart, Pinto."

Pinto gently brushed Jackie's eyes closed, picked up the dart and brought it to Samsa.

Samsa examined it carefully, deliberately avoiding the point. "Full dose, all right. Get the med kit in my tent back at camp."

"Got it." With that, the girl was gone, running up the trail away from the river.

Samsa examined Jackie minutely. He placed a hand on her chest to measure her breathing. After that, he held his hand under her trunk and stood silently.

"What are you doing?" Michael asked quietly.

"Shut up."

After a moment, Samsa released the trunk. "Pulse is good. Breathing is a little weak."

"That was a poison dart."

"You're a smart one."

"Why shoot me?"

"Let's see. You're riding the biggest piece of meat for twenty miles around—except for the dozen or so other pieces of meat just as big. You're not important, boy. She is. Too important to provide you a year's supply of steaks."

"You think I was going to eat her?"

"That would be a little ambitious. I think you were going

to trade her. Maybe to the Angels in Memphis or the Rubber Girls in Chattanooga. They would have taken her and then served you up as a garnish—which would have been fine by me but we'd still be out an elephant."

"Jackie's not one of your elephants."

"I know that. Since you're accidentally alive you can tell me where you stole her."

"I didn't steal Jackie. I don't think anybody could do that. If she could talk, she'd tell you herself."

Samsa snorted. "I expect she'd have a lot to tell me, too."

Michael fell silent.

"Where did you get her?"

"Jackie and I came from Saint Louis. We were trying to find the elephants at Hohenwald. She wanted her own herd."

"Well, you found them. We'll take it from here."

"She's—"

Samsa pointed the dart at him. "There's enough left in this for a little slip of a thing like you. Even if it didn't kill you, it'll paralyze you until morning. The Komodos would find you long before that."

Michael stared at the point of the dart. The tip had a drop of oil on it. He couldn't look away.

"Don't," Jackie said in a long exhalation.

Samsa looked over at the elephant. He looked back at Michael. "She didn't just talk, did she?"

"Is she going to be all right?"

Samsa looked back at her. "I think so. The curare didn't kill her so it will wear off in a while. Pinto is bringing back the antidote."

"Then pretty soon you'll find out for yourself."

Pinto returned with a professional looking bag. She gave it to Samsa and went to sit next to Jackie. She huddled next to her head. Michael hoped she had sense enough to move away when Jackie got up.

Michael tried to figure out the two of them. Samsa was an older man. What little hair he had left was streaked with gray and matched his beard. He was tall and thin as if strung together with wires. Pinto wasn't much more than Michael's own age. Through her loose shirt Michael could see a suggestion of young breasts, but her legs and arms still looked childish. Michael wondered if Pinto had bartered protection the same way he had with Uncle Ned. They didn't look related.

Samsa pulled out two glass ampoules, one with a powder and the other a liquid, a syringe and a wicked needle. He filled the syringe with the liquid and injected it into the ampoule with the powder and swirled it around to mix it. He caught Michael watching him.

"We don't have much call to use this so it's still in the original packaging." Samsa grinned at him. "We brew the poison ourselves."

"From what?"

"Poison arrow frogs down in the bayou. We go down there once or twice a year to catch what we need."

"I didn't know there were such animals."

"Pretty little things. Red. Blue. All sorts of colors. Skin carries a poison that will lay you out to dry if you mess with them. They didn't use to live down there but somebody's menagerie broke open—or was deliberately released—and some small group managed to survive the cooler winters. It's a nice weapon against humans—quiet. Quick. If you keep your wits about you, you can take down half a dozen people before they realize what's happening."

He finished shaking the ampoule and filled the syringe with the resulting mixture.

"Out of the way, Pinto," Samsa said. He swabbed a section of Jackie's hide and slipped the needle in. Then he withdrew the needle, broke it, and put the syringe and broken needle in a jar from the bag.

"She's still not going to be moving for a couple of hours but now her breathing won't be affected." He looked up at the hot sun. "We'll have to keep her cool." He looked at Michael. "Take your shirt off and wet it in the river. Keep it wet and on the elephant's head."

"Her name is Jackie."

"Jackie, then."

"Better untie me."

"You'll do fine with your hands tied together. Hop to it. Pinto? Help him but keep out of reach. Use your own shirt, too. I'll go get a couple of buckets."

Pinto kept a wary eye on Michael but he ignored her. The sun was hot even on his sweating body. He didn't want to imagine what Jackie felt like.

"Keep her ears wet, too," Pinto told him. "Elephants keep cool through their ears."

Michael grunted and bathed Jackie's ears.

"Did she knock you down?" Pinto asked as they passed one another on the way to the river.

"She saved my life," Michael said simply.

"Right."

Michael shrugged.

Samsa returned with two buckets and a rifle.

"I thought you liked poison," Michael said.

"I do. But it's hard to penetrate the hide of a crocodile with a dart."

"There are *crocodiles* in this river?"

"Not usually this far north but sometimes. The Komodos usually stay away, too. But not always. I'll keep watch, just in case."

Michael stopped and looked at Samsa. "You were a Keeper at Hohenwald."

"Director," Samsa corrected.

"So you let the elephants go when everybody died?"

Samsa cocked his head. "Eleven years ago."

"All the other elephants in Saint Louis died. Jackie and the Keeper decided she should look for the elephants down here."

"Did they, now?"

"Jackie's going to have a baby. Is the poison going to hurt it?"

Samsa sighed and looked over to her still form. "I should have picked that up right away." He turned back to Michael. "I hope not but there's no way to know. If she doesn't miscarry, it's a fair bet the baby will be all right." Samsa gestured to Michael. When Michael came close enough, Samsa untied his hands.

"I'm starting to believe you're not a poacher." He held up the gun. "But I still have the rifle."

Michael nodded and went back to filling buckets.

In the early afternoon, Jackie started twitching. An hour later, she was trying to get up. Samsa stood next to her, speaking soothingly. "Don't get up yet, girl." He gestured Michael and Pinto off the sand bank.

Jackie seemed to calm down and remained still. But it wasn't long until she heaved herself up, swaying and looking confused.

"It's okay, girl," Samsa said soothingly.

Jackie swung her trunk and knocked the rifle to the ground, then swung back, caught Samsa's leg and turned him over on his back. In a moment, she had a foot on his chest.

"You tried to kill my boy," she hissed.

Samsa tried to speak but couldn't.

Pinto ran to Jackie and tried to pull up her foot. Jackie ignored her.

"Are you all right, Michael?"

"Yeah."

"What do you want me to do with him?"

"Let him go," Michael said. "He's the director at Hohenwald."

Jackie slowly raised her foot. She carefully walked down the sandbar into the water and eased into it.

Pinto held Samsa's hand. She was crying. Michael squatted down next to him.

"She can talk," Samsa coughed out.

"I know," Michael said.

Dear Mom,

We found the other elephants. But the people that own them found us. Almost killed us, too. Me, anyway.

Samsa and Pinto were out tracking the herd. There is one big herd of six adult females and no calves. There are two other groups. One has three females and one calf. The other has four females and two calves.

Male elephants don't hang around except when they're in muss. Or muth. Or something. There are four males in the area.

All of them are Indian elephants except one: Tika. Tika is an african elephant. She's huge. She was the big elephant we saw at the stream. Samsa says it's possible for african and indian elephants to mate but she won't have any of the males. She's real strickt with her group. Maybe that's why they don't have calves.

Samsa let the elephants free when it looked like everybody was going to die, him included. But he didn't. Now there are fifteen people who help Samsa watch the elephants. They don't eat meat. They protect the elephants from people. Maybe they want to be elephants themselves.

They have their own little village near here. Samsa seems to run things from what I've seen. They want Jackie to come to the village. Jackie's not interedsted. She wants to join the herd. I think she's suspicious of them. They won't let me stay in the village. Maybe they still think I'm a poacher.

Love, Michael

"You need both legs to follow the elephants," said Samsa reasonably.

"I can get around pretty good with my crutch. Let me do something."

"You can't run. Sometimes the elephants charge and if you can't get up a tree quick enough, there won't be quite enough of you left to bury. We've lost people that way." Samsa and Pinto left before Michael could protest further.

Jackie was resting near the camp. She watched them from a distance. Michael had no doubt she could hear every word.

Michael hobbled over to her. He sat down next to her. She reached up and pulled down the branch of a birch tree and began methodically pulling the leaves off and eating them.

"They won't let me come with them," Michael said.

"So I heard."

The fog had come up the trail from the river and everything was swathed in mist. Michael felt cold and half blind. "How are you feeling?"

"Tired. Laying in the sun for half a day takes a lot out of you."

"Do you think there really are crocodiles in the river?"

"Do you think they're lying?"

Michael looked back to the fog. "I guess not. Do you know which band you're going after?"

Jackie didn't answer for a moment. "Tika's band, I think."

"Won't she be the hardest?"

"Probably."

"Then why her?"

Jackie was quiet a moment. "Silly reasons. It's surprising she even has a band with Indians in it. When you're desperate for company you'll take anything I suppose."

Michael didn't speak immediately. His chest hurt and his throat felt thick. He stared up the trail where Samsa and Pinto had gone. Was that how he felt about them? Desperate? Was that how Jackie felt about him?

He went to their gear and opened up the hidden flap. He put together the rifle and took the exploding shells.

"What are you going to do?" Jackie stared at him.

"Follow them."

It was awkward to carry the rifle while he was still forced to use the crutch. He thought maybe he'd try to get down to one of the old cities and look for a leg. Or build one. He had a vague memory of a story about someone with a peg leg. That would be enough for him.

The trail was clear and Samsa and Pinto had left footprints so they weren't hard to follow. He'd catch up to them or he wouldn't. Either way he was doing *something*.

He could tell the trail was coming close to the river by the way the trees began to thin. Michael listened and he could hear splashing—probably the elephants. He found a tall tree, leaned the crutch against the trunk and slung the rifle over his back and started to climb.

From near the top, he had a commanding view of the

river, the elephants, and Samsa and Pinto watching the elephants. He could also see the sunken logs slowly drifting toward the splashing of the elephants. He unslung the rifle and aimed it at one of the logs. The telescopic sight showed the crocodile clearly. He turned on the laser and saw the bright red spot appear on the animal's back. Then he watched.

Samsa and Pinto were watching the elephants. Samsa had a rifle but it was slung. He was talking, or maybe arguing, with Pinto. One of the crocodiles stopped, watching the bank. Then, it submerged.

Let's see, thought Michael. Think like a croc—or a dragon. Go for the little target, not the big one. Where would I attack from if I were a crocodile?

The water erupted near Pinto.

Right there. For a moment, the crocodile was frozen in midleap, the red spot clearly showing on his neck. Michael squeezed off three shots. He saw the water and blood spurt where they hit.

Then time caught and the crocodile started to close his jaws on Pinto when the explosive rounds triggered.

There was no flash or sound but the crocodile fell to the ground, dragging Pinto down with him. Samsa pulled Pinto out of the animal's limp mouth. They scrambled back up the bank, blood showing on Pinto's legs. But the croc was unmoving.

The elephants roared out of the water and ran into the forest. Michael stayed there for some time but the river was empty save for the remaining crocs staying safely off shore.

He climbed down and made his way back to camp. Samsa was treating Pinto's wounds.

Michael put the rifle down and sat next to it.

"I have some use," he said.

Samsa was sitting across from him when Michael awoke.

"I want the rifle."

Michael sat up. "I'd like to live in the village and use it to help you. But what I'd really like is to have my leg back. But that's the way it is."

Samsa shook his head. "We don't know you. I can't have

any weapon around that can kill an elephant in the hands of someone I don't know."

"You mean like the darts?"

"That's different." Samsa watched him a moment. "We could dart you and take it."

Michael pulled out the pistol and held it loosely. He didn't point it at Samsa but he didn't deliberately point it away. "You could pry it from my cold dead hands, I suppose."

"I know where that expression comes from. Do you?"

"Does it matter?" Michael was quiet for a moment. "I think it should be enough that Jackie trusts me."

"I don't think so. Jackie hasn't seen enough humans to know who to trust."

"Do tell," said Jackie from behind Samsa.

Michael looked up at Jackie. "You tell me what you want done with the rifle."

"Keep it," said Jackie shortly. "Likely you're a better shot with it than he is. Certainly, you're more trustworthy."

"I am the caretaker of the elephants," Samsa said in a controlled voice.

"That's not your job," said Jackie. "It's mine."

They didn't tell Samsa or Pinto or anyone else they were leaving. The village was up the hill and out of sight behind a bend in the trail. Michael certainly wasn't going out of his way to say goodbye. Even so, Michael could feel watchful eyes on him as they turned from the trail that led up the hill to the elephant scat covered trail that followed the bottomland.

"Tell me," Jackie said conversationally that afternoon. "Do you think Samsaville is on the map?"

Michael laughed for a long time.

The quality of their travel changed. Before, Michael had felt essentially alone in the forest. Other elephants were an abstraction. Other humans were absent. The very idea of a village was absurd.

But now Samsaville—the name stuck—loomed in his mind. He thought Jackie might think similarly about the elephants.

Dear Mom,

> *Jackie and I have left the other people and went to look for the elephants on our own. I'm not sure what's going to happen now. Maybe Jackie would be better without a one legged crippled kid.*
> *I miss you and Dad. I miss Gerry. I even miss Uncle Ned. I miss my leg. It hurts at night.*
> *Jackie's worried about joining the elephants. She doesn't say so but I can tell. Maybe Samsa will follow us. Maybe he'll dart me or worse. Maybe Tika won't let us join. Maybe something bad will happen.*
> *Whatever happens, I love you.*

Michael

They found Tika two days later. It was mid-morning. The herd was grazing on the edge of a clearing. Worn buildings marked the clearing as having once been a farm. Michael looked at the ancient stubble of corn shocks and rusting machinery. This farm had never seen a robot. It had been abandoned long ago.

Tika had already turned to face them before Jackie and Michael left the forest. She must have heard them coming, thought Michael. Or smelled them.

Jackie stopped well short of them and started grazing on the opposite side of the clearing. After an hour or so, Tika returned to grazing with the other females. But her attention never wavered from Jackie.

Afternoon came and the herd disappeared into the forest. Michael slid down to the ground and made himself a lunch out of dried fruit and crocodile jerky.

"Samsa is watching us," Jackie muttered and she stood near Michael. "Up on the ridge. I can smell him."

Michael nodded. "Is he going to shoot me?"

"I can't smell a gun but that doesn't mean much."

"Anybody else?"

Jackie shook her head. "Not as far as I can tell."

"Nothing to be done, then."

Michael chewed the crocodile jerky. Not bad. Sort of like chicken. "I wonder why the dragons don't come across the bridges. Do you think there's something here they don't like?"

"Maybe the elephants kill them. I know I would."

"You *did.*"

"True." Jackie thought for a moment. "It's a mistake to think this ecology here is complete. Humans left it very recently. It could be the Komodos just haven't reached this far yet. The Komodos have to migrate north from the coast every spring and return every fall. It's going to take time for them to penetrate new areas. Any place they go can only be as far as they can return to in time to avoid the winter."

"They could learn to winter up here."

"Unlikely."

"*They're* unlikely, right? Who knows what they can do?"

Jackie was silent for a moment. "That's not something I want to think about."

Michael shivered. "Me, neither."

The next week followed the same ritual. The elephants came to the abandoned farm and grazed, moving over to new areas as they stripped the old of leaves. By the week's end, Jackie and Tika had circled the entire clearing. Still standing opposite one another, Jackie was now where they had first sighted Tika and Tika was grazing where Jackie had first entered the clearing.

"Today we have to follow them," said Michael. He spit out the last of the meat. He was tired of crocodile jerky.

"It's too soon."

"Look around you." Michael pointed at the trees. "There's nothing left. They're not going to come back here just to say hello."

Tika chivvied her herd back to the clearing's entrance. Jackie followed at a respectful distance. Tika kept turning to check on them.

"This might work out," Jackie whispered.

They followed the band for hours. The smell of Samsa and the other humans faded. The trail became wilder and more curved until they couldn't see the band for minutes at a time. Then they turned a corner in the trail and Tika was facing them.

Jackie stopped dead still. Michael had been leaning forward, resting his head on Jackie's head and watching. He froze, not wanting to draw attention to himself.

Tika approached cautiously, trunk half raised and sniffing the air. Jackie raised her trunk slightly. When the two of them were close enough, they sniffed each other with their trunks. Tika seemed to relax.

Michael watched. It came to him that Tika wanted Jackie in her band—maybe because she was pregnant. Maybe because there were dangers enough out here for everybody to share.

Tika suddenly whipped her trunk over Jackie's head and caught Michael squarely in the side, sweeping him off Jackie's neck and down on the ground in front of Tika.

Michael fell the ten feet in a moment of frozen astonishment and landed hard on his back, knocking the wind out of him. Desperately, he tried to force himself to breathe, cough, anything. But his lungs stubbornly refused to fill.

Tika raised her leg over him.

Michael saw the details of her foot, the broken toenail, the puckered scar.

Jackie screamed *"No!"* and stepped over him, shoving Tika away.

Tika stumbled back and then shoved back.

Jackie stood foursquare over him, her head and trunk down.

Michael's breath caught and he sat up, watched twenty tons of animals shoving above him.

"Move," Jackie cried.

Michael scrambled away. *A tree! Where's a tree?* He saw an oak and hopped over to it, clawed his way up the trunk and into the branches high enough to escape Tika.

Jackie fell back in front of the tree, facing Tika.

Tika trumpeted at her.

It was as if she shouted in English: *You we want. But not with him.*

Jackie trumpeted back. *Not without him.*

"Jackie," he shouted. "Go with them. I'll be okay."

Tika fell back, staring at the two of them.

"No," Jackie said. "Both of us or not at all."

Michael found himself crying.

Part 5

Dear Mom,

It's been a while since I wrote but I've been busy. Little Bill is just as stubborn as his mother. Jackie says he outgrew the cute phase when he was two. Now she thinks it's just unpleasant. But I like him. He reminds me of his mother.

I think Tika's finally accepted me. It took long enough. She's allowed me to stay all this time by just ignoring me. But a few weeks ago before we left Panacea one of her toenails got infected and needed to be lanced and cleaned. It was pretty clear it had to be done before we started north. Jackie stood next to me to make sure I didn't get hurt. But Tika brought over her foot and didn't twitch when I cleaned out the wound. It must have hurt. It looks lots better now.

That was just after I shot two Komodos that had decided to make a meal out of Tika's leg. The Komodos aren't much problem in the winter. They're all asleep somewhere. But between the time they wake up in the spring and the time they start north, they're pretty hungry and mean. I can't say for sure what made Tika change her mind. But she seemed pretty happy that Jackie and I were walking next to her when we went North this year.

Things are still changing. The Komodos are tough but they seem to have a hard time with the brush lions. We're not sure. Where we find brush lions, there aren't any Komodos and where we find Komodos there aren't any brush lions. We don't know exactly what's going on.

And the fire ants keep spreading north.

Good news this spring. Both Tanya and Wilma are pregnant. The bull that visited around Christmas must have done his job. More young ones for Little Bill to play with.

We're not far from Samsaville. It'll be nice to see Pinto and Samsa. I'm trying to persuade Jackie we should go far enough north to see Gerry. But she doesn't like going through dragon country.

> All for now,
> Love,
> Michael

Michael finished signing his name and closed the notebook. It was almost filled. This would be book number seven. He hefted it in his hands. He wondered if he was a little off in his head to be writing his dead mother all these years. He was sixteen now. Michael shrugged. He still liked doing it. Maybe Jackie would have an opinion on it.

He put down his pack and watched the river flow by. Mostly he just enjoyed the play of sunlight and color on the water. It was a careful observation, too. Keeping track of floating logs nearby that might leap out at him. The crocodiles had become more numerous in the last couple of years. Michael didn't know what they were eating but so far none had tasted elephant on his watch.

Little Bill came down to the edge of the bank. *Little?* Michael smiled to himself. Bill's head was two feet taller than he was.

"Jackie's-Boy! Jackie's-Boy!" he piped, a tiny voice for such a large body. Michael wondered when, and if, the elephant's voice would ever break into the deep timbre of an adult. Michael's had. Well, mostly. Sometimes it still cracked.

"Just Michael," he said. "Like I always say. Just Michael."

"Jackie's-Boy is what Tika calls you."

Michael chuckled, wondering not for the first time, how an elephant spoke without being able to speak. The world was filled with mysteries. "Does she now?"

"Are you ready to go?" piped Bill. "Tika sent me to get you. She wants you and Jackie to go first."

Michael reached down and pulled up his artificial leg and fastened it on. "Really? *Tika* wants us to lead?"

"Sure. At least as far as Cobraville."

"Ah. She wants us to cross the fire ants first, eh?"

"Yeah."

"Will wonders never cease?"

Little Bill didn't answer. Instead, he made a leg. Michael shouldered the rifle and climbed up over his neck. He looked around. The blue bowl of the sky above him, the warm sun, his gray family patiently waiting for him half a mile away. He felt like singing.

Lovingly, he patted the top of Little Bill's head.

"Well, then. Musn't grumble," he said with a grin. "Let's go."

Eight Miles

SEAN McMULLEN

Sean McMullen (www.seanmcmullen.net.au) lives in Melbourne, Australia. He began publishing in the 1980s, and nine early stories are collected in Call to the Edge *(1992). Taken together they give evidence of an impressive and wide-ranging SF storytelling talent emerging. His first two novels were published in Australia,* Voices in the Light *(1994) and the sequel,* Mirrorsun Rising *(1995), and were part of the projected Greatwinter series. He combined and rewrote the first two Greatwinter novels as* Souls in the Great Machine *(Tor, 1999). The sequel,* The Miocene Arrow, *and another,* The Eyes of the Calculor, *were published in 2001. He is also one of the leading bibliographers of Australian SF, and has won the William Atheling, Jr. Award three times in the 1990s. His bibliographies are an essential underpinning of the* Melbourne University Press Encyclopedia of Australian Science Fiction & Fantasy *(1998).*

"Eight Miles" was published in Analog. *It is about as hard SF as the steampunk subgenre, which most often is more fantasy than SF, gets. McMullen says about it: "a ballooning story from the 1840s. Back then they could build balloons to go twice as high as Everest, but humans tended to die at about five or six. It is about a man trying to push the envelope, but even with leading edge 1840s life support it is rather tricky. Why eight miles? His passenger has breathing problems at lower altitudes."*

Consider a journey of eight miles. One could walk it in less than an afternoon; in a carriage, it would take an hour, or one could conquer the distance in one of Stevenson's steam trains in fifteen minutes or less. Set two towers eight miles apart, and a signal may be transmitted by flashing mirrors in less time than modern science is able to measure. Eight miles is not all that it used to be, yet seek to travel eight miles straight up and you come to a frontier more remote than the peaks of Tibet's mountains or the depths of Africa's jungles. It is a frontier that can kill.

My journey of eight miles began in London, in the spring of 1840. At that time I was the owner and operator of a hot air balloon. It was reliable, robust, and easy to fly, and I provided flights to amuse the jaded and idle rich. It was a fickle income, but when I had clients, they paid well for novelty.

Lord Cedric Gainsley was certainly rich, and when his card arrived I assumed that he wished to hire my balloon to impress some friends with a flight above London. I kept it packed aboard a waggon to launch from wherever the clients wished. Its open wicker car could carry six adults; indeed, the idea of six people of mixed sexes packed in close proximity seemed to add to the allure of a balloon flight.

My first moments in Gainsley's London rooms told me that he was no ordinary client. The walls of the parlour were decorated by maps alternating with sketches of mountain peaks and ruins. The butler showed me into a drawing room completely lined with books. This was nothing unusual, for many gentlemen bought identical collections of worthy books to display to visitors. At that time it was also fashionable to collect, so Gainsley collected. In and on display cases were preserved insects, fossil shells, mineral crystals, old astronomical instruments, clocks dating back to the fourteenth century, lamps from the Roman Empire, and coins from ancient Greece. Seven species of fox were represented by stuffed specimens.

As I began to look through Gainsley's library, however, I realised that many books had been heavily used, to the point of being grubby. They were mainly concerned with the natural sciences.

"Does geology interest you?"

I turned to see a tall man of perhaps forty handing a top hat to the butler. He wore a black tailcoat with a fashionably narrow waist, but was just slightly unkempt. A rich man who did not want to draw attention to himself might look that way.

"Geology—you mean the books?"

"Yes, they made me rich. I learned to tell when minerals were present, in places where other men saw only wilderness."

The butler cleared his throat.

"Lord Cedric Gainsley, may I introduce Mr. Harold Parkes," he improvised, not entirely sure of the protocol when the baron had opened the conversation first.

"Thank you, Stuart. Now have Miss Angelica ready and waiting for my summons."

"Very good, my lord."

Once we were alone, Gainsley waved at a crystal brandy decanter and told me to make myself at home. He paced before the fireplace as I poured myself a glass, and showed no interest in a drink for himself. I took a sip. It was very good—far better than I was used to.

"How high can your balloon ascend, Mr. Parkes?" he asked.

"I take pleasure seekers a mile above London," I began. "My rates—"

"Your rates are not a problem for me. Could you ascend, say, two miles?"

I blinked.

"At two miles the air is thin and cold, sir. Besides, the view of London is not as good as from a lower altitude."

"Two miles, and hold that height for six hours."

I blinked again. Pleasure flights seldom lasted more than one hour. People got bored. More to the point, the balloon needed to carry fuel for its burner to maintain the supply of hot air. That was a constraint.

"I must ask some questions, sir. How many passengers, what weight will they total, and what weight of food and drink will they carry? You see, to stay aloft for so long, the balloon must carry some fuel to keep the air heated. With the weight of fuel for six hours, I may not even be able to get off the ground."

"Yourself, myself, a young woman of one hundred and forty pounds, and food and drink not exceeding ten pounds. Nothing more."

"Then it is possible, but not certain."

"Why not?"

"Nothing in ballooning is certain. Above us is a dangerous and unforgiving frontier."

Gainsley thought about this for a time.

"You are a man of science, Mr. Parkes, like me. You invented the mercury ascent barometer, and you calibrated it to five miles."

"With the help of Green and Rush, yes. They took it on their record-breaking flight some months ago."

"Yet you are in difficult circumstances."

"There is not a big market for ascent barometers. Many of my other inventions turned out to be impractical, but proving them impractical nearly bankrupted me. Pleasure flights are not my preferred career, but they are lifting me out of debt."

I had once had visions of becoming the George Stephenson of the skies by inventing the airborne train, and I spent all my money installing a purpose-built Cornish steam engine with small windmill blades beneath a hot air balloon.

Alas, although it did drive the balloon in any direction on a calm day, in wind it was useless. As I found out, a balloon is effectively a huge sail, and the wind was more than a match for any steam engine small enough to be carried aloft.

"Mr. Parkes, my flights are to be no pleasure jaunt, and I need an innovative balloonist, one who can solve technical problems as they arise," Gainsley now explained. "I intend to study the effects of extreme altitude on a very special person. I will pay you fifty pounds for each ascent, and I shall also pay for the fuel to inflate your balloon with hot air. My condition is that you work for nobody else while in my hire, and that you exercise absolute discretion regarding the flights and the nature of my research."

His rates were certainly better than I was currently making from pleasure flights. In fact, as a business proposition it was too good to be true. Once I had agreed, he pulled at a red velvet tassel that hung beside the fireplace. The butler appeared within moments.

"My lord?"

"Stuart, fetch Miss Angelica now."

Angelica was a young woman a little below average height, with a delicate, angular face. She was wearing a dark blue woollen cloak and close-fitting bonnet, but I could see nothing more of her attire. There was something odd about her eyes. They were listless, almost lacking in life.

"Miss Angelica has been in my service for some months," said Gainsley. "I named her Angelica because she comes from very high altitudes."

"A fallen angel?"

"Quite so. It is my little joke. Now then, put your glass down, make sure you are seated comfortably, and prepare yourself for a shock."

Gainsley unpinned her cloak and let it fall to the floor. Such were my expectations that it took some moments to realise that she was neither clothed nor naked. Angelica was covered in fine, dark brown fur, except for her face. She had three pairs of breasts, each no larger than that of a girl in early pubescence. Her chest was surprisingly broad and deep, however, and I would estimate that her lung capacity was greater than mine. Her ears were pointed, in the manner of a fox. I sat staring for some time.

"Well?" asked Gainsley.

The young woman showed no sign of shame, which was a very strong clue. She was probably used to being on display.

"I have seen the like before," I replied uneasily.

"Indeed? Where?"

"At fairgrounds, in the novelty tents. Women with beards, boys with six and seven fingers, I have even seen a child with two heads. By some accident of birth the human template was not applied to them correctly by nature. For this young lady, it is the same."

"You are wrong," said Gainsley. "She is a werefox, for the lack of a better word. She speaks no language, sleeps on the floor, and is not familiar with clothing."

I managed not to make a reply, which is just as well because it would surely have been sarcastic.

"You clearly do not share my opinion," he prompted.

"Indeed not, sir."

"Then how would you account for her condition?"

"A feral child, abandoned by her parents. She was born covered in fur, so they cast her out. Perhaps wild beasts raised her."

"I thought that too, at first. I did indeed find her in a fairground. Her manager said she had been bought from a dealer, who also sold dancing bears. When she was captured in India's northern mountains she had been more active and entertaining; she could even do little tricks. At low altitudes she became very lethargic, however, and was only of value as a passive curiosity. It was not until some days later that I realised the truth. I returned to the fair and bought her."

"And what is that truth?"

"The girl is adapted to very great altitudes. At sea level the richness of the air overwhelms her, much as a diet of that brandy would overwhelm either of us. I believe there is a whole race of humans who live on the highest of mountains, adapted to the thin air."

The idea was fantastic. I looked back to the girl. Her lungs were certainly large in proportion to her body, and the fur would have protected her from the cold.

"I am not sure what role you have planned for me," I said at last. "I know nothing of mountaineering."

"Ah, but your balloon will be a substitute for the mountains. A trip to India would take years, but my business interests do not allow me to leave England for more than days. Your balloon can take us two miles high in . . . how long?"

"Twenty minutes, perhaps thirty. It depends on the load."

"Splendid. We can do the flight above my estate, north of London, and be down in time for dinner. At two miles I can observe how Angelica reacts to thin air and cold. If it restores her senses, I might even be able to speak with her, to question her about her people."

Gainsley helped Angelica back into her cloak, then rang for the butler to escort her away. Once we were alone again he walked over to the window and gestured to the crowded street outside.

"Look upon my prosperous neighbours, Mr. Parkes," he said. "Merchants, bankers, financiers, landed gentry. What do they do, other than grow rich and live well?"

"Visit the theatre, attend the races, go to balls?" I guessed. "Some take balloon rides above the races. That is all the fashion just now."

"Theatre, balls, races," Gainsley muttered, shaking his head. "Within a year of their deaths, such people are all but forgotten. I want to be like Isaac Newton, James Cook or Joseph Banks—I want to be remembered for discovering something stupendous. Miss Angelica will make my name."

"You have lost me, sir."

"I have a theory, Mr. Parkes. In my theory of adaptive morphology I assert that humans take other physical forms under extremes. For example, in polar regions they may become seals if they dwell there too long."

"The silkie legend of the Scots: people turning into seals."

"Yes, and I think that extreme altitudes might render us into a form like that of Angelica."

* * *

Gainsley's estate was not far to the north of London, and he sent his draught horses to draw my transport waggon there. Kelly and Feldman were my tending crew, and they spent most of the night setting the frame, and unpacking and checking the balloon itself. I was up two hours before dawn, adjusting my altitude barometer and installing it in the wicker car.

Inflating a balloon on the ground is not a problem. One has unlimited fuel to supply the hot air, and to keep that hot air maintained. Once aloft, it is a different matter. The little furnace in the wicker car is fuelled by lamp oil that the balloon must carry, so this oil must be used sparingly. It was the work of a half hour to inflate the bag sufficiently that it stood up by itself. Then I sent word to the manor house that we were ready to ascend. Gainsley emerged with Angelica, leading her by a chain attached around her waist. She was dressed in the manner of a boy.

We rose very rapidly, drifting right over the roof of the manor house. The wind was southerly and very light, and the sky was clear. At first Gainsley made a big show of looking over the side and exclaiming at the sight of his estate, far below. He almost seemed to forget why we were there, and chattered about ascending with an artist next time, to have his lands painted from above. I had the barometer calibrated to display altitude in quarters of miles. At a mile and a half Gainsley suddenly remembered why he had paid for the ascent.

"A mile and one half; almost eight thousand feet," he said, peering at my barometer.

"We are ascending slowly, at about five miles per hour," I reported.

"Six minutes from the prescribed height," he replied. "Angelica was apparently found at eleven thousand feet. Can you hold that altitude?"

"That I can, sir. Bleeding a little hot air from the balloon will reduce our buoyancy and stabilise our height."

I released some hot air and we continued to ascend, but at a much slower rate. According to my barometer, we settled at twelve thousand feet. By my estimate we were drifting north northeast at three miles per hour. The direction of the wind was different up here.

It was at this altitude that the visions began. Actually the term visions does not do them justice—they were more like memories that were not mine being implanted in my mind. I seemed to have walked beside canals built across deserts of red sand beneath an unnaturally dark blue sky with a pale and tiny sun. In the distance I could see a city, but it was more of a metropolis of immense crystals of saltpetre, feldspar, and quartzite than like London.

I had paid Angelica no attention until now, being occupied with tending the furnace, checking the barometer, and monitoring the direction and progress of our drift relative to the ground. It was Gainsley who took me by the arm and pointed to her. Angelica had begun the ascent sitting on the floor of the wicker car, paying no heed to what was going on around her. Now she was on her feet, looking over the edge of the car. As I watched, she turned away and scrutinised my altitude barometer. For a full minute at least she stared at the mercury. Then she raised a hand slowly before making a horizontal chopping motion.

"Sign language," said Gainsley. "She is telling us that she understands what is happening. We have been rising, but now we have stopped."

"More than that," I said with a very odd prickle in my skin. "She understands my altitude barometer on first viewing."

In London, at sea level, Angelica had showed not the slightest interest in the machines and furniture that surrounded her. Even the mechanics of doors were beyond her. Now she was able to read a barometer, and that ability was beyond ninety-nine in every hundred of my fellow Britons.

I noticed her eyes. For the first time they were alert, calculating, even intelligent.

"Angelica, can you hear me?" asked Gainsley.

At the sound of her assigned name she turned her head.

"Angelica, speak to me," urged Gainsley. "Speak. Speak English, French, Hindi, anything."

He put a hand to his ear, to signify that he expected an answer. Angelica did not reply.

At the pace of a slow walk we drifted over the country-side. Far below I could see farmhouses and other manors. Gainsley continued to coax and question Angelica. She proved disappointing. He showed her pictures of mountains, foxes, and even a sketch of herself. She displayed vague interest, but did not speak.

"How long have we been aloft?" he asked me.

"One hour and thirty minutes."

"And what endurance have we?"

"Very little. The seal of the bag is imperfect—some hole that my crew missed—so hot air slowly leaks out. I balance that by stoking up the furnace and working the bellows, but the air is cold and thin up here, and it is using too much lamp oil."

Gainsley scowled, but did not argue. This was a ship, after a fashion, and I was the captain. He returned to his questioning of Angelica. The wind swung around and began to blow us back toward London. There was little for me to do, other than feed in hot air every so often to maintain height. I watched as Angelica became even more alert. She examined the magnetic compass, Gainsley's pocket watch, and even the furnace. After studying the last-mentioned for some minutes and watching me at work, she gently pushed me aside, bled in some lamp oil, and applied herself to the bellows.

"Astounding," I gasped. "She deduced its operation, merely from watching."

"Very high intelligence," said Gainsley.

"And an understanding of machines."

Now Angelica scrutinised the barometer, where the mercury indicated that we had risen another quarter mile. To my complete astonishment she touched her finger to the new level of mercury.

"She understands the operation of this balloon as well as the altitude barometer," I said. "Very few of my passengers could claim that."

"Up here, in rarefied air, she is transformed," Gainsley observed.

"How can this be?"

"Remember my theory, adaptive morphology? I think she

comes from a civilization in very high mountains. Ascending into cool, thin air frees her mind from the effects of the sludge that we breathe."

Finally, I declared that we would have to descend. By then Angelica had not spoken a single word, but she had demonstrated awesome intelligence. My balloon was one of the most advanced vehicles available, yet she understood its workings and instruments.

"Only four hours of exposure to the thin air, yet her brain cleared," said Gainsley in triumph.

"She did not speak."

"Yet she understood the balloon's workings."

"Her werefox race must have its own language," I suggested.

It was at this point, just as we began our descent, that Angelica began tapping at the altitude barometer and making upward movements with her other hand. The part of the scale that she was indicating was for eight miles. This part of the scale was where I had marked uncalibrated altitude projections. She looked to me, her eyes alive and full of pleading. I held up the empty lamp oil barrel and shook my head. She seemed to comprehend, for she now sat quietly on the car's wicker floor and closed her eyes, resigned to the oblivion of sea level.

Using the varying directions of the wind at different altitudes, I managed to steer us back over Gainsley's estate, then bring us to earth just a mile from where we had ascended. Kelly and Feldman presently arrived with the waggon, then Gainsley's groom brought a light carriage. He was quick to get Angelica into the carriage and away from sight, but with this done he returned to speak with me as I helped my men pack the balloon away.

"How high may we ascend?" he asked, "and how long may we stay there?"

"Hot air has its limitations," I explained. "My balloon must carry its own fuel. Going higher means using more fuel. Using more fuel means less is left over to sustain the hot air and maintain our height."

"Could you build a balloon to reach eight miles?"

I almost choked on my own gasp. The question was akin to asking whether a new type of gun could shoot a duck even more dead than dead.

"There is no point," I replied. "Above five miles the air is so rarefied that one may not breathe."

"But could you build a balloon to do it?"

"Using hydrogen, yes, but to what end? It would be our dead bodies that achieve the feat."

"Then how high may we go?"

"I think you mean how high in safety. Four miles is my answer."

"Why four?"

"Remember, the air thins as we ascend. I have ascended three and one half miles. It was distressing, but endurable. My lips and those of my companion turned blue, and fatigue set in very quickly. Four miles is double what we achieved today."

"Have others gone higher?"

"Yes. Some months ago the aeronauts Charles Green and Spencer Rush reached five miles. They found it near impossible to breathe, however, and consider themselves lucky to have survived."

"Five miles. The height is comparable to the highest of mountains to the north of India."

"So I have read."

"So we too could do it?"

"Yes, but it would be appallingly dangerous."

"I fought Napoleon, just a quarter century ago. How can this be more dangerous than trading volleys with his soldiers?"

"Death is death, whatever the cause. Why ascend five miles in search of it?"

"Because at four or five miles we may well clear Angelica's mind to a greater degree. She may even be able to speak. Begin planning for another hot air flight tomorrow, but also draw up plans for a balloon filled with hydrogen."

"Do you realise that hydrogen is even more volatile than gunpowder?"

"Of course, Mr. Parkes, I am a man of science. Send the bills for whatever you need to me."

"So am I to be kept in your employment?" I asked.

"Yes, yes, board and lodging, plus whatever rate you were earning by taking people on pleasure flights. The same for your men."

That night I dreamed, and my dreams were lurid. My mind was filled with visions of vast, gleaming things that glided through blackness, and blossoms of fire that became twinkling clouds of glitter. I awoke, not so much distraught as puzzled. The dreams had become part of my memory. What was more confusing was that I had other memories that were not part of the dreams. There were splendid cities full of graceful crystalline towers and wide promenades, yet all of them were strewn with dead creatures. At first I thought that the bodies were of vermin, but many of them were wearing straps and belts, gold braid, ceremonial swords, and even helmets. Perhaps they had built the cities, these creatures that wore no clothes but fur. They closely resembled Angelica.

We made another dozen hot air ascents while the hydrogen bag was being fabricated. We did not manage much more in communicating with Angelica, but the visions continued to pour into my head every time we ascended. I said nothing, because practical men are not meant to have visions and I wanted to keep Gainsley's trust. Would you travel on a ship whose captain said that he could see water sprites, mermaids, and harpies? I can only compare my visions to leafing through randomly chosen books in a library. I saw nothing of the whole picture, just snatches of fragments.

A gasworks at the edge of London provided the hydrogen, which saved the cost of buying a hydrogen reactor, and chemicals to fuel it. The first hydrogen flight saw us ascend from the city in the half-light before dawn. We remained at four miles for only a quarter hour, because Gainsley quickly weakened, then lost consciousness. I descended rapidly, and when he revived he confessed that his lungs had been weakened by some childhood disease. On the other hand Angelica had been vastly improved by even the brief exposure to the thin air, however, and had even scrawled some characters and diagrams on a notepad. Alas, we could make no sense of them.

On the way down I had a number of ideas. Gainsley had been complaining about his lungs preventing him from staying at four miles. I offered to take Angelica to five miles without him and report what she did, but he would not hear of it. Whatever she did, he wanted to be there to see it.

"If only I could make the ascent myself," he sighed.

"Impossible. Even at four miles we are on borrowed time. You especially."

"Green and Rush did it."

"Only briefly. They were on borrowed time too."

"Yet they lived."

"They lived because they descended in haste. People must acclimatise slowly to very high altitudes. Mountaineers I have spoken to say that it takes weeks."

"Find a way. Two hundred pounds, and I will pay for whatever you need."

"Two hundred pounds, you say?"

"I do pledge that."

"Then there may be a way. I have been reading about the nature of air, my lord. You may have heard of the experiments with glass jars and candles. Burn a candle in one, and it will go out when the oxygen is exhausted. Introduce a mouse to that depleted air, and it soon suffocates."

"Explain further."

"Suffocation interests me, being a balloonist. I performed this experiment, then piped some pure oxygen into that depleted air. The mouse revived."

Gainsley thought about this for some time, smiling and nodding every so often.

"How heavy is the mechanism for supplying oxygen?" he asked at last.

"I need a bigger reactor to supply enough oxygen for humans, but it need not be very heavy. Just a tank, some pipes, spigots, and a sealable chute."

"Then build it, build it! I shall pay for the materials and labour."

"And the two-hundred-pound bounty?"

"It is yours."

* * *

The problem of staying alive at extreme altitudes occupied my mind a great deal in the days that followed. Oxygen is the essential ingredient of air that gives us life, yet it occupies only one part in five of air's volume. Provide air that is five parts in five oxygen, and one might well survive in much thinner air. I paid a visit to Darkington and Sons, Pneumatic Systems and Valves of Sheffield. Jeremy Darkington was about Gainsley's age, but he was dressed as a tradesman and spoke with a hybrid Yorkshire-Cockney accent. He was a skilled metalworker who had made good by supplying valves for steam trains.

While he sat behind his desk, I unpacked my chemicals. I uncorked a bottle and poured a little solution into a glass, then opened a jar of dark purple crystals. I dropped one into the glass, where it began to bubble with great vigour.

"Permanganate of potash added to peroxide of hydrogen will release oxygen," I explained as we watched the reaction turn the liquid to a greenish purple froth.

"I know t'reaction," he replied.

I now laid out drawings before him.

"I wish to have a reactor built. Peroxide will be fed in here, potash here. Oxygen will be released into this pipe as they react, and when they are spent, the solution will be vented through this tap before fresh materials are introduced to give off more oxygen."

He examined the drawings, scratching his head from time to time, but generally nodding. At last he looked up.

"Can be built, but what end for it? There's oxygen all about."

"I have an application that calls for pure oxygen. An industrial application."

"Ah."

"How much to build it, and how long?"

"Summat busy for present . . . thirty pounds. Just now there's batches of valves for Mr. Stevenson's new engine fleet . . . a fortnight?"

"Done! Put my contract on your books."

My reactor looked viable in principle, but the only way to

test it was by means of a flight. That was risky. Still, it was worth the risk.

My father had two sayings that I lived by. *Luck is opportunity recognised,* was sensible enough, except that opportunity generally eluded me. *That which is too good to be true is never true,* was a little less positive, yet it had kept me out of trouble on many occasions. Gainsley and his schemes seemed too good to be true, yet he paid generously enough.

I was returning from Sheffield and was within ten miles of Gainsley's manor house when a rainstorm swept over the countryside. Because it was late in the afternoon, I decided to spend the night at a small inn on the edge of a hamlet. I was dining on a pork pie when a bearded man approached me. He was dressed as an itinerant labourer, but that illusion vanished as soon as he began to speak.

"So, you are Gainsley's latest balloonist," he said in a soft, almost conspiratorial voice with a French accent.

"I do not know you, sir," I responded warily.

"My name is Norvin, and I know you to be Harold Parkes."

Clearly he had something serious to discuss. I gestured to a chair.

"You said I was Lord Gainsley's latest balloonist, yet the baron never flew before I took him aloft."

"He has had four balloonists. Routley, he died in a mysterious duel in 1831. Sanderson died of food poisoning, two years later. Elders fell from the carriage of a train in 1837, and was found beside the tracks with his neck broken. I would wager my last pound that it was broken before he fell."

I felt a stab of alarm, but the stranger showed not a trace of hostility.

"You said four balloonists," I prompted.

"I was on a fishing boat, supposedly being taken back to France. One mile out to sea, I was padlocked to a length of iron rail and heaved over the side."

"Yet here you are, alive."

"When on hard times I supplemented my income by liberating goods guarded by padlocks. Thus my pick wire is always upon my person. It was a near thing, picking a lock in darkness, under water."

I was aware that those balloonists he had named had died, for we are a small fraternity. Now I speculated.

"The balloonist Edward Norvin was French and a veteran of the Napoleonic Wars. He vanished in 1836."

"So I did, Monsieur Parkes. The seventeenth day of July at one hour before midnight. One does not forget days like that in a hurry. I grew a beard and developed a new identity."

"Can you prove that Gainsley was involved?"

"Can *you* prove that Gainsley and yourself have had *any* business dealings?" he asked in turn.

I raised my finger and opened my mouth to reply . . . but said nothing. All of our dealings had been in cash. My men Kelly and Feldman now lived on the Gainsley estate, as did I. Nobody knew. The colour quite probably drained from my face. Norvin smiled and took a sip from his tankard.

"You are having dreams and visions, Monsieur Parkes," he continued. "The visions begin to tumble through your mind when ascending with Gainsley and Angelica. They begin at about ten thousand feet, the altitude that the fox-woman's mind becomes more clear. It is as if she were emerging from a drunken stupor, raving randomly."

"But she has never said a thing."

"She is not like us. She speaks with her mind; her words are images of thoughts. I would say that you have said nothing of this to Gainsley as yet."

"Why?"

"You are still alive."

I did not want to hear any of this, yet it was true.

"I saw landscapes that were all red and green under a violet sky," Norvin continued. "There were cities of silver crystal, their streets strewn with bodies although the buildings were intact. It looked like a scene of plague. My perspective was odd. It was as if I were being dragged about, being made to look at the bodies. The only moving figures were wearing helmets and coveralls that resembled a Seibe diving suit—except that the helmets were made of glass and had no air hoses."

Now I began to feel really frightened. Norvin was describing precisely what I had seen, both in the ascent visions and in my dreams. I decided to be honest, in order to gain his trust.

"I have also had dreams filled with vast, gleaming things that floated in blackness against constellations of unfamiliar stars," I confessed.

Norvin nodded. "I have had similar dreams and visions. Tell me more."

"I—I cannot describe the gleaming things because they are like nothing in my experience, yet they moved with the stateliness of huge ships. They blossomed into white fire that yellowed, then became twinkling, gleaming clouds of fragments."

"Warships of the air, perhaps, fighting at night. I saw great crowds cheering Angelica. There had been a battle. She was a hero. She was their leader."

"A woman as leader? Preposterous."

"Why so? The young Queen Victoria is currently monarch of your vast empire. In the sixteenth century, Queen Elizabeth ruled you, and she was indeed a warrior queen. In France we had Joan of Arc."

Again we sat in silence. By now I was in a cold sweat, in spite of the fire roaring in the hearth.

"It is my opinion that Angelica came from somewhere very, very high," Norvin speculated. "Perhaps from Tibet, in regions that have never been explored. Regions that *cannot* be explored, because we cannot breathe there. I have studied maps, such as they exist. I have read accounts by the explorers Celebrooke and Webb. They reported mountains five miles high. I think that *our* visions are of cities high in those mountains. It is a region the size of France of which we know nothing. What of the bodies in the visions? What is your thought on them?"

"A plague. Angelica fled for her life. Down, out of the cool, pure air. Down into the thick, warm soporific atmosphere of humans. For her it would have been like lying in a bath of warm whiskey. Her brain is permanently addled by the dense air. Back in the mountains she would be restored, but in my balloon, four miles above this tavern, her mind also begins to clear in the thin air."

"No plague," said Norvin. "I have had four years to think about the content of my visions. Angelica was not fleeing a plague, she was *exiled*. There was a war. She was their Napoleon, and she lost."

"That is just too fantastic—" I began.

"Gainsley hopes to learn the secrets of her people's weapons and crafts by listening to the babblings of her mind. As her mind clears, she speaks delirious visions in the minds of all those nearby. *That* is why he employs you. He wants to learn secrets that could change the world. He has sketched machines and weapons that he does not yet understand, and each flight allows him to gather more fragments from her mind. His problem is that he must always have a balloonist with him, because he is prone to faint in thin air. That is why he killed the others. He does not want anyone to accumulate as many of Angelica's visions as he has. You told him nothing about the visions, so perhaps he assumes you have a deafness of the mind."

Now I laughed.

"This is preposterous! What would Napoleon or Wellington know about metalworking, cannon manufacture, flintlock mechanisms, or even weaving cloth for uniforms? It is artisans who know those things, not generals."

"Really? How do you make gunpowder?"

"Why, take sulphur, charcoal, and saltpetre, and mix them in proportions suited to the usage. Sixty percent saltpetre . . ."

Suddenly I realised what he meant. Some important secrets were very, very simple. Again I shivered in the warmth of the room.

"One single breakthrough can change a world, Monsieur Parkes. Simple ideas, simple enough for even generals and monarchs to understand. Gunpowder can win wars. Invent the bond market, and you can finance wars more easily. Have you ever thought about how accounting changed the world? What about replacing a ship's steering oar with a rudder? All of those things can be comprehended by any idiot—or politician."

"But surely not all of those things lead to war."

"Think again. Suppose you were a governor of some colony, and you were brought word that the local natives were being taught to cast cannons and build warships. What would you do?"

"Why, send a fleet of gunboats before any ship was launched."

"Precisely. Angelica's people will not take kindly to us if we catch up with their sciences. They will put us back in our place, make no mistake, and they will destroy our civilization to do it. Good day to you, Monsieur Parkes."

He stood up to go. I stood too.

"Wait! What are you proposing?"

"To you, sir, I am proposing nothing."

"Then why speak with me?"

"Why, Monsieur Parkes? Because when I do what I have to do, I want at least one person to know that I acted out of honour."

I had not told Norvin everything. I was actually the first balloonist in the employ of Gainsley to use an altitude barometer. On no other flight had Angelica been able to point to eight miles on the scale, because my predecessors did not have barometers. Eight miles. Much of the Earth is unexplored, but we do at least know that mountains do not rise to forty-two thousand feet. Not on our world, anyway. If Angelica were adapted to such a height, it meant that she had once lived on another world. Mars, perhaps. It was a small planet, so its air might be thin.

I did a lot of research in libraries. Polar caps and seas had been observed on Mars in the midseventeenth century, and in 1665 the Italian astronomer Cassini had measured its day to be not much different to that of Earth. It was a world like our own, I quickly established. Now I turned to the literature of the fantastic. Godwin's *The Man in the Moon* had been published over two hundred years earlier, introducing us to the idea of travel between worlds, and the great Voltaire made use of the idea in *Micromegas*. Clearly, planets were other worlds, possibly with inhabitants. If a suitable ship could be built . . . but perhaps it already had.

For me the conclusion was inescapable: The whole of our planet was Angelica's island of exile, her Elba.

We had been to half of the height that she was adapted to. Her mind had cleared, but not to any great extent. What might she reveal when fully conscious, with a mind as sharp as a newly wrought cavalry sabre? Eight miles. It was a very long way up. The balloon could do it, but I could not. Not without my new oxygen reactor. My oxygen reactor that had only ever been tested at sea level.

Then there was Gainsley. Had Norvin been telling the truth? Had Gainsley killed those other balloonists? Anyway, what to do about Gainsley? Eight miles was double the altitude that was causing him distress. Even with pure oxygen, I would be pushing my own powers of endurance to the very limit. Gainsley had no place on the flight, and I told myself that I was excluding him for his own good. In case he was as dangerous as Norvin had said, I decided to take my father's old Tower flintlock pistol on the next flight.

The day of the next ascent began perfectly. The air was calm, and the balloon stood tall and stately above the gasworks. The first flights had all been from the privacy of Gainsley's estate, and had been in hot air balloons. Our initial flight from the gasworks had been done unannounced, and had taken everyone by surprise. This time we had crowds, and the newspaper people were there. Gainsley announced to the public that he would ascend alone, so Angelica and myself had been hidden in the wicker car during the night. We remained crouched down as the balloon filled and the sky lightened.

The people of northern London seemed determined to make a big occasion of the flight. Gainsley had declared that the ascent was purely scientific, and that he intended to chart the properties of the atmosphere at extreme altitudes. He would measure wind direction, temperature, barometric pressure, humidity, and even the intensity of sunlight. A band began to play and people cheered. As Gainsley began speaking about the importance of science and progress, I heard two workmen nearby say that the balloon was full, and that the hydrogen lead should be tied off.

Gainsley had had the balloon tied down to the roof of the gasworks. One of his trusted men was ready beside a release lever, and pulling upon this would send us on our way. The rope passed through the base of the wicker car, however, and was secured to the main ring at the base of the gas bag. Unknown to everyone, I had brought a butcher's cleaver aboard.

Three blows severed the rope.

The balloon ascended with the speed of a sprinting man. For some moments the band struck up a triumphant march, but above the music I could hear Gainsley's cries of outrage. A large part of the crowd seemed to think that the launch had gone according to plan, so cheering erupted. I remained crouched down, out of sight. Angelica was as passive as ever.

So far luck was with me, and that had me worried. I preferred to have my bad luck at the beginning of a flight, and the good at the end. I had feared that the outraged and frustrated Gainsley or his men might shoot at me, but the huge crowd of witnesses meant that this was not an option. I monitored my watch, and at thirty minutes I stood. The barometer indicated that we were at twelve thousand feet and climbing rapidly. Looking down, I saw that we were above the edge of London, but drifting northeast very slowly, out over fields.

We rose through the first four miles in fifty minutes. Angelica began to take an interest in her surroundings again, and to gaze over the side. As expected, visions were flickering in my mind, but this time I paid them little heed. At five miles I activated the oxygen reactor. I had left it rather longer than was probably safe, but its efficiency in thin air was unknown, and I wanted the chemicals to last as long as possible.

We were now at the height of the mountains at the northern frontier of India. If Angelica were from there, this would be her preferred altitude. As I expected, however, her mind did not clear completely. This was bad tidings for me.

I knew that I would not last long, even with the oxygen. We were at a height that I should have allowed weeks to adapt to. By moving very little I tried to conserve my vitality, but my condition was definitely deteriorating.

There were new visions that were not from my mind. I was at a balcony, and thousands were cheering. All around me stood werefox people, wearing no clothing, but decorated with gold braid, studded straps, ceremonial swords, and belts that glowed with tiny lights. Some had apparently dyed their fur in green, purple, blue, and yellow patterns. Angelica stood next to the barometer, still tapping the scale at the eight-mile mark.

Not of this world, that was for certain now. At this height she should have collapsed without the oxygen tube, yet she now looked the most alive and vibrant that I had ever seen her. By rising so high into the atmosphere, we were definitely simulating the air of her own world.

Her images kept flooding into my mind. Angelica was in something like a courtroom, presided over by judges whose fur was dyed black. Many werefoxes gestured and pointed at her. I understood the wordless trial, I cannot say how. Earth's air is thick and laden with oxygen, so she was sentenced to exile on our world. Here there was too much oxygen, too much pressure, too much heat. At sea level she walked in a stupor, aware of who she was but unable to put words together. It was a subtle punishment, like being perpetually, helplessly drunk.

Now another thought reached me. At a certain height, freedom. The barometer indicated that we were in excess of six miles altitude when her random thoughts ceased to flood through my mind. It was a distinct relief, as I was now having trouble operating the oxygen reactor that was keeping me alive. I was again lucky, for the device was functioning precisely as it had been designed. When next I checked the barometer, we had passed seven miles.

It is difficult to convey the sense of serenity seven miles above the English countryside. There were no birds or insects, and even the cloud tops were small, remote things far, far below. Those sounds that I could hear were muted in the thin air and were no more than the creaking of the wicker car and the bubbling of the permanganate of potash and peroxide of hydrogen. It was very, very cold. Although I was dressed in heavy furs and woollens, the cold passed through them like needles of ice.

The light was like nothing I had ever seen, and I was aware that I was the first human ever to see the sky from this altitude. Every breath was an effort, in spite of the pure oxygen from the tube in my mouth. Angelica's thoughts began to trickle into my mind again. These were not the random scatter of memories from her mind as it emerged from the fog of sea-level breathing, but sharp, precise, focussed thoughts. She was communicating with me. The trickle became a deluge.

My last glance at the barometer was at eight miles. We went higher. How high, I shall never know, but it might have been in the vicinity of forty-five thousand feet. Thoughts flooded into my mind: specifications, philosophy, principles, tolerances, laws, limits, battles, honours, defeats. Angelica now tended the oxygen reactor as I lay on the floor of the car, holding the tube to my mouth. One last jar of peroxide was left when she looked down at my face. A corona of light seemed to blaze around her head, and tendrils of purple discharge crackled around us. I was wondering if the electrical sparks might ignite the hydrogen in the bag above us when there was a flash of the most intense and pure white light imaginable.

I opened my eyes to a sky of deep violet in which a small, pale sun was shining amid thin, scattered clouds. In the distance was a gleaming white crystalline city of spires, columns, buttresses, and arches, a city that was a work of art in itself. Before me was a canal lined with stone in which purplish water flowed. It stretched straight, all the way to the horizon from the city. The fields to either side of this canal were filled with low, bushy trees on which yellow fruit grew.

"This is not real," I said aloud.

Angelica materialised beside me.

"Of course not. We are in my mind."

"Then where am I?"

"Beneath a balloon, eight miles above the countryside. If we do not descend in another minute you will die, but minutes can become hours in the mindscape, so do not worry."

"You can talk."

"No, I cannot. I have merely imagined that I can talk. It preserves your sanity."

"Then . . . what shall we talk about?"

"People that I can see in your memories of history books and lessons. Napoleon, Wellington, Caesar, Alexander, Hannibal."

"Edward Norvin says you are like Napoleon in exile on Elba. He says you must not be allowed to escape, or you will start new wars and cause unimaginable suffering."

"He did not discuss Hannibal."

"No. Should he have?"

"Were he being fair, yes. Hannibal fought bravely and cleverly for his Carthaginian people against the Roman state. He lost, after a long and devastating war. His defeat was more due to the stupidity of his government than Roman supremacy in the battlefield. He fled into exile. Rome despoiled Carthage and annihilated its people so completely that the entire civilization ceased to exist. Even its fields were poisoned, so that no city could ever be built there again."

"I know the story well."

"So let us go back two millennia."

The landscape dissolved, then we were somewhere on Earth, at night, in a town that reminded me of paintings done in Egypt. I was sitting with an imposing, dynamic-looking man, in some sort of outdoor tavern. He looked tired, even haggard, but by no means defeated. He smiled at me and raised an eyebrow.

"Angelica?" I asked.

"Hannibal to you. Look behind me, what do you see?"

"A man with two mugs on a tray. He is adding powder to one of them. Poison?"

"Of course."

The assassin came up to us, bowed, gave us our drinks, then hurried away. He had Norvin's face.

"Remember, I am Hannibal," said Angelica. "If you reach across and fling the contents of my mug into the dust, I may live to raise another army of Rome's enemies. This time I may defeat Rome. Think of what would be gained and lost."

I thought. Rome had many accomplishments, but it also had a lot to answer for.

"But Hannibal suicided to avoid capture and humiliation."

"You think so? Victors write the histories. I should know."

"Will it be any better under your rule?" I asked.

"I would like to think so. The Carthaginians were more merchants than conquerors."

The figure of Hannibal began raising the poisoned wine to his lips. Without being entirely sure why I did it, I reached across and struck it from his fingers.

The scene dissolved into a modern workshop. We were standing beside a workbench, upon which an unusual piston assembly had been dismantled.

"Powered by a very ordinary steam engine, this piston and valve system can slowly withdraw air from a chamber the size of a small room. It can reduce the atmospheric pressure to one tenth that at sea level."

"The pressure at eight miles?"

"Yes. I could dwell within it, and have full control of my mind."

"Do you want me to build it?"

"That is the wrong question, Mr. Parkes. Do you want to build it? I have pleaded my case, now *you* are my judge. What is my sentence?"

Once more the scene began to dissolve, but this time only blackness followed.

We were at four miles when I revived. Breathing was not easy, but a trickle of oxygen seemed to be still issuing from the reactor. Angelica was back to her old vegetative self, sitting on the floor.

In my haste to plan the abduction of the balloon, I had made no real plans for the return to earth. While still a few yards from the ground I released the rope and grapple. It snared a tree in a windbreak, then the car came to earth gently in what was actually one of my better landings. I helped Angelica from the car, and pausing only to discard my heavy coat and gloves, I hurried her to a nearby stand of trees. We had come down in a field not far from the edge of London, and I estimated that we had travelled no more than fifteen miles laterally. Gainsley and his men would arrive soon, to fetch Angelica back and have me dead. My thought was to hide until a large crowd had assembled, for he would not want to kill me in front of witnesses.

A pair of farm labourers arrived at the balloon after a few minutes. Although fearful of the huge gas bag at first, they soon began striking poses in front of the wicker car. One even put on my heavy fur coat, as if he had been the aeronaut.

It was now that Gainsley arrived, riding hard with his butler, groom, and two other men. My worst fears were justified when he shouted an order and all four of his men produced rifles and fired at the man in my coat. He fell to the ground. His companion raised his hands. It was clear that Gainsley had mistaken the two men for myself and Angelica. He soon realised his error.

"The man and woman—Where are they?" he screamed, dismounting and seizing the surviving labourer by the smock while pressing one of those tiny American percussion cap pistols between his eyes.

"Dunno, sir," the man answered. "Me an' Fergus, we found the balloon 'ere. We thought we'd guard it until the owner got back."

"My balloon was stolen by the man who owns that coat. Where is he?"

"Dunno sir, the coat was on the grass when we arrived."

The temptation for Gainsley to kill him was probably near to overwhelming, but by now another horseman was approaching. One death could have been a mistake. A second would send Gainsley to the gallows, baron or not. He ordered his men to dismount and reload as the rider drew up.

"Ho there, sir, we are pursuing dangerous criminals who

stole this balloon," was as much as Gainsley managed to say before the rider produced a pistol and shot him between the eyes.

It was at this point that I recognised Norvin. Gainsley's four men had not yet managed to reload their Enfield rifles, so they attempted to mob him. They had not realised that he was armed with one of the new pepperbox pistols by Cooper of London. It could fire six shots from six barrels in as many seconds, so at close quarters it made one man as effective as six. Two more men were shot down before one of the others used his rifle butt to club Norvin from the saddle. He fell, but shot a third while lying on his back in the grass. The survivor raised his hands.

"Mercy, sir, you'd not shoot an unarmed man, would you?" he cried.

"How much mercy did you show me, Monsieur Garrard?" asked Norvin, who then shot him down.

By now the farm labourer had got to his feet and was running for his life. Norvin calmly took a percussion lock rifle from his saddle, aimed with smooth, professional style, and fired. The side of the man's head burst open as a ball seven tenths of an inch across did its work. Even at a distance I could see the gleam of tears on Norvin's cheeks. He was a good man, being forced to kill. He was a Frenchman killing a Napoleon for the greater good. He probably thought he was saving the world. Knowing only what he did, which of us would not do the same?

I lay absolutely still. True, I had my father's flintlock, but I am no flash shot, and would have trouble hitting a steam train from the platform. Norvin had killed six men with as many shots, and still had one shot remaining in his pistol. Apparently satisfied that he had killed Gainsley and his men, and that Angelica and myself were the dead farm labourers, he mounted and rode away. We remained hidden amid the trees until more people arrived at the balloon and discovered the massacre. When the authorities arrived I emerged and played the part of a yokel who had come late to the scene, and of course Angelica was quite convincing as a village idiot. It was no great effort for us to slip away and walk back to London.

That was two years ago, and since then I have prospered. I have my own workshop, where a steam engine chugs night and day to maintain the world's only altitude chamber. It is the size of a small room, and within it lives Angelica, in conditions of pressure that can be found at eight miles. Otherwise, it is furnished very comfortably in red and green leather upholstery, Regency furniture, a small library, a desk where she draws diagrams of things for me to build, and a workbench where she builds tiny, intricate metal machines like surreal insects with wings of blue and silver lace. Food and drink passes in through an equalisation chamber. What comes out is mainly diagrams.

I am building a voidcraft. The thing resembles a streamlined steam train with no wheels. It stands on grasshopper-like legs driven by pistons plated in gold. In place of a cabin there is an airtight double chamber with portholes. One side is for Angelica, the other is mine, and they are at very divergent atmospheric pressures. I tell the artisans that help with construction that it is a new type of armoured balloon, and in their ignorance they believe me.

The parts were made at a thousand different workshops in Britain, continental Europe, and even America. It is a beautiful thing, with a body of brass pipes, steel tubes, crystal mechanisms mounted in gaslight enclosures, and riveted boilers in which nothing boils. Even in its incomplete state, it is awesome in its performance. Last night we rolled back the moveable roof of the workshop, ascended into the night, and looked down upon the gaslit, smoky haze of London in comfort . . . from eight miles. How easily the frontier becomes the commonplace. Angelica spoke within my thoughts, asking whether I wished to fly on to the Moon, but I was not ready for that. Like lungs acclimatising to the air at great altitudes, my mind needed time to adjust to such wonders.

Currently, I am having four quite different engines built to add to our craft. To me they make no sense, but Angelica insists that they will work. The clever and industrious Mr. Brunel has contracts to make some of the parts. If only he knew that he was really building boilers to confine matter more black than soot that has no real existence as we know it. The electrical experimenter Faraday is supplying many of our electromagnetic and electrostatic controls, while the jewelers Pennington and Bailey fabricate crystals to almost-conduct electricity, and Harley Brothers Watchmakers build control clockwork that they do not understand.

The voidcraft of rivets and iron plate will be able to travel to the stars, even though my mind cannot comprehend the distances in any more than the most general sense. It will be armed with a tube being built in two sections in the work-shops of Glasgow and Sheffield, a tube that will one day enclose a fragment of a star's heart. With it one can vaporise a warship at ten miles using not one thousandth of the power available. Angelica will be the captain, navigator, and gunner, yet when she leaves, I will be with her. After all, what engine can work without a humble stoker and oiler?

Norvin was right in a sense. Angelica is a Napoleon from an unimaginably advanced race, and Earth is the Elba where she was exiled. Norvin also feared her, but in this he was mistaken. It is with worlds too distant to comprehend that Angelica has her quarrel. After all, why would a Napoleon want to conquer a little Elba when so much more is within reach?

Ghosts Doing
the Orange Dance

(The Parke Family Scrapbook Number IV)

PAUL PARK

Paul Park lives with his wife, Deborah Brothers, and their children in North Adams, Massachusetts. He teaches at Williams College. He became prominent in SF in the late 1980s with the publication of his first three novels, The Starbridge Chronicles: Soldiers of Paradise *(1987),* Sugar Rain *(1989), and* The Cult of Loving Kindness *(1991). He went on to write a variety of challenging novels in and out of genre, and short stories, collected in* If Lions Could Speak *(2002). His major project in the last decade has been the four-volume fantasy of an alternate world where magic works:* A Princess of Roumania *(2005) and its sequels,* The Tourmaline *(2006),* The White Tyger *(2007), and* The Hidden World *(2008).*

"Ghosts Doing the Orange Dance" was published in F&SF *in a slightly longer version. It is an ambitious work of SF post-modern fiction, set in the relatively near future, combining autobiography, family history, continual hints of the fantastic, stories within stories, and finally settling down as science fiction. All the clues are present for a multiplicity of interpretations. It rewards the reader's careful attention.*

1. Phosphorescence

Before her marriage, my mother's mother's name and address took the form of a palindrome. I've seen it on the upper left-hand corner of old envelopes:

> Virginia Spotswood McKenney
> Spotswood
> McKenney
> Virginia

Spotswood was her father's farm in a town named after him, outside of Petersburg. He was a congressman and a judge who had sent his daughters north to Bryn Mawr for their education, and had no reason to think at the time of his death that they wouldn't live their lives within powerful formal constraints. He died of pneumonia in 1912. He'd been shooting snipe in the marshes near his home.

For many years my grandmother lived a life that was disordered and uncertain. But by the time I knew her, when she was an old woman, that had changed. This was thanks to forces outside her control—her sister Annie had married a lawyer who defended the German government in an international case, the Black Tom explosion of 1916. An American gunboat had blown up in the Hudson River amid suspicions of sabotage.

The lawyer's name was Howard Harrington. Afterward, on the strength of his expectations, he gave up his practice and retired to Ireland, where he bought an estate called Dun-low Castle. Somewhere around here I have a gold whistle with his initials on it, and also a photograph of him and my great-aunt, surrounded by a phalanx of staff.

But he was never paid. America entered the First World War, and in two years the Kaiser's government collapsed. Aunt Annie and Uncle Howard returned to New York, bankrupt and ill. My grandmother took them in, and paid for the sanatorium in Saranac Lake where he died of tuberculosis, leaving her his debts. In the family this was considered unnecessarily virtuous, because he had offered no help when she was most in need. Conspicuously and publicly he had rejected her husband's request for a job in his law firm, claiming that he had "committed the only crime a gentleman couldn't forgive."

She had to wait forty years for her reward. In the 1970s a West German accountant discovered a discrepancy, an unresolved payment which, with interest, was enough to set her up in comfort for the rest of her life.

At that time she was director of the Valentine Museum in Richmond. She used to come to Rhode Island during the summers and make pickled peaches in our kitchen. I was frightened of her formal manners, her take-no-prisoners attitude toward children, and her southern accent, which seemed as foreign to me as Turkish or Uzbeki. She had white hair down her back, but I could only see how long it was when I was spying on her through the crack in her bedroom door, during her morning toilette. She'd brush it out, then braid it, then secure the braids around her head in tight spirals, held in place with long tortoiseshell hairpins.

She wore a corset.

One night there was a thunderstorm, and for some reason there was no one home but she and I. She appeared at the top of the stairs, her hair undone. She was breathing hard, blowing her cheeks out as she came down, and then she stood in the open door, looking out at the pelting rain. "Come," she said—I always obeyed her. She led me out onto the front lawn. We didn't wear any coats, and in a moment we were soaked. Lightning struck nearby. She took hold of my arm and led me down the path toward the sea; we stood on the bluff as the storm raged. The waves were up the beach. Rain wiped clean the surface of the water. For some reason there was a lot of phosphorescence.

She had hold of my arm, which was not characteristic. Before, she'd never had a reason to touch me. Her other hand was clenched in a fist. The lenses of her glasses were streaked with rain. The wind blew her white hair around her head. She pulled me around in a circle, grinning the whole time. Her teeth were very crooked, very bad.

2. The Glass House

It occurs to me that every memoirist and every historian should begin by reminding their readers that the mere act of writing something down, of organizing something in a line of words, involves a clear betrayal of the truth. Without alternatives we resort to telling stories, coherent narratives involving chains of circumstance, causes and effects, climactic moments, introductions and denouements. We can't help it.

This is even before we start to make things up. And it's in spite of what we already know from our own experience: that our minds are like jumbled crates or suitcases or cluttered rooms, and that memory cannot be separated from ordinary thinking, which is constructed in layers rather than sequences. In the same way history cannot be separated from the present. Both memory and history consist not of stories but of single images, words, phrases, or motifs repeated to absurdity. Who could tolerate reading about such things? Who could even understand it?

So our betrayal of experience has a practical justification. But it also has a psychological one. How could we convince ourselves of progress, of momentum, if the past remained as formless or as pointless as the present? In our search for meaning, especially, we are like a man who looks for his vehicle access and ignition cards under a streetlamp regardless of where he lost them. What choice does he have? In the darkness, it's there or nowhere.

But stories once they're started are self-generating. Each image, once clarified, suggests the next. Form invents content, and so problems of falsehood cannot be limited entirely to form. A friend of mine once told me a story about visiting his father, sitting with him in the VA hospital the morning he died, trying to make conversation, although they had never been close. "Dad," he said, "there's one thing I've never forgotten. We were at the lake house the summer I was twelve, and you came downstairs with some army stuff, your old revolver that you'd rediscovered at the bottom of a drawer. You told Bobby and me to take it out into the woods and shoot it off, just for fun. But I said I didn't want to, I wanted to watch *Gilligan's Island* on TV, and you were okay with that. Bobby went out by himself. And I think that was a turning point for me, where I knew you would accept me whatever I did, even if it was, you know, intellectual things—books and literature. Bobby's in jail, now, of course. But I just wanted you to know how grateful I was for that, because you didn't force me to conform to some. . . ."

Then my friend had to stop because the old man was staring at him and trying to talk, even though the tubes were down his throat. What kind of deranged psychotic asshole, he seemed to want to express, would give his teenage sons a loaded gun of any kind, let alone a goddamned .38? The lake house, as it happened, was not in Siberia or fucking Wyoming, but suburban Maryland; there were neighbors on both sides. The woods were only a hundred yards deep. You could waste some jerkoff as he sat on his own toilet in his own home. What the fuck? And don't even talk to me about Bobby. He's twice the man you are.

Previously, my friend had told variations of this childhood memory to his wife and his young sons, during moments of personal or family affirmation. He had thought of it as the defining moment of his youth, but now in the stark semiprivate hospital room it sounded ridiculous even to him. And of course, any hope of thoughtful tranquility or reconciliation was impeded, as the old man passed away immediately afterward.

Everyone has had experiences like this. And yet what can we do, except pretend what we say is accurate? What can we do, except continue with our stories? Here is mine. It starts with a visit to my grandfather, my father's father, sometime in the early 1960s.

His name was Edwin Avery Park, and he lived in Old Mystic in eastern Connecticut, not far from Preston, where his family had wasted much of the seventeenth, the entire eighteenth, and half of the nineteenth centuries on unprofitable farms. He had been trained as an architect, but had retired early to devote himself to painting—imitations, first, of John Marin's landscapes, and then later of Georgio di Chirico's surrealist canvases; he knew his work derived from theirs. Once he said, "I envy you. I know I'll never have what you have. Now here I am at the end of my life, a fifth-rate painter." His eyes got misty, wistful. "I could have been a third-rate painter."

He showed no interest in my sisters. But I had been born in a caul, the afterbirth wrapped around my head, which made me exceptional in his eyes. When we visited, my grandfather was always waking me up early and taking me for rambles in old graveyards. Once he parked the car by the side of the road, and he—

No, wait. Something happened first. At dawn I had crept up to his studio in the top of the house and looked through a stack of paintings: "Ghosts Doing the Orange Dance." "The Waxed Intruder." "Shrouds and Dirges, Disassembled."

This was when I was seven or eight years old. I found myself examining a pencil sketch of a woman riding a horned animal. I have it before me now, spread out on the surface of my desk. She wears a long robe, but in my recollection she is naked, and that was the reason I was embarrassed to hear the heavy sound of my grandfather's cane on the stairs, why I pretended to be looking at something else when he appeared.

His mother, Lucy Cowell, had been no larger than a child,

and he also was very small—five feet at most, and bald. Long, thin nose. Pale blue eyes. White moustache. He knew immediately what I'd been looking at. He barely had to stoop to peer into my face. Later, he parked the car beside the road, and we walked out through a long field toward an overgrown structure in the distance. The sky was low, and it was threatening to rain. We took a long time to reach the greenhouse through the wet, high grass.

Now, in my memory it is a magical place. Maybe it didn't seem so at the time. I thought the panes were dirty and smudged, many of them cracked and broken. Vines and creepers had grown in through the lights. But now I see immediately why I was there. Standing inside the ruined skeleton, I looked up to see the sun break through the clouds, catch at motes of drifting dust. And I was surrounded on all sides by ghostly images, faded portraits. The greenhouse had been built of large, old-fashioned photographic exposures on square sheets of glass.

A couple of years later, in Puerto Rico, I saw some of the actual images made from these plates. I didn't know it then. Now, seated at my office desk, I can see the greenhouse in the long, low, morning light, and I can see with my imagination's eye the bearded officers and judges, the city fathers with their families, the children with their black nannies. And then other, stranger images: My grandfather had to swipe away the grass to show me, lower down, the murky blurred exposure of the horned woman on the shaggy beast, taken by firelight, at midnight—surely she was naked there! "These were made by my great-uncle, Benjamin Cowell," he said. "He had a photography studio in Virginia. After the war he came home and worked for his brother. This farm provided all the vegetables for Cowell's Restaurant."

Denounced as a Confederate sympathizer, Benjamin Cowell had had a difficult time back in Connecticut, and had ended up by taking his own life. But in Petersburg in the 1850s, his studio had been famous—Rockwell & Cowell. Robert E. Lee sat for him during the siege of the city in 1864. That's a matter of record, and yet the greenhouse itself—how could my grandfather have walked that far across an unmowed field? The entire time I knew him he was very lame, the result of a car accident.

Middle-aged, I tried to find the greenhouse again, and failed. My father had no recollection. "He'd never have told him," sniffed Winifred, my grandfather's third wife. "He liked you. You were born in a caul. He liked that. It was quite an accomplishment, he always said."

Toward the end of her life I used to visit her in Hanover, New Hampshire, where they'd moved in the 1970s when she was diagnosed with multiple sclerosis. It was her home town. Abused by her father, a German professor at Dartmouth, she had escaped to marry my grandfather, himself more than thirty years older, whom she had met in a psychiatric art clinic in Boston, a program run by his second wife. It surprised everyone when Winifred wanted to move home, most of all my grandfather, who didn't long survive the change. He had spent the 1930s in Bennington, Vermont, teaching in the college there, and had learned to loathe those mountains. In addition, I believe now, he had another, more complicated fear, which he associated with that general area.

Because of her illness, Winifred was unable to care for him, and he ended his life in a nursing home. He was convinced, the last time I saw him, that I was visiting him during half-time of the 1908 Yale-Harvard game. "This is the worst hotel I've ever stayed in," he confided in a whisper, when I bent down to kiss his cheek. But then he turned and grabbed my arm. "You've seen her, haven't you?"

I didn't even ask him what he meant, he was so far gone. Later, when I used to visit Winifred in New Hampshire, she got in the habit of giving me things to take away—his paintings first of all. She'd never cared for them. Then old tools and odds and ends, and finally a leather suitcase, keyless and locked, which I broke open when I got home. There in an envelope was the drawing of the horned woman riding the horned beast.

There also were several packages tied up in brown paper and twine, each with my name in his quavering handwriting. I brought them to my office at Williams College and opened them. The one on top contained the first three volumes of something called *The Parke Scrapbook*, compiled by a woman named Ruby Parke Anderson: exhaustive genealogical notes, which were also full of errors, as Winifred subsequently pointed out. Folded into Volume Two was his own commentary, an autobiographical sketch, together with his annotated family tree. This was familiar to me, as he had made me memorize the list of names when I was still a child, starting with his immigrant ancestor in Massachusetts Bay— Robert, Thomas, Robert, Hezekiah, Paul, Elijah, Benjamin Franklin, Edwin Avery, Franklin Allen, Edwin Avery, David Allen, Paul Claiborne, Adrian Xhaferaj. . . .

But I saw immediately that some of the names were marked with asterisks, my grandfather's cousin Theo, Benjamin Cowell, and the Reverend Paul Parke, an eighteenth-century Congregationalist minister. At the bottom of the page, next to another asterisk, my grandfather had printed CAUL.

3. The Battle of the Crater

Not everyone is interested in these things. Already in those years I had achieved a reputation in my family as someone with an unusual tolerance for detritus and memorabilia. Years before I had received a crate of stuff from Puerto Rico via my mother's mother in Virginia. These were books and papers from my mother's father, also addressed to me, though I hadn't seen him since I was nine years old, in 1964. They had included his disbarment records in a leather portfolio, a steel dispatch case without a key, and a bundle of love letters to and from my grandmother, wrapped in rubber bands. I'd scarcely looked at them. I'd filed them for later when I'd have more time.

That would be now. I sat back at my desk, looked out the open window in the September heat. There wasn't any air conditioning anymore, although someone was mowing the lawn over by the Congo church. And I will pretend that this was my Proustian moment, by which I mean the moment that introduces a long, false, coherent memory—close enough.

I really hadn't thought about Benjamin Cowell during the intervening years, or the greenhouse or the horned lady. My memories of Puerto Rico seemed of a different type, inverted, solid, untransparent. In this way they were like the block of pasteboard images my mother's father showed me at his farm in Maricao, and then packed up for me later to be delivered after his death, photographs made, I now realized, by Rockwell & Cowell in Petersburg, where he was from.

I closed my eyes for a moment. Surely in the greenhouse I'd seen this one, and this one—images that joined my mother's and my father's families. Years before on my office wall I'd hung "Ghosts Doing the Orange Dance" in a simple wooden frame, and beside it the military medallion in gilt and ormolu: General Lee surrounded by his staff. Under them, amid some boxes of books, I now uncovered the old crate, still with its stickers from some Puerto Rican shipping line. I levered off the top. Now I possessed two miscellaneous repositories of words, objects, and pictures, one from each grandfather. And because of this sudden connection between them, I saw immediately a way to organize these things into a pattern that might conceivably make sense. Several ways, in fact—geographically, chronologically, thematically. I imagined I could find some meaning. Alternately from the leather satchel and the wooden crate, I started to lay out packages and manuscripts along the surface of my desk and the adjoining table. I picked up a copy of an ancient Spanish tile, inscribed with a stick figure riding a stag—it was my maternal grandfather in Puerto Rico who had shown me this. He had taken me behind the farmhouse to a cave in the forest, where someone had once seen an apparition of the devil. And he himself had found there, when he first bought the property, a Spanish gold doubloon. "You've seen her, haven't you?" he said.

"Who?"

A lawyer, he had left his wife and children to resettle in the Caribbean, first in the Virgin Islands and then in San Juan. He'd won cases and concessions for the Garment and Handicrafts Union, until he was disbarred in the 1950s. Subsequently he'd planted citrus trees in a mountain ravine outside of Maricao. His name was Robert W. Claiborne.

In my office, I put my hand on the locked dispatch case, and then moved down the line. In 1904, his father, my great-grandfather, had published a memoir called *Seventy-Five Years in Old Virginia*. Now I picked up what looked like the original manuscript, red-lined by the editor at Neale Publishing, and with extensive marginal notes.

Years before I'd read the book, or parts of it. Dr. John Herbert Claiborne had been director of the military hospital in Petersburg during the siege, and subsequently the last surgeon-general of the Army of Northern Virginia, during the retreat to Appomattox. A little of his prose, I remembered, went a long way:

> We were descendents of the cavalier elements that settled in that State and wrested it from the savage by their prowess, introducing a leaven in the body politic, which not only bred a high order of civilization at home, but spread throughout the Southern and Western States, as the Virginian, moved by love of adventure or desire of preferment, migrated into the new and adjoining territories. And from this sneered-at stock was bred the six millions of Southrons who for four long years maintained unequal war with thirty millions of Northern hybrids, backed by a hireling soldiery brought from the whole world to put down constitutional liberty—an unequal war, in which the same Southron stock struck undaunted for honor and the right, until its cohorts of starved and ragged heroes perished in their own annihilation. . . .

In other words, what you might call an unreconstructed Southerner, gnawing at old bones from the Civil War. I glanced up at a copy of the finished book on the shelf above my desk. And I could guess immediately that the typescript underneath my hand was longer. Leafing through it, I could see whole chapters were crossed out.

For example, in the section that describes the siege of Petersburg, there is an odd addendum to an account of the Battle of the Crater, which took place on the night and early morning of July 30, 1864:

But now at certain nights during the year, between Christmas Night and New Year's Day, or else sometimes during the Ember Days, I find myself again on the Jerusalem Plank Road, or else re-treading in the footsteps of Mahone's doughty veterans, as they came up along the continuous ravine to the east of the Cameron house, and on to near the present location of the water works. From there I find myself in full view of the captured salient, and the fortifications that had been exploded by the mine, where Pegram's Battery had stood. On these moon-lit nights, I see the tortured chasm in the earth, the crater as it was,—two hundred feet long, sixty feet wide, and thirty feet deep. To my old eyes it is an abyss as profound as Hell itself, and beyond I see the dark, massed flags of the enemy, as they were on that fatal morning,—eleven flags in fewer than one hundred yards,—showing the disorder of his advance. Yet he comes in great strength. As before, because of the power of the exploded mine, and because of the awful destruction of the Eighteenth and Twenty-second South Carolina Regiments, the way lies open to Cemetery Hill, and then onward to the gates of the doomed city, rising but two hundred yards beyond its crest. As before and as always, the Federals advance into the gap, ten thousand, twelve thousand strong. But on the shattered lip of the Crater, where Mahone brought up his spirited brigade, there is no one but myself, a gaunt and ancient man, holding in his hand neither musket nor bayonet, but instead a tender stalk of maize. Weary, I draw back, because I have fought this battle before, in other circumstances. As I do so, as before, I see that I am not alone, and in the pearly dawn that there are others who have come down from the hill, old veterans like myself, and boys also, and even ladies in their long gowns, as if come immediately from one of our 'starvation balls,' in the winter of '64, and each carrying her frail sprig of barley, or wheat, or straw. On these nights, over and again, we must defend the hearths and houses of the town, the kine in their fields, the horses in their stalls. Over and again, we must obey the silent trumpet's call.

This is not Burnsides's Corps, but in its place an army of
the dead, commanded by a fearsome figure many times
his superior in skill and fortitude, a figure which I see
upon the ridge, her shaggy mount trembling beneath her
weight. . . .

This entire section is crossed out by an editor's pen, and
then further qualified by a note in the margin—"Are we intended to accept this as a literal account of your actual experience?" And later, "Your tone here cannot be successfully
reconciled."

Needless to say, I disagreed with the editors' assessments.
In my opinion they might have published these excised sections and forgotten all the rest. I was especially interested in
the following paragraph, marked with a double question
mark in the margin:

Combined with unconsciousness, it is a condition that
is characterized by an extreme muscular rigidity, particularly in the sinews of the upper body. But the sensation
is difficult to describe. [. . .] Now the grass grows green.
In the mornings, the good citizens of the town bring out
their hampers. But through the hours after mid-night
I must find a different landscape as, neck stiff, hands
frozen into claws, I make my way from my warm bed,
in secret. Nor have I once seen any living soul along the
way, unless one might count that single, odd, bird-like,
Yankee 'carpet-bagger' from his 'atelier,' trudging
through the gloom, all his cases and contraptions over
his shoulders, including his diabolical long flares of
phosphorus. . . .

4. A UFO in Preston

Benjamin Cowell had made his exposures on sheets of glass
covered with a silver emulsion. There were none of his photographs in Edwin Avery Park's leather valise. Instead I
found daguerreotypes and tintypes from the 1850s and ear-

lier. And as I dug farther into the recesses of the musty bag, I found other images—a framed silhouette of Hannah Avery, and then, as I pushed back into the eighteenth century, pen and pencil sketches of other faces, coarser and coarser and worse-and-worse drawn, increasingly cartoonish and indistinct, the lines lighter and lighter, the paper darker and darker.

The sketch of the Reverend Paul Parke is particularly crude, less a portrait than a child's scribble: spidery silver lines on a spotted yellow card: bald pate, round eyes, comically seraphic smile, suggesting the death's head on an ancient grave. It was in an envelope with another artifact, a little handwritten booklet about three by six inches, sewn together and covered in rough brown paper. The booklet contained the text of a sermon preached at the Preston Separate Church on July 15, 1797, on the occasion of the fiftieth anniversary of the Rev. Parke's public ministry.

For the Reverend Parke, the most powerful and astonishing changes of his lifetime had been spiritual in nature, the various schisms and revivals we refer to as the Great Awakening. Independence, and the rebellion of the American Colonies, seemed almost an afterthought to him, a distant social echo of a more profound and significant rebellion against established doctrine, which had resulted in the manifest defeat of the Anti-Christ, and the final destruction of Babylon.

Moving through the sermon, at first I thought I imagined an appealing sense of modesty and doubt:

> . . . whilst I endeavored not to trust in one thing I found I was trusting in Something else: and they Sem all to be but refuges of lies as when I fled from a lion I met a fox or went to lean on the wall a Serpent wood bite me and my own hart dyed and my every way I Could take and when I could find no way to escape and as I thought no Divine assistance or favour: I found Dreadful or it was my hart murmuring in emity against God himself that others found mercy and were Safe and happy: whilst I that had Sought as much was Denied of help and was

perishing: but this Soon Subsided and other Subjects drew my sight. If any one was known to err in principle or practisee or Did Not walk everly there was Strickt Disapline attended according to rule, bee the sin private and publick, as the Case required: and the offender recovered or admenished that theire Condition be all ways plaine, their Soberiety and Zeal for virtue and piety was Such theire Common language and manners was plaine.

Even though my office window was open, the heat was still oppressive. I sat back, listening to the buzz of the big mowers sweeping close across the lawn. This last part seemed full of redirected misery, and it occurred to me to understand why, having given me my ancestor's name, my parents had never actually used it, preferring to call me by a nickname from a 1950s comic strip. I slouched in my chair, letting my eyes drift down the page until I found some other point of entry. But after a few lines I was encouraged, and imagined also a sudden, mild stir of interest, moving through the ancient congregation like a breeze:

. . . in Embr Weeke, this was pasd the middle of the night when I went out thoug my wife would not Sweare otherwise but that I had not shifted from my bed. But in Darkness I betoke myself amongst the hils of maise and having broken of a staff of it I cam out from the verge and into the plouged field wher I saw others in the sam stile. Amongst them were that sam Jonas Devenport and his woman that we had still Givn mercyfull Punishment and whipd as I have menshoned on that publick ocation befor the entire congregation. But on this night when I had come out with the rest: not them but others to that we had similarly Discomforted. So I saw an army of Sinners that incluyded Jho Whitside Alice Hster and myself come from the maise with ears and tasills in our hands. On that bar ground of my unopned mind these ours wood apear as like a Morning without ligt of Gospill truth and all was fals Clouds and scret Darkness. Theire I saw printed on the earth the hoof of mine enimy: a deep print

up on the ground. In the dark I could still perceive her
horns and her fowl wind. Nor thougt I we could hold her
of with our weak armes. But together lnking hands we
strugld upward up the hill by Preston Grang nto the appel
trees led by that enimy common to al who movd befor us
like a hornd beast togther with her armee of walking corses
of dead men. Nor could I think she was not leding us to
slaghter by the ruind hutts of the Pecuods theire: exsept
When I saw a Great Ligt at the top of the hill coming
throug the trees as lik a cold fire and a vessel or a shipe
com down from heavn theire and burning our fases as we
knelt and prayd. Those hutts bursd afire and a Great Ligt
and a vessill on stakes or joyntd legs was come for our de-
livrance: with Angels coming down the laddr with theire
Great Heads and Eys. Nor could I Scersely refrain my
Mouth from laughter and my tongue from Singing: for the
Lord God omnipotent reigneth: or singing like Israel at the
Red Sea: the hors and his rider he has thrown into the Sea.
If any man doubt it theire is stil now upon that hill the
remnts of that battel. Or I have writ a copy of that Shipe
that otherwse did flie away and leving ondly this scrape of
scin ript from man's enimny in that hour of Tryumph. . . .

In my office, in the late afternoon, I sat back. The diagram was there, separately drawn on a small, stiff card, the
lines so light I could hardly make them out. But I saw a
small sphere atop three jointed legs.

Then I unwrapped the piece of skin, which was tied up in
a shred of leather. It was hard as coal and blackish-green,
perhaps two inches by three, the scales like goose-bumps.

I looked up at my grandfather's painting above my desk,
"Ghosts Doing the Orange Dance." I had examined it many
times. The ghosts are like pentagrams, five-pointed stars,
misty and transparent. They are bowing to each other in a
circle, clutching the oranges in their hands. In the misty landscape, under the light of what must be the full moon behind
the clouds, there are cabinets and chests of drawers where
other ghosts lie folded up.

But now I noticed an odd detail for the first time. The

furniture is littered across a half-plowed field. And in the background, against a row of faux-gothic windows, there are men and women hiding, peering out from a row of corn placed incongruously along the front. Their faces glint silver in the moonlight. Their eyes are hollow, their cheeks pinched and thin.

I got up to examine the painting more closely. I unhooked it from the wall and held it up close to my nose. Then I laid it among the piles of paper on my desk.

These similarities, these correspondences between my mother's family and my father's—I give the impression they are obvious and clear. But that is the privilege of the memoirist or the historian, searching for patterns, choosing what to emphasize: a matter of a few lines here and there, sprinkled over thousands of pages. Turning away, I wandered around my office for a little while, noticing with despair the boxes of old books and artifacts, the shelves of specimens, disordered and chaotic. A rolled-up map had fallen across the door. How had everything gotten to be like this? Soon, I thought, I'd need a shovel just to dig myself out.

But through the open window I could smell cut grass. I turned toward the screen again, searching for a way to calm myself and to arrange in my mind these disparate narratives. Because of my training as a literary scholar, I found it easy to identify some similarities, especially the repeating motif of the corn stalk, and the conception of a small number of unworthy people, obliged to protect their world or their community from an awful power. And even in the scene of triumph described by the Reverend Parke—achieved, apparently, through some type of extraterrestrial intervention—was I wrong to catch an odor of futility? This was no final victory, after all. These struggles were nightly, or else at certain intervals of the year. The enemy was too strong, the stakes too high. Our weapons are fragile and bizarre, our allies uncertain and unlike ourselves—no one we would have chosen for so desperate a trial.

I sat back down again, touched my computer, googled Ember Days, idly checked my email, not wanting to go home.

The buzz of the lawnmower was gone. The campus was underutilized, of course. The building was almost empty.

I cleared a place on my desk, crossed my arms over it, laid down my cheek. Not very comfortable. But in a few minutes I was asleep. I have always been a lucid dreamer, and as I have gotten older the vividness of my dreams has increased and not diminished, the sense of being in some vague kind of control. This is in spite of the fact that I sleep poorly now, never for more than a few hours at a time, and if a car goes by outside my bedroom, or if someone were to turn onto her side or change her breathing, I am instantly awake. As a result, the experience of sleeping and not sleeping has lost the edge between them. But then at moments my surroundings are sufficiently distorted and bizarre for me to say for certain, "I am dreaming," and so wake myself up.

With my cheek and mouth pressed out of shape against the wooden surface, I succumbed to this type of double experience. I had a dream in which I was sufficiently alert to ponder its meaning while it was still going on. Not that I have any clear preconceptions about the language of dreams, but in a general way I can see, or pretend I can see, how certain imagery can reflect or evoke the anxieties of waking life—the stresses on a relationship or a marriage, say, or the reasons I was sitting here in my office on a sweltering afternoon, instead of going home. I dreamed I was at one of those little private cave-systems that are a roadside feature of the Shenandoah Valley Interstate—I had visited a few with Nicola and Adrian when he was four or five and we were still living in Baltimore. But I was alone this time. I felt the wind rush by me as I stood at the entrance to the main cavern, a function of the difference in temperature outside and inside. It gives the illusion that the cave is "breathing," an illusion fostered in this case by the soft colors and textures of the stone above my head, the flesh-like protuberances, and the row of sharp white stalactites. Perhaps inevitably I now realized I was in the mouth of a sleeping giant, and that the giant was in fact myself, collapsed over my office desk. And as I ran out over the hard, smooth surface, I realized further that I had taken the shape of a small rodent; now I jumped down to the floor and made a circuit of the room, trying to find a hole to hide in, or (even better!) a means of egress through the towering stacks of books.

5. A Detour

When I woke, I immediately packed my laptop, locked my office. It was late. I went down to my car in the lot below Stetson Hall, seeing no one along the way. I passed what once had been known as the North Academic Building—subsequently they'd made the basement classroom into a storeroom. The glass they had replaced with bricks, so that you couldn't look in. But even so I always walked this way, in order to remember my first trip to Williams College years before, and the class where I had met my wife. In this dark, cannibalized building, Professor Rosenheim had taught his 100-level course on meta-fiction. Andromeda Yoo (as I will call her for these purposes) had been a first-year student then.

These days we also live in a town called Petersburg, though the coincidence had never struck me until now. It is across the border in New York State, and there are two ways to drive home. One of them, slightly longer, loops north into Vermont.

Usually I take the shorter way, because I have to stop and show my identification and vaccination cards at only one state inspection booth and not two. There's hardly ever a line, and usually you just breeze through. Of course I accept the necessity. The world has changed. Even so, there's something that rubs against the grain.

But that afternoon I headed north. On my way along Route 346, it occurred to me suddenly that I recognized the façade in the painting of the star-shaped ghosts. It belongs to a gingerbread construction, a mansion in North Bennington called the Park-McCullough House, at one time open to the public, and not far from the campus where Edwin Park taught architecture and watercolor painting in the 1930s, until he was dismissed (my father once claimed) for some kind of sexual indiscretion.

But apparently, much later, subsequent to his marriage to Winifred, he had revisited the place. I knew this because of a strange document in a battered envelope, part of the contents of his leather valise, a scribbled note on the stationery of the Hanover nursing home where he had ended his life, and then a few typed pages, obviously prepared earlier, about the time, I imagined, that he had painted "Ghosts Doing the Orange Dance." And then some more pages in a woman's writing—when I first glanced at them, I had discounted the whole thing as some sort of meandering and abortive attempt at fiction. Now, as I drove home, I found I wasn't so sure.

The note was attached to the pages with a paperclip, and the thin, spidery lines were almost illegible. Yet even though the letters were distorted, I could still see vestiges of my grandfather's fine hand: "Ghosts; ghosts in the moon."

And here is the typed text of the manuscript: "Now that I'm an old man, dreams come so hard I wake up choking. Now at midnight, with my wife asleep, I sit down hoping to expunge a crime—a tiny crime I must insist—that I committed in the Park-McCullough mansion on one autumn night when I was there alone.

"In 1955 I moved to Boston and married Winifred Nief, who had been a patient of my deceased wife. Within a few years I retired from my architectural practice and removed to Old Mystic to devote myself to painting. About this time I became a member of the Park Genealogical Society, an organization of modest ambitions, though useful for determining a precise degree of consanguinity with people whose names all sound like variations of Queen Gertrude the Bald. Its standards of admission, as a consequence and fortunately, are quite lax.

"Starting in the early 1960s, the society had its annual meeting each Halloween weekend in the Park-McCullough House, a boxy Second-Empire structure in Bennington, which was no longer by that time in private hands. At first

I had no wish to go. Quite the contrary. Winifred was bored speechless by the prospect, and I couldn't blame her. But something perverse about the idea nagged at me, and finally I thought I might like to revisit that town, without saying why. Enough time had passed, I thought.

"Winifred said she might like to drive down to Williamstown and visit David and Clara. She could drop me off for the afternoon and pick me up later. I had no desire to see the children go out trick-or-treating. In those days I didn't concern myself with my son's family, except for Paul, though in many ways he was the least interesting of the four. He'd been born in a caul, which my daughter-in-law had not seen fit to preserve. The youngest daughter was retarded, of course.

"Winifred dropped me off under the porte-cochere on a beautiful autumn day. Among a dozen or so genealogists, it was impossible for me to pretend any relation to the former owners, who by that time had died out. But we traipsed around the house, listening with modest interest to the shenanigans of the Parks and the McCulloughs—Trenor Park had made his money in the Gold Rush. Even so, he seemed a foolish sort. Success, even more than accomplishment, is the consolation of a mediocre mind.

"The house itself interested me more, designed by Henry Dudley (of the euphonious New York firm of Diaper & Dudley) in the mid 1860s, and displaying some interesting features of the Romantic Revival. It was a shameless copy of many rather ugly buildings, but I have often thought that true originality in architecture, or in anything, can only be achieved through a self-conscious process of imitation. I was especially taken with the elegant way the staff's rooms and corridors and staircases were folded invisibly into the structure, as if two separate houses were located on the same floor plan, intersecting only through a series of hidden doors. In fact there were many more secret passageways and whatnot than were usual. I was shown the secret tunnel under the front. There was a large dumbwaiter on the first floor.

"The docent told me stories of the family, and stories also about screams in the night, strange sounds and footsteps, lights turned on, a mysterious impression on the mattress of the great four-poster in the master bedroom. These are standard stories in old houses, but it seemed to me that an unusual quantity had accumulated here, a ghost in almost every room, and this over a mere hundred years of occupation. For example, there was a servant who had disappeared after his shift, never to be heard of again. A fellow named John Kepler, like the philosopher. He had left a wife and child in the village.

"I had thought I would go to the morning session and then use the afternoon to stroll about the town. As things turned out, I found my leg was bothering me too much. I could not bear to walk the streets or even less to climb the hill to the campus, for fear I might be recognized. I berated myself for coming within a hundred miles of the place, and so I took refuge in the mansion past the time everyone else had departed, and the staff was preparing for a special children's program, putting up paper spiderwebs and bats. The docents were so used to me they left me to my own devices. Waiting for Winifred to pick me up, I found myself sitting in an alcove off Eliza McCullough's bedroom, where she had written her correspondence at a small, Italianate, marble-topped table.

"I sat back in the wicker chair. I've always had an instinct for rotten wood, and for any kind of anomaly. I happened to glance at the parquet floor beneath my feet and saw at once a place where the complicated inlay had been cut apart and reassembled not quite perfectly. In old houses sometimes there are secret compartments put in for the original owners, and that secret is often lost and forgotten in the second generation or the third. And in this house I thought I could detect a mania for secrecy. I put my foot on the anomaly and pressed, and was rewarded by a small click. I could tell a box was hidden under the surface of the floor.

"I confess I was nervous and excited as I listened at the door for the footsteps of the staff. Then I returned and knelt down on the floor. I could see immediately the secret was an obvious one, a puzzle like those child's toys, plastic sliding squares with letters on them in a little frame, and because one square is missing, the rest can be rearranged. Words can be spelled. The little squares of parquetry moved under my fingers until one revealed a deeper hole underneath. I reached in and found the clasp, and the box popped open.

"The hole contained a document. I had already been shown a sample of Eliza Park-McCullough's handwriting, the distinctively loopy, forceful, slanting letters, which I recognized immediately. I enclose the pages, pilfered from the house. But because they are difficult to read, I also transcribe them here:

> God I think I will go mad if I don't put this down. Esther tells me to say nothing, to tell nothing and say nothing, but she does not live here. Nor will she come back she says as long as she lives. And the rest are all gone and will not come back for an old woman, nor can I tell them. It would be prison if they knew or an asylum. So here I am alone in the nights when the servants go back behind the wall, and I take the elevator to the second floor. And I cannot always keep the lights burning and the victrola playing and the radio on, and then I am alone. It has been twenty years since Mr. McCullough died and left me here, a crippled bird who cannot fly to him! So in the night I drink my sherry and roll my chair back and forth along the hall. I spy from the front windows, and I can almost see them gather on the lawn, not just one or two. But they nod shyly to each other as they join in the dance. The lamps that they carry glow like fireflies. But they are also lit from above as if from an enormous fire behind the clouds, an engine coming down. Some nights I think it must land here on the roof, and if I could I would climb to the top of the house, and it would take me up. Or else I lie on my bed and listen for the sounds I know must come, the clink of the billiard balls on the green baize, and the smell of cigar smoke even though it has been two years since I had them take the balls and cues away. I asked them to burn them. I am sure they thought me insane, but I'm not insane. Nor was I even unhappy till the monster came into this house, and if I'm punished now it is for giving him his post and not dismissing him. But

how could I do that? John McCullough, do you forgive me? It was for his high forehead and curling brown moustaches and strong arms like your arms. Do you know when I first saw him, when he first stood there in the hall with his cap in his hands, I thought I saw your ghost. No one is alive now who remembers you when you were young, but I remember. That boy was my John brought back, and when he lifted me in his arms and carried me upstairs before the elevator went in, when he put me down in my wheel-chair at the top of the stairs, I scarcely could let go his neck. Do they think because I'm paralyzed that I feel nothing? Even now, past my eightieth year I can remember how it felt when you would carry me up those stairs and to my room, me like a little bird in your arms, though I could walk then and fly, too. Do not think I was unfaithful when I put my face into his shirt when he was carrying me upstairs. And when he put me down and asked me in his country voice if there was anything more, why then the spell was broken.

I do not say these things to excuse myself. There is no excuse. Though even now I marvel I was able to do it, able to find a way that night when they were all asleep and I was reading in my room. Or perhaps I had gone asleep. 'Is that you?' I cried when I heard the click of the billiard balls and smelled the cigar. I thought it was you, the way you put the house to bed before you came up. I pulled myself into my chair and wheeled myself down the hall. 'Is that you?' And when I saw him coming up the stairs, you ask me why I didn't ring the bell. I tell you it was all a dream until he spoke in his loud voice. I had no money about the place. Perhaps he thought I'd be asleep. He smiled when he saw me. He was drunk. I am ashamed to say I do not think he would have hurt me. But I could not forgive him because he knew my secret. I could tell it in his smiling face as he came down the hall. He knew why I could not cry out or ring the bell. Oh my John, he was nothing like you then as he turned my chair about and rolled me down away from the servants' door.

'Is that right, old bird?' he said. He would not let go of my chair. Once he put his hand over my mouth. And he went through my jewel case and he turned out my closets and my drawers. He could not guess the secret of this box where I keep the stone. Then he was angry and he took hold of my arms. He put his face against my face so that our noses touched, and he smiled and I could smell his cologne and something else, the man's smell underneath. I could not forgive him. 'There in the closet,' I said, meaning the water closet, though he didn't understand me. I let him wheel me over the threshold, and then I reached out on the surface of the cabinet where Mr. McCullough's man had shaved him every morning. There was no electric light, and so I reached out my hand in the darkness. The man's head was near my head and I struck at him with the razor. Oh, I could not get it out of my head that I had committed a great crime! It was you, John, who put that thought into my head, and I did not deserve it! I pulled myself into my room again. I found a clean night-gown and took off my other one and lay down on my bed. When I made my telephone call it was to Esther who drove up from the town. I think I was a little insane, then. She scrubbed the floor with her own hands. She told me we must tell no one, and that no one would believe us. She said there was a space where the dumb-waiter comes into the third floor, a fancy of the builder's she'd discovered when she and Bess were children. It is a three-sided compartment set into the top of the shaft. Esther does not live in the real world, though that is hard to say of your own child. She said the stone would keep the man away. But otherwise he would come back. She laughed and said it would be an eye for him. We'd put it into his head and it would be his eye. We'd claim he'd stolen it and run away. We'd claim a rat had died inside the wall.

"I sat reading these notes as it grew dark. Then I folded up the pages and slipped them into my jacket. I sat at Mrs. McCullough's desk and stared out the window. Darkness was falling. I poked at the floor with the end of my cane. Winifred was late. The box in the parquetry was closed.

"The docent's name was Jane Mears, and she was a beautiful, shy woman, with soft hair, if you care about that sort of thing. She stood in the doorway with a question on her lips. I asked her whether there was any story of a famous jewel that appertained to the house. And she told me about a massive stone, a ruby or sapphire or topaz or tourmaline the size of an orange that Trenor Park had won in a poker game in San Francisco. According to the story, it was delivered to his hotel room in a blood-spattered box, the former owner having shot himself after he packed it up.

"'It disappeared around 1932,' she said.

"I didn't say anything. I was not like other members of my family, or like my cousin Theodora who had died. I had never heard the voices. There had been no membrane over my eyes when I was born, no secret screen of images between me and the world. But even so I was interested in the anomaly, the corpse at the top of the shaft, a jewel in his mouth, as I imagined. A ghost's footprint in the dust, or else the men and women who had come out of the corn to follow my great-great-great-grandfather up Bartlett Hill in Preston, where there was a machine, or a mechanical robot, or an automaton with the cold light behind it and the stag running away.

"When Winifred drove up, I was waiting in the drive. She had stories to tell me about my son's family. I asked her to take the long way round, to circle by the campus, and we drove through North Bennington and watched the children dressed as witches and Frankensteins. There was a little ghost running after his mother, carrying a pumpkin.

"I motioned with my finger, and Winifred drove me toward the Silk Road and the covered bridge, then past it toward the corner where my car had spun out of control. She chattered about her day, and I responded in monosyllables. She made the turn past the tree where I had lost control. She didn't know, and at first I didn't think I would say anything about it. But then I changed my mind. 'Stop,' I said, and I made her pull over onto the side of the road. I gave her some foolish story, and left her in the car while I limped back in the darkness to deliver my gift."

6. Andromeda Yoo

As I sped home at dusk, I wondered if I should retrace my grandfather's steps and drive up to the Park-McCullough House along Silk Road—it wasn't so far out of the way. Perhaps I could find the tree he was talking about. But I passed the turnoff and continued, pondering as I did so the differences and connections between this narrative and the previous ones. That Halloween night, I thought, there had been no ghosts in the cornrows, and no cornrows at all, lining the front of the mansion or surrounding the elaborate porte-cochere. But then why had my grandfather chosen that image or motif for his portrait of the house? Though it was obvious he had read the Reverend Parke's sermon, he had no way of knowing how it corresponded or overlapped with various documents from my mother's family—manuscripts he'd never seen, composed by people he'd never met.

But after I had crossed into New York State, I left behind my obsessive thoughts of those dry texts. Instead I imagined my wife waiting for me. And so when I arrived home at my little house beside the river, there she was. She had brought Chinese food from Pittsfield, where she worked as a lawyer for Sabic Plastics.

What was it my grandfather had said? ". . . A beautiful, shy woman with long black hair, if you care about that sort of thing. She stood in the doorway with a question on her lips . . ."—when I first read the description I had thought of my wife. Driving home, remembering that first reading, I thought of her again, and wondered how I would answer her question, and whether she would be angry or impatient, as the docent at the Park-McCullough House, I imagined, had had every right to be. But Andromeda was just curious; she often got home late after supper, and in the long September light, everything tended to seem earlier than it was. We made Bombays-and-tonic and went to sit on the deck looking down toward the swamp willows, and ate seaweed salad and chicken with orange sauce out of the white containers with wire handles—very civilized. Andromeda raised her chopsticks, a further interrogation.

And so I told her about the mystery, the ghosts in the corn. As I did so, I remembered the first time I saw her in Professor Rosenheim's class, fresh-faced, eager to engage. Rosenheim had given them an early novel of mine, *A Princess of Roumania*, and it was obvious to me that Andromeda had liked it very much. The class itself was about meta-fiction, which is a way of doubling a story back upon itself, in a fashion similar to my grandfather's description of the double nature of the Park-McCullough mansion with its manifest anomalies. It was possible to see these kinds of patterns in my own work, although I always warned students against complexity for its own sake, and to consider the virtues of the simple story, simply told.

Rosenheim had invited me up from Baltimore to discuss *A Princess of Roumania*, a novel that had become infected almost against my will with references to the past, with descriptions of locations from my own life, and people I had once known or would come to know—all writing, after all, is a mixture of experience and imagination, fantasy and fact. I had accepted his offer because the trip enabled me to revisit the town where I'd grown up, and where part of the novel was set. Already by that time, Baltimore had ceased to feel like home.

And so I spent the weekend visiting as if for the first time the locations where I had set *A Princess of Roumania*. It was strange to see how I had misread my own memory, how little the text recalled the actual places. Lakes had become ponds. Rivers had become streams. Subdued, I met Rosenheim the night before the class, and we sat in a bar called "The Red Herring," and it was there that he first told me about his student, Andromeda. "You'll see what I mean tomorrow. None of this will be difficult for her. She'll figure out not just what you said, but what you meant to say. If only the rest had half her brains," he said, peering at me through glasses as thick as hockey pucks.

But then he roused himself, brandishing in his right hand the text of something else I had been working on, a "memoir," or fragment of science-fiction, which I would finish many years later, and which, ill-advisedly maybe, I had emailed to his class a couple of days before. "How dare you?" he said. "How dare you send this without my permission? Did you think I wouldn't find out about it?

"Did you think I'd be jazzed about this?" he complained, indicating the phrase "whispered drunkenly" in the text. "Did you think I'd want them to think I'm an alcoholic? Though in a way it's the least of my problems: Right now they are reading this," he whispered drunkenly, conspiratorially, "and they have no idea why. Right here, right here, this is confusing them," he said, pressing his pudgy thumb onto the manuscript a couple lines later, a fractured and contradictory passage. "Andromeda Yoo is reading this," he said, his voice hoarse with strain. "You . . . you'll see what I mean tomorrow."

Now, years later, as we sat with our drinks in Petersburg, she was supremely sensible. "I agree with you. There must be something else besides the sermon, some other manuscript." She smiled. "You know, this is like what I do all day. I took a Bible history course in college, and I think the thing that made me want to be a lawyer was the discussion of the Q Gospel—you know, how you can deduce the existence of a missing source. It's all meta-fiction, all the time. That's what I learned in college. So that's what we have here. Where's the actual text?"

For the purposes of this memoir, I have narrated it verbatim, as if I carried the document with me, or else had committed it to heart. But that's not so. "It's in my office," I told her. Some birds were squawking down by the stream.

"What do you think your father means by a 'sexual indiscretion'? It couldn't have been just sleeping with students. That's what Bennington College was all about, wasn't it? Its founding philosophy. In the 1930s? Didn't you get fired for *not* doing that?"

"I don't think my father knows anything about it. He's just guessing."

This was true, or at least it was true that I thought so. "But it must have been something pretty humiliating," continued Andromeda. "I mean, thirty years later he couldn't even walk around the town."

"I guess."

"Although maybe the only reason he joined the genealogical society was to go back there, to have an excuse. The way he talks about it, it's not like he had any real interest."

"You're wrong about that," I said. "He made me memorize a list of all the Parks, although we tended to stop before Gertrude the Bald."

"Hmm—so maybe it's about the jewel. But the problem is, there must be at least one other source for this business about the cornfields, something that doesn't involve anything about the Claibornes. Because there are two sources from that side, aren't there? Doctor Claiborne *and* his son? Was there anything about it in the court-martial?"

"Maybe, but I don't know anything about that yet. I was saving it for later. I haven't told anyone."

She frowned. "Who would you tell?"

"Well, I mean the people who might be reading about this. I've told them about Doctor Claiborne and the Battle of the Crater. But the court-martial, I guess I'm already fore-shadowing it a little. Part of it, anyway."

Andromeda looked around. There was no one in the neighbor's yard. Not a living soul, unless you counted the cat jumping in and out of the bee's balm.

"That sounds crazy," she said indulgently. "Particularly since now you've mentioned it to me."

"Never mind about that," I interrupted. "We don't want to pay attention to everything at once. One thing after another. Speaking of which, isn't there something else you want to tell me? I mean about this. Now might be a convenient time."

I didn't like to bully her or order her around, especially since it felt so good to talk to her, to let our conversation develop naturally, as if unplanned. All day I had been listening to people's voices inside my head, ghosts long departed, and in some sense I had been telling them what to say.

The sun had gone down, and we watched the bats veer

and blunder through the purple sky. The yard was deep and needed mowing. Suddenly it was quite cold.

She turned to me and smiled. "Okay, so let's get it over with," she said, raising her glass. "You know that Bible Studies class I told you about? Well, the second semester was all about heresy. And when you talk about this stuff, I'm so totally reminded of these trials in this one part of northern Italy. It was kind of the same thing—these peasants were being prosecuted for witchcraft. But they were the opposite of witches, that's what they claimed. They talked about a tradition, father to son, mother to daughter, going back generations. On some specific nights their souls would leave their bodies and go out to do battle with the real witches and warlocks, who were out to steal the harvest and, you know, poison the wells, make the women miscarry, spread diseases, the usual. I remember thinking, Jesus, we need more people like this. And they never gave in, they never confessed, even though this was part of the whole witchcraft mania of the sixteenth century. I'm sure they were tortured, but even so, they were just so totally convinced that the entire Inquisition was part of the same diabolic plot to keep them from their work—they'd seen it all before."

Andromeda Yoo was so beautiful at that moment, her golden skin, her black hair down her back. I felt she understood me. "Another interesting thing," she said, "was that these people were never the model citizens. There was always something dodgy or damaged about them. You could tell it in the way they talked about each other, not so much about themselves. And of course the judges were always pointing out that they were sluts and whores and drunks and sodomites and village idiots. But they had a place in the community. Everyone was on their side. They had to bring people in from neighboring counties just to have a quorum at the executions."

"That's a relief," I murmured.

She got up from her chair and came to stand behind me, bent down to embrace me—I didn't deserve her! "I'm glad I got that off my chest," she said, a puzzled expression on her face. "Now, where were we?"

And we proceeded to talk about other things. "What do you think he left next to the tree?" she asked. "I'll bet it was the jewel. The tourmaline the size of a pumpkin or whatever. I'll bet that was what was in the secret box under the floor."

"That's crazy. It never would have fit."

"What do you mean? That's what it was for. Do you really think Esther would have left it in the dead man's mouth? Or in his eye—Kepler's eye, wasn't that it? No, she wanted to see where it was hidden. That was probably how she'd found the compartment at the top of the shaft—looking for the jewel. Maybe she had hired the guy in the first place, or she was his lover—no, scratch that. She was probably a lesbian. That's what her mother probably meant about not living in the real world."

"Really. But then why wouldn't she have stolen it that night? Why leave it in the box?"

"I'm not sure. But that's what your grandfather meant about a tiny crime. He just had it for a few minutes. He'd taken it on impulse, and he had time to think during the drive. How could you dispose of such a thing?"

Andromeda had been adopted from a Korean orphanage and then orphaned again when her American parents died in a fire. And they themselves were also orphans, had met in an orphanage, possessed no family or traditions or history on either side—I don't think I had ever known their names. Maybe they had never even had any names. This was one of the things I found comforting about Andromeda, together with her calmness and common sense. She was so different from me.

Our bedroom, underneath the eaves, was always warmer than the rest of the house. Later, I had already dozed off when I heard her say, "I think it probably has to do with his cousin, Theodora. Didn't she kill herself?"

"Yes, when she was a teenager. It was a terrible thing. He was an only child, and she was his only cousin, too. My father always said it was some kind of romantic disappointment. Maybe a pregnancy."

"You mean a 'sexual indiscretion.'"

"I suppose so. But not the same one. The dates don't work out."

"Well, what do you know about her? Is there anything in your boxes?"

"I think there's a photograph. A locket."

"Where?"

I had hung up my pants before we lay down, and put my wallet on the dresser with some loose change, a pocket knife, and a number of other small objects. The locket wasn't among them. It's not as if I carried it around. "I don't know," I said.

But then I felt something in my closed fist. "Wait," I said, opening my hand, revealing it on my palm. It was round and gold, as big as an old-fashioned watch, and had an ornate "T" engraved on the lid. Inside there were two photographs, a smiling young woman on one side, and an older man in a bowler hat on the other, my grandfather's uncle Charlie, perhaps.

"Turn on the light," Andromeda said. "I can't see anything."

There was a reading light beside the bed. I switched it on. Andromeda lay naked on her back, one hand scratching her pubic hair. She turned onto her side, raised herself on one elbow, and her breasts re-formed. "Look at the depth of the case," she said. "Maybe there's some kind of secret message inside, under the photograph. There's enough room for a letter folded six or seven times. Look—that's a place where it might lever up," she said, sliding her fingernail under the circle of gold that held the image. Because of her legal work for Sabic Plastics, she had all kinds of special expertise.

Theodora Park had a pleasant, happy face with a big round nose like a doorknob. I thought to myself she might have made a good clown in the circus, though no doubt that was partly because of her distended lips, the white circles on her cheeks, and the fright wig she was wearing underneath the potted geranium that served her for a hat.

"Look," said Andromeda, her beautiful young (Why not? What the hell?) body curved around the locket, which we held between us. And under her fingernail, whether it was just a rick of the light, but the woman in the photograph seemed to shift and move and change expression—a sudden, exaggerated grimace, while at the same time the man in the bowler hat and big moustache frowned in disapproval. And that was certainly enough, because Andromeda's black eyes filled with tears. "No," she said, "oh, no, no, no, no, no, no, no. . . ."

7. Second Life

In fact no one was there when I got home. I feel I can pretend, as long as it is obvious: I had lived by myself for many, many years, and the house was a wreck. Andromeda Yoo is a confabulation, though I suppose she carries a small resemblance to the underdressed avatar of a woman I once met in a sex club in Second Life, or else the lawyer who handled my wife's divorce long ago—not just that poor girl in Rosenheim's class.

No, the other stuff—the peasants from the Friuli—I had discovered for myself, through a chance reference in one of my sister Katy's books. I've always had an interest in European history. Nor do I think there is any surviving information about Theo Park, any diary or letter or written text that might explain her suicide, or if she suffered from these vivid dreams. There isn't a living person who knows anything about her. And I suppose it can be a kind of comfort to imagine that our passions or our difficulties might at some time be released into the air, as if they never had existed. But it is also possible to imagine that the world consists of untold stories, each a little package of urgent feelings that might possibly explain our lives to us. And even if that's an illusion or too much to hope for, it is still possible to think that nothing ever goes away, that the passions of the dead are still intact forever, sealed up irrevocably in the past. No one could think, for example, that if you lost an object that was precious to you, then it would suddenly stop existing. It would be solipsistic arrogance to think like that. No, the object would always be bumping around somewhere, forgotten in someone else's drawer, a compound tragedy.

I got myself a gin and tonic—that much is true—and sat at the kitchen table under the fluorescent light, studying a pack of well-thumbed photographs of my son when he was small. My wife had taken so many, I used to say you could make of a flip-book of his childhood in real time—enough for both of us, as it turned out. More than enough. I could look at them forever, and yet I always felt soiled, somehow, afterward, as if I had indulged myself in something dirty. In the same way, perhaps, you can look at photographs of naked women on the Internet for hours at a time, each one interesting for some tiny, urgent fraction of a second.

I went upstairs to lie down. In the morning, I telephoned the offices of *The Bennington Banner*, where someone was uploading the biweekly edition. I didn't have a precise date, and I didn't even know exactly what I was looking for. But a good part of the archives was now online, and after a couple of hours I found the story. On the first of November, 1939, a Bennington College student had died in a car accident. The road was slippery after a rainstorm. She hadn't been driving. The details were much as I'd suspected.

"What do you think about what's happening in Virginia," said the woman on the phone.

"Virginia?"

The Bennington Banner is about small amounts of local news, if it's about anything. But this woman paid attention to the blogs. "There's some kind of disturbance," she told me. "Riots in the streets."

Subsequent to this conversation, I took a drive. I drove out to the Park-McCullough House. The place was boarded up, the grounds were overgrown. After ten minutes I continued on toward the former Bennington College campus and took a left down the Silk Road through the covered bridge. Along the back way to the monument I looked for likely trees, but it was impossible to tell. When I reached Route 7, I continued straight toward Williamstown. I thought if there was a message for me—a blog from the past, say—it might be hidden in my grandfather's painting, which was, I now imagined, less a piece of De Chirico surrealism than an expression of regret.

It had rained during the night, and toward three o'clock the day was overcast and humid. In my office, I sat in the wreckage with my feet on the desk. I looked up at the painting, and I could tell there was something wrong with it. I just had a feeling, and so I turned on my computer, IM'd my ex-wife in Richmond, and asked her to meet me in Second Life.

Which meant Romania, where she was working, supposedly, as some kind of virtual engineer. In Second Life, her office is in a hot air balloon suspended above the Piata Revolutiei in Bucharest; you'd have to teleport. It was a lovely place, decked out with a wood-burning stove, but she didn't want to meet me there. Too private. Instead we flew east to the Black Sea coast, past Constanta to the space park, the castle on the beach, where there was always a crowd. We alighted on the boardwalk and went into a café. We both got lattés at the machine, and sat down to talk.

God knows what Romania is like now. God knows what's going on there. But in Second Life it's charming and picturesque, with whitewashed buildings painted with flowers and livestock, and red tile roofs. In Second Life my ex-wife's name is Nicolae Quandry. She wears a military uniform and a handlebar mustache—a peculiar transformation from the time I knew her. It's hard not to take it personally, even after all these years—according to the *Kanun*, or tribal code, women under certain circumstances can take a vow of celibacy and live as men, with all the rights and privileges. Albanian by heritage, Nicola—Nicolae, here—had a great-aunt who made that choice, after the death of her father and brothers. Of course her great-aunt had not had a grown autistic son.

It was always strange to see her in her hip boots, epaulettes, and braid. She had carried this to extremes, because once I had told her that her new name and avatar reminded me of Nicolae Ceausescu, the Romanian dictator whom I'd researched extensively for my novel—not that she looked like him. He was a drab little bureaucrat, while she carried a pistol on her hip. With Saturn hanging low over the Black Sea, its rings clearly visible, she stood out among all the space aliens

that were walking around. "My psychiatrist says I'm not supposed to talk to you," I typed.

"Hey, Matt," she typed—my name in Second Life is Matthew Wirefly. "I figured you would want to bring Adrian a
birthday present."

It was hard to tell from her face, but I imagined she
sounded happy to hear from me, a function of my strategy in
both marriage and divorce, to always give her everything
she wanted. Besides, everything had happened so long ago.
Now I was an old man, though you wouldn't necessarily
have known it from my avatar. "Yes, that's right," I typed. "I
bought him a sea turtle at the aquarium. I'll bring it to his
party. Where's it going to be?"

"Oh, I don't know. Terra Nova. You know how he likes
steampunk."

Actually, I didn't know. I'd thought he was still in his sea-
mammal stage, which had lasted ten years or so. The previous year he'd had his party on the beach in Mamaia Sat, and
I'd ridden up on the back of a beluga whale.

Now we typed about this and that. A man with six arms
wandered by, gave us an odd look, it seemed to me. The
name above his head was in Korean characters.

After a few minutes I got down to business. She had never
known my grandfather, but I tried to fill her in. After a certain amount of time, she interrupted. "I don't even believe
you have a psychiatrist," she typed. "What do you pay him?"

"Her," I corrected. "Nowadays they work for food."

"Hunh. Maybe you could ask her to adjust your meds.
Remember when you thought the graffiti on the subway was
a message for you? 'Close Guantanamo'—that's good advice! 'Call Mark'—you're probably the only person who
ever called. And you didn't even get through."

Good times, I thought. "Hey, I misdialed. Or he moved.
Hey, *le monde n'est qu'un texte*."

"Fine—whatever. That's so true. For twenty years I've
thanked God it's not my responsibility anymore, to act as
your damn filter."

She knew what I meant, and I knew what she meant. It's

possible for me to get carried away. But I hadn't ever told her during the eight years of our relationship, and I didn't tell her now, that I had always, I think, exaggerated certain symptoms for dramatic effect.

Once, when New York City was still New York City, I'd belonged to a squash club on Fifth Avenue. Someone I played with got it into his head that I was Canadian, introduced me to someone else—I let it go. It seemed impolite to insist. Within weeks I was tangled up in explanations, recriminations, and invented histories. When I found myself having to learn French, to memorize maps of Montreal, I had to quit the club.

This was like that. When Nicola and I first got together, I pretended to have had a psychiatric episode years before, thinking that was a good way to appeal to her—a short-term tactic that had long-term effects. It was a story she was amusingly eager to believe, a story confirmed rather than contradicted by my parents' befuddled refusal to discuss the issue, a typical (she imagined) Episcopalian reticence that was in itself symptomatic. And it was a story I had to continue embellishing, particularly after Adrian was first diagnosed.

But like all successful lies, it was predominantly true. These things run in families, after all. And sometimes I have a hard time prioritizing: "What's happening in Richmond?" I asked her. "What's happening down there?"

Nicolae took a sip from her latte, wiped her mustache. Above us, from the deck of the space park, you could see the solar system trying to persevere, while behind it the universe was coming to an end. Stars exploded and went cold. "Matt," she typed. "You don't want to know. It would just worry you. I don't even know. Something downtown. Abigail has gone out and I—fuck, what could you do, anyway?" She touched the pistol at her hip.

After we logged off, I sat for a while in peace. Then I got up on my desk so I could look at the picture, "Ghosts Doing the Orange Dance."

Kneeling, my nose up close, I saw a few things that were

new. No, that's not right. I noticed a few things I hadn't seen before. This is partly because I'd just been to the house, circled the drive. But now I saw some differences.

My grandfather had never been able to paint human beings. Trained as an architect, he had excelled in façades, ruins, urban landscapes. But people's faces and hands were mysterious to him, and so instead he made indistinct stylized figures, mostly in the distance. Shapes of light and darkness. Star-shaped ghosts with oranges in their hands. The haunted house in the moonlight, or else a burning light behind the clouds, descending to the roof. Men and women in the corn, beyond the porte-cochere. A single light at the top of the house, and a shadow against the glass. Kepler's eye. I wondered if this was where the dumbwaiter reached the third floor.

Down below, along the garden wall, a woman lay back against a tree trunk. Her face was just a circle of white, and she had long white hair. She was holding an orange, too, holding it out as if in supplication. Her legs were white. Her skirt had ridden up.

I thought I had not seen that tree against that wall that morning, when I had stopped my Toyota on the drive. My grandfather was good at trees. This was a swamp willow, rendered in miniature, so that the branches drooped over the woman's head. I thought there was no tree like that on the grounds of the Park-McCullough House. So instead I went to look for it.

8. In Quantico

Naturally, after forty years I didn't find anything valuable. But there was a willow tree along the Silk Road, set back on the other side of a ditch. He must have been going very fast.

I dug down through the old roots. And I did find something, a key ring with two stainless steel keys, in good condition. One of them, I assumed, was a secret or back-door key to the abandoned McCullough mansion. The other was much smaller, more generic, the kind of key that could open many cheap little locks. After a detour to my office, I took it home. I unpacked my satchel, took out my laptop. I arranged various stacks of paper on the kitchen table. And then I used the little key to unlock the steel dispatch case that had come to me from Puerto Rico. I knew what I'd find, the various documents and exhibits from the court-martial of Captain Robert Watson Claiborne, USMC.

After dinner (Indian takeout and a beer), I began my search. The trial had taken place at the Marine barracks at Quantico, Virginia, during the second and third weeks in January, 1919. There were about eight hundred pages of testimony, accusations and counter-accusations regarding my grandfather's behavior aboard the USS *Cincinnati* during the previous November, the last month of the European war. Captain Claiborne was only recently attached to the ship, in command of a detachment of Marines. But during the course of twenty-seven days there were complaints against him from four Marine Corps privates and a Navy ensign, when the vessel was anchored off Key West.

Colonel Dion Williams, commander of the barracks at Quantico, presided over the court, and the judge advocate was Captain Leo Horan. On the fourth day of the trial, my grandfather took the stand in his own defense. Here's what I found on page 604 of the transcript, during Captain Horan's cross-examination:

463. Q. In his testimony you heard him say in substance that he came into your room on the occasion when he came there to see a kodak, and that you and he lay on your bunk or bed and that he slept, or pretended to fall asleep, and that at that time you put your hands on his private parts.
A. That is not true.
464. Q. Did you fondle his person?
A. I did not fondle his person. I only touched him in the manner as one might touch another, as one would come in contact with another lying down next to each other on a bed, the approximate width of which was about as that table (indicating).

465. Q. I see. Referring to another matter, will you tell the court, Captain Claiborne, what kind of a school this was you say you started at Sharon, Connecticut?

A. A school for boys.

466. Q. Average age?

A. Average age was twelve or thirteen.

467. Q. I see. Did you sleep soundly on board the Cincinnati, as a general rule?

A. I did.

468. Q. I see. The alleged conduct of you toward Ensign Mowbray—do you now deny that that might have been in an unconscious manner?

A. I do.

469. Q. I see. About this radium-dialed watch: as I recall your testimony, you had a little pocket watch?

A. I had quite a large pocket watch, a normal watch, too large to be fixed into any leather case which would hold it onto the wrist.

470. Q. Mr. Mowbray's statement about seeing a wrist-watch, radium dialed, on your wrist the night of the first sleeping on the divan is a fabrication?

A. Yes.

471. Q. I see. Now, taking up the matter of this first hike, before you turned in with Walker, will you tell the court how far you went on this hike, approximately?

A. About three or four miles. We went through Key West and out into the country.

472. Q. On these hikes they went swimming along the beach?

A. On that hike they went in swimming at my orders.

473. Q. Yes. What happened afterward?

A. They came out and dried themselves and put on their clothes and took physical exercise.

474. Q. How were they clad when they took this physical exercise?

A. Some of them had on underwear and some of them did not. The majority of them had on underwear.

475. *Q. How were you dressed at the time that the men were undressed going through this physical drill on the beach?*
A. I don't recall.
476. *Q. I want a little bit more than that. Do you deny that you were undressed at the time?*
A. I either had on part of my underwear, or my entire underwear, or had on none.
477. *Q. In front of the guard, were you?*
A. I don't recall.
478. *Q. But you do admit that you may have been entirely naked.*
A. I may have been.
479. *Q. You admit that? They went through these Swedish exercises, whatever they were? Physical drill?*
A. Physical drill, yes.
480. *Q. I see. Now, Captain Claiborne, you admit to sleeping soundly on board ship, as a general rule? No problem with somnambulism, or anything of that sort?*

Counsel for the accused (Mr. Littleton): If the court please, I began by saying I would desist from making any objections in this case. Nevertheless, I could not then anticipate that counsel would profit from my forbearance by making these insinuations about the conduct of the accused, in these matters that are irrelevant to the complaints against him. I did not anticipate that counsel would undertake to go all over the world asking this sort of question about conduct which, if Captain Claiborne had not acted as he did, would have constituted a dereliction. I am going to withdraw my statement that I will not object, and I am going to insist upon the rules in reference to this witness. He needs protection in some way from the promiscuous examination regarding every Tom, Dick, and Harry in the universe. I insist that the counsel shall confine his examination to things which are somewhere within the range of these charges. We cannot be called on to suffer the imputation which a mere question itself carries.

The judge advocate: Are you objecting to that question, the last question about somnambulism?

Counsel for the accused (Mr. Littleton): Yes, the last question is the only one I could object to. The others were all answered. I am objecting to it on the basis that it is irrelevant.

By a member: Mr. President, I also would like to arise to ask the point of these questions, so that we may know, at the time they are asked, whether they are relevant or not.

Counsel assisting the judge advocate: If the court please, we would be very ready and willing to tell you what our purpose is, but it would disclose the purpose of the cross examination, and I don't think we are required to state before the court and before the witness what our purpose may be in bringing out this subject of somnambulism. But it is perfectly proper cross examination, inasmuch as the witness has testified to sleeping soundly at the time of these alleged incidents.

The accused: I am perfectly willing to answer the question.

Counsel assisting the judge advocate: The witness and the judge advocate are at one on that now, if the judge advocate will ask that question.

The court was cleared.

The court was opened. All parties to the trial entered, and the president announced that the court overruled the objection.

481. Q. Very well, Captain Claiborne. Have you ever suffered from somnambulism?

Counsel for the accused (Mr. Littleton): I object—

The judge advocate: Let me rephrase the question. Did you experience an episode of somnambulism while on board the U.S.S. Cincinnati, between the first and twenty-seventh of November of last year?

A. I can't remember exactly what day. But I had a sensation of being awake and dreaming at the same time. This is not unusual with me, and from time to time I have had this experience ever since I was a boy. This is only the most extreme example, and I imagine that I was affected by a sort of nervous excitement, due to the end of the hostilities in Europe, and of course my own catastrophic reversal of fortune. This was in the very early morning when I saw myself at the top of a great cliff, while below me I could see the streets of a town laid out with lines of lamp-posts, glowing in a sort of a fog. I thought to myself that I was overlooking a town or city of the dead. There were houses full of dead men, and hospitals full of soldiers of every nationality, and also influenza patients who were laid outside in an open field or empty lot. I thought there were thousands of them. At the same time there was a long, straight boulevard cutting through the town from north to south. I saw a regiment or a battalion march along it toward a dark beach along the sea, which had a yellow mist and a yellow froth on the water. Other men climbed toward me up a narrow ravine. I thought to myself that I must fight them to protect the high plain, and I had a stick in my hand to do it. As they clambered up I struck at them one by one. The first fellow over the ledge was Captain Harrington, whom I replaced on board the Cincinnati, *because he had died of the influenza in October—the bloom was on his face. It was a fight, but I struck and struck until the stick burst in my hand. Then I woke up and found myself outside on the balcony, long past midnight—*

482. Q. By balcony I presume you mean the ship's rail—

A. No, no, I mean the balcony of my hotel where I was staying with my wife. I mean I had left the bed and climbed out onto the balcony, dressed only in my shirt. It was four A.M., judging from my wrist-watch. This was in New York City before Christmas, less than a month ago, several weeks after I had been detached from the ship.

Counsel assisting the judge advocate: Captain Claiborne, please restrict your answers to the time covered in the complaint, prior to the twenty-seventh of November.

Counsel for the accused (Mr. Littleton): Again I must object to this entire line of questioning, on the grounds that it is irrelevant.

The judge advocate: I withdraw the question—

The president: The objection is overruled. The court would like the witness to continue.

The member: This was during the third week in Advent, was it not? During what is commonly called the "Ember Days"?

The president: The stick that was in your hand, the court would like to know what type of stick it was.

The member: Captain Claiborne, will you tell the court whether you were born still wrapped inside an afterbirth membrane, which is a trait or condition that can run in certain families—

The judge advocate: Mr. President, I must agree with my esteemed colleague, the counsel for the accused—

The president: The objection is overruled. The witness will answer the question. Now, Captain Claiborne, the court would like to know if you experienced any stiffness or muscular discomfort prior to this event, especially in your neck or jaw.

A. *Well, now that you mention it, I did have a discomfort of that kind.*

The president: The court would like you to expand on your answer to an earlier question, when you described your encounter with Captain Harrington. You said the bloom was on his face, or words of that effect. Did you see any marks or symptoms of the influenza epidemic on him at that time?

Counsel for the accused (Mr. Littleton): I object—
The judge advocate: Mr. President—
The president: The objection is overruled. The witness will answer the question.
A. Now that you mention it, there is a great deal more
I could say about the events of that night, between the
time I recognized Captain Harrington and the time I
came to myself on the balcony above Lexington Avenue. If the court wishes, I could proceed. Captain
Harrington was the first but by no means the last who
were climbing up along the precipice, and all of them
bore traces of the epidemic. Pale skin, dull eyes, hair
lank and wet. Hectic blossoms on their cheeks, and in
this way they were different than the soldiers marching below them in the streets of the necropolis, most
of whom, I see now, were returning from France. I
remember Captain Harrington because I was able to
dislodge his fingers and thrust him backward with a
broken head. But soon I was forced to retreat, because
these ones who had climbed the cliffs and spread out
along the plain were too numerous for us to resist. I
had no more than a company of raw recruits under
my command. Against us marched several hundred
of the enemy, perhaps as many as a battalion of all
qualities and conditions, while behind them I could
see a large number of women in their hospital gowns.
Severely outnumbered, we gave way before them. But
I brought us to the high ground, where we attempted
to defend a single house on a high hill, a mansion in
the French style. The weather had been calm, but
then I heard a roll of distant thunder. A stroke of lightning split the sky, followed by a pelting rain, and a
wind strong enough to flatten the wide, flat stalks
as the fire burned. By then it was black night, and
whether from some stroke of lightning or some other
cause, but the roof of the house had caught on fire. By
its light I could see the battle in the corn, while at the
same time we were reinforced quite unexpectedly in a

*way that is difficult for me to describe. But a ship had
come down from the clouds, a great metal airship or
dirigible, while a metal stair unrolled out of its belly . . .*

9. Ember Days

My grandfather was immediately acquitted of all charges.
The president of the court, and at least one of its members,
came down to shake his hand. Nevertheless, he did not lin-
ger in the Marine Corps, but put in for his release as quickly
as he could. In some ways he was not suited to a soldier's
life. You can't please everyone: There were some—among
them his brother-in-law, Howard Harrington—who thought
his acquittal had not fully restored his reputation.

Subsequently he ran a music school in Rye, New York,
hosted a classical music radio program in New York City,
and even wrote a book, before he left the United States to
practice law in the Caribbean. Prior to his disbarment he
was full of schemes—expensive kumquat jellies, Nubian
goats delivered to the mainland by submarine during the
Second World War—all of which my grandmother dutifully underwrote. His farm in Maricao was called the Haci-
enda Santa Rita, and it was there that we visited him when I
was nine years old, my father, my two older sisters, and
myself. My mother hadn't seen him since she was a teenager, and did not accompany us. She could never forgive the
way he'd treated her and her brother when they were children. This was something I didn't appreciate at the time,
particularly since he went out of his way to charm us. He
organized a parade in our honor, roasted a suckling pig. And
he showed an interest in talking to me—the first adult ever
to do so—perhaps from some mistaken idea of primogeni-
ture. In those days he was a slender, elegant, white-haired
old man.

Later I was worried that my own life would follow his
trajectory of false starts and betrayals and dependency.
Early on he had staked out the position that ordinary standards of civilized behavior had no hold on people like him.
On the contrary, the world owed him a debt because of his

genius, which had been thwarted and traduced at every turn—a conspiracy of jealous little minds. It was this aspect of her father's personality that my mother hated most of all, and regularly exposed to ridicule. A moderately gifted musician, he had the pretensions of genius, she used to say, without the talent. Moreover, she said, even if he'd been Franz Liszt himself, he could not have justified the damage that he caused. When I asked why her mother had stayed with him, she retorted that you don't turn a sick dog out to die. But I suspected there was more to her parents' marriage than that, and more to his sense of privilege. Laying the record of his court-martial aside, I imagined that any summary of his life that did not include the valiant battle he had waged—one of many, I guessed—against the victims of the Spanish Influenza epidemic of 1918, would seem truncated and absurd. Maybe the goats and the kumquats were the visible, sparse symptoms of a secret and urgent campaign, the part of the ice above the water.

When my mother talked about her father, I always thought she was advising me, because it was obvious from photographs that I took after him. She had no patience for anything old, either from her or my father's family, and she was constantly throwing things away. My father's father never forgave her for disposing of the caul I was born in, and she never forgave him for pressing on me, when I was seven, a bizarre compensation for this supposed loss. He had wrapped it up for me, or Winifred had: a sequined and threadbare velvet pouch, which contained, in a rubberized inner compartment, his cousin Theo's caul, her prized possession, which she had carried with her at all times. She had embroidered her name in thick gold thread; furious, my mother snatched up the pouch and hid it away. I only rediscovered it years later, when she asked me to move some boxes in the attic.

When I was a child I kept the thought of this velvet pouch as a picture in my mind, and referred to it mentally whenever I heard a story about something large contained in something small, as often happens in fairy tales. I had seen it briefly, when my grandfather had first pressed it into my hands. It was about six inches long, red velvet worn away along the seams. Some of the stitches on the "T" and the "h" had come undone.

But I wondered when I was young, was I special in any way? Perhaps it was my specialness that could explain my failures, then and always. At a certain moment, we cannot but hope, the ordinary markers of success will show themselves to be fraudulent, irrelevant, diversionary. All those cheating hucksters, those athletes and lovers, those trusted businessmen and competent professionals, those good fathers, good husbands, and good providers will hang their heads in shame while the rest of us stand forward, unapologetic at long last.

Thinking these inspirational thoughts, in the third week of September—the third sequence of ember days of the liturgical year, as I had learned from various wikipedias—I drove up to the Park-McCullough House again. As usual that summer and fall, I had not been able to fall asleep in my own bed. Past two o'clock in the morning, Theodora Park's velvet purse in my pocket, I sidled up to each of the mansion's doors in turn, and tried the second key I had found among the roots of the willow. Some windows on the upper floor were broken. Ghosts, I thought, were wandering through the building and the grounds, but I couldn't get the key to work. Defeated, I stepped back from the porte-cochere; it was a warm night. Bugs blundered in the beam of my flashlight. The trees had grown up over the years, and it was too much to expect that a ship or dirigible would find the space to land here safely. The same could be said of Bartlett Hill in Preston, which I had visited many years before. Logged and cleared during Colonial times, now it was covered with second- or third-growth forest. From the crest overlooking the Avery-Parke Cemetery, you could barely see the lights and spires of Foxwoods Casino, rising like the Emerald City only a few miles away. I found myself wondering if the casino was still there, and if the "ruind hutts of the Pecuods" had "burst afire" as a result of the ship coming down, or as some kind of signal to indicate a landing site. Whichever, it was certainly interesting that in Robert Claiborne's account

f the battle on the French-style mansion's lawn, "the roof of
he house had caught on fire."

Interesting, but not conclusive. As a scholar, I was trained
o discount these seductive similarities. I had not yet dared
o unbutton the velvet pouch or slip my hand inside, but with
my hand firmly in my pocket I stepped back through the
broken, padlocked, wrought-iron fence and stumbled back
o the main road, where I had left my car. And because, like
three-quarters of the faculty at Williams College, I was on
unpaid leave for the fall semester, I thought I would drive
down to Richmond and see Adrian, who was now thirty
years old—a milestone. That was at least my intention. I
had a reliable automobile, one of the final hydrogen-cell,
solar-panel hybrids before Toyota discontinued exports. I
would take Route 2 to 87, making a wide semicircle around
the entire New York City area, before rejoining 95 in central
New Jersey. I would drive all night. There'd be no traffic to
speak of, except the lines of heavy trucks at all the check-
points.

So let's just say I went that way. Let's just say it was possible to go. And let's just say that nothing happened on that
long, dark drive, until morning had come.

Beyond the Delaware Bridge I saw the army convoys
headed south along I-95. North of Baltimore it became clear
I couldn't continue much farther, because there was no access to Washington. There were barricades on the interstate,
and flashing lights. Shortly before noon I got off the 695
bypass to drive through Baltimore itself—sort of a nostalgia tour, because Nicola and I had lived on North Calvert
Street and 31st, near the Johns Hopkins campus, when Adrian
was born. I drove past the line of row houses without stopping. Most of them were boarded up, which could not fail to
depress me and throw me back into the past. I took a left and
turned into the east gate of the Homewood campus. I wanted
to see if my old ID would still get me into the Eisenhower
Library, so I parked and gave it a try. It was a bright, cool
day, and I was cheered to see a few students lying around the
lawn.

I needn't have worried—there was no one at the circulation

desk. Once inside the library, I took the stairs below street level to one of the basements, a peculiar place that I remembered from the days when I had taught at the university. The electricity wasn't functioning, but some vague illumination came from the airshafts, and I had my flashlight. With some difficulty I made my way toward the north end of that level, where a number of books by various members of my family were shelved in different sections that nevertheless came together in odd proximity around an always-deserted reading area. Within a few steps from those dilapidated couches you could find a rare copy of Robert W. Claiborne's book *How Man Learned Music*. A few shelves farther on there were six or seven volumes by his son, my uncle, on popular science or philology. In the opposite direction, if you didn't mind stooping, you would discover three books on autism by Clara Claiborne Park, while scarcely a hundred feet away there were a whole clutch of my father's physics textbooks and histories of science. Still on the same level it was possible to unearth Edwin Avery Park's tome (Harcourt, Brace, 1927) on modernist architecture, *New Backgrounds for a New Age*, as well as other books by other members of the family. And filling out the last corner of a rough square, at comfortable eye-level, in attractive and colorful bindings, stood a row of my own novels, including *A Princess of Roumania*. It was one of the few that had come out while I was living in Baltimore, and I was touched to see they had continued to acquire the later volumes, either out of loyalty or bureaucratic inertia—certainly not from need—up to the point where everything turned digital.

It is such a pleasure to pick up a book and hold it. I will never get used to reading something off a screen. I gathered together an assortment of texts and went back to the reading area, rectangular vinyl couches around a square table. Other people had been there recently; there were greasy paper bags, and a bedroll, and a gallon jug of water. The tiled floor was marred with ashes and charred sticks, and the skylight was dark with soot. But I had proprietary instincts, and would not be deterred. I put down my leather satchel and laid the books down in a pile, squared the edges, and with my flash-light in my hand I played a game I hadn't played in years, since the last time I was in that library.

The game was called "trajectories," my personal version of the *I Ching*. I would choose at random various sentences and paragraphs, hoping to combine them into a kind of narrative, or else whittle them into an arrow of language that might point into the future. For luck I took Cousin Theo's velvet pouch out of my pocket, ran my thumb along the worn places. I did not dare unbutton it, thinking, as usual, that whatever had once been inside of it had probably dried up and disappeared. The pouch, I imagined, was as empty as Pandora's box or even emptier. How big was a caul, anyway? How long did it take for it to crumble into dust?

I set to work. Here was my first point of reference, from my uncle Bob (Robert W. Jr.) Claiborne's book on human evolution, *God or Beast* (Norton, 1974), page 77:

> . . . To begin with, then, in that the women to whom I have been closest during my lifetime have all of them been bright, intellectually curious, and independent-minded. My mother was involved in the women's rights movement before World War I, and until her retirement worked at administrative jobs; at this writing she is, at eighty-six, still actively interested in people, ideas, and public affairs. My sister is a college teacher and author. . . .

And on page 84:

> Thus it seems to me very probable that, like both baboon and chimp males, the human male has a less powerful tendency to become involved with the young than does the female. I can't prove this, and indeed am not certain that it can ever be either proved or disproved. Nonetheless, it seems to me at least arguable that the emotional rewards of fatherhood are somewhat less than those of motherhood. Be that as it may, however, the rewards exist and I, for one, would hate to have forgone them.

In these passages I could see in my uncle a wistful combination of pedantry and 1960s masculinity. As I read, I remembered him telling me about a trip to visit his father in the Virgin Islands when he was a teenager. He had found him living with an alumnus of the music school, a boy also named Robert, whom he had already passed off to the neighbors as his son, Robert Jr. Loud and gleeful, sitting on his leather sofa in the West Tenth Street apartment, my uncle had described the farcical misunderstandings and logistical contortions that had accompanied his stay.

But what about this, a few more pages on? Here in the flashlight's small tight circle, when I brought it close:

> The point bears repetition, because it is important, and because no one else is willing to make it (I've checked.) . . .

I thought this was a promising place to start, and so I laid the book down, picked up another at random. It was *The Grand Contraption*, a book about comparative cosmologies that my father—the husband, as it happens, of the "college teacher and author" mentioned above—published in 2005. Here's what he had to say to me, on page 142:

> . . . Once more the merchant looked around him. Far away on the road someone walked toward the hill, but there was still time. A little smoke still came out of the eastern pot. There was no sound but he went on, softly reciting *Our Father*. He crossed himself, stepped into the center of the triangle, filled his lungs, and bellowed into the quiet air, "Make the chair ready!"
>
> But it is time for us to leave the demons alone. Even if supernatural beings are an important part of many people's vision of the world, they belong to a different order of nature and should be allowed some privacy.

I didn't think so. Looking up momentarily, glancing down the long dark layers of books, reflecting briefly on the diminished condition of the world, it didn't occur to me that privacy was in short supply. It didn't occur to me that it had any value whatsoever, since a different order of nature was what I was desperate to reveal.

But I was used to these feelings of ambivalence. Leafing forward through the book, I remembered how studiously my father had competed with his own children. After my sister started publishing her own histories of science, he switched from physics to a version of the same field, claiming it was the easier discipline, and therefore suitable to his waning powers. Princeton University Press had been her publisher before it was his. And after I had started selling science fiction stories in the 1980s, he wrote a few himself. He sent them off to the same magazines, claiming that he wanted to start out easy, just like me. Though unprintable, all his stories shared an interesting trait—they started out almost aggressively conventional, before taking an unexpected science-fiction turn. At the time I'd wondered if he was trying to mimic aspects of my style. If so, could it be true that he had found no emotional rewards in fatherhood?

Disappointed by this line of thought, I glanced down at the book again, where my thumb had caught. The beam of the flashlight, a red rim around a yellow core, captured these words: "The point bears repetition."

That was enough. I closed *The Grand Contraption* with a bang that reverberated through the library. Apprehensive, I shined the light back toward the stairway, listening for an answering noise.

After a moment, to reassure myself, I opened a novel written by my father's mother, Edwin Avery Park's first wife. It was called *Walls Against the Wind*, and had been published by Houghton Mifflin. On the strength of the advance, my grandmother had taken my father on a bicycle tour through Western Ireland in 1935. This, from the last pages:

'I'm going to Moscow,' Miranda told him. 'They have another beauty and a different God—' The tones of her voice were cool as spring rain. 'It's what I have to do. It's all arranged.'

'Yes . . . I wish you'd understand.'

'I'm going almost immediately. I'm going to work

there and be part of it.' Her voice came hard and clipped like someone speaking into a long-distance telephone. 'Will you come to Russia with me?' she challenged her brother. 'Will you do that?'

Adrian flung back his head, unexpectedly meeting her challenge. His eyes were blue coals in the white fire of his face.

'All right,' he said. 'I'll go with you.'

She wanted them to go to Russia. It was the only thing she wanted to do. There was a fine clean world for them there, with hard work and cold winters. It was the kind of world she could dig into and feel at home in. She did not want to live in softness with Adrian. Only in the clean cold could the ripe fruit of his youth keep firm and fresh. She gave him her hand across the table. Perhaps it would work out—some way. Russia. In Russia, she thought, anything can happen. . . .

Anything could happen. Of course not much information had come out of Russia for a long time, not even the kind of disinformation that might have convinced a cultivated Greenwich Village *bohemienne* like my grandmother that Russia might be a bracing place to relocate in the 1930s. Now, of course, in Moscow there wasn't even Second Life.

But maybe my thinking was too literal. Parts of what had been Quebec, I knew from various websites, were experimenting with a new form of socialism. Maybe, I thought, my impersonation of a Canadian in New York City long before had constituted some kind of preparation, or at least some caul-induced clairvoyance. Maybe my grandmother's text was telling me to move up there, to escape my responsibilities or else bring them with me to attempt something new. Or if that was impossible, maybe I was to reorganize my own life along socialistic or even communistic lines, clear away what was unneeded, especially this bourgeois obsession with dead objects and the dead past. The world would have a future, after all, and I could choose to share it or else not.

And of course all this frivolous thinking was meant to

hide a disturbing coincidence. Adrian was my son's name. Furthermore, my wife had miscarried a few years before he was born, a girl we were intending to name Miranda. But I don't think, in my previous trajectories, I had ever glanced at this particular book. The library contained several other romances by Frances Park.

Was I to think that if Miranda had lived, she would have been able to reach her brother as I and his mother had not, break him out of his isolation? Briefly, idly, I wondered if, Abigail now dead in some unfortunate civil disturbance, I could swoop down on Richmond like Ulysses S. Grant. . . .

After a few moments, I tightened my flashlight's beam. What did I possess so far? A deluded vision of a fine clean world, with hard work and cold winters. Demons, rapid transformations, and the diluted pleasures of fatherhood. Almost against my will, a pattern was beginning to materialize.

But now I turned to something else, a Zone book from 2006 called *Secrets of Women*, page 60:

> . . . In addition to these concerns about evidence, authenticity, and female corporeality, a second factor helps explain why anatomies were performed principally or exclusively on holy women: the perceived similarities between the production of internal relics and the female physiology of conception. Women, after all, generated other bodies inside their own. God's presence in the heart might be imagined as becoming pregnant with Christ.

It was true that I had many concerns about evidence, authenticity, and female corporeality, although it had not occurred to me until that moment to wonder why anatomies had been performed (either principally or exclusively) on holy women. These words had been written by my sister, Katy Park, who had been a history professor at Harvard University. She had left Boston in 2019, when the city was attacked, but up until her death she was still working in Second Life. Her lectures were so popular, she used to give them in the open air, surrounded by hundreds of students and non-students. For a course in utopias, she had created painstaking reproductions of Plato's Republic, Erewhon, Islandia, and Kim Stanley Robinson's Orange County. Or once I'd seen her give a private seminar in Andreas Veselius's surgical amphitheater, while he performed an autopsy down below.

She had not had children. But her words could not but remind me of my ex-wife's pregnancy, and how miraculous that had seemed. Anxious, I took the laptop from my satchel and tried to contact Nicola in Richmond, but everything was down. Or almost everything—there was information available on almost any year but this one.

So maybe it wasn't even true, that I could choose to share in the world's future. It wasn't a matter of simple nostalgia: For a long time, for many people and certainly for me, the past had taken the future's place, as any hope or sense of forward progress had dried up and disappeared. But now, as I aged, more and more the past had taken over the present also, because the past was all we had. Everywhere, it was the past or nothing. In Second Life, frustrated, I pulled up some of the daily reconstructions of the siege of 1864-65—why not? I could see the day when my New Orleans great-great-grandmother, Clara Justine Lockett, crossed the line with food and blankets for her brother, who was serving with the Washington Artillery. Crossing back, she'd been taken for a spy, and had died of consumption while awaiting trial.

Or during the previous July, I could see at a glance that during the Battle of the Crater, inexplicably, unforgivably, General Burnsides had waited more than an hour after the explosion to advance, allowing the Confederates to re-form their ranks. If he had attacked immediately, before dawn, he might have ended the war that day.

Exasperated by his failure, I logged off. I picked up a book my mother had written about my younger sister, published in 1967 when she was nine years old. As if to reassure myself, I searched out a few lines from the introduction where my mother introduced the rest of the family under a selection of aliases. Katy was called Sara. Rachel was called Becky. I was called Matthew:

If I were to describe them this would be the place to do it. Their separate characteristics. The weaknesses and strengths of each one of them, are part of Elly's story. But it is a part that must remain incomplete, even at the risk of unreality. Our children have put up with a lot of things because of Elly; they will not have to put up with their mother's summation of their personalities printed in a book . . .

This seemed fair and just to me, though it meant we scarcely appeared or existed in our own history. I wouldn't make the same mistake; finding nothing more of interest, I laid the book aside. Instead I picked up its sequel, *Exiting Nirvana* (Little, Brown, 2001, in case you want to check).

In that book, Elly has disappeared, and Jessy has resumed her real name. Autism is already so common, there is no longer any fear of embarrassment. But when I was young, Jessy was an anomaly. The figure I grew up with was one child out of 15,000—hard to believe now, when in some areas, if you believe the blogs, the rates approach twenty percent. Spectrum kids, they call them. In the 1960s the causes were thought to be an intolerable and unloving family. Larger environmental or genetic tendencies were ignored. But toward the end of her life, my mother resembled my sister more and more, until finally in their speech patterns, their behavior, their obsessions, even their looks, they were virtually identical.

Now I examined the pictures. My autistic sister, like her grandfather, had not excelled in portraiture. Her frail grasp of other people's feelings did not allow her to render faces or gestures or expressions. But unlike him, for a while she had enjoyed a thriving career, because her various disabilities were explicit in her work, rather than (as is true for the rest of us, as is true, for example, right now) its muddled subtext. For a short time before her death she was famous for her meticulous acrylic paintings of private houses, or bridges, or public buildings—the prismatic colors, the night skies full of constellations and atmospheric anomalies. When I lived in Baltimore, I had commissioned one for a colleague. Here it was, printed in color in the middle of the book: "The House on Abell Avenue."

I looked at the reproduction of Jessy's painting—one of her best—and tried to imagine the end of my trajectory, the house of a woman I used to know. I tried to imagine a sense of forward progress, but in this I was hindered by another aspect of the game, the way it threw you back into the past, the way it allowed you to see genetic and even stylistic traits in families. Shared interests, shared compulsions, a pattern curling backward, a reverse projection, depressing for that reason. This was the shadow portion of the game, which wouldn't function without it, obviously. But even the first time I had stumbled on these shelves, I had been careful not to look at my own books, or bring them to the table, or even think about them in this context. There had been more future then, not as much past.

I was not yet done. There were some other texts to be examined, the only one not published by a member of my family, or published at all. But I had collected in a manila envelope some essays on the subject of *A Princess of Roumania*, forwarded to me by Professor Rosenheim after my appearance in his class. To these I had added the letters I'd received from the girl I called Andromeda, not because that was her name, but because it was the character in the novel she had most admired. While she was alive, I had wanted to hide them from my wife, not that she'd have cared. And after her death I had disposed of them among the "R" shelves of the Eisenhower Library, thinking the subject closed.

I opened the envelope, and took out Rosenheim's scribbled note: "I was disappointed with their responses to *A Princess of Roumania*. I was insulted by proxy, me to you. These students have no sympathy for failure, for lives destroyed just because the world is that way. They are so used to reading cause and effect, cause and effect, cause and effect, as if that were some kind of magic template for understanding. With what I've gone through this past year. . . ."

I assumed he was referring to the painful breakup of his own marriage, which he'd mentioned in the bar. Here is an excerpt from the essay he was talking about:

The novel ends before the sexual status of Andromeda can be resolved. It ends before the confrontation between Miranda and the baroness, Nicola Ceausescu, her
surrogate mother, though one assumes that will be covered in the sequels. And it ends before the lovers con-
summate their relationship, which we already know won't
last. Park's ideas about love are too cynical, too "sad" to
be convincing here, though the novel seems to want to
turn that way, a frail shoot turning toward the sun. Similarly, the goal of the quest narrative, the great jewel,
Kepler's Eye (dug from the brain of the famous alche-
mist) is too ambiguous a symbol, representing enlighten-
ment and blindness at the same time. . . .

"How dare he put 'sad' in quotation marks?" commented
Rosenheim.
And on the same page he had scribbled a little bit more
about his prize student, who apparently hadn't made such
mistakes, and who had requested my address on North Calvert Street in Baltimore ("You made quite an impression. I
hope she ends up sending you something. I've gotten to know
her a little bit outside of class, because she's been baby-
sitting for the twins . . .").

Dear Mr. Park: What I liked most about the book was
the experience of living inside of it as I was reading it,
because it was set where I live, and I could walk around
to those places, there was never anyone there but me.
Although I noticed some mistakes, especially with the
street names, and I wondered . . .

Dear Mr. Park: What I liked best about the book was
all those portraits of loving fathers and understanding
husbands, so many different kinds. I hadn't known there
were so many kinds . . .

Dear Mr. Park: I know we're supposed to like the
heroine, but I can't. I find the others much more convincing, because they are so incomplete, holes missing, and

the rest of them pasted together like collages. I mean
Nicola Ceausescu, but especially Andromeda . . .

I couldn't read any more. How was it possible to care
about these things, after all these years? Tears were in my
eyes, whatever that means. Now I tried to remember the face
of a woman I'd met only once, with whom I'd swapped a
half a dozen letters and perhaps as many emails, before she
and Rosenheim had died together in a car crash, when he was
driving her home. There was no suggestion of a scandal.
A drunk had crossed the line. I'd read about it in the newspaper.

Because I had been up all night, I stretched out on the
vinyl sofa and fell asleep. I had switched off the flashlight,
and when I woke up I was entirely in darkness, and I was no
longer alone.

No—wait. There was a time when I was lying awake. I
remember thinking it was obvious that I had made an error,
because the sun had obviously gone down. The light was
gone from the stairwells and the air shafts. I remember worrying about my car, and whether it was safe where I had
parked it. And I remember thinking about Adrian and Nicola,
about the way my fantasies had pursued in their footsteps
and then changed them into distortions of themselves—all,
I thought, out of a sense of misplaced guilt.

As I lay there in the dark, my mind was lit with images of
her and of Adrian when he was young. Bright figures running through the grass, almost transparent with the sunlight
behind them. Subsequent to his diagnosis, the images darkened. Nowadays, of course, no one would have given Adrian's autism a second's thought: It was just the progress of the
world. No one cared about personal or family trauma anymore. No one cared about genetic causes. But there was
something in the water or the air. You couldn't help it.

Now there was light from the stairwell, and the noise of
conversation. For a moment I had wondered if I'd be safe in
the library overnight. But it was too tempting a refuge; I
packed away my laptop, gathered together my satchel and
my flashlight. I stuffed my velvet pouch into my pocket, and

moved into the stacks to replace my books on their shelves. I knew the locations almost without looking. I felt my way.

I thought the owner or owners of the bedroll had returned, and I would relinquish the reading area and move crabwise through the stacks until I found the exit, and he or she or they would never see me. I would make a break for it. Their voices were loud, and at first I paid no attention to the words or the tone, but only to the volume. The light from their torches lapped at my feet. I stepped away as if from an advancing wave, turned away, and saw something glinting in the corner. I risked a quick pulse from my flashlight, my finger on the button. And I was horrified to see a face looking up at me, the spectacled face of a man lying on his side on the floor, motionless, his cheek against the tiles.

I turned off the flashlight.

Was it a corpse I had seen? It must have been a corpse. In my mind, I could not but examine my small glimpse of it: a man in his sixties, I thought—in any case, younger than I. Bald, bearded, his cap beside him on the floor. A narrow nose. Heavy, square, black glasses. The frame had lifted from one ear. In the darkness I watched him. I did not move, and in my stillness and my fear I found myself listening to the conversation of the strangers, who had by this time reached the vinyl couches and were sitting there. Perhaps I had caught a glimpse of them as they passed by the entrance to the stacks where I was hiding, or perhaps I was inventing details from the sound of their voices, but I pictured a boy and a girl in their late teens or early twenties, with pale skin, pale, red-rimmed eyes, straw hair. I pictured chapped lips, bad skin, ripped raincoats, fingerless wool gloves, though it was warm in the library where I stood. I felt the sweat along my arms.

Girl: *"Did you use a condom?"*
Boy: *"Yes."*
Girl: *"Did you use it, please?"*
Boy: *"I did use it."*
Girl: *"What kind did you use?"*
Boy: *"I don't know."*

Girl: "Was it the ribbed kind?"

Boy: (inaudible)

Girl: "Or with the receptacle?"

Boy: "No."

Girl (anxiously): "Maybe with both? Ribbed and receptacle?"

Boy: (inaudible)

Girl: "No. I didn't feel it. Was it too small? Why are you smiling at me?"

Girl (after a pause, and in a nervous sing-song): "Because I don't want to get pregnant."

Girl (after a pause): "I don't want to get up so early."

Girl (after a pause): "And not have sleep."

Girl (after a pause): "Because of the feeding in the middle of the night. What are you doing?"

Boy (loudly and without inflection): "You slide it down like this. First this way and then this. Can you do that?"

Girl (angrily): "Why do you ask me?"

Boy: "For protection. This goes here. Yes, you see it. You point it like this, with both hands."

Girl: "I don't want to use it. Because too dangerous."

Boy: "For protection from any people. Because you are my girlfriend. Here's where you press the switch, and it comes out."

Girl: "I don't want to use it."

Girl (after a pause): "What will you shoot?"

Girl (after a pause): "Will you shoot animals? Or a wall? Or maybe a target?"

Boy: "Because you are my girlfriend. Look in the bag. Those are many condoms of all different kinds. Will you choose one?"

Girl (after a pause): "Oh, I don't know which one to choose."

Girl (after a pause): "This one. Has it expired, please?"

Boy: (inaudible)

Girl: "Is it past the expiration date?"

As I listened, I was thinking of the dead man on the floor. His body was blocking the end of the stacks, and I didn't want to step over him. But I also didn't want to interrupt the young lovers, homeless people somewhere on the spectrum, as I guessed, and armed. At the same time, I felt an irrational desire to replace in their proper spaces the books I held in my hands, because I didn't think, if I was unable now to take the time, that they would ever be reshelved.

I couldn't bear to tumble them together, the Parks and the Claibornes, on some inappropriate shelf. And this was not just a matter of obsessiveness or vanity. Many of these people disliked each other, had imagined their work as indirect reproaches to some other member of the family. Even my parents, married sixty-five years. That was how "trajectories" functioned, as I imagined it: forcing the books together would create a kinetic field. Repulsed, the chunks of text would fly apart and make a pattern. Without even considering the dead man on the floor, the library was full of ghosts. At the same time, I had to get out of there.

Of course it was also possible that the spectrum kids would end up burning the place down, and I was surprised that the girl, who seemed like a cautious sort, had not noticed the possibility. Light came from a small fire, laid (as I could occasionally see as I moved among the shelves, trusting my memory, feeling for the gaps I had left—in each case I had pulled out an adjoining book a few inches, as if preparing for this eventuality) in a concave metal pan, like an oversized hubcap. Evidently it had been stored under the square table in the reading area, though in the uncertain light I had not seen it there.

I still had one book in my hand when I heard the girl say, "What is that noise?"

I waited. "What is that noise?" she said again.

Then I had to move. I burst from my hiding place, and she screamed. As I rounded the corner, heading toward the stairwell, I glanced her way, and was surprised to see (considering the precision of the way I had imagined her) that she was older and smaller and darker than I'd thought—a light-skinned black woman, perhaps. The man I scarcely dared glance at, because I imagined him pointing his gun; I turned my head and was gone, up the stairs and into the big atrium, which formerly had housed the reference library. Up the stairs to the main entrance, and I was conscious, as I hurried, that there were one or two others in that big dark space.

Outside, in the parking lot, I found no cars at all.

It was a chilly autumn night, with a three-quarter moon. I stood with my leather satchel over my shoulder, looking down toward St. Charles Avenue. The Homewood campus sits on a hill overlooking my old neighborhood, which was mostly dark. But some fires were burning somewhere, it looked like.

I had my mother's book in my hand. Because of it, and because a few hours before I had been looking at "The House on Abell Avenue," I wondered if my friend still lived in that house, and if I could take refuge there. Her name was Bonni Goldberg, and she had taught creative writing at the School for Continuing Studies long ago. What with one thing and another, we had fallen out of touch.

All these northeastern cities had lost population over the years since the pandemics. Baltimore had been particularly hard hit. North of me, in gated areas like Roland Park, there was still electricity. East, near where I was going, the shops and fast-food restaurants were open along Greenmount Avenue. I could see the blue glow from the carbide lanterns. But Charles Village was mostly dark as I set off down the hill and along 33rd Street, and took the right onto Abell Avenue.

Jessy had painted the house from photographs, long before. According to her habit she had drawn a precise sketch, every broken shingle and cracked slate in place—a two-story arts & crafts with an open wraparound porch and deep, protruding eaves. A cardinal was at the bird feeder, a bouquet of white mums at the kitchen window. Striped socks were on the clothesline—I remembered them. In actuality they had been red and brown, but in the painting the socks were the pastels that Jessy favored. It was the same with the house itself, dark green with a gray roof. But in the painting each shingle and slate was a different shade of lavender, pink, light green, light blue, etc. The photograph had been taken during the day, and in the painting the house shone with reflected light. But above it the sky was black, except for the precisely rendered winter constellations—Orion, Taurus, the Pleiades. And then the anomaly: a silver funnel cloud, an Alpine lighting effect known as a Brocken Spectre, and over to the side, the golden lines from one of Jessy's migraine headaches.

I was hoping Bonni still lived there, but the house was burned. The roof had collapsed from the south end. I stood in the garden next to the magnolia tree. In Jessy's painting, it had been in flower. I stood there trying to remember some of the cocktail parties, dinner parties, or luncheons I'd attended in that house. Bonni had put her house portrait up over the fireplace, and I remembered admiring it there. She'd joked about the funnel cloud, which suggested to her the arrival of some kind of flying saucer, and she'd hinted that an interest in such things must run in families.

Remembering this, I found myself wondering if the painting, or some remnant of it, was still hanging inside the wreckage of the house. Simultaneously, and this was also a shadow trajectory, I was already thinking it was a stupid mistake to have come here, even though I'd seen very few people on my walk from the campus, and Abell Avenue was deserted. But I was only a block or so from Greenmount, which I imagined still formed a sort of a frontier. And so inevitably I was accosted, robbed, pushed to the ground, none of which I'll describe. If it's happened to you recently, it was like that. They didn't hit me hard.

I listened to them argue over my laptop and my velvet purse, and it took me a while to figure out they were talking in a foreign language—Cambodian, perhaps. They unbuttoned the purse, and I could hear their expressions of disappointment and disgust, though I couldn't guess what they were actually touching as they thrust their fingers inside. Embarrassed, humiliated, I lay on my back on the torn-up earth—it is natural in these situations to blame yourself. A cold but reliable comfort—if not victims, whom else does it make sense to blame? You have to start somewhere. Besides, these people in an instant had done something I had never dared.

It won't amaze you to hear that as I lay there, a dazed old man on the cold ground, I was conscious of a certain stiffness in my joints, especially in my shoulders and the bones of my neck. As my attackers moved off across a vacant lot, I raised myself onto my elbows. I was in considerable pain, and I didn't know what I was supposed to do without money or credit cards. I thought I should try to find a policeman or a community health clinic.

How was it possible that what happened next took me by surprise? It is, once again, because how you tell a story, or how you hear it, is different from how you experience it, different in every way. Cold hands grabbed hold of me and raised me to my feet. Cold voices whispered words of comfort—"Here, here."

Walking from Homewood I'd seen almost no one, as I've said. St. Paul, North Calvert, Guilford—I'd passed blocks of empty houses and apartments. But now I could sense that doors were opening, people were gathering on the side streets. I could hear laughter and muted conversation. Two men turned the corner, arm in arm. Light came from their flashlight beams. In the meantime, the woman who had raised me up was dusting off my coat with her bare palms, and now she stooped to retrieve my own flashlight, which had rolled away among the crusts of mud. She pressed it into my hands, closed my fingers over it, and then looked up at me. In the moonlight I was startled to see a face I recognized, the black woman in the library whom I had overheard discussing prophylactics. She smiled at me, a shy, natural expression very rare inside the spectrum—her front teeth were chipped.

Overhead, the moon moved quickly through the sky, because the clouds were moving. A bright wind rattled the leaves of the magnolia tree. People came to stand around us, and together we moved off toward Merrymans Lane, and the parking lot where there had been a farmers' market in the old days. "Good to see you," a man said. "It's General Claiborne's grandson," murmured someone, as if explaining something to someone else. "He looks just like him."

The clouds raced over us, and the moon rode high. As we

gathered in the parking lot, a weapon was passed along to me, a sharp stick about three feet long. There was a pile of weapons on the shattered asphalt: sticks and stones, dried cornstalks, old tomatoes, fallen fruit. My comrades chose among them. More of them arrived at every minute, including a contingent of black kids from farther south along Greenmount. There was some brittle high-fiving, and some nervous hilarity.

"Here," said the spectrum girl. She had some food for me, hot burritos in a greasy paper bag. "You need your strength."

"Thanks."

Our commander was an old man like me, a gap-toothed old black man in an Argyle vest and charcoal suit, standing away from the others with a pair of binoculars. I walked over. Even though my neck was painfully stiff, I could turn from my waist and shoulders and look north and east. I could see how the land had changed. Instead of the middle of the city, I stood at its outer edge. North, the forest sloped away from me. East, past Loch Raven Boulevard, the land opened up around patches of scrub oak and ash, and the grass was knee-high as far as I could see. There was no sign of any structure or illumination in either direction, unless you count the lightning on the eastern horizon, down toward Dundalk and the river's mouth. The wind blew from over there, carrying the smell of ozone and the bay. Black birds hung above us. Thirty-third Street was a wide, rutted track, and as I watched I could see movement down its length, a deeper blackness there.

The commander handed me the binoculars. "She's brought them up from the Eastern Shore on flatboats," he said.

I held the binoculars in my hand. I couldn't bear to look. For all I knew, among the pallid dead I would perceive people that I recognized—Shawn Rosenheim, perhaps, a bayonet in his big fist. And one young woman, of whose face I'd be less sure.

"She'll try and take the citadel tonight," murmured the commander by my side. Behind us, the road ran over a bridge before ending at the gates of Homewood. St. Charles Avenue was hidden at the bottom of a ravine. The campus rose above us, edged with cliffs, a black rampart from the art museum to the squash courts. And at the summit of the hill, light gleamed from between the columns of the citadel.

I had to turn in a complete circle to see it all. But I was also imagining what lay behind the hill, the people those ramparts housed and protected, not just here but all over the world. Two hundred miles south, in Richmond, a boy and his mother crouched together in the scary dark.

"I fought with your grandfather when I was just a boy," said the commander. "That was on Katahdin Ridge in 1963. That was the first time I saw her." He motioned back down the road toward Loch Raven. I put the binoculars to my eyes, and I could see the black flags.

"Her?"

"Her."

I knew whom he meant. "What took you so long, anyway?" he asked. I might have tried to answer, if there was time, because I didn't hear even the smallest kind of reproach in his voice, but just simple curiosity. I myself was curious. What had I been doing all these years, when there was work to be done? Others, evidently, started as children—there were kids among us now.

I was distracted from my excuses by the sight of them building up a bonfire of old two-by-fours and plywood shards, while the rest of us stood around warming our hands. I heard laughter and conversation. People passed around bottles of liquor. They smoked cigarettes or joints. A woman uncovered a basket of corn muffins. A man had a bag of oranges, which he passed around. I could detect no sense of urgency, even though the eastern wind made the fire roar, while lightning licked the edges of the plain. The crack of thunder was like distant guns.

"Here they come," said the commander.

Story Copyrights